Two billionaire brothers…brides wanted!

Gorgeous Greek brothers Akis and Vannis Giannopoulos have the world at their feet.

They have everything they need…except love.

Until their lives—and hearts!—are turned upside down when two feisty women arrive on their luxurious Greek island…

Akis meets his match, and the only woman who can discover the man beneath the suit and tie, in

The Millionaire's True Worth

And look out for

A Wedding for the Greek Tycoon

Available from September 2015

Let Rebecca Winters whisk you away with this riveting and emotional new duet!

THE MILLIONAIRE'S TRUE WORTH

BY
REBECCA WINTERS

Published in Great Britain 2015
by Mills & Boon, an imprint of Harlequin (UK) Limited,
Eton House, 18-24 Paradise Road, Richmond, Surrey, TW9 1SR

© 2015 Rebecca Winters

ISBN: 978-0-263-25148-7

23-0715

Harlequin (UK) Limited's policy is to use papers that are natural, renewable and recyclable products and made from wood grown in sustainable forests. The logging and manufacturing processes conform to the legal environmental regulations of the country of origin.

Printed and bound in Spain
by CPI, Barcelona

Rebecca Winters lives in Salt Lake City, Utah, USA. With canyons and high alpine meadows full of wildflowers, she never runs out of places to explore. They, plus her favorite vacation spots in Europe, often end up as backgrounds for her romance novels, because writing is her passion, along with her family and church.

Rebecca loves to hear from readers. If you wish to e-mail her, please visit her website at www.cleanromances.com.

CHAPTER ONE

"CHLOE? I'M SORRY I can't be your maid of honor, but you know why."

Following that statement there was a long silence on Chloe's part. But Raina had her job plus the many responsibilities thrown onto her shoulders since the death of her grandfather. She was now heiress to the Maywood billion-dollar fortune and was constantly in the news. When she went out in public, the paparazzi were right on her heels.

Chloe's family were high-profile Greek industrialists, a favorite target of the European paparazzi. Her marriage would be the top story in Athens. "If I were your maid of honor, the media would make a circus out of your special day." Raina feared it would take the spotlight off her dear friend. For Chloe's sake, she couldn't risk it.

Too much had happened in the intervening years. It had been eight years, in fact, since Chloe had lived with Raina and her grandparents during her senior year of high school. But they'd stayed in touch by phone and the internet.

Three years ago Raina's grandmother had died and Chloe had come to California with her parents for the funeral. Just nine months ago Raina's grandfather had died and once again Chloe and her family had flown over to be with her for his funeral. Their close friendship had helped her get through her grief, and Chloe's family had begged Raina to come back to Greece with them.

"Please tell me you understand, Chloe. I have no desire to intrude on your joy."

"I don't care about me."

"But I *do*."

After a resigned sigh Chloe said, "Then at least stay at the house with me and my family. After all you did for me when I lived with you, my parents are anxious to do everything they can for you."

"Tell you what. After you've left on your honeymoon I'll be thrilled to spend time with them before I fly back to California."

"They'll want you to stay for several months. Think about it. We could have such a wonderful time together."

"I will think about it. As for right now I can't wait to be at your reception. The photos you sent me in your wedding dress are fabulous!"

"But you won't get to see me married at the church."

"Much as I'm sorry about that, it's better this way. I've already booked a room at the Diethnes Hotel. You can reach me on the phone there or on my cell phone. Chloe? You promise you haven't told your fiancé my plans?"

"I swear it. Of course he knows all about you, but he doesn't have any idea that you are coming to Greece."

"Good. That's how I want things to stay. This is going to be *your* day! If the press finds out I'm there, I'm afraid it will ruin things for you. Later this year I'll fly over to meet him, or you can fly to California."

"I promise. He's so wonderful, I can't eat or sleep."

"That doesn't surprise me. *Ta le-me*, Chloe," she said, using one of the few Greek expressions she still remembered, before hanging up.

Six years ago Raina had been in the same excited condition as her friend. Halfway through college she'd met Byron Wallace, a writer. After a whirlwind romance they were married. But it didn't take long to see his selfish nature and suspect her new husband of being unfaithful. Armed with proof of his infidelity even before their two-year marriage anniversary, she'd divorced him, only to lose her grandmother to heart failure.

In her pain she vowed never to marry again. She'd told as much to her beloved, ailing grandfather who'd passed away from stomach cancer.

Chloe's phone call a month ago about her impending marriage had come as a wonderful surprise. Since the death of Raina's grandfather, it was the one piece of news that put some excitement back into her life.

The head of her team at the lab was aware she hadn't taken a vacation in several years. He urged her to take the time off for as long as she wanted. "Go to Greece and be with your friend," he'd said. "We'll still be here when you get back."

Raina thought about it. A change of scene to enjoy Chloe's nuptials might be exactly what she needed.

* * *

Maybe it was the stress of everything she'd had to do before her flight to Athens, Greece. All Raina knew was that she had developed a splitting headache. She needed a strong painkiller. After filing out of the coach section to clear customs wearing jeans and a T-shirt, she retrieved her medium-sized suitcase and left the terminal late morning to find a taxi.

"The Diethnes Hotel, please," she told the driver. The man at the travel agency in Carmel-by-the-Sea, California, had booked the budget hotel for her. From there she could walk to Syntagma Square and the city center without problem.

Chloe had phoned her from Athens yesterday to exclaim over the gorgeous seventy-eight-degree temperature, perfect for her June wedding that would take place tomorrow. Considering the prominence of the Milonis and Chiotis families, it promised to be one of the country's major society events of the summer.

Raina, a strawberry blonde with wavy hair cut neck length, looked at the clear blue Greek sky, a good omen for the impending festivities. Chloe was the sweetest girl in the world. Raina hoped she was marrying an honorable man who'd be true to her.

Raina hadn't been so lucky in that department, but four years had passed since the divorce and she refused to let any remaining clouds dampen the excitement for her friend. Every woman went into marriage praying it would last forever. *A woman had that right, didn't she?*

Once she'd been shown to her room and had unpacked, Raina went back downstairs for directions to the nearest pharmacy for headache medicine. The concierge told her there was a convenience store in the next block many of the American tourists frequented.

Raina thanked him and made her way down the street.

Akis Giannopoulos smiled at his best friend. "Are you ready to take the big plunge?"

Theo grinned. "You already know the answer to that question. If I'd had my way, I would have kidnapped Chloe and married her in private several months ago. But her mother and mine have had an agenda since the engagement. Wouldn't you know the guest list includes a cast of thousands?"

"You're a lucky man." Akis was happy for him. Theo and Chloe seemed to be a perfect match. "Can I do any last-minute service for you before you become a married man?"

"You did more than enough helping me make all the hotel arrangements for our out-of-town guests. I suggest you go back to the penthouse. I need my best man relaxed before the big day tomorrow. Will your brother be there?"

"Vasso phoned me earlier. He'll make it to the wedding, but then he has to get back to the grand opening so he'll miss the reception."

"Understood. So, I'll see you at the church in the morning?"

Akis hugged him. "Try to keep me away."

The two men had been friends for a long time. Naturally Akis was thrilled for Theo, but he was surprised to discover just how much he would miss the camaraderie they'd shared as bachelors. Having done so many things together, Akis was feeling a real sense of loss.

Theo's life would now be swept up with Chloe's. Falling in love with her had changed his friend. He was excited for this marriage. Akis marveled that Theo wanted it so much.

How could he feel so certain that marrying Chloe was the right thing for him?

Marriage meant a lifelong commitment. The woman would have to be so sensational. Akis couldn't fathom finding such a woman.

Aware he was in a despondent mood that wasn't like him, he left the bank Theo's family had owned for several decades and decided to walk to the penthouse in order to shake it off. After the wedding rehearsal that had taken place this morning, exercise was what he needed.

Tourists had flooded into Athens. He saw every kind and description as he made his way to the Giannopoulos complex. After turning a corner, he almost bumped into a beautiful female in a T-shirt and jeans coming in his direction.

"Me seen xo rees, thespinis," he apologized, getting out of her way just in time.

She murmured something he didn't quite hear. For a moment their eyes locked. He felt like he'd suddenly come in contact with an electric current. She must have felt it, too, because he saw little bursts of violet coming from those velvety depths before she walked on. By the way she moved, she had a definite destination in mind. The last thing he saw was her blondish-red hair gleaming in the sun before she rounded the corner behind him.

Raina slowed down, shocked by what had just happened. Maybe it was her bad headache that had caused her to almost walk into the most gorgeous male she'd ever seen in her life. Not in her wildest dreams could she have conjured such a man.

She needed medicine fast!

Luckily the sign for the convenience store was in Greek and English. Alpha/Omega 24. Translation— everything from A to Z. That was a clever name for the store. Its interior looked like "everywhere USA." There was a caution sign saying Wet Floor in both languages as you walked in.

She tiptoed over the newly mopped floor in her sandals to the counter. The male clerk, probably college age, helped her find the over-the-counter medicine section for headaches.

After picking it out plus a bottle of water, she followed him back to the counter to pay for the items with some euros. While she waited, she opened the water and took two pills. On her way out, the clerk asked her where she was staying. Raina told him she was just passing through and started for the exit. But somehow, she didn't know how, she slipped and fell.

"Whoa—" Pain radiated from her ankle. The clerk rushed from behind the counter to help her get up. When she tried to stand, it really hurt. Hopefully the medicine would help tamp down the pain.

He hurried into a back room and brought out a chair so she could sit down. "I'm calling the hospital."

"I don't think there's a need for that."

He ignored her. "This is the store's fault. You stay there."

She felt the fool sitting there while there were customers coming in and out. The other clerk who'd mopped the floor waited on them. In a few minutes an ambulance drove up in front. By then she'd answered a few questions the clerk had asked in order to fill out an incident form.

Because she was incognito, she gave her grandmother's name with her information so no one would pick up on her name. To her dismay there was a small crowd standing around as she was helped outside. Great! Exactly what she didn't want.

"Thank you," she said to the clerk before being helped into the back by one of the attendants. "You've been very kind and I appreciate it."

Two hours later her sprain had been wrapped. She needed to put ice on it and elevate her leg to cut down the swelling. The ER doctor fitted her with crutches and sent them with her in the taxi, letting her know the bill would be taken care of by the store where she'd fallen.

After the wedding reception, Raina would make certain her insurance company would reimburse the store. After all, the accident was her fault.

For the time being, she needed to lie down and call room service for her meals and ice. How crazy was it that she would have to go to the reception tomorrow evening on crutches. No matter what, she refused to miss her dear friend's celebration.

After flying all this way, how even crazier was it that all she could think about was the man she'd come close to colliding with earlier in the day. She'd never experienced anything like that before. The streets of Athens were crowded with hundreds of people. How was it that one man could rob her of breath just looking at him?

With a champagne glass in hand, Akis stood at the head table to toast the bride and groom. "It was a great honor Theo Chiotis bestowed on me when he asked me to be his best man. No man has had a better friend." Except for Vasso, of course. "After meeting and getting to know Chloe, I can say without reservation that no man could have married a sweeter woman. To Theo and Chloe. May you always be as happy as you are today."

After the crowd applauded, other friends of the bridal couple made their toasts. Akis was thankful his part in the long wedding-day festivities was officially over. When he felt a decent interval of time had passed, he would slip out of the luxurious Grand Bretagne Hotel ballroom unnoticed and leave for the penthouse.

To love a woman enough to go through this exhaustive kind of day was anathema to Akis. No man appreciated women more than he did, but his business affairs with thirty-year-old Vasso kept him too busy to enjoy more than a surface relationship that didn't last long.

Though he congratulated himself on reaching the age of twenty-nine without yet succumbing to marriage, Theo's wedding caused Akis to question what was going on with him and his brother.

The two of them had been in business since they were young boys. To this point in time no enduring love interest had interfered with their lives and they'd managed to make their dream to rise out of poverty come true. Besides owning a conglomerate of retail stores throughout Greece, they'd set up a charity Foundation with two centers, one in Greece, the other in New York City.

Their dirt-poor background might be a memory,

but it was the one that drove them so they'd never know what it was like to go hungry again. Unfortunately their ascent from rags to riches didn't come without some drawbacks. For various reasons both he and Vasso found it difficult to trust the women who came into their lives. They enjoyed brief relationships. But they grew leery when they came across women who seemed to love them for themselves, with no interest in their money. He thought about their parents who, though they were painfully poor and scraped for every drachma, had loved and were devoted to one another. They came from the same island with the same expectations of life and the ability to endure the ups and downs of marriage. Both Akis and Vasso wanted a union like their parents', one that would last forever. But finding the right woman seemed to be growing harder.

Akis's thoughts wandered back to the words he'd just spoken to the guests in the ballroom. He'd meant what he'd said about Chloe, who was kind and compatible. She suited Theo, who also had a winning nature. They both came from the same elite, socioeconomic background that helped them to trust that neither had an agenda. If two people could make it through this life together and be happy, he imagined they would.

Every so often he felt the maid of honor's dark eyes willing him to pay attention to her. Althea Loris was one of Chloe's friends, a very glamorous woman as yet unattached. She'd tried to corner him at various parties given before the wedding. Althea came from a good family with a modest income, but Akis sensed how much she wanted all the trappings of a marriage like Chloe's.

Even if Akis had felt an attraction, he would have wondered if she'd set her eyes on him for what he could give her monetarily. It wasn't fair to judge, but he couldn't ignore his basic instinct about her.

There was nothing he wanted more than to be loved for himself. An imperfect self, to be sure. Both he and Vasso had been born into a family where you worked by the sweat of your brow all the days of your life. The idea of a formal education was unheard of, but he hadn't worried about it until the summer right before he had to do his military service.

An Italian tourist named Fabrizia, who was staying on the island that July, had flirted with Akis at the store where he worked. He couldn't speak Italian, nor she Greek, so they managed with passable English. He was attracted and spent time swimming with her when he could get an hour off. By the time she had to go home, he'd fallen for her and wanted to know when she'd be back.

After kissing him passionately she'd said, "I won't be able to come." In the next breath she'd told him she'd be getting married soon to one of the attorneys working for her father in Rome. "But I'll never forget my beautiful grocery boy. Why couldn't you be the attorney my parents have picked out for me?"

Not only had his pride taken a direct hit, her question had made him startlingly aware of his shortcomings, the kind that went soil-deep. The kind that separated the rich from the poor. From that time on, Akis had enjoyed several relationships with women, but they didn't approach the level of his wanting to get married.

Too bad his brother had to leave after the wedding

at the church and couldn't attend the reception. He was away on important business at the moment so he couldn't rescue Akis with a legitimate excuse to leave early. Akis would have to manufacture a good one on his own.

Thankfully the speeches were almost over. Chloe's father was the last person to speak. After getting choked up because he was losing his precious daughter to Theo, he urged everyone to enjoy the rest of the evening and dance.

Akis watched as Theo escorted Chloe to the floor for the first dance. Soon other couples joined them. That meant Akis had to fulfill one last duty. It was expected that he ask Althea, who was more than eager to find herself in his arms.

"I've been waiting for this all day, Akis."

He knew what she was saying, what she was hoping for, but he couldn't force interest that wasn't there. The long, exhausting wedding day was almost over. Akis couldn't wait to leave, but he needed to choose his words carefully. "Unfortunately I still have business to do after the reception is over."

Her head jerked up. "Business? Tonight?"

"My work is never done." As the music was coming to an end, he danced her over to her parents' table and let her go. "Thank you, Althea. Theo asked me to mingle so if you'll excuse me, there's one more person I should dance with before I leave." The lie had just come to him.

While she looked at him with genuine disappointment, he smiled at her parents before he moved through the crowded room toward the rear of the ballroom. In order to prove he hadn't told an untruth, he looked for any woman at one of the tables who didn't have an escort, whom he could ask to dance.

At the round table nearest the rear doors he saw a woman sitting alone. Another couple sat across from her, but it was clear she didn't have a man with her. Knowing Althea was still watching him, he walked toward the stranger. Maybe she was waiting for someone, but he'd take his chances.

Closer now he could make out classic features beneath hair an incredible light gold with a natural hint of red. He'd only seen hair that color on one other woman. His breath caught. She wore a pale blue silk suit jacket with a small enamel locket hanging around her neck. He imagined she was in her mid-twenties. He saw no rings.

Akis approached her. "Excuse me, *thespinis.* I see you're alone for the moment. As best man of this wedding, if you'd permit, I'd like to dance with you."

Her eyes lifted to his.

Those eyes. They were the same eyes he'd looked into yesterday, but tonight he discovered they were a stunning shade of lavender blue and he found himself lost in them.

"I'm sorry, but I don't speak Greek."

Her comment jarred him back to the present. What was this American beauty doing at Theo's wedding reception? Switching to unpolished English he said, "We passed in the street yesterday."

"I remember almost bumping into you," she murmured, averting her eyes. He noticed with satisfaction that a nerve throbbed in her throat above her locket. She was as excited as he was by this unexpected meeting. "I came close to knocking you down because I wasn't watching where I was going."

He smiled. "No problem. Just now I asked you to dance, but perhaps you're waiting for the man who brought you."

A delicate flush filled her cheeks. "No. I came alone. Thank you for the invitation, but I was just getting ready to leave."

He wasn't about to let her go a second time. "Surely you can spare one dance with me? I need rescuing."

"Where's your wife?"

"I've never had a wife. As for a girlfriend, I haven't had one in months." It was the truth.

"Then who was the woman with the long black hair you were dancing with moments ago?"

So she'd noticed. "You're very observant. She was the maid of honor. It would have been unkind not to dance with her."

With a twinkle in her eyes, she leaned to the right and retrieved a pair of crutches from the floor. She stood them on end. "Unless you're prepared for your feet to be impaled by one of these, I'll do you a favor and exit the room."

She'd surprised Akis. This had to be a very recent injury. Her legitimate excuse to turn him down only fed his determination to get to know her better. Yesterday he'd wanted to pursue her, but hadn't dared for fear of alarming her. "Then let me help you."

Without hesitation he took the crutches from her and waited until she got to her feet. She was probably five foot seven, with enticing curves. The matching suit skirt covered womanly hips and slender legs. His gaze fell lower to the left ankle that had been wrapped. She wore a sandal on her foot and a low-heeled shoe on the other.

"Thank you." She reached for the crutches and fit them beneath her arms. The delicate fragrance emanating from her assailed him. "Why don't you ask the other woman at my table to dance? I'm sure her partner won't mind."

"I'd rather help you to your room."

"I'm not staying here."

That was interesting. He'd helped Theo make arrangements for all their out-of-town guests to stay here. "Then I'll walk you outside and take you wherever you'd like to go."

"As long as you're offering, I wouldn't say no if you hailed a taxi for me. I'm craving my hotel room so I can elevate my leg."

"I'll do better than that." Akis accompanied her from the ballroom and down the hall to the foyer. The woman at his side managed her crutches with little trouble. En route he phoned his driver and told him to come to the hotel entrance.

As they walked outside, flashes from the cameras of the paparazzi blinded them. Chloe and Theo's wedding would be the top story making the ten o'clock news on television. Video of prominent guests and the best man attending the reception filmed by TV news crews would be included.

Some of the paparazzi called out questions about the beautiful woman with Akis. He hated the attention though he was used to it, and kept walking her to the smoked-glass limo without answering them. He took her crutches so she could get in, then he followed and shut the door before sitting opposite her. "Are you all right?"

"I am. Are you?"

"I am now. The press is unrelenting. Tell me where you're staying and I'll let the driver know."

"The Diethnes."

A lot of tourists on a budget frequented two-star hotels like that one. Until he and Vasso had started making money, he could never have afforded to stay at any hotel. Period. Akis gave his driver directions and they pulled away from the Grand Bretagne. "When did you have time to injure your ankle?"

She let out a sound of exasperation. "It happened right after you and I passed on the sidewalk. I had a headache and was on my way to a store for some medicine. While I was inside, I slipped on the wet floor. It was such a stupid accident, totally my fault for not paying attention. The clerk was incredibly kind and called the ambulance for me."

Akis mulled over her answer. Had she decided it would be easier to attend the reception rather than the wedding because of her injury? If she'd been at the church, he wouldn't have been able to take his eyes off her during the ceremony.

"Are you in pain?"

"Not really. It's more a dull ache until I rest it."

"I'm sorry you had to fall, especially the day before the wedding."

"Funny about life, isn't it?" she murmured. "You never know what's going to happen when you get up in the morning." The almost haunted tone in her voice intrigued him.

"How true. When I left for the wedding, I didn't

know I was going to meet the lovely stranger who'd passed me on the street yesterday."

"Or be chased by the maid of honor tonight," she said in a wry tone. "Am I mistaken, or were you taking flight?"

"You noticed that."

"It was hard not to." She chuckled without looking at him. "I would imagine a man with your looks and minus a wedding ring needs rescuing from myriads of females."

He blinked. "*My* looks?"

"You know very well you're the embodiment of a Greek god."

Akis frowned. "Which terrifying one are you referring to?"

At this point she laughed. "I didn't have any particular god in mind. It's something American women say when they've met an exceptionally good-looking man."

"Then they haven't seen one of our Greek statues up close or they'd run for their lives in the other direction."

Her laughing continued. He decided she was somewhat of a tease.

"I don't know. Despite your fearsome expression, the female pursuing you tonight didn't seem turned off by you. Quite the opposite, in fact."

That's exactly what Althea had been doing for weeks. Maybe he'd misjudged her, but it didn't matter because he hadn't been attracted. "You saved me from being caught. For that, I'm in your debt."

"I'm in yours for giving me a lift to the hotel," she came right back. "We're even."

Akis had never met a woman like her. "Are you a friend of Theo's or Chloe's? I don't even know your name."

"Let's keep it that way."

Her remark shouldn't have bothered him, but it did…

They continued down the busy street. "Oh— Look—" she cried softly. "See that store on the right? Alpha/Omega 24?" He nodded. "That's the one where I fell. My hotel is in the next block."

Raina couldn't believe that the incredible man she'd seen on the street yesterday was none other than Theo's best man. It was an amazing coincidence. She was actually upset with herself for having any feelings about seeing him again tonight.

Since her divorce, there'd been no man in her life and she'd purposely kept it that way. She didn't want to fall in love again and take the chance of being hurt. For this man to have already made an impact on her without even trying was disturbing. After the pain she'd been through because of Byron, she never wanted to experience it again.

When the driver drove up in front of the hotel, Raina was relieved that the striking Greek male sitting next to her had gone quiet and didn't pressure her for more information. That was good.

She found that when she used a man's tactics of a little false flattery on him, the fun went out of it on his part. Knowing Raina could see through his strategy, his interest had quickly waned. She wanted to leave Greece with no complications. Already she knew this man was unforgettable. The sooner she could get away from him, the better.

"Thanks again for the lift," she said in a cheery voice, needing to escape the potency of his male charisma.

He opened the door and took her crutches to help her from the back of the limo. She put them underneath her arms and started for the entrance. After pushing the hotel door open, he accompanied her as far as the foyer. She kept moving toward the elevator. While she waited, she turned in his direction.

"Like you, I appreciated being rescued." The lift door finally opened. "Good night." She stepped inside without looking back, praying for it to close fast in case he decided to go upstairs with her.

Raina willed her heart to stop thudding. She hadn't been kidding when she'd said he looked like a Greek god. From his black hair and eyes to his tall, powerful build, he was the personification of male perfection. She hadn't been able to take her eyes off him all evening. His image would be all over the television tonight, causing legions of women to swoon.

Chloe had raved about Theo's looks, but he couldn't hold a candle to his best man. What had she called him? Akis something or other. He had a self-assured presence, bordering on an arrogance he probably wasn't aware of.

The maid of honor who'd danced with him earlier had looked pained when he'd left her side and made a beeline to Raina's table. Here Raina had tried so hard to be invisible during the reception. But at least no one recognized her.

So far the only photos taken of her were because

the best man with his Greek-god looks had helped
her out to the limo. Until now Raina had managed to
escape any notoriety. The paparazzi were following
him, not her. Chloe's beautiful day had gone perfectly
without a marring incident of any kind. If ever a bride
looked euphoric…

Grateful for the reception to be over, she let herself into the room. To her surprise there was a light
blinking on the phone. It couldn't possibly be Chloe.
Maybe it was the front desk. She used her crutches to
reach the bedside and sat down to find out if something was wrong.

When she picked up, she listened to the message
from Nora Milonis, Chloe's mother. She was sending
a car for Raina in the morning and insisted she spend
the rest of her time in Athens with them. *Be ready at
9:00 a.m.* Absolutely no excuses now that the wedding was over!

She'd known the invitation was coming. It warmed
her heart and put her in a much better mood.

Once she'd called for ice and was ready for bed,
she elevated her leg and turned on the TV. But her
mind wandered to the man who'd brought her home.

He spoke English with a deep, heavy Greek accent
she found appealing. The man hadn't done anything,
yet he'd disturbed her senses that had lain dormant
since she'd discovered her husband had been unfaithful to her. The way he'd looked at her both yesterday
and tonight had made her feel alive for the first time
in years and he hadn't even touched her!

Why this man? Why now? She couldn't understand
what it was that made him so fascinating to her. That
was the trouble. She didn't want to find him fasci-

nating because it meant a part of her wanted to see him again.

She'd planned to fly back to California soon, but her sprained ankle prevented her from leaving for a while. How wonderful that she'd be able to spend time with Chloe's parents after all! Raina needed family right now, even if it wasn't her own.

The doctor had warned her to keep it supported close to a week for a faster recovery. She'd planned to do work on her laptop and get in some reading.

Anything to keep her mind off Theo's best man.

CHAPTER TWO

"*KALIMERA*, GALEN."

The clerk's head lifted. "Kyrie Giannopoulos—what a surprise to see you in here this morning! I didn't expect a visit before next week."

Galen reminded Akis of himself at an earlier age. He was eager for the work and anxious to please. So far, Akis had had no complaints about him. "I came by to find out if you were on duty the day before yesterday when an American woman slipped and fell."

"Yes. Mikos and I were both here. How did you know?"

"That's not important. Tell me what happened."

Akis listened as his employee recounted the same story the exciting woman had told him last night. "Did she threaten to sue?"

"No. She claimed it was her fault."

"Did you fill out an incident report?"

"Yes. It's on the desk in the back room. I told the ambulance attendant the store would be responsible for the bill."

"You did exactly the right thing. Thank you."

Akis walked behind the counter and entered the small room, anxious to see what was written.

He reached in the Out basket and found the injury report.

June 3, 1:45 p.m.
Ginger Moss: American, age 26
Athens address: The Diethnes Hotel.
Customer fell on wet floor after purchasing
some headache medicine. She limped in pain. I
called an ambulance. She was taken to St. Mi-
chael's Hospital.
Signed: Galen.

Ginger… He liked the name very much. He liked everything about her *too* much. She'd caused him a restless night despite the fact that the whole wedding day had been exhausting. Ginger Moss had that effect on a man.

Akis had felt her magic and couldn't throw it off. Now that he was armed with her name, he planned to seek her out so he could get to know her better. Since he didn't know her agenda, he had no idea how long she'd be in Athens. The only way to find out was to head over to her hotel.

Galen poked his head in the door. "Is everything all right, boss?"

"You two are doing a fine job."

"Thanks. About that American woman who slipped and fell?"

Akis turned his head to look at his employee. "Yes?"

"Mikos had just mopped the floor before she came in. We did have the caution sign set out on the floor."

"Good." He nodded to his two employees and went

back out to the limo. "I'll walk to the Diethnes from here," he told the driver. "Follow me and wait in front until you hear from me again."

A few minutes later he entered the hotel lobby and told the concierge he'd like to speak to one of their guests named Ginger Moss. The other man shook his head. "We don't have a tourist staying here with that name."

Akis unconsciously ran a hand through his hair in surprise. "You're sure? Maybe if I explain that the woman I'm looking for was using crutches when I dropped her off here last night."

"Ah... The one with hair the color of a Titian painting and a figure like the statue in the museum. You know—the one of the goddess Aphrodite carrying a pitcher?"

Yes—that was the precise one Akis had envisioned himself.

He thought back to last night. She'd been elusive about everything. What kind of a game was she playing? He closed his eyes tightly for a moment, remembering her comment about him resembling a Greek god. *Touché*.

"Would you ring her room and tell her the man who helped her home last night is in the lobby and wishes to talk to her?"

His shoulders hunched. "I can't. She checked out an hour ago."

"You mean permanently?" he barked the question.

"Of course."

"Did she leave a forwarding address?"

"No. I'm sorry."

"Did she go by taxi?"

"I don't know. I was busy at the desk."

"What name did she register under?"

"Unless you have a judge's warrant, I can't tell you."

Trying to tamp down his frustration, he thanked the man and hurried outside to the limo where his driver was waiting.

"Shall I take you to the office?

"Not yet. I have a phone call to make first." Akis climbed in the back and phoned Theo's parents. He reached his friend's mother. After chatting for a moment about the perfect wedding, she mentioned Althea and her disappointment that Akis had needed to leave the reception so soon. Akis reminded her that something pressing in business had come up. Then he got to the point.

"Did you invite an American woman named Ginger Moss to the wedding reception?"

"Moss? No," she claimed after reflection. "That's an unusual name, and it certainly wasn't on our list or I would have remembered. Why?"

So that was the reason why Theo hadn't arranged for her to stay at the Grand Bretagne. "I'm trying to find her."

After a silence, "Is she the person who caused you to walk away from Althea so fast last night?"

Akis didn't mind her teasing insinuation. Theo's parents were like a second family to him. For the last year both of them had kept reminding him it was time he got married, too. "No. As I was leaving the ballroom, I ran into the woman who was on crutches and needed help out to a taxi."

"Hmm. Why don't you check with Chloe's parents? They must have invited her. If they haven't heard of her, either, maybe she was a friend of Chloe's or Theo's. Perhaps they invited her too late to receive an invitation."

"Maybe," he muttered. "She hadn't been at the church or *I* would have remembered," he said quietly. "Thanks. We'll all have to get together after they get back from their honeymoon."

"Wonderful, but don't you dare be a stranger while they're away!"

"I won't," Akis promised, but his mind was on the woman he'd asked to dance last night. He could have sworn there'd been feelings between them. Sparks. Some nuance of chemistry that had happened immediately while they were on the sidewalk and wouldn't leave him alone. Yet she'd run off this morning.

No matter what, he intended to find her. It bothered him that she'd given him the slip when she knew he wanted to get to know her better. Maybe it was his pride that made him want to prove she had feelings for him, too. One thing was certain. He wasn't going to let her disappear on him.

Without wasting another moment, he phoned Chloe's house. The housekeeper said she'd put through the call to Chloe's father because Kyria Milonis was occupied.

The more Akis thought about it, the more he decided this woman had to be a friend of Chloe's. Otherwise Theo would have talked about her long before now. He wouldn't have been able to help himself because even if he was head over heels in love with Chloe, this Ginger, or whoever she was, stood out from the rest.

Why had she sat at the last table near the doors last night? It was almost as if she hadn't wanted to be seen. Her behavior was a mystery to him. Vasso would be shocked by the strength of his brother's desire to find the tantalizing female. Nothing like this had ever happened before. No one was more shocked than Akis himself. In case she'd be leaving Athens soon, he had to work fast.

"Akis, my boy!" came the booming voice of Chloe's father. "Great to hear from you! We're going to miss the kids. The place feels empty. Come on over to the house for lunch. My wife will be thrilled. We'll eat by the pool."

The perfect place to vet Chloe's parents. "I'll be there soon, Socus. Thank you."

After getting settled on a patio lounger by the pool with her leg raised, Raina smiled at Chloe's mother who hovered around her like her grandmother used to do. She loved her friend's parents and drew great comfort from being with them. They couldn't seem to do enough for her.

"We were always sorry that you didn't come to live with us after Chloe's school year with you ended. It was all Chloe had talked about."

"I would have come, but as you know my grandmother wasn't well and I was afraid to leave her. Then I started college and met the man who became my husband. When our marriage didn't work out, I divorced him. Then, of course, my grandmother died and I needed to take care of my grandfather, who was diagnosed with stomach cancer. There was never a good time to come to Greece."

Chloe's father patted her hand. "You've had a great load on your shoulders."

"My grandparents raised me. I loved them so much and owed them everything. But I have to tell you, the year Chloe spent with me was the happiest of my life. It was like having a sister. My grandparents adored her."

Nora smiled with tears in her eyes. "She loved the three of you. Why don't you consider this your temporary home and stay with us for a time? There's nothing we'd like more. Chloe would be ecstatic."

"That would be wonderful, but I have a job waiting for me when I get back."

"You like your work?"

"Very much," but she was prevented from saying more because a maid appeared beneath the striped patio awning. She said something in Greek and suddenly the best man walked out on the terrace.

"Akis!" Nora cried with warmth in her voice.

Raina's heart skipped several beats. In a short-sleeved white crew neck and matching cargo pants, he robbed her of breath, with his rock-hard physique and arresting Greek features.

He hadn't seen Raina yet and said something in Greek to Chloe's parents with an aura of authority she was sure came naturally to him. He sounded intense, with no accompanying smile. After he stopped talking, they both started to chuckle and turned to Raina.

The man's dark head jerked around in her direction. His penetrating gaze caused her body to fill with heat. To her dismay she lay helpless on the lounger in another T-shirt and jeans with her leg propped, hardly an exciting sight. The look of shock on his face was priceless.

"You're here," he muttered, rubbing his chest absently. "I went to the hotel but the concierge said you'd already checked out. Theo's parents claimed they didn't know you, so I decided to come over here to find out if you were a friend of Chloe's."

The knowledge that he'd been trying to find her excited her. Again she was struck by his heavily accented English. For want of a better word, she found it endearing. Raina nodded to him, stunned that he'd gone to such lengths to find her. "Friends from a long time ago. Her parents sent a car for me this morning so we could visit."

"Which has been long overdue," Nora stated in English.

He still looked thunderstruck. Raina could read his mind. "Did you think I had invited myself to the reception?"

"No, but I got the feeling you didn't want to be noticed," he drawled. She had the feeling nothing got past him.

"While you two talk, I'll tell Ione to serve lunch out here." Nora got up from the deck chair and Chloe's father followed her, leaving them alone.

Raina swallowed hard. She never imagined seeing him again and wasn't prepared for this overwhelming response to the very sight of him.

He pulled up a deck chair and sat down next to her. His black eyes played over her from head to toe, missing nothing in between. Her pulse raced. "How's the pain this morning?"

"I took an ibuprofen and now it's hardly noticeable. At this rate I'll be able to fly home soon."

"What's the rush?"

"Work is waiting for me." *I don't dare spend any more time around you. I didn't come to Greece to meet a man who has already become too important to me.*

He leaned forward with his hands clasped between his hard muscled legs. "What kind?"

Oh, boy. She could tell she was in for a vetting. The less he knew about her, the better. She was afraid to be open with her feelings for fear of being hurt again. After having made a huge mistake in choosing Byron, she feared she didn't have wise judgment when it came to men.

Byron had been relentless in his pursuit of her. She'd been so naive and so flattered by his attention, she'd fallen into his grasping, narcissistic hands like an apple from a tree. His betrayal of her even before their marriage had scarred her for life, forcing her to grow up overnight.

Never again would she allow herself to be caught off guard, even if this man thrilled her to the core of her being. Raina would rather leave Greece without feeling any tug of emotion for this dark-haired stranger. He was already dangerous to her peace of mind.

"I work in a lab with a team of people." That was as much as she was willing to reveal. "What do you do for a living?"

He studied her intently. "My brother and I are in business. That's how I met Theo. So now that we have that out of the way, how did you meet Chloe?"

Raina could tell he was equally reticent to talk

about himself. That was fine with her. He could keep his secrets, whatever they were. "My senior year of high school, she came to live with me in California for the school year so she could learn English. That year there were three other students from other countries living with some of the students' families."

"Was it a reciprocal arrangement?"

"Yes. After graduation I was supposed to spend the next year with her family, but too many things at the time prevented me from coming here to live with them."

Needing some space to gather her composure before he asked her any more questions, she sat up and swung her legs to the ground. He anticipated her movements and handed her the crutches lying by the side of the lounger. "Thank you," she said, tucking them beneath her arms. "If you'll excuse me, please, I need to use the restroom."

"Of course."

Raina could see in his eyes she hadn't fooled him, but what did it matter. She hurried through the mansion to her suite of rooms. The fabulous Milonis estate had been built along neoclassical lines in its purest architectural form. So different from the home where she'd been raised in Carmel.

When she eventually returned to the patio, she discovered Akis in the swimming pool. Their lunch had been brought out to the patio table. While he was doing laps at tremendous speed, she sat down in one of the chairs around the table and dug into the salad filled with delicious chicken, feta cheese and olives.

Chloe's parents were nowhere in sight. Raina had hoped they'd come out to provide a buffer against his questions, but no such luck. Chloe's parents were a very hip couple she adored. Raina could see why. Too bad they thought they were aiding a romantic situation by staying away.

As her eyes looked out at the pool, Akis suddenly raised his head. The wet black hair was swept back from his forehead to reveal his extraordinary male features. The moment he saw her, he levered himself from the aquamarine water and reached for a towel, giving her more than a glimpse of his splendid body. He must have borrowed someone's black trunks. They hung low on his hips.

"Last night you resembled one of your disgruntled gods," she teased to fight her attraction. "Today you've morphed into Poseidon."

Akis finished drying himself off before he sat down in a chair opposite her and plucked a big olive from the salad his white teeth bit into with relish. Between his olive skin and black hair, he was a work of art if there was such a label to describe a beautiful man. To her consternation, everything he said and did intrigued her.

"Oddly enough you haven't changed since last night," he remarked. "The concierge said you resembled Aphrodite, a description that fits you in every detail except for your crutches."

She laughed to let him know she didn't take him seriously. To believe him would be a huge mistake. "Careful," she cautioned. "You might just turn my head if you keep up that malarkey."

One dark brow lifted. "Malarkey?"

"An English expression for nonsense."

His jet-black eyes came alive. "You mean my methods are working?" By now he'd devoured a roll and most of his salad.

"Absolutely. But since I won't be in Greece long, maybe your time would be better spent talking to someone of your own kind and background."

In an instant his jaw hardened. Uh-oh. She must have struck a nerve.

"*My own kind?*" The words came out more like a soft hiss.

She choked on her iced tea. What had she said to provoke such a reaction? "Surely you must realize I meant no offense. Perhaps the maid of honor wasn't to your liking last night, but I saw a lot of lovely Greek women at the reception—women who live here and would enjoy your attention."

Akis sat back in the chair. "Meaning you don't?"

"I didn't say that!" Their conversation had taken a strange twist.

"Let's start over again." He cocked his head. "We weren't formally introduced. My name is Akis Giannopoulos as you already know. What's yours?"

She took a deep breath. "Raina."

"Ah. Raina what?"

She shrugged her shoulders. "Does it matter when we'll never see each other again?"

"That's the second time you've used the same excuse not to tell me."

"I simply don't see the point." He grew on her with every moment they spent together. This wasn't supposed to happen!

An ominous silence surrounded them. "Obviously not. If you'll excuse me, I'm going to change clothes in the cabana."

She'd made him angry. Good. Raina wanted him to leave her alone. But as she watched him stride to the other side of the pool, she experienced a strange sense of loss totally at odds with her determination to separate herself from him.

Raina wanted to escape any more involvement because she had a premonition this man had the power to hurt her in a way not even Byron had done. Akis made her feel things she didn't want to feel. To give in to her desire to be with him could bring her joy, but for how long? When the excitement wore off for him, would he find someone else? Raina was afraid to trust what she was feeling. She quickly grabbed her crutches and hurried to find Chloe's mother who was in the kitchen.

"Thank you for the delicious lunch, Nora. Now if you don't mind, my ankle has started to ache again. I'm going to go to my room and lie down for a while. Please say goodbye to Mr. Giannopoulos for me. He came over to your home to visit with you and is still out in the pool."

Her eyes widened. "Of course. Can I get you anything?"

"Not a thing. You've done too much for me already. I just need to rest my leg for a while."

"Then go on." The two women hugged and she left the kitchen for her suite of rooms. In truth Raina needed to get her mind off Akis. Since she hadn't had family around for a long time, it felt wonderful to be spoiled by two people who showed her so much love. Hopefully when Raina went back outside later, she'd find Akis gone.

With Chloe and Theo touring the fjords in Norway

for the next two weeks, she hoped Akis wouldn't drop by until after the couple had returned from their honeymoon. After a few days' reunion in order to meet Theo, Raina would fly back to Monterey.

Akis took his time dressing. He knew instinctively Raina had said and done things to discourage him. Why? One of her stiletto-like jabs had worked its way under his skin and had taken hold.

How much did she know about him? Had she been insinuating that he wasn't good enough for her? Was it something Chloe had told her about his roots?

His own kind and background? Was he being paranoid?

Raina had rushed to explain what she'd meant when she'd told him he'd be better off spending time with his own kind and background instead of an American who'd be leaving soon. Even if he'd felt her sincerity and were willing to believe her explanation, the words had sunk deep in that vulnerable spot inside him and wouldn't go away.

He and Vasso were the brothers who'd climbed out of poverty without the benefit of formalized education. No college, no university degrees to hang on the wall. Akis wasn't well read or well traveled. He came out of that class of poor people who didn't have that kind of money, nor the sophistication. Whatever he and his brother had achieved had come through hard work.

No matter how much money he made now, it didn't give him the polish of someone like Theo who'd attended the finest university to become a banker like his father and grandfather before him. Akis could hold his own, but he was aware of certain inadequacies that would never change.

By now he got along fine in English, but being with her made him realize how much he didn't know about her language. He wasn't like Theo, who'd spent a year in England and spoke English with only a trace of accent.

Chloe could answer a lot of his questions, but she wasn't available and wouldn't be home for a fortnight. That presented a problem. Before long her former high school friend would be back in California. This woman worked in a lab? What kind? She could have meant anything.

His head was spinning with questions for which there were no answers. Not yet anyway.

When he left the cabana, he wasn't surprised to find Raina had disappeared on him. She couldn't get away from him fast enough. On his way into the house he ran into Nora. Though tempted to ask questions he knew she could answer, he didn't want to drag her into something that was strictly between him and Raina.

"The wedding was beautiful. Now you can relax for a little while. Thank you for lunch."

"You're always welcome here. You know that. Raina's ankle was hurting and she went to her room. She asked me to say goodbye to you."

"I appreciate that. She did seem a little under the weather."

He kissed her cheek and left the house for the limo where his driver was waiting. "Take me to the office."

During the ride he sat back trying to figure out what was going on with her. She'd told his employee at the store her name was Ginger Moss, but the concierge denied any knowledge of it. Why in the hell had she done that?

Once back at the Giannopoulos business complex off Syntagma Square, he walked through the empty offices to his private suite. It was a good thing it was Sunday. In this mood he'd probably bite the heads off the staff.

Vasso would be back tomorrow, but Akis needed to talk to him. His brother was busy overseeing a new store opening in Heraklion. If not for the wedding, Akis would have gone with him.

He rang Vasso's cell phone number. It was four o'clock in the afternoon. He should still be at the grand opening to make sure everything went smoothly. "Pick up, Vasso." But it went through to his voice mail. Akis left the message for him to call ASAP. While he waited to hear from him, he caught up on some paperwork.

When his brother hadn't phoned him by seven-thirty, Akis couldn't take it anymore and decided to drive back to the Milonis estate. Before the night was out he would find out why she didn't want to let him into her life. Was it because she thought he was beneath her socially? Wasn't he good enough for her? If that was the case, then she needed to say that to his face.

Raina was different than any woman he'd ever met. He was deeply attracted not only to her looks but to her personality, as well. She could fight it all she wanted, but they had a connection. He just had to tear down that wall she'd put up. It was important to him.

Ione, the Milonises' housekeeper, met him at the

door and explained that Chloe's parents had gone out for dinner, but they'd be back shortly.

"What about their houseguest?"

"Thespinis Maywood is in the den watching television."

Maywood...

So she hadn't run away quite yet. Pleased by the information he said, "I'll just say hello to her, then. Thanks, Ione." Without hesitation he walked past her and found his way to the room in question. Having been over here many times, he knew where to go.

The door was already open so he walked in to find her lying on the couch in front of the TV with a couple of throw pillows elevating her leg. She was dressed in the same jeans and T-shirt she'd worn earlier.

"That was quite a disappearing act you performed earlier," he stated from the doorway.

Her eyes met his calmly, as if she'd known he would show up again and was amused by it. Challenged by her deliberate pretense of indifference to him he said, "What does one call you? Ginger when you're with strangers, but just Raina with close friends?"

A sigh escaped her lips. After turning off the TV with the remote, she sat up and moved her legs to the floor. "I take it you went to the store where I fell." She stared hard at him. "I must admit I'm shocked that the clerk would give you my name. That's privileged information."

"Agreed, but it was false information. In case you were worried, I happen to own that store."

"What?" Those incredible lavender eyes of hers had suddenly turned a darker hue. At last something had shaken her out of her almost condescending at-

titude. Did she really not know how he earned his living? Because of her relationship with the Milonis family, he found it hard, if not impossible, to believe.

"I read the incident report written up in the back room. You gave my employee the name of Ginger Moss, age twenty-six. What name will I find if I ask you to show me your passport? It will be important when I pay your hospital bill. They'll need more information to correct the discrepancy on the record."

"My insurance will reimburse you." She rested her hands on the top of her thighs. "I sometimes go by the nickname Ginger."

"Because of your hair?"

Her eyes fell away. "Yes."

"Even if I were to believe you, that's neither here nor there. I want to know why you felt you had to maintain your lie with me when you're a close friend of the woman who married my best friend."

The silence deafened him.

"I'll find out the truth before long. Why not be honest with me now and get it over with?" he pressed.

"Is that the only reason you came over here again?"

"What do *you* think?"

More color filled her cheeks. "I—I wish I hadn't told you where I'd fallen."

"Since I found you here at Chloe's, it's a moot point."

She stirred restlessly. "You want me to apologize?"

Akis had her rattled, otherwise she wouldn't have asked those questions. He rubbed his lower lip with his thumb. "You want the truth from me? Do you think that's fair when you've exempted yourself from being forthcoming with me?"

She moistened her lips, drawing his attention to them. All night he'd wondered what she'd taste like. "I meant no harm."

"If that's the case, then why the deception?"

"Look—" She sounded exasperated. Her cheeks grew more flushed as she got to her feet and fitted the crutches beneath her arms. "I haven't had a meaningful relationship with a man for a long time because it's the way I've wanted it."

He walked over to her. "But clearly there've been a lot of men who've wanted one with you. You think I'm just another man you can ignore without telling me why?" She looked away quickly, letting him know he'd guessed the truth. "A woman with your looks naturally attracts a lot of unwanted attention. It must be galling to realize that whatever you did to put me off, fate had a hand in my showing up at Chloe's home. Prove to me my interest in you isn't wanted and I'll leave now."

She looked the slightest bit anxious. "Akis—I just don't think it wise to get to know you better."

"Why? Because you haven't been honest with me and there *is* a man back home you're involved with?"

"No," she volunteered so fast and emphatically, he believed her. "There's no one. This conversation is ridiculous."

"It would be if I didn't know that you're interested in me, too. But for some reason, you're afraid and are using the excuse of having to fly to California to put me off. I want to know why."

"I'm not afraid of you. That's absurd."

"Last night you cheated me out of a dance. I don't

know about you, but I need to feel your mouth moving beneath mine or I might go a little mad with wanting."

"Please don't say things like that," she whispered.

"Because you know you want it, too?"

Her breathing sounded shallow. "Maybe I do, but I'm afraid."

"Of me?" He brushed his lips against hers.

"No. Not you. I'm afraid of my own feelings."

"Shall we find out if they're as strong as mine?" He wrapped her in his arms, crutches and all. His lips caught the small cry that escaped hers, giving him the opportunity to coax a deeper kiss from her. First one, then another, until she allowed him full access and the spark between them ignited into fire.

"Akis—" she cried softly before kissing him back with a hunger that thrilled him. He'd kissed other women, but nothing prepared him for the surge of desire driving both of them as they swayed together.

"I want you, Raina," he whispered against her creamy throat, "more than any woman I've ever wanted in my life." He came close to forgetting her sprained ankle until a moan sounded in her throat, prompting him to release her with reluctance and step away.

She steadied herself with the crutches for control. Those enticing lips looked swollen and thoroughly kissed. "That shouldn't have happened." The tremor in her voice was achingly real.

"But it did because we both wanted it." He took a quick breath. "I want to spend time with you, and from the way you kissed me, I know you want the same thing." His comment coincided with the arrival of Chloe's parents, who walked in on the two of them.

"Weren't you over here earlier?" Socus teased him in his native tongue. "No wonder our guest didn't mind that we had an important business dinner to attend."

Akis shook his head. "She didn't know I was coming over again."

"We're glad you're here, Akis," Nora said in English. "We don't want her to leave. Please do what you can to persuade her to stay until Chloe and Theo get back."

Socus chimed in. "If we had our way, we'd insist on your living with us for a long time, young woman."

Raina's eyes misted over. "You're such dear people and have been wonderful to me. But I'm afraid I have too many responsibilities at home to remain here for any length of time."

"Your ankle needs at least a week to heal before we let you get on a plane," Chloe's father declared. "But we can talk more about this in the morning. Good night, you two."

After they left the room Akis said, "Your ankle could use more rest. There's nothing I'd like better than to help you pass the time."

He sensed she knew she was defeated, but that didn't stop her from darting him a piercing glance. "What about your work?"

"My brother will fill in for me. We do it for each other when necessary." He stood there with his hands on his hips. "You look tired, so I'm going to leave. If I come over in the morning, will I still find you here?"

Her eyes flashed. "Perhaps the question should be, will you show up since you have a disparaging opinion of me?"

"You mean after you told me I should stick with my own kind and background?"

She stirred restlessly. "I can see you still haven't forgiven me for an innocent remark."

"There was nothing innocent about it. But the way you kissed me back a few minutes ago confirms my original gut instinct that you know something significant has happened to both of us. Good night, *thespinis*."

He left the house for the limo. On the way to his penthouse his cell phone rang. One look at the caller ID and he clicked on. "Vasso? How come it's taken you so long to get back to me?"

"Nice talking to you, too, bro."

His head reared. "Sorry."

"The phone died on me and I just got back to my hotel to recharge it. What's wrong? You don't sound like yourself."

"That's because I'm not."

"The opening went fine."

Akis was in such a state he'd forgotten to ask. "Sorry. My mind is on something else."

"Was there a problem at the wedding? I saw you on the evening news helping a beautiful woman on crutches into the limo."

So Vasso saw it. "She's the reason I called. When will you be back?"

His brother laughed. "I'll fly in around 7:00 a.m. and should be at the office by nine."

"If you're that late, I'm afraid I won't be there."

"That sounded cryptic. Why?"

"Something happened at the reception."

"You sound odd. What is it?"

"I've...met someone."

"I'm not even going to try to figure that one out. Just tell me what has you so damned upset."

"Believe it or not, a woman has come into my life."

"There've been several women in your life over the years. Tell me something I don't know. Are we talking about the woman on crutches?"

"Yes. This one is different." Both brothers had led a bachelor life for so long, not even Akis believed what had happened to him since he'd seen Raina on the street.

"Are you saying what I think you're saying?"

"Yes."

"You're serious."

"Yes."

Vasso exhaled sharply. "She feels the same way?"

His teeth snapped together. "After the way she kissed me back tonight, I'd stake my life on it."

"But you only met her last evening."

"I know. She looks like Aphrodite with lavender eyes."

"I'll admit she was a stunner." Laughter burst out of Vasso. "But you sound like you still need to sleep off the champagne."

"I swear I only had a sip."

"Come on, Akis. Quit the teasing."

"I'm not." For the first time in his life Akis was swimming in uncharted waters where a woman was concerned.

A long silence ensued. "How old is she?"

"Twenty-six."

"From Athens?"

"No. California."

"She's an American?"

"Yes. On the day of the wedding rehearsal, we almost bumped into each other on the sidewalk after I left Theo at the bank. I couldn't get her out of my head. On the night of the reception, to my surprise she was sitting at a table in the back of the ballroom.

"When I asked her to dance, she didn't understand because she said she didn't speak Greek. But she couldn't dance anyway because she was on crutches. I helped her out to the limo and took her to her hotel."

"Just like that you spent the night with her? You've never done anything like that before. Wasn't that awfully fast?"

"I didn't stay with her and you don't know all that happened. When I couldn't find her at the hotel today and learned she'd checked out, I checked with Theo's family. They hadn't heard of her so I decided to go over to Chloe's for help. When I went walked in, to my shock I found her relaxing at the side of the pool."

"She was at Chloe's?"

"Yes. It seems Chloe spent a school year with her back in high school on one of those exchange programs to learn English."

"How come you've never heard of her?"

"I once remember Theo telling me that Chloe had an American friend she lived with in high school, but I never made the connection."

"What's her name?"

"Raina Maywood. But when she fell and sprained her ankle in our number four store, she gave Galen a different name before going to the ER. I had a devil of a time tracking her down."

"Wait, wait—start over again. You're not making sense."

"Nothing has made sense since we first saw each other."

"Akis? Are you still with me?"

"Yes."

"What's your gut telling you?"

"I don't know," he confessed.

"Maybe she wanted to meet you. It wouldn't be hard to connect the dots. After all, she knows the circles Chloe's family runs in. Maybe when Chloe invited her to come to the wedding, she told her about Theo's best man and promised to introduce you."

"There's a flaw in that thinking, Vasso, because it didn't happen that way. By sheer chance I asked her to dance. Otherwise we would never have met. After I took her to her hotel, she made it close to impossible for me to find her."

"But she *did* end up at Chloe's, so it's my guess she hoped you'd show up there at some point. Even if that part of the evening wasn't planned, what if all along her agenda has been to come to the wedding and use Chloe's parents to meet you? Is that what you're afraid of? That she's after your money?"

"Hell if I know."

"It stands to reason Chloe would have told her all about Theo's best man. There's no sin in it, but the way things are moving so fast, don't you think you need to take a step back until more time passes? Then you can see what's real and what isn't. Think about it."

Akis *was* thinking. His big brother had touched on one of Akis's deepest fears. The possibility that somehow she'd engineered their meeting like other women in the past had done tore him up inside. He wanted to believe that everything about their meeting and the unfolding of events had been entirely spontaneous.

But if Chloe had discussed him with Raina, then her comment about his background made a lot of sense. He and Vasso were the brothers who'd climbed out of poverty to make their way in the world. They lacked the essentials that other well-bred people took for granted—like monetary help from family, school scholarships, exposure to the world.

They'd been marked from birth as the brothers who'd come out of that class of poor people who would be lucky to survive. Whatever he and Vasso had achieved had come through sheer hard work.

Akis could hold his own, but he was aware of certain inadequacies that would never change.

If in the past the situation had warranted it, he and Vasso had always given each other good advice. But this one time he didn't want to hear it even though he was the one who'd called his brother.

Akis didn't want to think Raina might be like Althea who was looking for a husband who could keep her in the style of Chloe's parents.

"Isn't that why you phoned me, because you're worried?" his brother prodded. "She's seen the kind of wealth Chloe comes from. You remember how crazy Sofia and I were over each other when we lived on the island without a drachma to our name?"

"How could I forget?"

"But she turned down my wedding proposal because she said she could do better. It wasn't until our business started to flourish that she started chasing me again and wouldn't leave me alone. At that point I wasn't interested in her anymore."

"I remember everything," Akis's voice grated. Both he and Vasso had been through the painful experience of being used. It had made them wary of stronger attachments. A few years ago when they'd set up two charities to honor their parents, one of the women they'd hired as a secretary to deal with the paperwork had made a play for Vasso. But it turned out she wanted marriage rather than the job.

Akis had run into a similar situation with an attractive woman they'd hired to run one of their stores. She'd called Akis one evening claiming there was an emergency. When he showed up at the store, it turned out the emergency was a ploy to get him alone.

Most women they met were introduced to them by mutual friends. After a few dates it was clear they had marriage and money on their minds. But the essential bonding of two minds and hearts of the kind he saw in Theo and Chloe's relationship always seemed to be missing.

"Sorry to be such a downer, but Chloe's friend did lie about her name, which I find strange. When are you going to see her again?"

"I told her I'd be over tomorrow."

"Did she tell you *not* to come?"

He grimaced. "No." But earlier she'd told him he'd be better off to find a woman of his own kind and background because she was leaving Greece. She'd been keeping up that mantra to hide what was really wrong.

"Okay. As I see it, maybe she's taking advantage of

her friendship with Chloe. Then again, maybe there is
no agenda here. All I can say is, slow down."

Akis took a deep breath, more confused than ever
over her mixed signals. Why would she have flown all
the way to Greece, yet she hadn't attended the wedding of her good friend at the church? Bombarded by a
series of conflicting emotions, he felt a negative burst
of adrenaline, not knowing what to believe.

"I don't want to think about it anymore tonight.
Thanks for listening. I'll see you in the morning."
He clicked off.

Without that kiss he might have decided it wasn't
worth it to pursue her further, except that he didn't really believe that. It had taken all his willpower not to
chase around the corner after her with some excuse to
detain her. But this evening he hadn't been thinking
clearly. The need to feel her in his arms outweighed
every other thought. *It still did...*

"Kyrie?" his driver called to him. "We've arrived."

So they had. Akis thanked him and climbed out of
the limo. On his way up to the penthouse, he went over
the conversation with his brother. Vasso had given him
one piece of advice he would follow from here on out.

Slow down.

CHAPTER THREE

By the time Raina had unwrapped her ankle to shower on Monday morning, she had to admit it felt a lot better. Resting it had really helped because there was little swelling now. It didn't need to be rewrapped as long as she walked with crutches and was careful.

After dressing in a blouse and jeans, she brushed her hair and put on her pink lipstick. Every time she thought about Akis Giannopoulos, she got a fluttery feeling in her chest, the kind there was no remedy for.

Her lips still throbbed from the passion his mouth had aroused. For a little while she'd been swept away to a place she'd never been before. After having no personal life for so long, she supposed something like this had been inevitable. Maybe it was good this hormone rush had happened here in Greece. Before long she'd be leaving, so whatever it was she felt for this man, their relationship would be short-lived.

Since she couldn't do any sightseeing this trip, her only option was to stay at Chloe's. Such inactivity for a man like Akis would wear thin. When he found himself bored, he'd find a plausible reason to leave.

Breakfast came and went. She lounged by the pool

and read a book she'd brought. Every time Nora or a maid came out to see if she wanted anything, she expected Akis to follow. By lunchtime she decided he wasn't coming.

After kissing her as payback for the way she'd treated him last night, he'd left the house. It wouldn't surprise her if he'd had no intention of coming back today. Raina ought to be relieved. Once she'd eaten lunch with Nora, there was still no sign of him.

Hating to admit to herself she was disappointed he hadn't come, she went to her bedroom to do some business on the phone with her staff running the estate in California. No sooner had she gotten off the phone than the maid knocked on her door. "Kyrie Giannopoulos is waiting for you on the patio."

At the news her heart jumped, a terrible sign that he mattered to her much more than she wanted him to. "I'll be right there." She refreshed her lipstick before using her crutches to make it out to the pool area where Akis was waiting for her.

His intense black gaze swept over her while he stood beneath the awning in an open-necked tan sport shirt and jeans. His clothes covered a well-defined chest and rock-hard legs. Whether he wore a tux, a bathing suit or casual clothes, her legs turned to mush just looking at him.

"I would have been here sooner, but my business meeting this morning took longer than I'd supposed. The housekeeper told me you've already had lunch. Have you ever been to Athens?"

"I came here once with my grandparents when I was young, but remember very little."

"What happened to your parents?"

"They were killed in a light plane crash when I was twelve."

"How awful for you."

"I could hardly believe it when it happened. I suffered for years. We had such a wonderful life together. They were my best friends."

"I'm sorry," he whispered.

"So am I, but I was very blessed to have marvelous grandparents who did everything for me."

"Thank heaven for that." He eyed her thoughtfully. "Are you up to some sightseeing then?"

Her breath caught. "Much as I'd love to tour Athens, I can't. You didn't need to come over. A phone call would have sufficed."

"You can see Athens from my penthouse terrace." She blinked. "The city will be at your feet. I have a powerful telescope that will enable you to see its famous sights up close from the comfort of a chair and ottoman for your leg."

"Go with him, Raina," Chloe's mother urged, having just walked out on the patio. "Socus and I went up there one night. You can see everything in the most wonderful detail. The Acropolis at twilight is like a miracle."

Raina couldn't very well turn him down with an endorsement like that from Nora. "You've sold me. I'll just go back to the room for my purse." Reaching for her crutches, she hurried away with a pounding heart. Retrieving her purse, she headed for the front door, but Akis was there first to open it for her.

"Thank you," she whispered, so aware of his presence it was hard to think. Once he'd helped her inside the limo out in front, he sat across from her. "I know you want to rest your leg so I've told the driver to take us straight to the Giannopoulos complex."

"We could have stayed at Chloe's and played cards. It would have saved you all this trouble."

The compelling male mouth that had kissed her so thoroughly last night broke into a smile, turning her heart over. "Some trouble is worth it."

She looked out the window without seeing anything. Going to his penthouse wasn't a good idea, but her hectic emotions had taken over her common sense. Raina wanted to be with him. She would only stay awhile before she asked him to take her back to Chloe's.

The driver turned into a private alley and stopped at the rear of the office building. Akis helped her out and drew a remote from his pocket that opened a door to a private elevator. In less than a minute they'd shot to the roof and the door opened again.

Adjusting her crutches, Raina followed him into his glassed in, air-conditioned penthouse. No woman's touch here, no curtains, no frills or knickknacks. Only chrome and earth tones. It was a man's domicile through and through, yet she saw nothing of his dynamic personality reflected.

The best man who'd tracked her down despite all odds didn't seem to fit in these unimaginative surroundings. But she could understand his coming home to this at night. Glorious Athens lay below them from every angle.

"Come out to the terrace. I have everything set up for you."

The telescope beckoned beneath the overhang. Working her crutches, she stepped out in the warm air and flashed him a glance. "Were you an eagle in another life? I like your eyrie very much."

"As far as I know, this is the only life I've been born to, but I was hatched in a very different place as you well know."

She frowned. No, she didn't know. Akis was trying to rile her. In retaliation she refused to rise to the bait.

He took her crutches so she could sit on the leather chair and prop her leg on the ottoman. After putting the crutches aside, he placed the telescope so she could look through it while she sat there. "I've set it on the Acropolis and the Parthenon."

"The cradle of Western civilization," she murmured. "This is the perfect spot to begin my tour. Thank you." One look and she couldn't believe it. "Oh, Akis—I feel like I'm right there. How fabulous! A picture doesn't do it justice. Do you mind if I move this around a little? There's so much to see, I could look through it for hours."

"That's why I brought you here. Enjoy any view you want. Since it's heating up outside, I'll get us some lemonade."

She was glad he'd left. The brief intimacy they'd shared last night hadn't lasted long enough. The fire between them had been building since he'd shown up at Chloe's house. But he was only gone for a few minutes and returned with a drink for both of them. The second he came back out, her pulse raced.

He lounged against the edge of a wrought-iron patio table and played tour director for the next two hours. Akis was a fount of information, responding to all her questions.

No one watching them would know how disturbed

she was to be this close to such a man who on the surface appeared so pleasant. Underneath his urbane facade Raina knew he was just biding his time until she tired of sightseeing and he had her full attention.

When she'd eventually run out of questions, she sat back with a sigh. "Thanks to you, I feel like I've walked all over this city without missing anything important. I'll remember your kindness when I watch the city recede from my plane window."

Akis moved the telescope out of reach, then flicked her a probing glance. "Forget about returning to California. You've only seen a portion of Athens. What you haven't seen is what I consider to be the best part of Greece. I'm prepared to show it to you. I understand Chloe's parents have extended you an open invitation to stay for a while."

She shook her head. "Why would you want to do anything for me when it's obvious you have issues with me?"

"Maybe because you're different from the other women I've met and I'm intrigued."

"That's not the answer and you know it."

One black brow lifted. "You can't deny the chemistry between us. I'm still breathless from the explosion when we got in each other's arms last night."

Raina's hands gripped the arms of the chair. "So am I."

"After such honesty, you still want to run from me?" he said in a husky tone.

"Physical attraction gets in the way of common sense."

He folded his arms. "What is your common sense telling you?"

"I think your questions about me have fueled your interest."

"Is that wrong?"

"Not wrong, just unsettling. I know you've been upset with me since the night of the reception when I wouldn't tell you my name and gave your employee a different name. I already told you the reason why."

"Just not all of it," he challenged in that maddening way, causing her blood pressure to soar.

"What's the matter with you?" she cried softly. "Earlier today you accused me of knowing something about your origins, when in truth I know next to nothing about you except that you were the best man!" Her voice shook with emotion. "If there's some sinister secret you're anxious to hide, I promise you I don't know what it is."

His eyes narrowed on her features. "That's difficult for me to believe when you've been Chloe's best friend for years."

She nodded. "We became best friends and have seen and stayed in touch with each other over the years. I knew she was crazy about Theo months ago, but I only heard she was getting married a month ago. She was so full of excitement over the wedding plans, I didn't even know the last name of her fiancé's best man, let alone any details about you. If that offends your male pride, I'm sorry."

He shifted his weight. "I'm afraid it's you *I've* offended without realizing it. Shall we call a truce and start over? Nora wants us to come back and eat dinner with them by the pool. Afterward they're going to show us the wedding video."

"You can tell they're missing Chloe," she said.

"That's what happens when there's an only child."

Raina knew all about that and agreed with him. "Their family is very close. Just being with them this little bit makes me surprised they allowed her to leave home for the school year."

"If she hadn't been happy with you, I'm sure she wouldn't have stayed." While she felt his deep voice resonate, his gaze traveled over her. "Surely you can understand how much they want to pay you back for the way your family made her feel so welcome. If you want my opinion, I think you'll hurt their feelings if you fly to the States too soon, but it's your call."

Privately Raina feared the same thing. "I'm sure you're right. If I stay until Chloe and Theo get back, it'll give me a chance to rest my leg a little more." *More days to spend with Akis.*

Wasn't that the underlying factor in her decision just now, even though her heart was warning her to run from him as fast as she could? To love this man meant opening herself up to pain from which she might never recover.

"They'll be happy to hear it. Are you ready to go back?"

No, her heart cried, but her lips said "Yes."

After she finished her drink, he helped her with the crutches. Their hands brushed, sending darts of sensation running up her arms. He didn't try to take advantage, but it didn't matter. Every look or touch from him sensitized her body. As they left the penthouse for the drive back to the Milonis estate, she fought to ignore her awareness of him.

Later, after a delicious dinner, Akis took the crutches from Raina while she settled on the couch in the den. Nora sat next to her while Socus started the video. Akis turned off the light and sat in one of the upholstered chairs to watch. Cries of excitement, happiness and laughter from Chloe's parents punctuated the scene of the wedding day unfolding before their eyes.

The videographer had captured everything from the moment Chloe left the house for the church. Parts of the ceremony in the church left Raina in happy tears for her dear friend. She just knew they'd have a wonderful life together.

Other parts of the film covered the reception, including the dancing. The camera panned from the wedding couple to the best man dancing with the maid of honor. "You and Althea make a beautiful couple," Socus exclaimed.

Raina concurred. He was so handsome it hurt, but the inscrutable expression on his face was distinctly different from the adoring look on Althea's. Suddenly the camera focused on the guests. Raina saw herself at the table. Shock!

But there were more shocks when it caught Akis accompanying her from the ballroom. She'd had no idea they were being filmed.

Nora laughed. "Oh, Akis… Now I understand why you didn't spend the rest of the evening with poor Althea. You remind me of the prince at the ball who avoided the stepsisters because he wanted to know the name of the mystery woman on crutches and ended up running after her." Socus's laughter followed.

In that instant Raina's gaze fused with a pair of jet black eyes glinting in satisfaction over Nora's observation. Her body broke out in guilty heat.

"Wasn't I lucky that I found Cinderella at your house."

"We're very happy you did." Nora beamed.

"It saved me from prowling the countryside for the maiden with the crutches."

Chloe's mother chuckled. "Wait till Chloe and Theo watch this. They're going to love it."

"They will," Raina agreed with her before lowering her blond head. Chloe would appreciate the irony of the camera finding her friend from California in the crowd despite every effort Raina had made to stay away from the camcorders of the paparazzi.

While she sat there wishing she could escape to her bedroom, Akis got to his feet and turned on the light. "Thank you for dinner and an entertaining evening. Now I know Raina needs to rest her leg, so I'm going to leave."

"So soon?" Nora questioned.

"I'm afraid so. But I'll be by in the morning at nine. Earlier I told Raina I'd like to show her another part of Greece I know she'll enjoy while she's still recovering." His dark eyes probed hers. "But maybe you've decided you'd rather stay here."

He'd deliberately put her on the spot. Everyone was waiting for her answer. Not wanting to seem ungracious she said, "No. I'll be ready. Thank you."

"Good."

The pilot landed the helicopter on the pad of the Milonis estate. Akis could see Raina's gleaming blond hair as she stood on her crutches. It wasn't until you got closer that you noticed that hint of red in the strands. His gaze fell over her curvaceous figure that did wonders for the summery denims and short-sleeved small-print blouse she was wearing.

He opened the doors of the Giannopoulos company's recently purchased five-seater copter. "Let me take your crutches and handbag." Once she'd handed them to him, he put them aside, then picked up her gorgeous body by the waist. The instant there was contact, her warmth and fragrance enveloped him.

Without letting go of her, he helped her into the seat next to the window behind the pilot. That way he could keep an eye on her from the copilot's seat. "Are you all right?" Their mouths were only inches apart.

"Y-yes," came her unsteady voice before she looked away. A nerve jumped madly at the base of her creamy throat. The touch of skin against skin had affected her, too.

"Have you ever flown in a helicopter before?"

She nodded.

After laying the crutches on the floor, he put her purse in the storage unit, and then looked down at her.

"Are you all strapped in?"

"Yes. I'm fine. I just want to know where we're going."

"Are you afraid I'm planning to carry you off, never to be seen again?"

A secret smile appeared. "After the fierce look on your face as you headed toward my table at the hotel, the thought did occur to me."

Charmed despite his questions about what she was still hiding from him he said, "I'll give you a clue. We're headed for the Ionian Sea. Once we reach the water, I'll give you a blow-by-blow account using the microphone. But there's one more thing I have to do before takeoff."

Akis pulled out several pillows from a locker and hunkered down to elevate her leg. She wore sandals. His hands slid beneath her calf and heel to adjust the fit. He ran a finger over her ankle, pleased to notice she trembled. "There's no trace of swelling I can see," he said, eyeing her. "We'll make sure things stay that way today."

The urge to kiss her was overwhelming, but he restrained himself. Her thank-you followed him to his seat. He gave the pilot a nod, put on his sunglasses and strapped himself in. Before long Athens receded and they were arcing their way in a northwesterly direction. Over the mic he gave her a geography lesson and responded to her questions.

When they reached the island of Corfu surrounded by brilliant blue water, he had the pilot swing lower so she could take in the fascinating sight of whitewashed houses. Here and there he pointed out a Byzantine church and the remains of several Venetian fortresses.

He shot Raina a speaking glance. "I brought you here first. This is where Poseidon fell in love with Korkyra, the Naiad nymph."

"Ah. Poseidon…" Her lips curved upward. "Did Korkyra reciprocate his feelings?"

"According to legend she adored him and they had a baby named Phaiax. Today the islanders have the nickname Phaeacians. Another island in this group is fourteen miles south of here. We'll head there now."

"What is it called?"

"Paxos. When you see it, you'll understand why it's constantly photographed."

In a few minutes he heard a cry. "What a darling island!" That wasn't the word he would have chosen, but he was pleased by her response. "What kind of vegetation is that?"

"Olive groves. Some of the gnarled trees are ancient. The pilot will fly us over the western side and you'll see steep, chalky white cliffs. If you look closely, you'll spot its many caves along the coast line. When you go into them on a launch, they glow blue."

"How beautiful!"

"We have Poseidon to thank for its creation. He wanted to get away from stress on the big island of Corfu, so he used his trident to create this hideaway for him and his wife."

"Or maybe to hide his wife from Korkyra? What are you saying? That the stress of having a mistress and keeping his wife happy at the same time was too much, even for a god?" Like a discordant note, he heard brittle laughter come out of her. "That's hilarious!"

There was a story behind her hollow reaction, but now was not the time to explore it. "The Greek myths are meant to be entertaining. If you'll notice, there's another tinier island just beyond this one called Anti Paxos. When Poseidon wanted to be strictly alone, he came here to swim in the clear green water you can see below."

"I imagine that leading a double life would have worn him out."

Laughter burst from Akis.

"Wasn't *he* lucky to be a god and pick the most divine area in his immortal world to plan his next conquest." The pilot circled Anti Paxos for a closer look. "What a heavenly spot."

It was. Akis's favorite place on earth. He wanted to hide Raina away here, away from the world where the two of them could be together and make love for the rest of time.

Unfortunately they'd come to the end of the tour. He checked his watch. "We're going to head back to Athens via a little different route. We'll be crossing over a portion of Albania you should find fascinating. If you're thirsty or hungry, there's bottled water and snacks in the seat pouch in front of you."

"Um. Don't mind if I do. Would you or the pilot like something?"

That was thoughtful of her. "We're fine."

In a minute she said, "These almonds are the best I've ever tasted!"

"They're grown on these islands." Akis was addicted to them.

"How would it be to live right down there in paradise! If I did, I'm sure I'd become an addict."

Everything she said and did entrenched her deeper in his heart. She had a sweetness and vulnerability that made him want to protect her. Raina had become his addiction and already he couldn't imagine life without her. That's when he realized he was in serious trouble, but for once in his life he didn't care.

"If you'll extend your time in Greece, I can arrange for you to stay on Anti Paxos. Think about it and let me know after we get back to Chloe's house."

"Even if I could take time off from work, what about yours? Can you afford to be gone any longer?"

His heart leaped. So she *was* interested…

"My brother will cover for me."

"You're lucky to have him." She sounded sincere. "Is there more family?"

"No. Just Vasso."

"Is he younger? Older?"

The questions were coming at last. "Older by eleven months."

"You were almost twins!"

"Almost."

"Do you resemble each other?"

He turned to his pilot. "What do you think?" he asked in Greek. "Do Vasso and I look alike?"

The other man grinned before giving him an answer.

Akis translated. "He said, superficially."

"Is Vasso married?"

Why did she want to know that? "Not yet."

"Then maybe you should arrange for him to meet Chloe's bridesmaid."

His black brows furrowed. "I'm afraid my brother prefers to be the one in pursuit. What makes you so concerned for Althea?"

"Even Nora noticed how crestfallen she looked when you stopped dancing with her."

"According to Theo, she has lots of boyfriends."

"But she wanted *you*," Raina came back.

"Why do you say that?"

"I may have been farther away, but I could see her disappointment. Think how much she would have enjoyed a day like this with you."

"If you're trying to make me feel guilty, it isn't working."

She flashed him a quick smile. "Not at all. I was just thinking how fortunate I've been to be given a fantastic personal tour narrated by you. It's a real thrill."

"I'm glad you're enjoying it. But it's not over yet. We'll be flying over a portion of the Pindus National Park covered in black pines. The view from this altitude is extraordinary." While she studied the landscape, he'd feast his eyes on her.

For the next hour she appeared captivated by the unfolding scenery. Every now and again he heard a little gasp of awe as they dipped lower to view a new sight. Whatever his suspicions might have been in the beginning, her barrage of questions made him think her reactions to the beauty below them couldn't be faked.

Once they'd landed on the pad of the Milonis estate, he helped Raina down. Their bodies brushed, causing a tiny gasp to escape her lips. He knew exactly how she felt and didn't know how long he could stand it before he kissed her again.

Akis watched her disappear before he used the guest bathroom and phoned his driver to come to the house. He had plans for him and Raina later. After washing his hands, he walked out to the patio to phone his brother. No doubt he was still at the office. Akis needed to give him a heads-up that he wouldn't be coming in to work for a few days. He was taking a brief vacation in order to spend time with Raina.

To his frustration, his call went to Vasso's voice mail. Once again he had to ask him to call him back ASAP. Then he spoke to his private secretary to know if there were any situations he needed to hear about. But he was assured everything was fine. Vasso had been there until two o'clock, then he'd left.

After hanging up, he walked to the cabana and changed into a swimming suit. Akis needed a workout after sitting so long. Much as he wanted Raina to join him in the pool, he knew she couldn't. But on that score he was wrong. When he'd finished his laps and started to get out, he saw her at the shallow end, floating on her back. The crutches had been left at the side of the pool.

By rotating her arms, she was able to move around without hurting her ankle. He swam over to her, noticing her blond hair looked darker now that it was wet and swept back. The classic features of her oval face revealed her pure beauty. Those eyes shimmered like amethysts. *Incredible.*

"I'm glad you came out here."

"After today's tour, I thought I'd like to see what it was like to swim with Poseidon, god of the sea."

He sucked in his breath. "You're not afraid I might make you my next conquest?"

She kept on moving. "Do you think you can?"

He kept up with her. "After our kiss the other night, I think you know the answer to that."

"What will your wife say?"

"She doesn't rule my life."

"That would be the worst fate for you, wouldn't it? To be ruled by your passion for one woman? To be her slave forever?"

"Not if she's the right woman."

"How will you know when you've found her?" The pulse throbbing violently in the vulnerable spot of her throat betrayed her.

"I think I have. Stay in Greece until I can unveil all of the real you."

"The real me?"

"Yes. There's more to you than you want to let on."

A beguiling smile broke the corners of her mouth. "And what about you, swimming into my life? Who are you, really?"

He swam closer. "Who would you like me to be?" The blood pounded in his ears.

"Just yourself."

Raina...

She'd reached for the side of the pool and clung to it. "Akis," she said softly. "I'm frightened because my feelings for you are already too strong."

"Strong enough to meet me halfway and kiss me again?"

"I want to." Her voice throbbed. "But I'm worried I'll be enslaved by you."

Akis took a deep breath and moved through the water next to her. "Don't you know you're the one who has enslaved me? I need you, Raina."

Her eyes looked glazed. "You're not the only one," she confessed.

He clasped her to him and covered her trembling mouth with his own. This time he'd jumped right into the fire, heedless of the flames licking through his body.

Her curves melted against him as if she were made for him. He kissed her with growing abandon until he felt her hungry response. It wasn't like anything he'd ever known and he was afraid he'd never get enough.

"Raina," he whispered in a thick tone. "Do you have any idea how beautiful you are? How much I want you?"

She moaned her answer, too swallowed up in their

need for each other to talk. This was what Akis had been waiting for all his life, this feeling of oneness and ecstasy.

"Anyone for dinner?" came the sudden godlike voice of thunder.

Raina made a sound in her throat and tore her lips from his. "Socus has seen us."

"He has to know what's going on," Akis whispered against the side of her neck. "You're a grown woman."

"Yes, but I'm also a guest in their home. What must he think when we only met a few days ago?"

"That we're incredibly lucky and are enjoying ourselves."

She lifted anxious eyes to him. "Way too much." To his regret she eased away from him in her orange bikini to reach the steps of the pool. After grabbing her towel and crutches, she disappeared inside the house.

Akis threw his dark head back and drank in gulps of air. No doubt Chloe's father had seen the two of them locked together while the water sizzled around them.

Naturally Raina would bring out a protective instinct in the older man. She was their honored guest. Akis swam to the deep end. After levering himself over the edge, he headed for the cabana to shower and get dressed.

As he was pulling on his crew neck, his cell rang. He drew it from his pant pocket to look at the caller ID and clicked on. "Vasso? Did you get my message?"

"Yes, but we've got an electrical problem at the number ten store I've got to see about. I'm leaving the penthouse to take care of it now. Before you go away on vacation, I've left some papers for you to look at in the den."

"About that new property we were thinking about on Crete?"

"No. It's something else. Talk to you later." He hung up before Akis could question him further.

Something else? What exactly did that mean? Curious over it, Akis left the cabana in a slightly different mood than before and walked around the pool to the covered portion of the patio. Everyone was seated at the table waiting for him. Raina looked a golden vision wearing a pale yellow beach robe over her beautiful body.

"Ah, there you are," Nora exclaimed. "Now we can eat."

"I'm sorry to keep you waiting. My brother called me about a business problem. After dinner, I'll have to get back to the penthouse to deal with it." His gaze darted to Raina whose eyes were asking questions not even he could answer yet. "I'll phone you later about our plans for tomorrow." The night he'd planned with her would have to wait.

Raina watched Akis's tall, powerful body disappear from the patio in a few swift strides. Disappointment swept over her. She despised her weakness for remaining silent when he announced in front of Chloe's parents he'd call her later about plans for the next day. To them the silence on her part meant agreement and she'd be staying in Greece longer.

After the two of them had come close to kissing each other senseless out in the pool, he would naturally assume she couldn't wait to be with him again.

Socus had seen them kissing and had been left in no doubt what was going on between them.

That kiss had been her fault for taunting Akis. In some part of her psyche she'd wanted him to pull her into his arms. Otherwise she wouldn't have gotten into the pool. She knew she'd come to the edge of a cliff like the kind they'd flown over earlier in the day. One more false step and she'd fall so deep and hard for this man, she'd never recover. Raina couldn't forget a certain conversation with him.

What will your wife say?

She doesn't rule my life.

That would be the worst fate for you, wouldn't it? To be ruled by your passion for one woman? To be her slave forever?

Not if she's the right woman.

Raina didn't believe there was a right woman for a man as exciting and virile as Akis. In time he would tire of his latest lover and be caught by another woman who appealed to him. In an instant he'd go in pursuit.

The bitter taste of Byron's betrayal still lingered. It was time to end this madness with Akis. But she'd promised Chloe's parents she'd wait to leave Greece until after Chloe and Theo got home from their honeymoon.

Once dinner was over, she went to her room. Though it was early, she took a shower and got ready for bed. She knew Akis would phone her.

If you know what's good for you, don't get in any deeper with him, Raina.

CHAPTER FOUR

AKIS LET HIMSELF in the penthouse and walked back to the den. He saw some papers placed on the table next to the computer. They looked like printouts. His brother had handwritten him a note he'd left on top of the keyboard. Akis sat down in the swivel chair and started to read.

> Don't get mad at me for what I've done. You're so damn honorable, I knew you'd let your questions about Raina Maywood eat you alive. So I decided to put you out of your misery and play PI so she can't accuse you of stalking her. For what it's worth, you're going to bless me for what I've done.
>
> Start with the printout of the article from a California newspaper, then work through the rest. Any worry you've been carrying around about her intentions has flown out the window. There's so much stuff about her, it'll blow your mind.
>
> When you told me her last name was Maywood and that she was a friend of Chloe's from California, it got me thinking about the two he-

licopters we purchased. No wonder Chloe's parents allowed her to stay with Raina, the granddaughter of a man who was one of the pillars of the American economy.

Dazed at this point, Akis picked up the top sheet dated nine months ago.

An American icon of aerospace technology is dead at ninety-two. Joseph Maywood died at his estate in Carmel-by-the-Sea after a long bout of stomach cancer. At his side was his beautiful granddaughter, Laraine Maywood, twenty-six, now heiress to the massive multibillion-dollar Maywood fortune. His wife, Ginger Moss, daughter of famous California seascape artist Edwin Moss, passed away from heart failure several years earlier.

Kaching, kaching, kaching.

Pieces of the puzzle were falling into place faster than Akis could absorb them. Nonplussed, he sat staring at the ceiling. She was an *heiress…*

Adrenaline gushed through his veins.

The X Jet Explorer, built by Pacificopter Inc., was a company owned by the Maywood Corporation in California, USA. Suddenly pure revelation flowed through him. Akis jumped to his feet, incredulous. She was *that* Maywood.

Absolutely stunned, he reached for the next printout dated four years back.

Scandal rocks world-renowned Carmel-by-

*the Sea, a European-style California village
nestled above a picturesque white-sand beach
and home to beautiful heiress-apparent Laraine Maywood Wallace of the Maywood Corporation.*

Wallace? He swallowed hard. She'd been married.
He looked back at the paper and kept reading.

*Reputed to be a lookalike for the famous
French actress and beauty Catherine Deneuve
in her youth, she has divorced husband Byron
Wallace, the writer and biographer involved
in a sensational, messy affair with Hollywood
would-be starlet Isabel Granger who was also
involved with her director boyfriend.*

Akis groaned.

Only now could he understand Raina's brittle
laughter during an earlier conversation. *What are you
saying? That the stress of having a mistress and keeping his wife happy at the same time was too much,
even for a god?* He could feel his gut twisting.

Vasso had left a postscript on his note.

*You've got a green light, bro. No more worry.
She's interested in you, not your money.*

He scanned the other sheets, astonished over the
two charities she'd started in California in honor of
her grandparents, including all she'd accomplished as
CEO of the Maywood megacorporation.

These revelations had turned him inside out. It

shamed him that he'd been so hard on her in his own mind when she'd suffered such pain in her life. The loss of her parents and grandparents…the betrayal by a man who had never deserved her…

"I hoped I'd find you here. How come you don't seem happier?"

Akis had been so absorbed and troubled, he hadn't heard his brother enter the den. He turned in his direction. "I didn't think you'd be back this soon."

"There was a power-grid failure, but it was soon repaired. I'm going to ask you again. What's wrong?"

He rubbed the back of his neck. "I feel like I've trespassed over her soul."

Vasso shook his head. "What are you talking about?"

"This information changes everything." It had been a humbling lesson that had left him shaken.

"Of course it does, but your reaction doesn't make sense."

"I can't explain right now." He squeezed Vasso's shoulder. "You're the best. I'll get back to you."

He left the printouts on the desk and hurried out of the penthouse, calling for his limo. Before he left for Chloe's house, he phoned Raina. She picked up on the third ring.

"Akis? I'm glad you phoned. We were all worried. Is everything okay?"

How strange what a piece of news could do to change everything. She was no longer a mystery in his eyes and the tone in her voice reflected genuine anxiety. The fact that he'd doubted her and had assumed she had an agenda, shamed him. It caused him to wonder how many women he'd falsely labeled when they were as innocent as Raina.

"That all depends on you." He gripped the phone tighter.

"So…there was no emergency with your business, or—or your brother?" Her voice sounded shaky.

Touched by her concern he said, "No. The problem was a power-grid failure that was soon put to right." This emergency was one closer to home. One so serious, he could hardly breathe. "I'm on my way over to talk to you."

"No, Akis. I've gone to bed."

"Then I'll see you tomorrow. We'll do whatever we feel like. I promise not to touch you unless you want me to. I've never met a woman remotely like you. I want to get to know you better, Raina. It would be worth everything to me."

Silence met his question.

"I'm not a god. As you found out in the pool, I'm a mortal with flaws trying to make it through this life. By a stroke of fate you were at the reception when I needed a woman who would dance with me. I haven't been the same since you lifted those violet eyes to me and told me you didn't speak Greek."

"I lied," she murmured. "I know about ten words."

His eyes closed tightly. "If you want nothing more to do with me, then say no in Greek and I'll leave you alone." It would serve him right. He didn't deserve her attention. He held the phone so tightly while he waited, it was amazing it didn't break.

"Neh," he heard her say.

"That means yes, not no."

"I know. I'll be here in the morning when you come

over. I admit I'd like to get to know you better, even if it goes against my better judgment. Good night."

An honest woman.

Akis released the breath he was holding. *"Kalineekta, thespinis."*

Raina spent a restless night waiting for morning to come. After hearing from Akis last night, she'd had trouble getting to sleep. She turned on television just as the news came on. All of a sudden she saw herself and Akis leaving the Grand Bretagne to get into the limo. It was already old news, but still playing because he was so gorgeous.

She shut off the TV, but couldn't shut out the memory of their kiss in the pool. When Akis had called her, she'd sensed a change in him. That edge in his voice had gone. There was a new earnestness in the way he spoke that compelled her to give in. Not only for his reasons, but for her own.

Besides his exceptional male beauty and the desire he'd aroused in her, she'd never met such a dynamic man. He'd gone to great lengths to entertain her while she had to stay off her leg. Only a resourceful person would give her a tour of Athens through a telescope and a sightseeing tour by helicopter, making sure she was comfortable.

He'd been generous with his time and was obviously successful in business with his brother. If she didn't know anything else about him, she knew that much. Chloe's parents seemed very fond of him. When it came right down to it, the big problem was the fact that he was Greek and lived here. Before long she had to go home.

But until that day came, she had to admit to a growing excitement at spending time with him. She couldn't remember the last time she'd taken a true vacation. Not since before her marriage to Byron.

Yes, it was taking a big risk to be with Akis, but she was tired of the continual battle to protect her heart. Before her grandfather had died, he'd warned her not to stay closed up because of Byron. She was too young to go through life an old maid because of one wretched man who didn't know the first thing about being a husband.

"Oh, Grandfather—I wish you were here. I've met a man who has stirred me like no other. Maybe he'll hurt me in the end, but I'll hurt more if I don't go with my feelings for him and see what happens."

If she let Byron win, then she was condemning herself to a life without love or children.

Raina had listened to her grandfather's wise counsel, but it wasn't until she'd been with Akis that his words had started to sink in.

Until the other night when he'd taken her back to the hotel, she'd felt old beyond her years, incapable of feeling the joy of falling in love or anything close to it. But being with Akis had made her forget the past and live in the moment for a little while. To date, no other man had been able to accomplish that miracle.

Akis thrilled her. He did. For once, why not go with those feelings? She wasn't about to walk down the aisle with him, but she could have a wonderful time for as long as this vacation lasted.

Without wasting time, she sat on the side of the bed and phoned the Maywood jet propulsion lab in Salinas where she worked. She asked to be put through to Larry.

"Raina! Great to hear from you. Are you back?"

"No. That's why I'm calling. I've decided to stay in Greece for a couple of weeks. Is that going to present any difficulties for you? I've got my laptop. If you need some problem solving done, I can do it from here."

"No, no. It's about time you took a long vacation. I take it you attended your friend's wedding."

"Yes. It was fabulous." Akis was fabulous.

"You sound different. Happier. That's excellent news."

"It's because I'm having a wonderful time. By the way, I was given a tour of the Ionian Islands in our latest X Jet Explorer. Take it from me, it's a winner in every aspect."

"Wait till I tell everyone! The Giannopoulos Company was our first buyer from Greece. They took delivery of two of them just a month ago."

Raina sprang to her feet in surprise. She'd assumed Akis had chartered a flight through one of the helicopter companies. "Giannopoulos?"

"Yes. Two brothers—like Onassis—who came from nothing and have become billionaires. How did you happen to meet up with them?"

Chloe had never mentioned a word. She'd been too caught up in her wedding arrangements. "Very accidentally," Raina's voice shook as she answered him.

"I've heard they have several thousand stores all over Greece."

Her hand tightened on the phone. *You sprained your ankle in one of them, Raina.*

Stunned by the news, Raina sank back down on the bed. The knowledge that Akis had his own money meant he was the antithesis of Byron, who couldn't make it on his own without living off a woman's money. Her grandfather's shrewd brain was instrumental in making certain Byron's extortion tactics for alimony didn't work.

As for Akis, whether he knew about her background or not, it didn't matter. Finances would never get in the way of her relationship with him. For the first time in her adult life she had no worry in that regard. Akis had his own money and was his own person.

"Thanks for letting me take more time off, Larry." Once she hung up, Raina felt so light-hearted she wanted to whirl around the room, but that wouldn't be a good idea yet. She couldn't risk taking a chance in delaying her recovery.

After getting dressed in a clean pair of jeans and blouse, she took time with her hair and makeup, wanting to look her best for him. Once ready, she left the bedroom on her crutches and headed out to the patio where the family always gathered for meals.

Her senses came alive to see Akis at the table with Chloe's parents while they ate breakfast. He wore a simple T-shirt and jeans. All she saw was the striking male who'd swept into her world, moving mountains to find out where she was hiding.

Well, maybe not mountains above the sea, she smiled to herself, remembering that he wasn't Poseidon. Right then she discovered him staring at her. The longing in his jet-black eyes told her he wanted her for herself. No other reason. He got to his feet and came round to relieve her of the crutches.

"Good morning, *thespinis.*" His deep voice sent curls of warmth through her body.

"It's a lovely morning," she said as he helped her to sit. The soap tang from his body assailed her with its fresh scent.

Socus smiled at her. "What are your plans for today?"

Her gaze switched to Akis who sat across from her. "I'm going to leave the decision up to my tour director."

His eyes gleamed over the rim of his coffee cup. "In that case you'll need to pack a bag because we'll be gone for a while. For the first couple of days we'll lounge by the water to give your ankle a good rest. After that we'll do more ambitious things."

"That's good for you to be careful," Nora commented.

"I'll make sure of it." Akis finished his meal. "When you're ready, we'll leave in the helicopter."

Raina took a certain pride in knowing she'd helped on the project that had tested it before it was ready for the market. Who would have dreamed she'd end up with Akis taking her for a tour in one he'd recently purchased for his business?

After eating some yogurt and fruit, she stood up. "I'll just go put some things in a bag."

Akis came around and handed her the crutches. In a few minutes they made their way out of the house to the helicopter pad. It was like *déjà vu,* except that this time Raina knew she and Akis were functioning on a level playing field where all that mattered was their mutual enjoyment of each other.

He helped her on board and propped her leg. Soon the blades were rotating and they were off. Raina hadn't asked where they were going. The thrill of being taken care of by a good man was enough for her to trust in his decision making.

After a minute he turned to her. "We're headed back to Anti Paxos."

"That island must have great significance for you."

"It's home to me when I'm not working. En route we'll fly over Corinth and Patras, old Biblical sites."

"I get gooseflesh just hearing those names. My grandparents took me to Jerusalem years ago. We didn't have time in Greece to see the religious sites. They promised we'd come back, but because of my grandmother's ill health, that promise wasn't realized."

"Then I'm glad you can see some of the ancient Biblical cities from the air."

For the next hour, the sights she saw including the islands of Cephalonia and Lefkada filled her with wonder.

"Do you recognize your birthplace?" he spoke over the mic.

She chuckled. "I thought I was born in Carmel, California."

"Then you've been misled. The goddess Aphrodite was reputed to be born on Lefkada." With his sunglasses on, she couldn't see his eyes, but she imagined they were smiling.

"That put her in easy reach of Poseidon."

"Exactly."

Before long they circled Paxos and still lower over Anti Paxos before the pilot set them down on a stone slab nestled on a hillside of olive trees and vineyards. Through the foliage she could make out a small quaint villa.

Enchanted by the surroundings, she accepted Akis's help as he lifted her to the ground and handed her the crutches. The pilot gave him her suitcase and purse to carry. They both waved to him before Akis led her along a pathway of mosaic and stone lined by a profusion of flowers to the side of the villa.

"What's that wonderful smell?"

"Thyme. It grows wild on the hillside."

The rustic charm and simplicity in this heavenly setting delighted her.

Once inside, she saw that the living room had been carved out of rock. A fireplace dominated that side of the cottage. The vaulted ceiling and beams of the house with its stone walls and arches defied description. Here and there were small framed photos of his family and splashes of color from the odd cushion and ceramics. She felt like she'd arrived in a place where time had stood still.

He opened French doors to the terrace with a table and chairs that looked out over a small, kidney-shaped swimming pool. A cluster of flowers grew at one end. Beyond it shimmered the blue waters of the Ionian in the distance. You couldn't see where the sky met the sea.

She walked to the edge of the grill-work railing. "If I lived here, I wouldn't want to go anywhere else. What a perfect hideaway."

He stood behind her, but he didn't touch her. He'd promised he wouldn't, but the heat from his body created yearnings within her. "I like living in a cottage. It suits my needs."

Unlike the penthouse, this place reflected his personality.

"How old is the original house?"

"Two hundred years more or less. If you want to use the bathroom, I'll take your bags to the guest room."

"Thank you."

In a few minutes she'd seen the layout of the house. The kitchen and bathroom had been modernized, but everything else remained intact like dwellings from the nineteenth century. She adored the little drop-leaf table and chairs meant for two, built into a wall in the kitchen. On the opposite wall was a door that opened onto steps leading down to the terrace.

A room for the washer and dryer had been built in the middle of the hallway between the two bedrooms. He had everything at his fingertips. She sat in one of the easy chairs and put her crutches down beside her. Akis brought a stool over to rest her leg, then he went to the kitchen and started getting things out of the fridge.

"I'm going to fix our dinner."

"If you'll give me a job, I'll help."

"Don't worry about it today."

"Akis? I don't know if you've heard the story of Goldilocks and the Three Bears, but this cottage reminds me of their adorable house in the forest."

"We Greeks have our own fairy tales. My favorite was the one our father taught me and Vasso about

Demetros who lived with his mother in a hut much like this one was once. When I come here to be alone, I'm reminded of it. He fell in love with a golden-haired fairy, but she wasn't happy with him and went away.

"Vasso and I must have heard that story so many times we memorized the words. Demetros would cry for the rest of his life, 'Come back, come back, my fairy wife. Come back, my fairy child. Seeking and searching I spend my life; I wander lone and wild.'"

Strangely touched by the story she asked, "He never found her again?"

"No. She belonged to a fairy kingdom where he couldn't go."

"That's a sad fairy tale."

"Our father was a realist. I believe he wanted us to learn that you shouldn't try to hold on to something that isn't truly yours or you'll end up like Demetros."

That's what Raina had tried to do when she first felt like she was losing Byron, who'd married her for money. It wasn't until the divorce she'd learned he'd been unfaithful even while they were dating.

No wonder their marriage hadn't worked. He thought he could have a wife, plus her money and another life on the side. Byron had belonged to his own secret world and could never be hers. Her choice in men before she'd come to Greece had been flawed.

As she glanced at Theo's best man, she realized she was looking at the best man alive. The knowledge shook her to the foundations. "Your father sounds like a wise man," she murmured. "Tell me about him."

"He came from a very poor family on Paxos." Ah,

she was beginning to understand why these islands drew him. "My grandparents and their children, with the exception of my father, were victims of the malaria epidemic that hit thousands of Greek villages at the time. By the early nineteen-sixties it was eradicated, but too late for them."

"But your father didn't contract the disease?"

"No. Sometimes it missed someone in a family. A poor fisherman living in a tiny hut in Loggos, who'd lost his family, took my father in to help him catch fish they sold at a shop in the marketplace. When he died, he left my father the hut and a rowboat. Papa married a girl who worked in the olive groves. Her family had perished during the epidemic too. They had to scrape for a living any way they could."

"It's hard for me to believe people can live through such hardships, but I know they do. Millions and millions, and somehow they survive."

"According to our papa, our parents were in love and happy."

"The magic ingredients. Mine were in love, too."

He nodded. "First Vasso was born, then I came along eleven months later. But the delivery was too hard on Mama, who was in frail health, and she died."

"Oh, no," Raina cried softly. "To not know your mother... I'm so sorry, Akis. I at least had mine until I was twelve."

Solemn eyes met hers. "But you lost both parents. It seems you and I have that in common."

"But you never even knew her. It breaks my heart. How on earth did you all manage?"

"Our father kept on working to keep us alive by

supplying olives and fish to the shop. When we were five and six years old, we would help him and never attended school on a regular basis. Life was a struggle. It was all we knew.

"The village thought of us as the poor Giannopoulos kids. Most people looked down on us. Then things turned worse when our father was diagnosed with lymphoma and died."

A quiet gasp escaped. "How old were you?"

"Thirteen and fourteen. By then the woman's husband who owned the shop had also died and she needed help. So she let us work in her shop and helped us learn English. She said it was important to cater to the British and American tourists in their language. We studied English from a book when we could."

"You learned English with no formal schooling? That's incredible."

He stared hard at her. "You're talking to a man whose education is sorely lacking in so many areas, I don't even like to think about it."

"I see no lack in you. Anything but."

"Give it time and my inadequacies will be evident in dozens of ways, but I digress.

"While Vasso waited on customers and did jobs the woman's husband had done, I would go fishing and pick olives. Then it would be my turn to spell him off. I don't think we got more than six hours sleep a night for several years."

"No time to play," she mused aloud.

He made an odd sound in his throat. "We didn't know the meaning of the word."

Raina hated to see him do all the work and got up

to help him. For the first time she didn't use crutches because the kitchen was so close.

"Careful," he cautioned.

"My ankle doesn't hurt."

"Just do me a favor and sit in the chair at the table. The food is ready. I'll bring everything over so we can eat." He'd cut up fresh melon and made a shrimp salad. Lastly came some rolls and iced tea.

"When did you have time to stock the refrigerator?"

He sat down opposite her. "I pay a boy to do errands for me when I come to the island."

"No housekeeper?"

"I prefer to do the work myself."

"You're a jack-of-all-trades as we say in English."

"What does it mean exactly? Whether you've been aware of it or not, I've been picking up a few expressions from you, but I'll admit I'm not familiar with that one."

"Jack is a common name and it means that you can do everything well. Now that you've given me some idea of your background, I understand why." The minute she said the word, she saw the slightest hint of emotion cause his lips to thin.

Realizing she'd stumbled on to something significant when he already felt vulnerable she said, "Akis? At the pool when I told you to talk to someone of your own kind and background, you thought I was being condescending. Admit it."

"The thought did cross my mind."

"Since I knew nothing about your upbringing until just now, will you believe me when I tell you I only said what I did because—"

"Because you sensed I was extremely attracted and it made you nervous." His dark eyes devoured her as he spoke.

She squirmed on the wooden chair. "You're right. Please go on and finish telling me your life's story. I'm riveted. The food is delicious, by the way."

"Thank you." He leaned forward. "The widow we worked for started to suffer from poor health and gave us more and more responsibility. One day an American came in and told us the place reminded him of the convenience-store chains in America. He said they were all over the country. We looked into it and started to make innovations."

"Like what?"

"To keep the shop open twenty-four hours, which we took turns manning. Besides stocking it with a few other items tourists needed, we let patrons cash checks and provided free delivery for those living or staying nearby. In time we'd saved enough money to buy half the store. When she had to stop working, we bought her out."

"That's amazing! How old were you?"

"I was eighteen. Vasso had turned nineteen and had to serve nine months in the army. While he was gone, I ran things. After he got back, it was my turn for military service. We both served in the peacekeeping forces and undertook the command of Kabul International Airport."

"It's a miracle neither of you was injured, or worse."

He shook his head, dismissing it too fast for her liking. What was it he wasn't prepared to share? "The real miracle was that overnight we started making real money. After the early years when most nights we went to bed hungry, it was literally like manna falling from heaven.

"After selling the hut, we moved to an apartment in Loggos right along the harbor. When the widow died, we purchased the property and undertook renovations. In time we'd made enough money to buy failing shops of the same type in Gaios and Lakka, the other towns on the island. We patterned them after the chains we'd investigated and called them Alpha/Omega 24."

She looked at him in amazement. "When I think of two brothers who had the will to survive everything and succeed, I'm in absolute awe over what you accomplished. How did you end up in Athens?"

"You really want to hear?"

"I can't get enough. Please. You can't stop now."

Not immune to her entreaty, Akis brought some plums to the table for their dessert before he spoke. "When our staff was in place at all three stores and we felt confident enough to leave, we took a ferry to Corfu. From there we flew to Athens, our first commercial plane trip."

"Late bloomers on your way to do big business." The warmth of her smile melted him. "Were you excited?"

"We were so full of our plans for future expansion, not much else registered. Without the backing of an established bank, we didn't have a prayer. After two days we found a shop for sale we wanted to buy and started talking to bankers. We were turned down by everyone."

Her eyes reflected the hue of a lavender field. "Obviously that didn't stop you."

"No. At the last bank on our list we met Theo Chiotis in the loan department. He was working his way up in his family's banking business. Maybe it was because we were all the same age and he could tell we were hungry, or maybe we just caught him on a good day, but he was actually willing to examine the books."

"Bless Theo," she murmured.

Akis nodded. "He asked a lot of questions and went with us to look at the property the next day. As we explained how we would remodel and showed him pictures, he said he would take the matter up with the bank director and get back to us. We had no choice but to return to Paxos and go about our business."

"How long did you have to wait?"

"A week."

"It must have felt like an eternity."

Unable to resist, he covered her hand resting on the table and squeezed it before letting it go. "He told us the bank would give us the loan for the one store. If it turned a profit, they'd consider loaning us more money for other stores in the future. But the loan was contingent on our offering our other stores as collateral."

"Of course. Akis—you had to have been overjoyed!"

He sat back in the chair. "Yes and no. Athens was a big city, not a little village. We had to gamble that Athenians as well as tourists would patronize us. In no time our number four store was up and running. Vasso and I took turns manning it. Literally overnight we started making a profit we hadn't even imagined and we never looked back. We call it our lucky store.

Would it interest you to know that's the store where you fell?"

A gentle laugh escaped her lips. "The concierge at the hotel recommended it so I could buy some headache medicine. After spraining my ankle, I didn't think I was so lucky."

"Fate definitely had something in store for us."

"Certainly for you since you and Theo became best friends."

"Theo had the good sense to fall in love with Chloe. If there'd been no Theo, you and I would never have met." Akis didn't even want to think about that possibility. "While I clean up, why don't you go in the living room so you can stretch out on the couch? There's an evening breeze coming in off the terrace."

"What's that other smell besides thyme?"

"It's the woody scent of the maquis growing here mixed with rock rose and laurel."

"I think you've brought me to the Elysian fields where Zeus allowed Homer to live out his days in happiness surrounded by flowers."

Everything she said reminded him that she was highly educated and had seen and done things only experienced by a privileged few. She knew things you only learned from books and academic study. That was part of what made her so desirable. What could he give her in return?

That question burned in his brain as he cleared the table and put things away. "I take it you don't mind being whisked here."

Her mouth curved into a full-bodied smile, filling him with indescribable longings. "Your only problem, Akis Giannopoulos, will be to pry me away when it's time to leave. I love this island where you come to fill your lamp with oil."

The things that came out of that beautiful mouth.

He took a swift breath. "Raina Maywood? Before it's time for bed, it's time I heard the story of *your* life."

CHAPTER FIVE

RAINA GOT UP before he could help her and walked into the other room, but she didn't dare lie down on the couch. The way she was feeling about Akis right now, Raina would ask him to join her and beg him to love her, so she opted for the chair.

He was a man a breed apart from other men in so many vital ways. What an irony that she'd tried to run from him that first night! What if he hadn't pursued her? The thought of never knowing him was like trying to imagine a world without the sun. She waited for him to come in the living room.

When he did, he stretched out on the couch, using the arm for a pillow. After hearing about his beginnings, she felt doubly privileged to be with him like this in his own private sanctuary. He turned his head toward her. "You haven't told me much about your parents."

Somehow Raina knew that question would come first. "I was blissfully happy until they died. Dad was an engineer."

"Your father had the kind of education I would have given anything for. And your mother?"

"She went to college, but became a housewife after

I was born. My most vivid memory of her was playing on the beach. We built sand castles and talked about life while my grandmother painted. I was blessed with grandparents who were there for me when my parents died. I don't know how I would have survived otherwise. They brought happiness into my life again, but they knew I was lonely, even though I had friends.

"That's why they said I could have a student from a foreign country come and live with us during my senior year. I don't know how it happened that Chloe was the perfect pick for me. It was so fun helping her with her English. She was an only child, too, so we just clicked from the beginning.

"My parents' house was near my grandparents who lived close to the ocean. We had horses. I grew up riding and loving it. When Chloe came, we rode along the beach and we did a lot of hiking in the Big Sur Mountains. We made all these plans about what we'd do when I went to Greece. But after Chloe left, my grandmother's heart started to act up and I was afraid to leave her."

"I'm sorry," he murmured. "Was it hard to see Chloe go?"

"Yes, but thankfully I had college and became engrossed in my studies."

He turned on his side toward her. "I missed out on that experience a lot of people take for granted." Akis sounded far away just then.

She smiled at him. "You didn't miss anything." Mindful that his impoverished background had made him the slightest bit sensitive, she said, "What you learned growing up was something no professor or textbook could ever teach you. Every student could take lessons from your work ethic alone."

"Thanks, but I don't want to talk about me."

"I'm not patronizing you, Akis."

"I know that. Keep talking. I love to hear about you. What did you study?"

"My father took after his father and his father before him. I guess a little of it rubbed off on me. I did well in math and science so I went to graduate school and studied physics. After that I went to work for the Maywood Corporation at our jet propulsion lab in Salinas, not far from Carmel."

Incredulous, Akis jackknifed into a sitting position. "Where the helicopters Vasso and I bought are manufactured?"

Her eyes lit up in amusement. "My team did work on its sensor system, one that spanned the electromagnetic spectrum using state-of-the-art instrumentation."

He was aghast. "You rode in a helicopter whose electronics you helped design and you never said a word?"

"Maybe I didn't for the same reason you didn't tell me your number-four store was only one of many."

They'd both been gun-shy of revealing themselves. He got it. "I'm so impressed with the work you do, I can hardly believe you've decided to prolong your vacation here."

"If you want to know the truth, I've worried that you've taken your tour director duty too seriously and your brother might feel that you're neglecting business because of me."

After the information Vasso found on Raina, no doubt he was curious about what was going on and had left a message for Akis to call him. But he'd put off returning it because for the first time in his life, a woman filled his world and he couldn't concentrate on anything else.

"It's getting late, Raina. Before we go to bed, what would you like to do tomorrow?"

"Swim in that green water off your private section of beach. It tops anything I've seen in the Caribbean."

"I've never been to the Caribbean." It was yet another reminder of how worlds apart they were in experience. But her observation caused him to expel a satisfied breath. "That can be arranged. There are few cars on the island, but I have a run-down truck parked on the property to get me around if I need it. We'll drive down to the shore line. Getting there would be tricky with your crutches."

"After tomorrow I'm hoping I can throw them away."

"That can't come soon enough for me. I'm living to dance with you at a charming taverna in Loggos without being impaled." Her chuckle excited him. "We'll take the cabin cruiser over."

"Is the hut you were born in still there?"

"Yes. But today it's surrounded by a vineyard. The vintner uses it to store his tools and such."

"Did that bother you?"

"When Vasso and I found out what was planned, we were happy about it."

"You have amazing resilience." After a pause, "Can we explore one of those caves that glows blue?"

He was prepared to do anything for her. "Whatever your heart desires."

She got to her feet. "You'd better not say that around me. I might just take you up on it because this has been a day of enchantment and I'm border-line addicted already. Good night, Akis."

He watched her fit the crutches under her arms and make her way to the guest room. The urge to carry her to his room brought him to his feet. Needing some-thing constructive to do so he wouldn't follow her, he cleaned up the kitchen, then went out on the terrace to call Vasso. There was no answer. He left the message that he planned to be away from Athens with Raina for a few days. If there was a problem, let him know.

No sooner had he locked up and headed for his bedroom than the phone rang. He picked up on the second ring. "Vasso?"

"You're on vacation with her now?" Akis heard the incredulity in his voice.

"Yes."

"Where?"

"Anti Paxos."

"You're kidding! What has happened to you?"

Something that had already changed his life, but he couldn't say the words out loud quite yet. "Do you need me back at the office?"

"That's not the point. What's going on? Bottom line."

"I'm still trying to figure things out."

"Has she been honest with you?"

He sucked in his breath. "We're getting there."

"Akis—I'm really worried about you."

He didn't want to listen. "Why?"

"You've never been hurt soul-deep by a woman. The way you feel about her, she could be the first to do damage I don't even want to think about if it doesn't work out."

"You mean like Sofia did to you?"

"Yes, but I was younger then and got over it. I'm warning you to be careful."

"I thought you gave me the green light."

"So I did, but she's not just any woman. Hundreds of people depend on her as CEO. Don't forget she came for the wedding and has to go back."

Akis had forgotten nothing. The fear that she'd be able to walk away from him after their vacation was over would keep him tossing and turning during the nights to come. Once in a while the big brother in Vasso took over.

"What are you really trying to warn me about?"

"You've let her into your life where no other woman has gone. I guess I just don't want to see you get hurt. But don't mind me. Papa told me to look after you before he died. I guess I've forgotten you're a grown man now and can take care of yourself. Forgive me?"

"If you can forgive me for asking for a few more days off."

"What do you think?"

"I know it's asking a lot."

"Akis? Take care."

His brotherly warning had come too late. It had been too late by the time she'd flashed those violet eyes at him on the street.

After swimming for the better part of an idyllic day in aquamarine water so clear and clean you could see everything, Raina walked on white-gold silky sand to the little truck to go back to the villa. Akis had played gently with her, always careful so she wouldn't injure her ankle. He'd honored his promise to maintain his distance to the point she wished he hadn't carried it this far.

Once in the house, she washed her hair in the shower and blow-dried it. She'd picked up some sun and applied a frost lipstick, then donned a white sundress and sandals. All day she'd been waiting for evening. He was taking her to Paxos Island to show her where he'd grown up and worked. She brought her crutches, hopefully for the last time.

They drove to the only harbor on Anti Paxos, where he'd moored their cabin cruiser. In a lightning move he lifted her like a bride and placed her on one of the padded benches. While she put on a life jacket, he untied the ropes. She could hardly take her eyes off him, dressed in a collared navy knit shirt and cream-colored pants outlining his amazing physique.

He started the engine and they backed out of the slip at no-wake speed until they reached open water. Different kinds of boats dotted the marine-blue sea separating the two islands. Akis pointed out landmarks along the coastline till they reached Loggos. The small, quaint town with its horseshoe-shaped waterfront held particular significance for her. This was where Akis and his brother were born.

He found a slip along the harbor and berthed the cruiser. She removed the life jacket before he reached for her and set her down on the dock. Their bodies brushed, ramping up the temperature from a fire that had been burning steadily for days now.

"Here you go." He handed her the crutches. Once she was ready, they began an exploration of the beachfront with its tavernas and shops. He pointed out an apartment above one of the bars. "That was our first place to live after we sold the hut."

"I don't know your language, but I recognize the Alpha/Omega 24 sign up ahead. You lived close to your store."

"That's how we were able to be on duty day and night."

She turned to him. "I've got gooseflesh just being with you where the whole business began. Your number-one store. When you look back at the beginning, can you believe what you've accomplished this far?"

His smile quickened her heartbeat. "Watching your reaction makes it all worth it."

"I want to go inside."

"The interiors are the same, but we've kept the facades of our various stores in keeping with the surroundings."

He was right. Once they stepped over the threshold, it was like entering the shop in Athens. There were several people in summer gear doing some shopping. A middle-aged man and woman beamed when they saw Akis and hurried over to him, giving him a hug, obviously holding him in great esteem.

Akis introduced Raina to the married couple who ran the store. Their gaze fastened on her with unchecked curiosity. They held a long conversation with Akis in Greek. At the very end he shook his head and ushered her back outside.

"What was that all about?"

He stared at her through veiled eyes. "Aside from

giving me a rundown about how business was going, they said you were very beautiful like a film star and that we looked beautiful together. They saw the news the other night where I was helping you out of the hotel into the limo. They wanted to know if you were my fiancée."

To be Akis's fiancée would be the ultimate gift after fearing it was all an unattainable dream. Heat filled her cheeks. "It's evident they're fond of you. So am I," her voice throbbed, "and I'm having a wonderful time with you. Where are we going to have dinner? I'm in the mood for fish."

"We'll go to the taverna ahead where you can eat beneath the olive trees. Their appetizers serve as an entire meal."

His choice didn't disappoint her. The waiter brought *mezes* made of octopus, salad, sardines, calamari, shrimp and clams. They feasted until they couldn't eat another bite. He taught her how to say the names of the fish in Greek. It was hilarious because her pronunciation needed help with *gareedes*, the name for shrimp, causing them both to laugh.

"I'm humbled when I realize you picked up English and are fluent in it. You're brilliant, Akis."

"We had to learn it out of necessity, no other reason."

"Those who know your story would call it genius. I lived with Chloe for nine months, but I didn't pick up her language. I'm ashamed to admit I didn't really try. *Your* genius is that you knew what you had to do and you *did* it against all odds."

"But my pronunciation needs help."

"No, it doesn't." She put a hand on his arm without realizing it. "I love the way you speak English. It's so sweet."

His black brows met together. "Sweet?"

"It's part of your unique charisma. There's nothing artificial about you. Never change."

He reached for her hand and kissed the palm. Full of food and so happy, she felt delicious sensations run through her body at the touch of his lips against her skin. She wanted, needed to be close to him.

"Vasso?" a female voice called out, causing Raina to lift her head in the direction of the lovely woman who'd come over to their table. She was probably Raina's age.

Still grasping her hand, Akis turned around to the person who'd interrupted them.

"Akis!" She looked shocked before her gaze strayed to Raina.

At that point he had to let go of her hand and stood up. "Sofia Peri," he said in English, "meet Raina Maywood."

The other woman nodded to Raina.

"Sofia grew up here at the same time with Vasso and me," he explained.

From the other woman's troubled expression, Raina suspected there'd been an uneasy history. "Akis and his brother must look a great deal alike for you to mistake him."

"Yes and no. How is he?"

"Busy running the office while I'm on vacation. How are you and Drako?" His gaze flicked to Raina. "Her husband owns the best fishing business on Paxos."

Sofia averted her eyes. "This has been a good year for us."

"I'm glad to hear it. Nice to see you, Sofia. Give my best to Drako."

"It was nice to meet you, Sofia," Raina chimed in.

Clearly Sofia wanted to prolong the conversation, but Akis had sat down, effectively bringing their meeting to a close. When they were alone once more Raina said, "She's a very pretty woman."

"A very unhappy one," Akis responded. "When Vasso got out of the military he asked her to marry him, but she turned him down because she was looking for a man who could give her all the things she wanted."

Raina read between the lines. "Now that you and your brother have prospered, she's wishing she hadn't turned him down?"

He sat back in the chair and nodded. "From his early teens, Vasso was crazy about her and she him, but she wanted more from life. There was a period when I feared he'd never get over the rejection. But he did."

She let out a sigh. "Thank goodness time has a healing effect."

His eyes searched hers. "You say that like someone who has been hurt."

The subject had come up. Better to get it out of the way now. "I married at twenty when I was young and naive. A writer ten years older than I came to the house to get details about a book he was writing on my grandmother's father, Edwin Moss. My great-grandfather was a seascape artist who's been gaining in popularity.

"Because Byron was older and brilliant, I was too blinded by his attention to realize he only wanted me for what my money could do to support his research and career. He told me he wanted to put off having children for a while."

"You wanted children?"

"More than anything. I didn't understand why he wanted to postpone it until he was trapped in a scandal with a grade-B film starlet from Hollywood and the director with whom she was having an affair. As you can imagine I thanked providence there was no child born to us who would be torn apart."

Akis's striking Greek features hardened.

"In court I learned Byron had been having relations with her before and during my marriage to him. It got ugly before it was over. My grandparents helped me through the ordeal. Without them I don't think I would have made it. Your brother was fortunate enough to be passed over. In the long run he's the winner."

"I couldn't agree more." Akis put some bills on the table. "Let's get out of here. Back along the shoreline near the dock is an outdoor club for dancing. We'll see how your ankle holds up without the crutches, but the second it starts to hurt, we'll leave."

Twilight had turned the island into a thing of incredible beauty. Between the water and the lights, Raina was caught in its spell. But for the crutches, she would have hung on to him, unable to help herself.

Many of the shops had closed for the night. "Look —your store is full of people. I'm so proud of what you've done I could burst."

"I'm afraid I'm going to burst if I don't get you in my arms soon."

He didn't know the half of it. Soon she could hear

live music coming from the club. They played everything from bouzouki to modern, jazz and rock. Some of the people sat around watching the lights of the harbor and the incoming ferry while they enjoyed a cocktail. Other couples had taken to the dance floor.

Akis put her crutches next to her chair and ordered them a local drink. "Come on." He reached for her hand and pulled her onto the floor. "I've waited as long as I can."

So had she. Today she'd been transported to another world and melted in his arms, dying for the legitimate excuse to get as close to him as possible. Her heart thudded so hard, she was certain he could feel it. Their bodies fit and moved as one flesh.

When he wrapped both arms around her to bring her even closer, she linked her arms around his neck and clung to him. The male scent of him combined with the soap he'd used in the shower acted as an aphrodisiac. Raina had no idea how long they'd been fused together when his lips brushed against her hot cheek. "How's your ankle?"

"What ankle?" she murmured back.

She felt his deep sigh. "When I was a young boy, we'd walk past this club on our way home from work every night. For years and years I used to watch the people sitting around drinking and dancing, unable to relate to their lives.

"It took money and leisure time, neither of which I had. A man needed decent clothes and shoes. But more than anything else it took courage I didn't have to walk in here with a woman and feel I was as good as anyone else."

Her eyes closed tightly. She was haunted by what

he'd told her. "How long did it take you to realize your own value and bring a woman in here to dance the night away?"

"I never did."

Raina's hands had a mind of their own and slid to his cheeks where she could feel the slight rasp of his hard male jaw. She forced him to look at her, trying to understand. "I'm the first?"

"I've been waiting for the right woman, but the way I'm feeling about you at this moment, I need to get us away from here now. Let's go." She knew how he felt and would have suggested it if he hadn't.

They walked back to the table. He handed her the crutches. After leaving money on the table, they left the club without having tasted their drinks.

The water felt like glass during the ride to Anti Paxos in the cabin cruiser. A sliver of a moon lit up the dark sky. Raina wanted this romantic night to last forever. When he pulled into the slip at the harbor, he turned to her. "How would you like to sleep out on the cruiser tonight?"

"Can we? I'd love it!"

"Tell you what. We'll drive to the house and pack a bag. I'll grab some food and we'll come back. To-morrow we'll begin a tour of the different islands."

She removed her life jacket. "You're sure you want to do this for me when you've lived here all your life? Won't it be boring for you?"

"Being with you is like seeing everything for the first time because your excitement is contagious."

"This part of Greece is so glorious, I'm speech-less, Akis."

"I'm in the same state around you. Come on." He

picked her up and carried her to the dock. They reached the truck and drove to the house in record time. At the house she changed out of her sundress and put on her lightweight white sweats. After packing bags and food, they returned to the cruiser. She really was doing fine without the crutches and had never known this kind of happiness before.

Being with Akis made her realize what a pitiful marriage she'd had with Byron, whose selfishness should have warned her she was making a terrible mistake. Theo's best man *was* the best man she'd ever known, and the most generous.

"We'll cruise over to my private beach and lay anchor until morning. The seats go back and make comfortable beds if you want to sleep on deck. Or you can use the bedroom below."

"I want to stay on top and look at the stars." That way they didn't have to be separated.

"Then that's what we'll do."

Euphoria enveloped Raina as they followed the shoreline to his area of the island. After cutting the motor, he dropped anchor. Theirs was the only boat around. He turned on the lights. It felt like they were on their own floating island. When she looked over the side, she could see beneath water so clear it didn't seem real.

She turned around with her elbows on the railing and smiled at him. "I feel enchanted. It's this place. The air's so warm and sweet, and the sky is like velvet."

His gaze swept over her. He'd turned on music and strolled toward her still dressed in the same clothes he'd worn earlier. Akis was so handsome, her mouth went dry. "I want to dance with you again. This time we don't have an audience."

Raina propelled herself into his arms and he swung her around. He murmured words into her hair she didn't understand. "What did you say?"

"That you smell and feel divine." He crushed her against him, running his hands over her back and molding her to him. They slow-danced until she lost track of time. His mouth roved her cheek until she couldn't bear it any longer. Needing his kiss like she needed air, she met his lips with her own. They became lost in a sea of want and desire.

"I could do this with you forever," he whispered against her warm throat. "My father told me it could be like this with the right woman."

She rose up on tiptoe and kissed his face one dashing feature at a time. "In my darkest moment, my grandfather told me the same thing and warned me not to lose hope. He and my grandmother were happily married for sixty-nine years."

Akis smiled down at her. "Imagine that." Twining his fingers with hers, he walked her to the banquette across the rear of the cruiser and pulled her onto his lap. He smoothed some strands of her hair tousled by the breeze. "If I were your great-grandfather, I'd paint you like this and name it Aphrodite by moonlight."

Raina buried her face in his neck. "If Rodin were alive, I'd commission him to sculpt you cavorting in the swells of your Hellenic world. Have you been to Paris?"

"No. But I've seen pictures of *The Kiss*. All the boys on the island liked looking at those kinds of pictures."

"I think everyone does. Do you think Rodin got it right?" she teased.

"As much as he could working with cold marble."

His comment sent a wave of heat through her body as she imagined them the models for the sculptor's famous work.

"You're all warmth." He lowered his head and kissed her until she was lost in rapture. A low moan passed through him. "Raina—I want to eat you up, every last centimeter of you. But if I do that, there won't be anything left for me tomorrow, so I'm giving you a chance to escape me. There's a comfortable bed waiting for you below where I won't be joining you. At least, not tonight."

He helped her off his lap. The last thing she remembered was the black fire of his eyes as he said good-night.

Her legs almost gave way from the blaze of desire she saw burning there and practically stumbled her way to the steps leading down to the galley. She was still out of breath when she finally climbed under the covers. Akis was the one who had the incredible self-control she lacked. Hers had deserted her the first time he'd taken her in his arms.

The frightening realization had come to her that to know his possession would change her life forever.

Forever…

Akis was a male force no woman could resist. There was no one else like him.

As Akis had done many times before, he slept on the top deck of the cruiser. But he couldn't sleep yet. When his father had talked about meeting the right woman he'd said, "Akis? You're only in your teens and you'll meet a lot of women before you're grown up. When you find *the* one, you must treat her like a queen.

"Your mother was my queen. I cherished and respected her from the beginning. She deserved that because not only was she going to be my wife, she was going to be the mother of our children."

There was no question in Akis's mind that at the age of twenty-nine he'd found *the* one. What tormented him was the fear she wouldn't think *he* was the one. How could he possibly measure up to the educated men she worked with and knew? Maybe that was why Vasso had cautioned him to be careful. Because he knew there was a vast chasm of knowledge separating Akis from Raina.

But when he awakened that morning, he felt the sun's warm rays on his face chasing away the disturbing fears that had come during the night. A burst of excitement radiated through him knowing Raina was only as far away as the bedroom below.

After he'd made breakfast in the galley, he called to her. He'd taken a swim first and was still dressed in his trunks. And needing a shave. She appeared minutes later looking a knockout in leaf-green shorts and a sleeveless white top. Those amazing lavender eyes smiled at him.

"I'm glad you're up, Raina. How are you feeling?"

"Fantastic. Something smells marvelous."

"It's the coffee." But she'd just come from the shower and brought her own intoxicating scent with her. "How's the ankle?"

"I've forgotten about it."

"Good. Come and sit down." He'd made eggs and put out fruit and pastries. "After we eat, I'll take us to Lefkada Island, your birthplace."

She chuckled and sat down in one of the pullout seats beneath the table. "Didn't we pass over it?"

He nodded. "Katsiki Beach will be a sight you won't forget. We'll swim to our heart's content."

She munched on a pastry and sipped her coffee. "I know I'm still dreaming and pray I never wake up."

"I'll do my best to ensure that doesn't happen."

Raina's expression turned serious. "You've been so good to me and have done all the work. I don't begin to know how to repay you. I've never been waited on like this in my life, but have done nothing to deserve it. Before our vacation is over I intend to wait on you."

"We'll take turns."

"While you pull up the anchor and get us underway, I'll start now by cleaning up the kitchen."

He walked around and kissed her luscious mouth. "See you on top in a few minutes." This was happiness in a new dimension. To make it last presented the challenge. If he wanted the prize, it meant not making mistakes along the way. Vasso's words still rang in his ears. *Slow down.*

Once he'd pulled on a clean T-shirt from his bag in the bathroom, he bounded up the steps to the deck and got everything ready. Raina appeared a few minutes later with a couple of beach towels and sunscreen. Beneath her beach robe he glimpsed the mold of her lovely body wearing her orange bikini and had to keep himself from staring.

"You'll need to put this on." He handed her the life jacket.

"Even if you swim like a fish, you have to wear one, too."

He flashed her a smile. "Tell you what. For you, I'll wear a belt." He opened a locker and pulled one out.

"Put it on, please."

"Nag, nag."

"Your command of English is remarkable."

"I heard the word enough times when an American husband and wife came in the store. His wife would tell him what she wanted and he'd walk around muttering the word under his breath."

Raina laughed so hard, her whole body shook. "Welcome to the US."

His black brows lifted. "I'm afraid it's the same here."

She nodded her head, drawing his attention to the gleaming red and gold strands of her hair in the sunlight. "Certain things between men and women will never change no matter the nationality."

"Like getting into each other's space until there's no air between them."

Raina had a tendency to blush. To avoid commenting, she poured the sunscreen on her hands to apply to her face and arms. "Would you like some?"

"Thanks, but my skin doesn't look like fine porcelain."

Her eyes traveled over his face. "You're right. You have an olive complexion that highlights your black hair and makes you...drop-dead gorgeous." She put the sunscreen on the seat.

His brows furrowed. "Drop-dead?"

"It's an American expression for a man who's so attractive, a woman could drop dead from a heart attack just looking at him. And there's another expression women use. They say 'he's jaw-dropping gorgeous.'" She touched his unshaven jaw with her left hand. "You know. Sometimes when you see something incredible and your mouth opens in shock?"

Studying the curving lines of her mouth almost gave *him* a heart attack. "You mean the way mine did when you looked up at me on the sidewalk? Does an American man say 'she's jaw-dropping gorgeous'?"

An impish twinkle lit up her eyes. "The phrase can be used to describe a woman or a man. And there's another more modern expression. 'He's hot.'"

"Which also works for a female. I've heard that one. Thank you for the vocabulary lesson. I'm indebted to you." But no matter how hard he could try to catch up to her intellectual level, he would never succeed.

"Maybe you can teach me some Greek, but I know it's a very difficult language to learn."

"You mean right now?"

"If you're willing."

"Then you'll have to sit close to me while I steer the boat."

She shot him a side glance. "How close?"

He gripped her hand and pulled her over to the captain's seat. After sitting down, he patted his leg. "Right here."

"Akis—" She chuckled. "You won't be able to drive."

"Try me."

As she perched on his leg, he grabbed her around the waist. "The first word I want to teach you is the most important. If you never learn another one, it won't matter." He started the engine and they skimmed across the water.

"What is it?"

"Repeat after me. *S'agapo.*"

She said it several times until she got the intonation just right. "How am I doing?"

"That was perfect."

"What does it mean?"

"Say it to Nora and Socus and surprise them. By their reaction you'll know what it means."

"S'agapo. S'agapo." She kissed his cheek and slid off his leg. "You're a terrific teacher, but you need to concentrate on your driving. We've been going around in circles," she teased.

"That's what you've done to me," he quipped back. "You have me staggering all over the place in a dazed condition."

"Then I'm going to leave you alone until we get to that beach you told me about."

"And then?"

"What do you mean?"

"You can't leave me hanging like that. Once we've arrived at our destination, I want to know what you propose to do to me."

She let out a devilish chuckle. "I'm considering several options, all of which require your complete attention."

The way Akis was feeling right now, they weren't going to make it another ten yards. "Shall we forget going anywhere and head back to my beach?"

Her smile filled all the lonely places inside him. "What kind of a tour director are you?"

"I can't help it if my first passenger surpasses any

sight I could show her. If you don't believe me, just watch the way men look at you when you walk by. I'm the envy of every male."

She rested her head against the seat, soaking up the sun. "Women do the same thing when they see you."

"I'm talking about you. Did you know the newspapers have printed photos of us leaving the Grand Bretagne? The headlines read, 'Who was the beautiful mystery woman seen with one of the Giannopoulos brothers?'"

She turned in his direction. "Chloe's wedding made the publicity inevitable. Knowing her like I do, I'm sure she didn't want it. She's the sweetest, kindest girl I've ever known."

"I couldn't agree more. Theo has a similar temperament. They're a perfect match."

"Isn't that wonderful? Tell me more about him."

"He's a vice president of the bank now."

"Good for him, but I want to know why you like him so much."

The more he got to know Raina, the more he realized how extraordinary she was, not only as a woman, but as a human being. "You're a lot like Theo. You look beyond the surface to the substance of a person."

He could feel her eyes on him. "I'm so glad he saw inside of you and was willing to take a risk for you. That's because you're such a good man."

"He's saved my back more than once."

"In what way?"

"We signed up for the military at the same time and served together."

Raina sat up. "How did you manage that?"

"His father had connections. I couldn't believe it when he was assigned to my unit."

"I take it that's where your friendship flourished."

"In unexpected ways. We grew close as brothers." He would have told her more, but talking about it would touch on a painful subject he didn't want to bring up today. "When he introduced me to Chloe six months ago, I worried she might not be good enough for him. But nothing could have been further from the truth."

Raina's eyes closed for a moment. She was so crazy about Akis, the thought of his breaking her heart caused her to groan.

"I had the same fear when she phoned to tell me about Theo. I knew her heart from long ago and didn't want any man breaking it. But getting to know you, I'm convinced he must be her equal, otherwise he wouldn't have come to be like family to you. I'm anxious to meet him when they get back from their honeymoon."

He had to clear his throat. "We'll definitely make that happen, but we've got a lot of living to do before then."

She sat back again. "I'm loving all this, but I'm afraid I'm keeping you from your work."

"I'm entitled to a vacation and have covered for Vasso many times."

"I haven't had a real one in years. It sounds like we're a pair of workaholics. But I have to admit work has saved my life since my grandfather passed away."

Akis filled his lungs with the sea air. "What do you say we forget everything and concentrate on having fun. We're coming to one of the most famous beaches in all of Greece."

Raina got up and wandered over to the side. "Those tall green hills are spectacular."

"You can't access them unless you climb up the eighty steep steps descending along the cliff. Your ankle is doing better, but I wouldn't suggest you try that activity for another few weeks."

"It's enough just to cruise around them. I can't get over how crystal clear the water is. Against the golden sand, you think you've arrived in a magical kingdom. I don't see any other people around."

"Without a boat it's difficult access. Most of the tourists come in July and August. For the moment we've got the beach to ourselves. I'll take us in closer. We can swim to the shore, then come back and eat on board."

"I can't wait!"

Neither could he. Akis needed her in his arms. When he'd found the right spot, he dropped anchor. She'd already taken off her life jacket. Soon she'd shed her top and shorts to reveal a bikini-clad body she filled out to perfection. Raina turned a beaming face to him. "See you on shore!"

A second later she climbed over the side and dove in. Now that her ankle had healed, he discovered she swam like a fish and had amazing stamina.

That's when a warning light came on in his mind, holding him back. His father's words came back to him again.

When you find the one, you must treat her like a queen. Your mother was my queen. I cherished and respected her from the beginning. She deserved that because not only was she going to be my wife, she was going to be the mother of our children.

As if in slow motion, he removed his life belt, pulled off his T-shirt and plunged in after her. He could hear her squeals of delight. "The water is so warm! I've lived by the Pacific Ocean all my life, but you always have to get used to the colder temperature. I could stay in this all day! There's no kelp or seaweed. What's below us?"

"Rocks made of soft limestone."

She did a somersault and swam beneath the water. He kept track of her until she emerged further away. "They *are* soft." Her laughter was music to his ears before she started swimming parallel to the long shoreline.

He'd brought her here to spend time with her and love her, but his father's words wouldn't leave him alone.

CHAPTER SIX

RAINA TURNED AROUND and trod water while she watched Akis coming after her like a torpedo at high speed. While his strong arms cleaved the water, his powerful legs kicked up a fountain.

Her heart raced madly as he came to a stop in front of her and raised his dark head. She could never get enough of just looking at him. "I feel like a happy little girl who's finally out of school for the summer and has all day to play."

"Except that you don't look like a little girl. Do you have any conception of what kind of a problem that presents for me?"

The tremor in his voice told her what he was holding back through sheer willpower. 'It's not exactly easy for me, either. I've come out to play with a man."

Lines darkened his features. "How many men have been in your life?"

"You mean ones who were important?"

"Yes."

She might as well get it all said now. "There were two. Before Byron, there was a graduate assistant teaching my math class during my freshman year.

He held seminars for the most promising students and has since become a professor at a west coast college."

"What drew you to him?"

They swam around in circles, always facing each other. "His smarts. He had a different way of looking at a problem to solve it. I envied him that gift. He fed my ego by telling me I'd inherited my father's mathematical mind."

"Why didn't that relationship go anywhere?"

"I didn't find out he was married until I'd been dating him for a month."

"Did you sleep with him?"

"No. I was waiting for marriage."

"Raina…" She heard a tortured sound in his voice.

"It was over a long time ago. He didn't wear a wedding ring. At the end of the term I went to see if my grade had been posted. The head of the math department called me in and asked me if I knew Rod was married. I felt the blood rush to my feet. After I got my second wind, I thanked him for the information."

"What did you do?"

"Rod had a cubicle down the hall. We'd planned to go out to dinner that evening. I dropped in on him. He assumed I wanted to check on the time. I told him to do his wife a favor and take her out to dinner instead. And I added one more thing. I wouldn't be putting in a good word for him at the jet propulsion laboratory. Then I walked out and shut the door. That was the end of it."

A grimace darkened Akis's face.

"I made the same mistake with Byron by putting him on a pedestal. He was a published writer who'd traveled to Europe to do art research for more books.

I admired someone so intelligent and well-read. He was older and had knowledge on so many subjects. The fact that he wanted to do my great-grandfather's story was a huge plus.

"We could talk for hours about the art we loved. I thought we'd never run out of things to discuss. What I didn't see was his empty bank account and his proclivity for women he could prey on. Have you heard the expression 'once bitten, twice shy'?"

"No, but I don't need a translation," he stated.

"In my case I was *twice* bitten before I learned the lesson I'd been needing."

"Enough of the past, Raina. Let's swim back to the cruiser and have our picnic."

Relieved to get off the subject of her pathetic naivety, she swam next to him. He paced himself so she could keep up with him. He did everything right. How she loved him!

She *loved* him.

She loved him for who he was, nothing else. Raina could finally say it and not be afraid. She wanted to shout it to the world.

I'm in love with him.

Loving him wasn't a mistake.

When they reached the ladder, he got in the boat first, then helped her up and wrapped her in one of the beach towels. He kissed her on the side of her neck, on her chin and nose, her cheeks, eyelids, earlobes.

Before he reached her mouth she said, "I'm going to fix our lunch while you relax. After we're full, I'll give you a big kiss for dessert." Raina was afraid that if she stayed on deck with him another instant, she'd forget everything else.

"Coward," he whispered against her lips before letting her go.

She hurried down the steps to the bedroom and dressed in another pair of shorts and a top. There was nothing she could do about her hair until she showered later.

In the fridge she found the ingredients to fix a Grecian-style sandwich. She made a fresh pot of coffee and put everything on the table with a couple of oranges. Akis joined her. While they finished off their orange sections, he told her they were going to head to Cape Lefkas, the inhospitable part of the island with cliffs seventy meters high. The lighthouse was built on the old temple of Apollo. From there you could view incredible vistas including Kefallonia Island.

He got up from the seat first and pressed a passionate kiss to her mouth. "That's the sweetest dessert I ever tasted. Save me more because tonight I'll be starving."

Akis could have no idea of the depth of her hunger for him. She didn't know how much longer she could go on without loving him completely. If she did that, then she'd never want to leave him. But what did Akis want?

Her experience with Byron proved to her that living happily ever after with the same person you married didn't necessarily happen. She couldn't bear the thought of a long-term relationship not working out with Akis. For the moment they were in a short-term situation because soon she would have to go back to California and once again take on the weight of her responsibilities.

If he wanted a life with Raina to continue, could a

long-distance relationship back and forth from Greece to California work? A week fit in here and another week there throughout the year with months of separation in between?

Raina knew she was getting way ahead of herself, but every second spent with him was condemning her to be fatally in love with him for the rest of her life.

There was one thing Raina refused to do. Become so desperate that she'd marry someone else who came along in the future just to be married and have children. She could meet dozens of men and none of them would ever measure up to Akis. If her grandfather were still alive and could know this bigger-than-life man, he'd understand why Raina would never be able to settle for anyone else.

Her only choice was to spend this precious time with the man she loved and see what happened. *Stop analyzing this to pieces, Raina.*

He wanted to show her *his* Greece, so go with it and let come what may. She'd come to Athens for Chloe's sake and had found joy beyond belief. If it meant that she could only experience it for a little while, then it was worth it. Casting any worries aside, she hurried up on deck and felt two arms grab her from behind.

"It took you long enough. I've been waiting for this." He turned her around and lowered his head, covering her mouth with his own. Once again she was swept away. They'd started devouring each other when Akis unexpectedly lifted his lips from hers. "I can't get enough of you, Raina."

She let out a shaky breath. "I'm in the same condition."

His hands gripped her shoulders. "I thought I could do this, but I can't."

When she saw the torment in his black gaze, she shuddered. "What's wrong?"

With a sound of reluctance, he let go of her. "I'd intended to vacation with you, but it's not working. Do you mind if we go back to the house?"

Raina took a step away from him. "Is it me? Something I've done?"

His answer was a long time in coming. "It's nothing you've done. I want to make love to you more than you can imagine, but I don't have the right."

Afraid her legs wouldn't support her, she found the nearest banquette so she could sit. Filled with anguish, she couldn't look at him. "What are you talking about?"

"You're wonderful, Raina, and you've changed my life to the point I don't know where I am."

She threw her head back. "Since you asked me to dance at the reception, my life hasn't been the same, either. Taking a vacation probably wasn't a good idea, but I'll never regret the time we've spent together. If that's what you want, then by all means let's go back to Anti Paxos."

His face was an expressionless mask. "It isn't what I want, but I don't see another alternative for our situation."

She didn't know what was driving this latest decision. But if by situation he meant that not making love to her had ruined the trip for him, then she agreed there was no point in prolonging it.

"All right." In a quick move she reached for the life jacket and put it on. "While you get us under way,

I'll go below to clean things up in the kitchen and pack."

He didn't try to stop her. After getting the work done, she stayed below the whole time and rested her leg on the bed, knowing he would prefer to be alone. Her pain had gone beyond tears. When he cut the motor, she realized they'd returned to the harbor and was surprised the return trip had been so fast. There was only a slight rocking movement of the boat now that he'd pulled into the slip.

She heard footsteps in the hallway and checked her watch. It was seven-thirty. He peered inside the bedroom with an indecipherable expression in his dark eyes. "I'll take your bag to the truck. Are you ready?"

"Yes." Raina got up and followed him to the deck. "Just a minute. I need to stow the life jacket." Once she'd taken it off and put it under the bench, she reached for the hand he extended to help her onto the dock. She thought he'd let go, but he kept it grasped in the warmth of his until he helped her into the truck in the parking area.

They drove in silence to his villa nestled in the greenery. It already felt like home to her. When it came time to say goodbye to this place, the wrench would be excruciating. She got out with her purse and started ahead of him along the path leading to the house. No longer needing the crutches she'd left behind, she climbed the steps to the back door. Akis let them in.

He walked her to the guest bedroom and put her bag down. "While you freshen up, I'll start dinner." Whatever emotions had been building inside him, he hadn't made her privy to them.

"I won't be long."

She headed for the bathroom to shower and wash her hair. After using a towel to dry it, she put on her sundress. Raina had picked up a lot of sun. Even with the sunscreen, her skin felt tender. The straps of the dress wouldn't hurt so much.

Once she'd brushed her hair, she put on lipstick and felt ready to face Akis. Before the night was over she knew there'd be a conversation and she was dreading it. When she walked into the living room, she saw that he'd opened the terrace doors. The table had been set on the patio.

He flicked her a glance and told her to come and eat. Akis had put another salad together along with fruit, rolls and coffee. He helped her into her chair and took a seat opposite her. "You picked up a lot of sun today."

"I know. I'm feeling it now."

"Skin like yours needs special care."

Don't keep it up, Akis. I can't take it.

She'd lost her appetite, but ate a little of everything so she wouldn't offend him. "Thank you for taking me to Lefkada. I loved every minute of it, including the helicopter tours."

He eyed her over the rim of his coffee cup. "Do you still remember the word I taught you?"

"*S'agapo.* I promise to try it out on Chloe's parents as soon as we fly back." When there was no response, Raina got to her feet. She couldn't stand their stilted, unnatural conversation. "Since we're both through eating, I'll clear the table. I can't tell you how nice it is to be able to walk around without crutches."

"I can only imagine."

After two trips to the kitchen, she returned to the terrace, breathing in the fragrant air. It filtered through the house, arousing her senses. This was all too much. "If you'll excuse me, I'm going to phone Nora. I promised her I'd call her, but I forgot last night. I don't want her worried."

Akis had gotten to his feet. "Don't take too long. After you've assured her you're all right, come back to the living room. I want you with me. We need to talk."

He wanted her with him? She didn't understand him. Her heightened pulse rate refused to go back to normal. "Nora may not even be available. If not, I'll leave a message."

As it turned out, the call went through to the Milonises' voice messaging. She told them Akis had brought her to Anti Paxos and they'd been out in the cruiser to Lefkada. After saying she'd see them soon, she hung up and returned to the semidark living room. Akis was still out on the terrace.

His arms were stretched out against the railing, presenting a hard muscled silhouette against the starry sky.

"Akis?" she called quietly from the doorway.

He turned so he was facing her. "I made a promise to you before we flew here. But today I was so terrified I was going to break it, I had to do something to stop myself. The only thing I could think of was to bring you back here while I got myself under control."

She swallowed hard. "Did it occur to you that I wanted you to break it?"

"Yes," he said in a gravelly voice. "But I don't think you know what you're saying. If I touch you, I won't be able to stop. I want you so badly, I'm trembling. I thought I could vacation with you and handle it, but it isn't possible to control what I'm feeling. Tomorrow I'll take you back to Chloe's."

Her heart rebelled at his words. "What are you afraid of?"

"I don't want an affair with you and then have to say goodbye."

Raina could hardly breathe. "Why does it have to be an affair?"

"Because I want to make love to you. But you're the kind of woman a man wants to marry before he takes her to bed."

"And you don't want marriage because you prefer to remain a bachelor. Is that what you're saying?"

His chest rose and fell visibly. "More to the point, you wouldn't want to marry me. I could never be your equal."

"Why would you say something like that? I know we haven't known each other long. But if you feel as strongly about me as I do you, what is there to prevent us from marrying? Is there some dark secret you've been hiding?"

His hand went to the back of his neck. "Not a secret, but I'm not marriage material for a woman like you."

A slight gasp of pain escaped her lips because he'd delivered the words with a chilling finality. "What do you mean a woman like me? If this is your unique way of letting me know up front that marriage isn't in your future, I get the message. You're the one who brought it up, not me."

"After the pain your ex-husband put you through, I'm trying to be totally honest with you."

"Except you haven't told me why you're not marriage material. What am I to think about a cryptic comment like that?" Her anger flared. "However honorable you're trying to be, you have no clue about what I'm thinking or what drives me."

He moved closer until she could see his black eyes glittering. "I know a lot more about you than you think. You're the gorgeous young heiress to the Maywood fortune, the darling of the paparazzi from coast to coast. The Maywood estate in Carmel is one of the wonders of your state. Your corporation is one that helps keep the economy of California afloat. Your philanthropic projects are well known."

His admission stunned her so much she couldn't talk.

"According to the newspapers, besides your important work at its jet-propulsion laboratory, you run the entire corporation like a captain runs his ship, involved in every aspect. I happen to know that the Maywood tactical defense-system group works on air-defense issues, particularly air-vehicle survivability where the vulnerability of the US Air Force is concerned. Do I need to go on?"

By now her body was trembling. "So you've done your homework on me. I guess that means Chloe didn't keep her promise to me after all." The knowledge stung.

His expression grew fierce. "What promise?"

"That she wouldn't tell her husband-to-be that her old scandal-plagued heiress friend was coming to Greece. Did you know she'd asked me to be her maid of honor? Much as I would have loved to do that, I told her it wouldn't work. It was her special day. I didn't want my being there with all my baggage to ruin it for her. That's why she chose Althea."

Akis shook his head. "Neither Chloe nor Theo said anything to me. You've got this all wrong."

"Then how did you find out about me? No one was supposed to know I was coming. In order to keep the press from creating chaos at her wedding and swarming around me instead of focusing on her at the church, I chose to slip into Greece unnoticed.

"Out of consideration for her I flew on a commercial airline and stayed in a budget hotel in order not to be recognized. We agreed that I'd attend the reception as one of the guests. She made sure that there would be a place for me to sit at one of the tables in the rear of the ballroom while I watched."

"I believe you, Raina. Now you need to listen to me. I found out about you from a completely difference source."

"What source would that be?" Her voice sounded shrill, even to her own ears. "It's finally making sense that you singled me out for a dance in the ballroom. I honestly believed it was pure accident that we met. You were the best man and as such, *you* took on the job of entertaining me. I can hear the conversation now."

"Stop, Raina. It was my brother who told me about you."

She blinked in shock. "What do you mean, your brother?"

"He knew I had a lot of questions about you and he did some digging without my permission."

Adrenaline filled her system. "You two really do watch out for each other. What happened? When he found out my secrets and told you, did you decide to give me a thrill and ask me to dance?

"Was it because I'd had such a bad time of it with that awful husband of mine, you took pity on me? I was so vulnerable, you knew I wouldn't turn down the best man. And once again I was so desperate for attention, I bought it. No matter what I said or did, you kept coming and refused to be put off."

"If you'll let me explain—"

"Explain what?" She was borderline hysterical. "For the first time in my life I thought, here's a man who wants to get to know me better, just for me and no other reason! What a joke!

"You have no idea what a heady experience it was to see you barge in on Chloe's parents looking for me." Tears trickled down her hot cheeks. "Here I thought something extraordinary had happened that night. But all along you put on an exhibition that rivaled anything Poseidon could have done with all his power."

"*Raina*—"

"I have to hand it to you, Kyrie Giannopoulos." She kept on talking, too fired up to stop. "All this time you've been toying with me, shoring me up while I was in Greece because I was a pathetic mess. But it shook you up when I brought up the *m* word. That idea became too real to you."

"You don't know what you're talking about."

"No? Who better to take on the responsibility than the best man Akis? My sprained ankle gave you the perfect excuse to see to my comfort, but you played your part too well and it has rebounded on you."

She was running out of breath. "Let me tell you something. I never want to be someone's project." The tears were gushing now, but she didn't care. "I suppose I should be grateful to your brother. It's taught me there's absolutely no one in this world I can trust. For the first time in his life, my grandfather was wrong."

"Don't say anymore," he whispered from lips that looked as pale as his face.

"I won't. I'm through and am ready to leave."

"Agape mou—"

But she was too far gone to acknowledge his cry that came out in Greek. "Tomorrow I'll go back to Chloe's. You can remain here and you won't have to lift a finger for me. You've done more than enough. Who could have been more qualified than a Giannopoulos to carry the water without complaint?

"In case you don't understand the expression, it means you took on the job of giving this old maid a thrill out of the kindness of your heart. Congratulations to you and your brother who've gotten everything you want out of life, yet can still throw a few crumbs to those less fortunate."

Akis stood there dumbfounded while she ran down the hall to the guest room and shut the door. Because of his fear that he didn't have the credentials to be the kind of husband she deserved, he was afraid to propose marriage to her. But he'd handled this all wrong and had said things that had turned the most heavenly day of his life into a nightmare.

He couldn't let another minute go by allowing her to believe the worst about him. This was all his fault and he had to make it right no matter the cost.

As he walked down the hall, he could hear gut-wrenching sobs. The sound tore him apart. He rapped on the door. "Raina? I need to talk to you."

She refused to answer. He couldn't blame her, but there was no way he was going to let this go without her knowing the truth. Relieved that he'd never had the door fitted with a lock, he opened it and stepped inside.

Raina lay across the bed with her face buried in her arms, still dressed in the white sundress. Her body shook with tears that tortured him. He stole across the room and half lay on the bed facing her. Acting on instinct he slid a hand into her glossy hair.

"You've said a lot of things and I heard you out. Now it's my turn."

"You don't get a turn. Please leave me alone."

He smiled despite his pain. "I can't do that. You're going to have to listen to me even if you don't want to. Trying to peel away the layers of misunderstanding is going to take some time. But before we start over, there's one matter I need to clear up right now.

"Whatever secret you asked Chloe to keep, I swear to you she kept it so well that Theo never breathed a word of anything to me. Furthermore I didn't know of your existence until I arrived at Nora and Socus's house. They told me the beautiful woman with the sprained ankle I was looking for was Chloe's friend from America and that you were going to stay with them for a while."

He waited for a response. When it didn't come he said, "Did you hear what I just said? You'll have to take my word for it that everything going on with you and me was purely accidental."

In a surprise move she rolled onto her back with a

tear-blotched face, forcing his hand to slide from her hair. "If that's true, then when did your brother manage to tell you all about my life?"

"Not until the next night when Vasso phoned about the downed power grid. He told me he'd left some papers for me at the penthouse I should look at before I left on vacation. But he didn't explain the nature of them. I had to leave you when it was the last thing I wanted to do.

"You have to understand he's the older brother and has always had this thing about looking out for me. After I told him I'd met this amazing woman, it made him nervous because I've never been this taken with a woman in my life. He realized how important you were to me already. When he connected the Maywood name with our helicopter purchase, he searched the internet and wanted me to see what he'd found."

She groaned. "I can't get away from the notoriety no matter what I do."

"You did with me. What thrilled me was that you didn't know anything about me, either.

"In a world that worships money, Vasso and I are constantly stalked by the press. Their voracious hunger to pry into our lives has been a nightmare.

"Don't you see, Raina? For once in our lives, you and I were simply two ordinary people who met by accident and were seized by an attraction we couldn't control or dismiss."

Raina gazed at him in the semidarkness with her soul in those violet eyes. "To be fair, I discovered who you were in a roundabout way. When I called the lab to tell them I was going to prolong my vacation, I inadvertently informed Larry that I'd just ridden in our newest model helicopter and that it performed beautifully.

"That's when he told me that the famous rags-to-riches billionaire Giannopoulos brothers were the first from Greece to purchase them. Suddenly everything made sense…the Giannopoulos Complex and penthouse, this house set on property only people with great wealth can afford, a state-of-the-art cabin cruiser."

He put his arm around her and pulled her close. "You never said a word," he murmured against her lips.

"Neither did you."

"I didn't want anything to ruin our relationship."

"Neither did I."

He cupped her face in his hands. "Except for the last few minutes in the living room, I've never been happier in my life."

"Akis—" She moaned his name before he couldn't stand it any longer and plundered her mouth over and over again. She met him with an avid eagerness he could only dream about. For the next while they communed in the most primal way. Time passed as they bestowed kiss after kiss on each other until he was held in the thrall of ecstasy.

"You're my heart's desire, Raina," he murmured into the curve of her neck. "But I don't want to make a wrong move with you. No one needs to tell me you're not just any woman. I knew it the second we met."

Out of breath, she lifted her head and rolled away from him. Sitting on the edge of the bed she said, "When I came to Greece, I never imagined something like this happening. I was ready to leave the reception when you asked me to dance. It seemed like some trickery of magic that the best man found his way to my table. I'd watched you all evening.

"But even with all these emotions, I still feel like my happiness is going to be taken from me."

"Why?"

"Because I don't know if your feelings are as intense as mine, that they'll last…"

He got to his feet. "Don't you know I suffer from the same fear? We've both been taken by surprise. I don't want to do anything to ruin it. Before this goes any further, there's something I need to tell you about me that could alter your feelings where I'm concerned."

"In what way?"

"You told me you were hoping to have children after you got married, but children weren't part of your husband's plan."

Exasperated, she stood up. "What does that have to do with our situation? We're not contemplating marriage."

"You have no idea what's on my mind." Did that mean he'd entertained the thought? Her heart skipped a beat because tonight she'd wished he'd been her husband and they were on their honeymoon. "Even so, you deserve to know the truth about me."

She felt a moment of panic. "What truth?"

"I'm simply trying to say that if we were to become intimate, you wouldn't have to worry about getting pregnant."

She hugged her arms to her waist. "Because you wouldn't want children whether in or out of wedlock?"

"I didn't say that. While I was in the military, I

came down with mumps. I'm one of the thirteen percent of men who developed mumps-related orchitis.
It rendered me sterile."

A quiet gasp escaped. "You weren't vaccinated?"

"Afraid not."

"But that was ten years ago. Today there are any
number of specialists in that field. Have you been to
one recently?"

"No. I've never had a reason to be worried about it.
But after you told me the history with your husband,
I know having children means everything to you."

And no doubt to him.

Her heart bled for him. "I'm so sorry, Akis. Have
you had this conversation with the other women in
your life?"

"There've only been a few, but the answer is no."

"Why not?"

"Because no woman ever made me want to carry
her off where I could get her alone to myself for the
duration."

His admission just described her condition, causing
her body to quiver in reaction. "I'm touched that you
would reveal something so personal to me."

She had to assume that the only reason he'd told
her these things was so she wouldn't be expecting a
marriage proposal at the end of their vacation. There
was always adoption, but he wouldn't want to hear
that from her. The painful conversation had gone in
a different direction. Needing to change the subject
she said, "Where are we going to go exploring tomorrow?"

His head jerked upward. "You've changed your
mind about going back to Chloe's?"

"You know why I said it, but if you'd rather I did…"

In the next breath he grasped her upper arms and drew her to him. "You know damn well I want to spend as much time with you as I possibly can until you have to go back to California."

"That's what I want, too." Without conscious thought she pressed her mouth to his, wanting him to know her feelings for him ran deeper than he knew.

He kissed her long and hard before lifting his head. "I'm going to let you go to sleep. Tomorrow over breakfast we'll come up with an itinerary. If there's something you want to do, we'll do it."

CHAPTER SEVEN

IF THERE'S SOMETHING you want to do, we'll do it.

Akis's words went round and round in Raina's head for the rest of the night. He was a conflicted man. On the one hand he didn't want to make love to her because she was the kind of a woman you married first.

On the other hand, Akis seemed convinced that her desire for a baby prevented him from entertaining marriage to her or any woman for that matter. He'd set up an impossible situation where Raina couldn't win.

He'd all but broken down and told her he was in love with her. Every sign was there. If she could penetrate that part of his psyche and make him realize his sterility didn't matter to her in the way he thought...

She would reason with him. Marriage was a risk. How many women got married and then found out that they had a problem that would prevent them from getting pregnant? Those situations happened to thousands of couples.

After moving restlessly for most of the night, an idea came to her and she was able to fall asleep. The next morning she awakened with a firm plan in mind. She freshened up and dressed in shorts and a small print blouse.

Before she'd left California she'd packed a pair of sneakers, but hadn't used them while she'd been here. Glad she was prepared, she put them on, eager to give them a workout today.

As usual, Akis had gotten up ahead of her and had breakfast waiting on the patio. He got up from the chair where he was drinking coffee. "Good morning, *thespinis.*" His eyes played over as he helped her to be seated.

"It's another beautiful morning. Does it ever get cloudy here?"

He smiled. Akis was so attractive, her heart literally jumped. "It rarely rains in June. You've come at the perfect time."

"I'm so lucky, and this looks delicious, as always." She started with eggs and a roll covered with marmalade. "No wonder Chloe chose this month to be married. Where are they going to live? Do you know?"

"They've bought a home in the northwest area of Athens called Marousi."

"I'll bet Chloe is so excited to set up her own house. She has a real eye for decor." Even back in high school her friend had dreamed of being married and having children, but Raina stayed away from that subject.

Akis flicked her a glance. "Have you decided where you'd like to visit today?"

"I have. I'd like us to take the cruiser to Paxos. When we went there before, I had to use crutches. Today I feel like walking and would like to visit all your old haunts like your first home, the school where you went when you had time. How about the home where your mother grew up? Could we visit the church where your parents were married?"

He averted his eyes. "None of it is that exciting."

"Maybe not to you, but I can't think of anything I'd rather do more. Unless it brings back painful memories. Does it?" she asked quietly.

"Not at all, but I supposed you wanted to see some of the other islands like Kefallonia."

"Maybe tomorrow, or another time."

Akis seemed engrossed in thought. While he finished his coffee, she cleared the table, anxious to get underway. This could be the most important day of her life if all went well.

In a few minutes he announced he was ready to leave. She grabbed her purse and left the house with him. "I love this old truck, Akis."

"It has seen a lot of wear transporting baskets of olives to town over the years."

"How did you come by it?"

"I bought it off a farmer who was happy for the money."

She eyed him intently. "Knowing you I bet you paid him ten times what it was worth."

A tiny nerve throbbed at the side of his temple. "What makes you think that?"

"You're a generous person by nature."

"You don't know any such thing."

Why couldn't he accept a compliment? "The way you treat me tells me the important things about you."

He lapsed into silence while they drove to the harbor to take out the boat. Maybe she shouldn't have suggested they travel to Loggos.

Once they reached the dock, she fastened her life jacket and sat across from him. He started the engine and they were on their way. "Akis? We don't have to go to Paxos if you don't want to."

"It's fine," he said without looking at her.

No, it wasn't, but he was determined to take her there. Raina made up her mind to enjoy this journey back in time with him. She ached to know all the private little things about him that made him the marvelous man he was.

The few framed photos in his house showed his parents, a young, attractive man and woman. There were two baby photos of him and Vasso. Adorable. Her heart pained for the circumstances that had taken their mother's life early. Her eyes filled with tears.

What a great father they'd had. One who'd worked night and day for them and had taught them how to be men. Though she couldn't meet his parents, she yearned to picture their life together. How proud they would be of their sons.

"Raina? Are you all right?"

"Of course."

"I can see tears."

"The sun got in my eyes."

The trip to Loggos didn't take long. This part of the famous island looked like a crown of dark green with jewels studding its base. Akis pulled into a slip to moor the cruiser. She discarded the life jacket and got out to help him tie the ropes to the dock.

She looked up at him, trying not to feast her eyes on him dressed in tan chinos and a dusky-blue crew neck. "Where should we start?"

He'd been studying her features through veiled eyes. "The old hut is on this side of the village, but it's a brief walk by trail. We might as well go there first."

Excitement built up inside her to be exploring his backyard, so to speak. They walked through the lush grove of olive trees interspersed with cypress trees. He'd grown up here, played here. At least he had to have played here a little until he was put to work at five years of age.

Before long they came to a clearing where a vineyard sprawled on the steep hillside before her eyes. She took a deep breath before following him along a path through the grape vines to the hut made of stone. It was even smaller than she had imagined.

Akis! He'd been born right here!

A man working the vineyard called out to him. Akis said something in Greek and a conversation ensued. He turned to Raina. "The owner says we're welcome to go inside."

She was too moved to say words. He opened the wood door and they walked into a stone house with windows and a wood floor. Twenty by thirty feet? There were no partitions, only a lot of vintner equipment and stakes. A counter with a sink was in the other corner.

"This is it, Raina. Our living room was over in that corner, our beds on the other side. That door over there leads to a bathroom of sorts. We had to pump water to fill the old bathtub. The best way for me and Vasso to get clean was to bathe in the sea."

"Were you able to keep any furniture?"

"It wasn't worth it. When the owner took over, he must have gotten rid of it."

A lump lodged in her throat. "Grandpa always said home is where love is. You can't get rid of that."

Akis turned to her and put his hands on her shoulders. He squeezed them, but didn't say anything. They stayed like that until he gave her the sweetest kiss on the mouth. Then he grasped her hand and they went outside.

"We'll climb up the hillside and along the ridge. The church is perched at the top. Because of the foliage you can't see it from here."

He let go of her as they walked through the rest of the vineyard and came to the trail. Pretty soon she saw the glistening white Greek church ahead of them standing alone, small and elegant. Raina looked back to the sea with a sweep of forest-green olive groves running toward it. She'd never seen such scenery.

"What's that white complex in the distance near the water?"

"The Center Vasso and I had built. It's a hospital and convalescent center for people with lymphoma who can't afford that kind of care. All in honor of our father."

"He raised such wonderful sons, he deserves the recognition. Did you go to church all the time?"

"Papa took us when he could."

"When was the last time you came here?"

"Vasso and I come every year and visit our parents' graves on their wedding anniversary in July. They're buried in the cemetery behind the church."

"If I'd known I would have brought flowers."

"We don't have to worry about that. See all those yellow flowers growing wild beneath the olive trees? The broom is in bloom. We'll pick an armful."

Akis left the path. She followed him and within a minute they'd picked a huge bunch. She buried her face in them. "They smell like vanilla."

He flashed her a white smile. "One of my favorite scents."

Soon they reached the church and walked around to the back. He stopped in front of his parents' headstone filled with Greek writing and dates. There was an empty can left in the center. Akis reached for her flowers and put them with his before lowering their stems into the can. "There's no water, but they'll stay beautiful until tomorrow."

She stood still while he remained hunkered down for a minute. Then he got up and they walked around to the front of the church. After the dazzling white outside, Raina had to take a minute for her eyes to adjust to the darker interior. It smelled of incense. Akis cupped her elbow and they moved toward the ornate shrine.

"There's no one here."

"The priest lives close by on the outskirts of the village. He'll come toward evening to conduct mass for the workers."

"This church is so lovely and quiet. While you sit, do you mind if I walk around to look at the wall icons?"

He slanted her a glance. "I'll come with you." To her delight he gave her a short history of each one before they walked outside the doors into the sunlight. The rays were so bright, she reached in her purse for her sunglasses.

"Let's head down to the village and have lunch at my favorite taverna. Elpis, the older woman who owns it, knew my parents before I did."

Raina chuckled over his little joke. Deep inside she was filled with new excitement to meet someone with whom he had a past connection. "I bet you're her favorite visitor."

"When Vasso and I were young, she cooked *l oukoumades* fresh every day and saved half a dozen for us to eat on the way home from work. She knew we couldn't afford them."

"I love that woman already. What are they?"

"Donuts soaked in honey and cinnamon. She'll serve you one. No one on the island makes them like she does."

Raina was so happy, she was surprised her feet touched the ground as they made their way down to the harbor. He pointed out the school where he and Vasso attended when they could. His life story was incredible.

The second they appeared at the blue-and-white outdoor café she heard a woman call out to Akis and come running. She hugged and kissed him in front of the people sitting at the tables. This woman had done her part for two young boys who'd lost their mother and had to work so hard.

When Akis introduced her to Raina, the older woman with gray in her dark hair eyed her for a minute and spoke in rapid Greek. Raina asked him what she said. His eyes narrowed on her face.

"You are a great beauty."

"That was kind of her."

For the next half hour they were plied with wonderful food while several tourists took pictures of them. Raina winked at him. "You've been found out. Smile pretty for the camera, Akis."

"Every eye is on you," came his deep voice.

Pretty soon Elpis appeared with a sack for Akis.

Raina knew what was in it. "Efharisto," she said to the older woman who kissed her on both cheeks.

"You are his fiancée?"

Raina didn't have to think twice. "I want to be."

A huge smile broke out on her face. "Ahh." She looked at Akis and said something in Greek, poking him in the chest.

After she went back inside he pulled some bills out of his wallet and put them on the table. His black brows lifted. "Are you ready to leave?"

"If I can get up. I ate so much, I'm afraid I'm nailed to the chair."

He came around to help her. By the lack of animation on his face, she couldn't tell if he'd understood the expression or not. The whole time more people were taking pictures of them with their phones. Akis was a celebrity. A lot of people had seen pictures of the Milonis wedding on TV, but he and his brother had been in the news long before that because of what they'd achieved in business.

The sun had grown hotter. When they boarded the cabin cruiser and took off for Anti Paxos, Raina welcomed the breeze on her skin. She stood at the railing all the way to the smaller island, wondering what he thought about her comment to Elpis. It appeared to have caught Akis off guard. That had been her intention. She needed him to know how she felt. But his silence had unnerved her. By the time they'd made it back to his house, she'd started to be afraid.

After setting down her suitcase, he put the sack of donuts on the counter and stared at her. "Do you have any idea what you said to Elpis?" His voice sounded unsteady.

She clung to one of the chair backs. "Yes. I'm in love with you, Akis. I couldn't hold it in any longer. It was evident how deeply Elpis cares for you, and I didn't want her to think that I just sleep with you. If I embarrassed you I'm so sorry," she whispered. "The fault's on me."

He cocked his dark head to the side. "What if I were to take you up on it?" His eyes were slits. "Aren't you afraid I might be your third mistake?"

The question produced a moan from her. "No. For once in my life I know clear through to my soul that you're the real thing." Her voice shook. "The only fear I have is that you don't have that same profound feeling for me. I saw the expression in your eyes when I blurted that I wanted to be your fiancée. I could read it so clearly.

"It was as if you'd said to me, 'Raina? We've been having a heavenly time together, but to take it to the next step is a completely different matter.' Deep in your heart of hearts you yearn to find a woman who's like the woman your father married—someone sweet and innocent with no divorce in her background."

"That's not true!"

"Oh, yes, it is. I understand why your brother was concerned enough to find out what he could about me. Some foreign woman with scandal in her past flies into Athens and disrupts the tenor of your lives. I never had a sibling. But knowing the story of you and Vasso, any woman either of you chooses will impact both your lives because you're family. I envy you that."

He moved closer, putting his hands on his hips in that potent male way. Her heart thudded mercilessly in response. "Let's talk about what I bring to your life.

As I told you the night of the reception, my brother and I are in business together. That's the sum total of our existence."

Her eyes misted over. "You bring so much, I don't know where to start."

"Why not start with the obvious. You run an empire."

She shook her head. "*I* don't do anything. My grandfather put people in place who do all the work. Since his death I've been the titular head. If I walked away from it tonight, there wouldn't be as much as a ripple. As for my job in the lab, there are dozens of scientists who'd fill my spot in a heartbeat."

His jaw hardened. "You're telling me you could leave it all behind? Just like that?"

Raina tried to swallow. "That's what I'm telling you. My parents and grandparents are gone. There's nothing to hold me." She couldn't control the throb in her voice. "To put it all in the hands of the capable people already in place and come to you would be my greatest joy."

His eyes closed tightly for a moment. "We couldn't even have a baby that could grow up to run the Maywood Corporation one day."

"We could have several babies through adoption who could one day head the Giannopoulos Company. You could call it Giannopoulos and Sons, or Daughters."

A strange, anguished sound came out of him. "I could swear the gods are playing a monstrous trick on me."

Her spirits sank. "In other words, Aphrodite is a monster in disguise."

"No, Raina. Your grandfather left you a legacy you can't ignore."

"I won't ignore it, but you're making an erroneous assumption. The difference between you and me is this…I didn't create the Maywood Corporation with my bare hands. I didn't do one thing to build it from scratch a hundred years ago. I'm a recipient of all the hard work that my great-great-grandfather started. That's all.

"But you and your brother started your company from scratch. You poured blood, sweat and tears into it every day, *all* day for years. It's your monument to your parents who gave you life and a father who taught you what was the most important thing in life."

"So what are you saying?" he ground out.

"That you can't leave your brother to live with me in California. You wouldn't want to and I wouldn't want you to. Furthermore I hate the idea of flying back and forth so we can see each other for a weekend here and there. It would be ludicrous.

"Since I don't want an affair, either, the simple solution is to live here with you for as long as you want me. I'd rather be married to you, but if you can't bring yourself to do that, then I'll be your lover and deal with it. As long as I know where I stand with you, no one else's opinion matters to me."

"It *does* matter." He sounded exasperated.

"Then what you're saying is nothing will fix our problem, so I should plan to go back to California? If that's the case then so be it." She wheeled around and grabbed her suitcase.

"Where are you going?"

"To change into my swimming suit and enjoy your pool. I need to work off the calories from our delicious lunch. Thank you for allowing me a glimpse of your early beginnings. It meant the world to me. Let me know when you're ready to pack in this vacation and get back to work. I can be ready in no time at all."

He followed her down the hall to the bedroom. "Will you stay until Chloe gets back?"

So he *was* anxious to get back to Athens. "Where else?" she said over her shoulder and plopped her suitcase on the bed. "I don't want to disappoint her parents."

"Do you want to leave in the morning? I'll send for the helicopter."

Her back was still to him. "That's entirely up to you." She opened the lid and pulled out her bathing suit.

"Don't be like this, Raina."

She whirled around. "Like what?"

"You're not thinking with your head. No one with a background like yours just walks away from everything because the man she loves lives on another continent."

She drew in a quick breath. "This one does, but you don't know me well enough to understand. If I leave California for good, money will continue to pour into my personal account Grandpa set up for me. Most of that money will be used to do research for a cure for stomach cancer and heart disease.

"As for everything else, I'll be available over the phone whenever one of the heads of the various departments wants to discuss a problem. I'll step down as CEO but remain on the board. If there's a vote to be cast that requires my physical presence, then I'll fly over. That's it. Not at all complicated."

He stood in the doorway unconsciously forming his hands into fists. "What about the estate? How could you contemplate leaving your home?"

Her chin lifted. "Before I ever heard from Chloe that she was getting married, I'd decided to move to a condo and turn the mansion and estate into a hospital. One wing for heart failure patients and the other for stomach cancer patients who can't afford health care. When I fly back to Carmel, I'll get the process going."

"You'd get rid of everything and live in a condo?" He was clearly incredulous.

"I already told my grandpa what I was going to do when he was gone. He gave me his blessing. I don't need an estate. To live one day in every room would take me a year."

She hoped he'd laugh, but his expression was inscrutable. "Look at this villa—it's the perfect size for you. That's why I love it so much. When you took me to the penthouse, I couldn't see you in it."

"Vasso and I use it out of necessity when we do business and have to stay on site in Athens."

"Ah, that explains it. Where does he live?"

"In a villa about this size on Loggos. But it's a beach house on the other side of the village."

She blinked. "You see? He doesn't need masses of square footage to be happy, either. Why do you think I would be any different?"

"But to come here and live isn't you."

His arguments were getting to her. "Because I'm a lousy linguist? I know I only know twelve words and don't pronounce them well, but I can learn. Just like you learned English!"

"We had to learn it in order for our business to succeed."

"Well, I'll have to learn Greek for marriage to you to be successful. What's the difference?"

"What kind of work would you do here?"

"If you opened up a new store along the harbor here on Anti Paxos, I could help manage it. If you hired another clerk, I could learn Greek from him."

He shook his head. "A job like that isn't for a woman like you."

"Akis—you have a strange idea of who I am. I'm flesh and blood and need work like everyone else. I think it would be fun. Your mom and dad worked together."

"That was different."

"How?"

"Because you're a physicist!"

"That's not the only thing I do. I'm a master scuba diver and could give lessons to people on the island."

"You never told me that," he accused.

"Because it never came up."

"Be serious, Raina. You'd go crazy being stuck here."

"Not if you came home to me at night."

"I can't always be here."

There was an edge of resolution to his delivery. A brittle laugh rose from her lungs like a death cry.

"I'd hoped you would want me here so much that I could convince you. But it hasn't happened, so you win. There's still some daylight left. Why don't you send for your helicopter and we'll fly back to Athens by dark. I'll phone Chloe's parents and alert them."

His lips had thinned to a white line. "Is that what you want?"

"You know what I want, but it doesn't matter. Go ahead and call your pilot. I'll take a swim, but I'll be ready when he arrives. Now if you don't mind, I'd like my privacy to change."

At first she didn't think he was going to leave. She could feel the negative vibes emanating from him. If he didn't go, she was in danger of screaming the house down.

Finally he disappeared and she got ready for her swim. For the next hour she played in the pool and lay back on the lounger. She had no idea what Akis was doing. Until the last second she prayed he hadn't sent for the helicopter. But then she heard the faint sound of rotors and knew it was coming. A stake driven through her heart couldn't have done more damage.

"Raina—you're back!" Chloe's mother clasped her with love and gave her kisses on both cheeks. "You've gotten a lot of sun."

"We've been so many places. It was wonderful." She hooked her arm through Nora's and they walked through the house to the guest bedroom. They'd left Akis and Socus having a private conversation at the helicopter pad.

"I have good news for you."

"What is it?"

"Chloe and Theo are having such a wonderful time, they're going to extend their honeymoon another week. Which means you have to stay with us longer than you'd first thought. She knows you're here and won't hear of your leaving Greece until after they get back."

Raina gave her a hug. "How about this? I'll fly home in the morning to do business. But I'll fly back when Chloe and Theo have arrived and we'll have our reunion."

"You promise?"

"Of course. I plan to leave early in the morning. Since it's getting late, I'm going to go to bed now."

"I'll have breakfast waiting for you before you leave."

"You don't need to do that."

"I want to."

"Thank you, dear Nora." She hugged her hard, already feeling a loss so excruciating, she didn't know how she would handle it.

After Nora left, Raina got ready for bed. The nightmare flight from the island with a taciturn Akis had pretty well destroyed her. When they'd landed on the pad, he'd helped her down and had whispered goodbye to her.

Just like that he'd let her go from his life. His words about Althea at the reception came back to haunt her. *You saved me from being caught. For that, I'm in your debt.*

"You're welcome," she whispered to the air before she buried her face in the pillow and sobbed.

As soon as the helicopter took off for the penthouse, Akis phoned his brother. Vasso picked up on the third ring. "How's the vacation going?"

"It isn't. Everything's over."

"What do you mean? Where are you?"

"I'm headed for the penthouse."

"I'll meet you there in ten minutes."

Akis hadn't been in the apartment five minutes before his brother arrived, but he'd already poured himself a drink. He held up the glass. "Want to join me?"

"No. You look like hell. Sit down and talk to me."

"There's nothing to say. I just said goodbye to Raina. She's going back to California in the morning."

Vasso sat down next to him. "Why?"

"It won't work."

"What won't work?"

"Us!"

"Doesn't she love you?"

He poured himself another drink. "She says she does."

"So what's the problem?"

"Look at me, Vasso!"

"I'm looking."

"Do you see a man who's worthy of her?"

Vasso's brows knit together. "Worthy—give me a definition."

"I'm not in her league and couldn't be in a hundred years. She's everything I'm not. In time she'll start to notice all that's missing and fall out of love with me. I couldn't handle that, so I let her go tonight." Exploding with pain, Akis got up from the couch. "I've got to go."

"At this time of night?"

"I need to be alone. I'm going to fly back to Anti Paxos."

"I'll come with you."

"No. I release you of the promise you made Papa to watch out for me. It's time I took care of myself."

"Wait—"

"Sorry, bro. I need to be alone."

It wasn't until Raina heard her phone ring in the middle of the night that she realized she'd been asleep.

She came wide awake and grabbed it off the night stand without looking at the caller ID. "Akis?" she cried.

"I'm sorry, Raina. It's Vasso Giannopoulos."

His big brother was phoning her? Her heart ran away with her. She clutched the phone tighter. "What's happened to him? Has there been an accident?"

"Not an accident, but he needs help and you're the only one who can fix this. I know it's three in the morning, but I had to call you. When he left me at the penthouse, he was in the worst state I've ever seen in my life."

"Where is he now?"

"He flew back to Anti Paxos. I heard him mutter something about being afraid you were leaving Greece forever."

She took a deep breath. "I am. I have to be at the airport in three hours to make my plane."

"Then it's true." Vasso's voice sounded a little different than his brother's, but he spoke English in the same endearing way.

"He said goodbye to me earlier when he dropped me off at Chloe's. I took it as final."

After a brief silence he said, "This is my fault for telling him about you. I did it because I wanted him to stop worrying about you. I don't know what has gone on between you two, but I have serious doubts he'll be able to handle it if you leave."

"He told me what you did, but that's not what is wrong. It's a long story. He took me to eat dinner at the taverna Elpis owns. When she asked me if I loved him, I said I wanted to be his fiancée."

"You *what*?"

Raina didn't blame him for being totally shocked. "Don't worry. He shut me down. I think it's because he got mumps and because of his sterility can't give me or any woman a child. He wants to do the honorable thing and give me a chance to marry a man who can."

"I don't believe that's the reason," he bit out, sounding like Akis just then.

"If it isn't, then I don't know what it could be."

"Look, Raina. I don't mean to interfere, but you can't leave yet."

"There's no point in staying. I fought him all day long trying to break him down so he'd really listen to me. That hurts a woman's pride, you know?" Tears crept into her voice.

"His pride is much worse. Do you love him?"

She got to her feet. "I love him to the depth of my soul."

Raina heard a sharp intake of breath. "Then go after him to that place inside of him and wear him down until you get the answer you're looking for."

She bit her lip. "He's given me his answer."

"No. It's a smoke screen for what is really bothering him. Trust me. If you love him like you say you do, don't give up."

"That's asking a lot."

"I'll send a helicopter for you first thing in the morning."

Her nails bit into her palm. "I'm afraid."

"Your fear couldn't be as great as his. He's not as secure as he lets on."

"Why do you say that?"

"Because I've known him longer. And I'm afraid of what will happen if you disappear from his life. I'll have the helicopter there at six whether you decide to take it or not."

He clicked off and left her pacing the floor for what was left of the night. It would mean telling Chloe's parents that she would going to Anti Paxos before she flew back to the States.

For the next two hours she went back and forth deciding what to do. At five o'clock she called to cancel her flight and the limo. When she left the bedroom with her bag, she went straight out to the patio to tell Chloe's parents her plans had changed. Only Nora was up, pouring coffee.

"There you are. I'm still having a hard time letting you go."

"Nora—my plans have changed."

"What do you mean?"

"I've cancelled everything and am going to fly to Anti Paxos to talk to Akis. We had a problem yesterday. In good conscience I can't fly home until we've talked again. Forgive me for making you get up early."

"I was awake." She smiled and gave her a hug. "The path to love is filled with obstacles."

Raina eyed her hesitantly. "Am I that transparent?"

She laughed. "Come on and sit down. As my husband remarked the day Akis came barging out here looking for the woman with the sprained ankle, the second you saw each other, no one else existed but the two of you. It was fascinating really because we'd noticed Akis running from Althea at the reception."

"I know. I felt so sorry for her."

"To our knowledge, Akis has never chased after a woman in his life. Yet the minute he saw you at the table, everything changed in an instant. I wondered when it was going to happen to him. Those two devilishly handsome brothers have been free agents for so long, it's had us worried.

"Their distaste for publicity has caused them to retreat from all the lovely women who'd love to have a relationship with them. But you've been surrounded by publicity, too, so you understand how stifling it can be."

Raina nodded. "I was afraid some member of the press would recognize me at Chloe's wedding and ruin her wedding day. That's why I chose to wait until the reception to make an appearance."

Nora patted her hand. "Chloe told us everything. She's always said you're the sweetest, kindest person she's ever known. Socus and I found that out years ago."

If Nora didn't stop, Raina would be in tears again. "So are all of you."

While she forced herself to eat breakfast for Nora's sake, she heard rotors in the distance. Her heart turned over. Vasso was as good as his word. Maybe he knew something she didn't. At this point she was running on faith and nothing else. He knew Akis better than anyone in the world and he was urging her to go to him.

Socus joined them for breakfast. Nora filled him in

before the three of them walked out to the pad with her suitcase. After several hugs, she climbed on board and waved to them before the helicopter whisked her away.

Athens passed beneath her, the Athens she'd seen through the telescope from his penthouse. Tears ran down her cheeks unchecked. She loved him so terribly. What if Vasso was wrong and Akis wanted nothing more to do with her? But Raina couldn't think about it.

CHAPTER EIGHT

AKIS DIDN'T KNOW where to go with his pain. Vasso hadn't been able to help him. For once in their lives the brother he relied on had no answer for him. This was a crisis he had to figure out on his own. Vasso had helped him get to the helicopter at the complex and told the pilot to fly him to Anti Paxos.

When he reached his house, he headed straight for the truck. He didn't care it was dark out. He needed work. It had been his salvation for years. He'd clean the cabin cruiser until he dropped.

Midmorning he grew so tired he staggered down the steps to the cabin. One of Raina's crutches resting against the wall had fallen across the floor, causing him to trip. He collapsed onto the bed so exhausted and emotionally drained he stayed right where he'd fallen. The next thing he knew it was late afternoon. He could tell by the position of the sun through the window slat.

Groaning, he turned on his back. Not since the serious case of mumps that almost killed him had he felt this ill. But it was a different kind of sickness that started in the very core of his being. By now Raina would be flying somewhere over the US to her home of three hundred and sixty-five rooms. He'd gotten rid of her all right. He'd done everything to make certain she'd never come near again.

His stomach growled because it was empty, but he wasn't hungry. He hadn't eaten since their meal at the café yesterday when Raina had told Elpis she wanted to be his fiancée. To be that open and honest in front of the older woman had knocked him sideways. He still hadn't recovered.

When she'd told him she'd be his lover if that's what he wanted, he'd felt shame that he'd been so cruel to her. He'd seen her heart in those fabulous violet eyes. They haunted him now. He looked around the cabin. All he saw was emptiness.

Life without Raina wasn't life.

He couldn't comprehend how he'd gotten through it this far without her. Life would have no meaning if he didn't go after her and beg her forgiveness. Grovel if necessary. It terrified him that she might refuse to see him. She would have every right.

The first thing to do was make arrangements for their company jet to fly to Corfu. He'd leave for the States from there. He pulled out his cell phone and made the call, then he headed to the bathroom for a shower and shave, but he only made it as far as the hallway when he smelled coffee and ham of all things.

Akis had been in a traumatic state last night. His brother must have come to check up on him. Calling out his name he went to the kitchen and came close to having a cardiac arrest.

"Raina—"

She stood at the counter whipping up eggs. Her blond head swerved in his direction. "You look terrible. By the time you've taken a shower, dinner will be ready. I'm fixing you an American breakfast. Did you know breakfast is my favorite meal? I could eat it morning, noon and night."

He rubbed the back of his neck in disbelief that she was really here. "You're supposed to be on your way home."

"Well as you can see, I haven't left Greece yet. Vasso phoned and asked me to peek in on you before I go. He seemed to think you needed help."

Akis couldn't believe it. "Vasso actually phoned you?"

She nodded. "From the look of you, I can see why. Hurry. We're having omelets and they only taste good right out of the skillet. Cooking is another one of my accomplishments."

Raina had so many accomplishments, it staggered him. Still in shock that she was here on the cruiser instead of a jet liner, he showered and shaved in record time. He kept casual clothes on board in the drawer. After dressing in a pair of jeans and a T-shirt, he hurried back to the kitchen, afraid he'd been dreaming and she wouldn't be there.

"You look a little better. Sit down and I'll feed you." She slid the omelets onto two plates with ham and placed them on the table.

"How did you get here?"

"When I saw that the truck was gone, I walked to the harbor and there it was. I climbed on board and found you passed out on the bed. I thought maybe you'd had too much to drink."

"I rarely drink."

"So I went back on deck and walked around the village to buy a few groceries and a pan. You were still asleep when I returned. To pass the time I got busy and made some brownies."

"What are they?"

"A chocolate dessert."

"Now that I think about it, I can smell it. This omelet with the ham is divine, by the way."

"That's because you're hungry. I'll report back to Vasso that your appetite has returned." He watched her get up and put some chocolate squares on a plate before she brought it to the table. "If you're still starving, you can fill up on these."

One bite and he was hooked on them. In no time at all he'd eaten all five.

"They're good, aren't they? The convenience stores carry them. They sell like hotcakes."

"Like hotcakes?"

"Or pancakes. Same thing. Americans love them, but you can never stop with just one. If you sold them in one of your Alpha/Omega 24 stores, you'd be shocked how fast they'd disappear."

"Raina—" He couldn't take anymore. "We need to talk."

"I think we've said it all. Now that some food has brought you back to life, I can leave in good conscience."

"Where do you think you're going?" He got to his feet to bar the way.

"Now that I've made my pit stop for your brother, I'm walking back to the house. Vasso's helicopter is waiting to fly me to Corfu. I'll let him know his worry over you is unfounded and I'll take the plane home from there."

"First you're going to come to the bedroom with me where we'll be more comfortable."

"Oh. Now you've decided I can be your lover? Sorry. I'm taking that offer back."

A grimace broke out on his face. "There's only one reason why I haven't asked you to marry me."

"Because you can't give me a baby. I know."

"That's not it." He picked her up around the hips and set her on the counter. "This is better. Now you're on eye level with me." Akis could feel her trembling. "Look at me, Raina."

"I don't want to."

"I don't blame you. After the way I've treated you, you have every right to despise me. The truth is, I'm not an educated man with diplomas covering my walls. I don't know all the things you know and have learned."

"*That's* the reason you were willing to let me go? Just because some pseudoacademic can talk to me about the differences in Pointillism between Seurat and Signac means absolutely nothing to me!"

"You see? I don't know who they are. I don't know what Pointillism is."

"You think I want to talk to you about that?"

"If we went to a party at one of your friends, they'd see my deficits in a hurry and you'd wish you'd never brought me."

"Oh, Akis—if I took you to one of my parties, the women would fall all over themselves just to hear you speak English with your unforgettable Greek accent. The men would take one look at you knowing they couldn't measure up to you, and they'd be so jealous of your business acumen, they'd croak."

"Croak?"

"Yes. Like a frog."

"Don't tease me, Raina. You're brilliant. I can't do math, I can't speak intelligently about art or literature. I'm not well read and haven't traveled the globe. Chloe and Theo have most everything in common. They suit each other in so many ways. But you and I are poles apart.

"I couldn't take it if we married and you grew bored with me. You told me Byron made a wonderful companion. Even though he betrayed you, he had a cultural background that stimulated you in the beginning. I can't give you that and I'm afraid I'll lose you."

She lifted wet eyes to him. "So you decided to push me away before you gave us a chance to find out what our life could be like? Do you know you could teach a class on Greek history and mythology that would blow everyone's mind? I know your worth, Akis. You know things no one else knows. You can't let that be the thing that keeps us apart!"

He cupped her face in his hands. "I was afraid at first, but no longer. I want to be all things to you. You're my heart's blood. I don't want to take another breath if I can't be with you. I love you, Raina. I love you," he cried against her lips. "I want you for my wife if you'll have me."

"If I'll have you— Oh, Akis…" She launched herself into his arms. He carried her out of the kitchen and down the hall to the bedroom. When he laid her down, she pulled him to her. "I love you, my darling," she murmured over and over again between kisses. "I wish we were already married."

"So do I, but I know a man in high places who can arrange a special license for us tomorrow. We can be married at the church on Paxos. I'll arrange it with the priest."

"You don't want a big wedding?"

"Never. Do you?"

"I did all that once before. What I want is to be your wife and hibernate with you for several months before anyone knows except Chloe's family, and Vasso, of course."

"I owe him for getting you here. How did he manage it?"

"His call at three in the morning got my attention in a hurry, but he didn't have to beg me. The thought of leaving you was so terrible, I doubt I would have gotten on the plane." By this time she'd broken down in tears of joy.

"Don't you know I love our differences? No woman could love you the way I do, Akis. I'm so in love with you, a lifetime won't be enough to show you how much. We were meant to be together, my love."

"I know that," he admitted. "My psyche knew it at the reception. One look into your eyes and the hairs began prickling on the back of my neck. They've never stopped."

"I knew I was crazy about you when you ran to my table in desperation." Their joyous laughter turned into moans of need as their mouths met and clung. Time had no meaning as their legs entwined and they tried without success to appease their unquenchable desire for each other. Akis felt as if he'd been born for this moment.

An all-consuming need to prolong this ecstasy

caused him to burn out of control. For the next while he found himself drowning rapturously in her overwhelming response. It was so marvelous to feel this alive, to touch her, love her. She was all warmth and beauty.

But Akis knew that to stay in the bedroom any longer would mean they'd never come out. He relinquished her mouth. "We need to go back to the house and make our plans, Raina. I want to be married before I make love to you for the first time. My father told me it was the best way to start out a marriage. I'd like to be a good son and honor his final advice to me."

"Then we will, but you're going to have to be the one with the willpower. Mine has deserted me. *S'agapo, Akis.*"

His breath caught. "You know what it means?"

"When you told me it was the most important word I would ever say in Greek, I figured out what it meant and have been dying to try it out on you. How did I do?"

He drew her off the bed and crushed her in his arms, rocking her back and forth. "You sounded like a native just now."

"Then there's hope for me. I plan to learn your difficult language or die in the attempt."

"Don't talk about dying on me," he begged. "Not ever, and not in jest. This is the first day of our new life together. Kiss me one more time before we leave. I need you the way I need our Greek sun to shine. You're my life force, Raina. Do you hear me?" He shook her gently.

"I think you have that turned around. You swept

across the dance floor to my table, and then you swept *me* out of the hotel, crutches and all." She looked into his eyes. "My beloved Poseidon, I'll love you forever. Do you hear me?"

CHAPTER NINE

Six weeks later

RAINA HURRIED INSIDE the villa with all her packages and put them down on the couch in the living room. Before she did anything else, she needed to call Akis and let him know her plans had changed. But she got his voice mail and had to leave a message.

"Darling? I know I told you I'd be at the penthouse when you got back from Crete, but I decided that since it's Friday, I'd rather we spent the weekend at the villa so I'll see you when I see you. Hurry. *S'agapo.*"

She had no idea when he'd hear the message, let alone when he'd be home. It was already ten after five. Between her shock and excitement since her morning appointment at the doctor's office in Athens, she wouldn't be surprised if she were running a temperature.

To get ready for tonight she'd stopped at an internet café to look for the picture she wanted. When she found it, she printed it off. Next, she went to a high-fashion boutique and found the perfect Grecian gown of lilac chiffon that tied over one shoulder.

After running by a florist's shop, she headed for the hair salon near the Grand Bretagne hotel and asked the stylist to make her hair look like the picture on the printout and twine the small lavender flowers in it. From there she went to a shop to buy a dozen vanilla-scented candles. Last but not least, she stopped at a boutique for infants and bought a beautiful baby book, which she had wrapped.

Once her errands were done, she returned to the penthouse and took the helicopter to Anti Paxos.

Time was of the essence. She made his favorite chicken salad with olives and feta cheese and would combine it with crusty rolls and fresh fruit. With the dinner ready, she went out on the patio to set the table. In between the potted plants she placed the candles, and put the last three for a centerpiece. She hid the baby book behind a big clay pot filled with azaleas.

Now to get dressed. After her shower she put on the gown. While she was tying it at the shoulder, her cell rang. Giddy with joy, she reached for it and saw the caller ID. "Darling?" she cried the second she picked up.

"I just got your message. Vasso and I are headed for the island now. You didn't want to go out on the town tonight?"

"Not really. Do you mind?"

"What do you think? If I had my way, we wouldn't go anywhere else."

"I'm glad you feel that way. Are you hungry?"

"Starving."

"How soon do you think you'll be here?"

"Fifteen minutes. You sound like you've missed me."

She was breathless. "I know it's only been two days, but I feel like it's been a month!"

"I'm never going to spend another night away from you. Not having you in bed with me was torture I don't want to live through again."

"Neither do I. Hurry home and be safe." *We have a future awaiting you never thought was possible.*

It took a few minutes for her to light all the candles. The flames flickered in the scented air, sending out their marvelous fragrance Akis said he loved. Twilight had fallen over the island. She'd just lighted the table candles when she heard the blades rotating.

He'd be here any second. She walked to the terrace entrance to wait. In a minute she heard him call out, "Raina? Where are you?"

Taking a deep breath she said, "I'm out on the patio."

Her gorgeous husband appeared in the living room wearing a sport shirt and trousers, but he stopped short of coming any closer. She could see he was almost dumbstruck. Good. That was exactly the reaction she'd hoped for.

His black eyes had a laser-like quality as they examined her from the flowers on her head to the gold slippers on her feet. She saw desire in that all-encompassing gaze and almost fainted.

"You've been away, so I wanted to make your homecoming special. Tonight you're going to stay with me or I'll think you've forsaken me. Come and eat while I serve you. I have a special surprise."

She heard him whisper her name, but he looked absolutely dazed. She loved him so much she could hardly stand it.

"Would you like your surprise first, or later?"

His hand passed over his chest. "I don't think I could handle another one. The way you look tonight standing there like a vision from Mount Olympus, I'm having trouble breathing."

Raina sent him a come-hither smile. "That's more like it. I thought maybe you'd forgotten me."

He started to look nervous. "Is there something wrong?" She could see an anxious expression in his eyes. It was sweet really. Her darling husband was so wonderful, she needed to put him out of his misery.

"Of course not. You're always so generous and take such perfect care of me, can't your lover do something special for you without you worrying?"

His chest rose and fell visibly, evidence that he needed an answer. Afraid to carry this charade any further without an explanation he could live with, she walked over to the flowerpot and pulled out the wrapped package.

"If you'll sit down at the table with me, I'll give this to you."

Instead of the happiness she'd expected, he looked stricken. "It's our six-week anniversary. I planned to give you your gift tonight while we were out to dinner in Athens. But I left it at the penthouse."

"There's plenty of time for you to give it to me. Right now why don't you open yours." She walked over to the table and put the present on top of his plate, then she sat down opposite him.

Akis moved slowly, like he was walking through water. Then he sank down in the chair stiffly and reached for it, but he kept looking at her. Why was he behaving like this? She couldn't understand it.

When he pulled the baby book out of the wrapping, she thought he'd paled, but it was difficult to tell in the candle light. His black brows furrowed. "What kind of a joke is this?"

With that question, she finally understood how much he'd suffered because he thought he could never be a father.

"It's no joke. I've been nauseated every morning for the last week. I asked Chloe to get me in to see her OB this morning in Athens. He took a blood test. I'm pregnant with your baby."

His head reared. He stared at her. "But that's impossible."

"I told my doctor the same thing. He said that mumps for a certain percentage of men cause a drop in their sperm count. But research has come a long way since ten years ago when you came down with them. Since then, he says you've recovered." She put a hand on his arm and squeezed it. "You had to have recovered because I'm pregnant."

When the truth finally sank in, the chair scraped on the tile. He shot out of it and came around to pick her up in his arms, holding her like a bride. "We're going to have a baby! *Raina*—"

He carried her through the house to their bedroom and followed her body down onto the bed. His mouth kissed her so long and hard, she could scarcely breathe. "My precious love." Over and over he kissed every inch of her face and hair. The tie on her shoulder had come undone. She felt moisture on her skin. By now they were both in tears.

"I didn't know it was possible I could be this happy, Akis."

"I still can't believe it." His hand slid down her body to her stomach, sending darts of delight through her. He leaned over to kiss her through the chiffon. "Our baby is inside you."

"Incredible, isn't it. Do you want a boy or a girl?"

"Don't ask me a question like that. I don't care. I only know I want you to take care of yourself. I couldn't bear to lose you."

She hugged his head to her breast, kissing his black hair. "Please don't be afraid for me. I'm not your mother. I won't die after giving birth. I'm strong and in perfect health. The doctor has given me a prescription for nausea. I've had all day to consider names. I can't think of a girl's name yet, but I know what I want if we have a boy."

He lifted his head. His eyes were filled with liquid. "Tell me," he whispered, kissing her mouth.

"Patroklos Giannopoulos after your father. We can call him Klos for short. I looked up his name. It means glory of the father. It's a perfect name to revere the man who fathered you and Vasso."

"It might be a girl," he murmured, kissing her neck to hide the emotions she knew were brimming out of him.

"Of course. But I draw the line at *Phaiax.*"

All of a sudden that delightful, rumbling sound of male laughter poured out of Akis. He rolled her on top of him. "My adorable Naiad nymph. If we have a daughter, we'll name her Ginger after her earthly great-grandmother who raised you to be the superb woman you are."

"Hmm." Raina drew her finger across his lower lip. "Ginger Giannopoulos. I love it. Almost as much as

I love my husband who has given me a priceless gift. Darling—I know what this news means to you. I also know that you and Vasso share everything. Go ahead and call him, then I'll have your whole attention."

A half smile broke the corner of his mouth. "Am I that transparent?"

"It's a beautiful thing to see two brothers so devoted to each other. Your joy will be his. Here. Use my phone." It was lying on the bedside table.

Their conversation was short and so touching, she teared up again. When he hung up, he crushed her in his arms. "Thank God my brother phoned you in the middle of the night."

She clasped him to her. "I know now that Grandpa was inspired when he told me not to close off my heart. He knew something I didn't. I love you so much. I'm the luckiest woman on earth. The doctor says I probably got pregnant on our wedding night."

"Have you told Chloe?"

"No. I simply asked her to give me the name of her OB since I needed a prescription for birth control. I think news like mine should be reserved for the man who's made me the happiest woman in the world."

"We haven't seen them since the wedding. Let's invite them over on Sunday and tell them together."

"I'd love it, but right now I want to concentrate on you. Do you want to eat first?"

"Not yet. I need to inspect my pregnant wife from head to toe."

Heat swept into her cheeks. "You already did when you saw me standing on the patio."

"I'll never forget the sight of you in this gown with

those flowers in your hair and the air fragrant with vanilla. But there are other sights meant for me and me alone. Come here to me, Raina."

"I'm here. *S'agapo*, my wonderful, fantastic Akis."

* * * * *

What had she done? And what was she going to do now?

Justin McMillian had kissed her again, unexpectedly and thoroughly, as if she were his to command with a touch of his lips. Worse, she had been willing, eager, hungry. She'd wanted to gobble him up. A part of her still did.

Stupid. Stupid. Stupid.

For all Bailey knew, her reaction was exactly the response he wanted. Nothing good would come from spending time with Justin. Conflict of interest. Uh, yeah. Kissing was not exactly professional behavior. The inn's staff and their families were counting on her to win.

She needed to keep her distance from him. He could be playing her. Why wouldn't he? A charming hotelier and construction hottie who oozed sex appeal must be good at that kind of game.

Her gaze narrowed on Justin heading down the stairs. He looked like a fashion model, handsome in his worn jeans, Henley shirt and flannel jacket. His boots were durable enough to withstand the weeds and rocks below. Handsome, check. Capable, check. Under control, check.

The opposite of her.

***

The Coles Of Haley's Bay:
For this family, love is a shore thing…

HIS PROPOSAL, THEIR FOREVER

BY
MELISSA McCLONE

MILLS
BOON

Published in Great Britain 2015
by Mills & Boon, an imprint of Harlequin (UK) Limited,
Eton House, 18-24 Paradise Road, Richmond, Surrey, TW9 1SR

© 2015 Melissa Martinez McClone

ISBN: 978-0-263-25148-7

23-0715

Harlequin (UK) Limited's policy is to use papers that are natural, renewable and recyclable products and made from wood grown in sustainable forests. The logging and manufacturing processes conform to the legal environmental regulations of the country of origin.

Printed and bound in Spain
by CPI, Barcelona

Melissa McClone has published over thirty novels. She has also been nominated for a Romance Writers of America RITA® Award. She lives in the Pacific Northwest with her husband, three school-age children, two spoiled Norwegian elkhounds and cats who think they rule the house. They do! Visit her at www.melissamcclone.com.

To Margie Lawson and the Wonderblue Wordsmiths:
Allie Burton, Linda Dindzans, Amy Mckenna Rae,
Megan Menard, Laura Navarre and Sarah Tipton

Special thanks to Amy Mckenna Rae, Lisa Hayden,
Terri Reed and Kimberly Field

Chapter One

The hourly chime of tower bells rang through the Piazza del Duomo. Bailey Cole raised her face to let the Florence sunshine kiss her cheeks.

Glong. Glong. D-ding-a-ting-glong.

Not bells from the famous tower, her cell phone ring tone.

Bailey opened her eyes. Not Italy. Home.

Her home. Haley's Bay, Washington.

She rubbed her face, trying to wake up.

The phone kept ringing.

A glance at the digital clock made her blink: 5:45 a.m. Too early for a social call. Something must be…

Flynn. Bailey's heart slammed against her chest. Air whooshed from her lungs. Her brother in the navy had mentioned going somewhere in his email last week.

Please let him be safe.

She reached for her phone on the nightstand, read "Grandma" and her phone number on the screen.

Bailey's chest sank with the weight of a flag-draped coffin. She fumbled for the talk button. "Grandma? Is everything okay?"

"Your aunt Ida Mae called. Told me the craziest thing. Said there's a construction crew set up in front of the Broughton Inn."

Not Flynn. Bailey released a breath. "Did you say a construction crew?"

"They've been moving things out of the inn and loading them into a big truck since late last night." The words flew out of Grandma's mouth faster than her homemade molasses cookies disappeared from the jar. "Equipment is parked on the street. A bulldozer and a crane with a wrecking ball."

Bailey sat straight, the covers falling to her waist.

"What's Floyd Jeffries trying to pull? I just saw him two days ago. He didn't mention any construction, and a wrecking ball sounds more like demolition. He knows owners can't touch a historic building without approval." She scrambled out of bed. "He practically wrote the preservation laws."

"Maybe he forgot."

"No way." She turned on the lamp, waited for her eyes to adjust to the light. "I took over the historical committee from him. He knows every single rule and regulation."

"He could be expanding the owner's apartment now that he's in a relationship."

"Floyd didn't mention his girlfriend moving here. She's half his age and most of their relationship has been online. Something's going on. I need to find out what. Fast."

Bailey pulled her nightshirt over her head and took a step. Her foot twisted, then slid, jamming into the bedpost.

A sledgehammer pain sliced through her big toe. She sucked in a breath. Tears stung her eyes. The phone slipped from her hand. She swore.

"Bailey?" Her grandmother's voice carried from wherever the phone had landed. Lilah Cole had been a widow for the past fifteen years, and her grandchildren had become her focus. "Are you okay?"

Hell, no. Bailey was naked, her mangled toe throbbing. She picked the phone off the bed. "I'm getting dressed. Trying not to panic over the twenty-five thousand dollars' worth of artwork inside the inn."

She hit the speakerphone button and placed the cell phone on the dresser. She opened the top drawer. Panties and bras. Second drawer—pajamas. Third drawer, *empty*. She had been so into her new painting this week she hadn't done laundry.

She wiggled into a pair of underwear, then put on a bra, trying not to cry out and worry Grandma. "Floyd might be struck stupid by Cupid, but he loves the inn."

"So do you. I know you'll straighten him out."

"Gotta go. I'll call you later."

Bailey bunny-hopped on one leg to the bathroom. Clothes overflowed from the hamper. Paint-splattered white, long-sleeved coveralls hung on a hook. She gave the fabric the sniff test. The cotton smelled of paint and solvents. Oh, well, this was what she'd planned to wear today while she worked. She dressed.

Clean panties and bra. Dirty coveralls.

Could be worse, right? A glance in the mirror brought a tell-me-I'm-still-dreaming cringe. Nope. This was pretty bad.

She didn't look sleep-rumpled sexy. More like bizarre, deranged scarecrow. Her wild hair stuck up every which way. Bet she'd freak out folks around town if she carried a broom this morning.

Okay, maybe not, but she would likely scare them, broom or not.

She combed her fingers through the tangles and twisted her hair into a messy bun. A slight improvement, but getting to the Broughton Inn was more important than looking good. So what if she ended up being tonight's gossip at the Crow's Nest, the local dive bar? Wouldn't be the first time or the last. Bailey took a step.

"Ouch, ouch, ouch." She stared at her aching foot turning blue. Her toe was swollen. Not bee-sting swollen—hot-air-balloon swollen.

Forget regular shoes. Her monster toe would never fit inside. Her oversize fuzzy slippers would have to do.

She shoved on the right slipper, then maneuvered her aching left foot inside the other. A jagged pain sliced through her toe, zigzagged up her foot.

Bailey hopped to her desk, using the wall and doorways for support. She grabbed the Broughton Inn files in case Floyd wanted to argue about what he could do to the inn, shoved them and her purse into a yellow recyclable shopping bag covered with multicolored polka dots. The colors matched the paint splatters on her coveralls. The newest trend in low fashion. Yeah, right.

Bailey hobbled to the door, walking on the heel of her bad foot. Not easy, but she had to get to the inn. Driving was her only option. She rehearsed a quick strategy.

Don't panic.

Don't burst in, acting as if she owned the place.

Most of all, don't piss off Floyd.

Logic and common sense, not to mention laws, would prevail. But she was prepared to do battle. No one was touching the Broughton Inn or the artwork inside.

Bailey was a Cole. Stubborn, unrelenting, ready to fight.

Early Thursday morning, Justin McMillian stood outside the Broughton Inn, McMillian Resorts' newest acquisition. Slivers of sunlight appeared in the dawn sky like fingers poking up from the horizon, wanting a piece of the night. He wanted to take what was his today.

This past winter's remodeling fiasco in Seaside on the Oregon coast had destroyed his parents' confidence in Justin and his two sisters' ability to take over the family company. The project had gone over schedule and over budget due to hidden foundation issues. His parents had blamed Justin, Paige—one of the company's attorneys—and Rainey, an interior designer, when two different inspectors hadn't seen the problem. That fact hadn't stopped his parents from threatening to sell to the highest bidder and firing their three children if the next project didn't run smoothly.

But today, Justin's mouth watered with the taste of success. His parents would be apologizing long before the new Broughton Inn opened next year. This project would be different from the Seaside one. His parents would see how capable he and his sisters were, and McMillian Resorts would show Haley's Bay what luxury and first-class service were about. Something his family had perfected over the years with both small and large properties.

"Loaded and ready to go, boss." Greg, Justin's driver, motioned to the semitruck parked on the street in front. "Never seen so much junk. Loads of outdated furniture and way too much artwork for such a small inn."

"Floyd Jeffries didn't have a clue how to run a boutique hotel."

"Good thing we do."

We. McMillian Resorts. Unless his parents followed through on their threat. That was not. Going. To. Happen. "Text me when you reach the warehouse."

"Should take me three hours or so to reach Lincoln City, depending on traffic."

"Drive carefully. I don't want the artwork broken. We can sell the better stuff to local galleries."

Greg adjusted the brim of his Seattle Mariners cap.

"Raw eggs could be loose in the cab and wouldn't break when I'm driving."

"Let's not test that theory."

Greg stared at the old inn. "Quaint place. Suz and I honeymooned here."

"Cozy, maybe, but a dinosaur. With those million-dollar views, the new inn will be the crown jewel in our hotel portfolio."

"Hope so." Greg took a picture of the inn with his cell phone. "Better hit the road."

Greg glanced at the inn again, then he headed to his truck.

Interesting. Justin had never known the driver to be sentimental.

Wyatt, the site foreman, walked up, adjusted his gloves. "We're ready. Say the word and we'll fire up the engines."

"It's time." Nothing beat the first morning on a new job, except the last day. Justin rubbed his hands together. "Tear her down, boys."

With whoops and hollers, his crew jogged to their equipment. Engines revved, filling the early morning air with noise. The crane hopped the curb and headed for the inn. Next came the bulldozer.

Finally. Over the past year, Justin had spent every free moment developing plans for a new Broughton Inn, even though he'd been unsure whether Paige could pull off the deal with Floyd Jeffries. They'd approached him last year with an offer that Floyd turned down. But Paige had achieved the impossible by not giving up and closing the deal.

This project would prove he and his sisters could run the company as well as his parents. Better. The three of them had grown up living in hotels. They knew the business inside and out.

A dog barked.

Huh? Justin shouldn't be able to hear a dog. Except the equipment had stopped moving. Engines had been cut off.

"What the hell is going on?" he yelled.

Wyatt pointed to the inn's porch where someone stood by the front door, hands on hips and a pissed-off frown on her face. "That woman."

Was that a woman with a yellow shopping bag hanging from her shoulder or an escapee from the circus? She wore painter's coveralls, but the color splatters made her look as if she'd been caught in a paintball battle.

"Where'd she come from?" Justin asked.

"No idea."

"The woman must be some sort of nut job. A disturbed bag lady or a history fanatic. I'll see if she has demands."

"Demands?" Wyatt asked.

"A woman doesn't step in front of a wrecking ball unless she has a death wish, or wants something. Given the crazy way she's dressed, my money's on the latter. Call the police in case I'm wrong and she'd rather meet the Grim Reaper."

Justin walked toward the porch. He didn't want his crew near the woman.

"Stop. Don't come any closer." Her voice sounded more normal than he'd expected. "You can't tear down the inn."

Her hands moved from her hips to out in front of her, palms facing Justin, as if she could push him away using The Force.

Demands. Justin knew a few things about women, though his ex-wife might disagree. He kept walking. Given the crazy lady's appearance, he knew how to handle her. He flashed his most charming smile, the one that got him what he wanted most every time, whether for business or pleasure.

"Hello there." In two steps, Justin stood on the porch. He softened his voice. "Can I help you?"

A jade-green gaze locked on his. Wow. Talk about a gorgeous color. Her warm, expressive eyes made him think of springtime.

"I'm looking for Floyd." Her voice rose at the end; her words weren't a question but had a hint of uncertainty.

Hell. She must not know about Floyd selling out. Not Justin's problem. Eyes aside, he didn't know why he kept looking at her. Clothes, hair, demeanor. *Not his type* didn't begin to describe what was wrong with the woman.

A brown dog barked and ran figure-eight patterns around the bulldozer and crane. Where had the animal come from?

"Oh, no. That poor dog is so skinny." Her compassion surprised Justin. "Catch him. He looks like he's starving."

Oh, man. The guys still ribbed him for the time he shut down a demo for a missing ferret. Stupid thing took five and a half hours to find.

"Please," she said, her eyes clouding.

Demands and a plea. Tropical-storm-strength pressure built behind his forehead. Easy jobs must be handed to worthier men. "Have you seen the dog before?"

"No." Her gaze remained on the animal. The dog ran around and barked. "But I don't see a collar. Could be a stray. Or lost."

Justin wasn't about to chase the dog on open ground, but he couldn't have the thing running around the site inside the safety fencing. That would be too dangerous.

He glanced at Wyatt, who stood on the grass between the porch and the equipment. "Give the dog a leftover donut."

"No chocolate." The words exploded from her mouth like a cannonball. Worry reflected in her eyes. "That's bad for dogs."

Justin didn't know that. He'd never had a dog or any kind of pet. His parents allowed guests to bring dogs and cats to the hotels, but had never let their children have an animal, not even a goldfish.

"Fine. Nothing chocolate. A sandwich, maybe," he said to Wyatt. Justin wanted to get back to work. These stupid delays were killing him. "Then get the dog out of here."

While he got rid of the woman. A McMillian team effort. That was the way things got done at their company. Each person did his or her part. The effort led to success. But when one didn't do what was expected, like his ex-wife, the result was failure.

He faced the woman. "Where were we?"

"Floyd Jeffries. Do you know where I can find him?"

"Belize."

Her nose crinkled. "Floyd never mentioned a vacation."

"Floyd might not share his personal life with customers."

"I'm not a customer." She raised her chin. "I'm his partner in the gallery."

Gallery. Justin's headache ramped into a cyclone. That explained the artwork on its way to Oregon, the splattered coveralls and Green Eyes' odd smells. "You're an artist."

"Painter." She gave him a strange look. "If Floyd's away, what are you doing here?"

"I'm the inn's new owner."

She flinched as if his words punched her. No clown makeup was needed to make her eyes look bigger. Any larger and they would be twins to her gaping mouth. The caricature was complete. All she needed was a dialogue bubble over her head to star in her own comic strip.

She took half a step back. "Floyd sold the inn?"

"We recently closed on the deal."

"Where's the artwork?" Her words shot out as if catapulted. "The textiles, paintings, sculptures?"

"Gone."

Her face morphed into a look of horror, a worst-news-ever-face. "Where?"

The raw emotion in the one word drew him forward. She looked desperate. Of course she was. Junk or not, the art pieces he'd seen must have taken hundreds of hours to make. If someone made off with a set of his blueprints that took half that long, he'd go ballistic. Ridiculing the woman no longer seemed cool. If anything, he wanted to give her a hug.

He forced himself not to step closer. He…couldn't. She was a stranger, a nuisance. "The inn's contents were part of the purchase agreement."

She bit her lip. Trying to decide what to say, or buy time? For what, he didn't know. She blinked, then wiped her eyes.

She'd better not, not, not cry. His sisters always pulled that stunt. His ex-wife, too. Taryn had blamed him for their marriage failing, saying he loved his work more than her. She hadn't understood that his job paid for everything, including their house, her shopping sprees and the numerous trips she took to Portland and Seattle while he was away at a site.

His sympathy well was drained. Not a drop of compassion remained. No way would he let this woman manipulate him. Time to send overwrought clown lady on her way. He handed her his business card.

"Talk to Floyd. Call my office for his contact information." Justin's voice sounded distant, unemotional, as intended. "You need to leave now so we can get back to work."

She grabbed the porch rail, gave him a this-isn't-over look, then sat. "I'm not going anywhere."

Of course not.

Justin should have known she wouldn't make this easy, but a one-person sit-in? "We have a schedule to keep. It's time for you to go."

"You can rephrase your request over and over again, but my answer will be the same. I'm not letting you touch the inn, let alone destroy the second-oldest building in Haley's Bay."

Attitude poured from the woman as easy as milk from a carton. Too bad hers was sour. "I've called the police."

Neither her gaze nor her facial expression wavered. If he wasn't on the receiving end of her stare, he might have been impressed by her backbone.

"Good." That attitude of hers wasn't letting up. "Because you're stealing."

Justin laughed. The woman had nerve. He had to give her that. "I have a contract."

"So do I. You may have bought the inn, but not the rest."

"Okay, I'll bite."

"The artwork doesn't belong to Floyd or the inn. He sold the pieces on consignment for local artists like me."

"The inn's contents belong to us per the deal—"

"The artists had contracts. Nontransferrable contracts."

She talked faster as if her nerves were getting to her, and her words were making him wonder what the hell was going on here.

"I see the Oregon plates on your equipment. I hope whatever truck you were loading earlier isn't headed across the bridge toward Astoria." She leveled him with a stare. "Given the value of the artwork, the theft qualifies as a class-B felony. But I'm sure the police can place blame where it's due and make the necessary arrests."

The woman could be telling the truth or she might be delusional. Could this be nothing more than a ruse to stop the demolition? "Floyd never mentioned the art didn't belong to the inn."

"Due diligence, Mr....?"

"Justin McMillian." Her vocabulary told him she knew something about business. Her know-it-all manner annoyed him like the sound of nails on concrete, but her point made his hope sink. Had Paige cut corners in a rush to get the deal closed? Their parents had put so much pressure on them it was...possible. He held out his arm to shake hands. "Mc-Millian Resorts. And you are?"

The woman pursed her lips, making her look haughty and naughty, a dangerous combination. This one was trouble.

After leaving him hanging a moment too long, she shook his hand. "Bailey Cole."

Warm, rough skin. Not unexpected, given that she worked with chemicals. Up close, she was kind of pretty with her pink cheeks and full lips. She might look halfway decent cleaned up.

Bailey removed the bag from her shoulder. "I'm happy to provide copies of the contracts to prove rightful ownership of the art. I have the information right here."

Paperwork? Crap. So much for her being delusional. The foundation mess in Seaside wasn't looking so bad now. At least they'd finally completed that project and had a viable hotel in a desirable market. But if what she said was true, he and his sisters were in trouble. His parents would never let them run the company. Hell, his mom and dad would probably refuse to pay bail.

Time to regroup. Get Greg back with the truck. Call Paige to find out if this Cole woman's story checked out. Justin glanced around but didn't see any of the crew. He texted Wyatt.

"I'll call the artists to pick up—"

Justin cut Bailey off. "The artwork will be back shortly."

Her jaw jutted forward, hard as granite. "You do know that transporting stolen property across state lines carries additional charges."

She might be an artist and the poster child for *What Not to Wear*, but this woman was no delicate flower swaying in the wind. She was a tree, solid and unmoving, firmly rooted in the earth, a sequoia. A good thing they had chain saws in the truck.

"The artwork is in Washington." He hoped.

Sirens sounded. Blue and red lights flashed.

Good. The police would get her off the property—no chain saws needed—and his team could get back on schedule.

A young, tall uniformed officer got out of his police car and straightened his hat. He took long, purposeful strides toward them.

Justin smiled at the guy who would save his day.

The officer stopped on the walkway in front of the porch. His attention, including a narrowed gaze, focused solely on Bailey Cole. The woman must be a known troublemaker in town to receive such scrutiny from a cop.

"What the hell are you doing, Bailey? And what's wrong with your foot?"

Justin noticed her knee was bent so her foot didn't touch the porch. No wonder she'd wanted him to go after the dog.

"You're not here to give me a hard time." She stood. A grimace flashed across her face. "I'm not the one who called you. This guy did, even though he stole the artwork from the inn."

The officer looked at Justin. "Is this true?"

Justin's smile hardened at the edges. He should've known she'd try to pin this on him, but he needed to keep his voice respectful. "My company, McMillian Resorts, bought the inn from Floyd Jeffries. The contents of the inn were included in the property's purchase. She's trespassing."

"What part of consignment don't you understand?" Bailey's hands returned to her hips, elbows pointed out. "The artists retain ownership and Floyd only received a commission if a piece sold. The artwork wasn't his, so it couldn't be included in the sale. Thus, it's been stolen."

The pursed lips returned, distracting Justin from her accusation. He needed to focus. She hadn't called him a thief exactly, but she was walking the line. She was still on *his* property. Her violation was clear. They needed to move this along.

He glanced at the officer whose face looked skeptical. Strange, but the guy had similar coloring to Bailey. Dark hair and green eyes.

On the lawn, Justin's crew gathered within listening distance. No sign of the dog. The donut or sandwich must have worked. Progress. Time for more.

"We can discuss the return of the art—if necessary— once she's escorted off my property." Justin might not know the whole story behind the gallery, but he trusted his sister to have negotiated a legally binding contract on the building and its contents.

"Not yet," Bailey said. "I'm here to protect my property and the inn, Grady. His construction permit did not go through the historical society's approval process."

She knew this how? Justin looked from Bailey to the cop, noticed the "Cole" name tag on the officer's chest.

"I'm Grady Cole. Bailey's my sister. She knows more about the approval process than anybody in town except Floyd Jeffries."

Siblings. This was not Justin's day. No matter. This project was *not* going to hell on his watch.

The crew moved closer, cutting the distance in half from where they'd stood before. He couldn't show any weakness or worry. Not in front of his guys.

"No problem." Justin removed the paperwork from his back pocket. "I have a permit."

"We'll see." Grady flipped through the forms, not once, but twice before frowning. "This permit is from Long Beach. The approvals, too."

"Yes, that's where I was told to go." Justin's headache throbbed. Holding back sarcasm was becoming harder. How long was this going to freaking take?

Bailey's smile widened. If she'd been a cat, canary feathers would be hanging from the corners of her mouth.

A knot formed in Justin's stomach. Crap. She knew something he didn't. "I checked the paperwork myself. We're good."

"You used the Long Beach zip code, not the one for Haley's Bay." Grady returned the papers. "This permit isn't valid. The town's municipal office must be used for projects within the city limits. You're also missing an approval stamp from the historical committee, since this property is on its registry."

The knot wrapped around the donut Justin had eaten for breakfast. "No problem. Floyd told me to go to Long Beach to get the permit. I'll head over to your town hall and get that and approvals right now."

"I'm sorry, but it's not that simple," Grady said.

Warning lights flashed. A cement roller pressed against Justin's chest. A vise squeezed his brain.

Bailey opened her mouth as if to speak.

He raised his hand, cutting her off. He didn't want Miss Know-It-All telling him why his must-succeed project was grounded. He wanted her gone; more than that, he wanted her to tell him this was a giant misunderstanding and they could work it out in the next two hours. And then smile.

Not gonna happen. "Once I have the permits, I'll be free to work on my property."

"Not exactly, Mr. McMillian." Her gaze remained on his, unwavering. More sure of herself with every passing minute, but maybe—if he wasn't stretching it—she was sympathetic, too. "Broughton Inn is on the Federal Register of Historic Places."

"I know. I also know private owners are not bound by any restrictions if they want to improve the property."

"Not bound by restrictions only if federal money—

grants—haven't been attached to their property." The confidence in her words matched the determined set of her chin.

The knot-entangled donut in his stomach turned to stone. He had spoken to the former inn owner, taken notes, confirmed each detail about what being on the historical register meant for improvements and teardowns. The ticking-clock time frame of Floyd Jeffries wanting to close the deal was looking suspect. "We were assured—"

"Floyd lied. You got taken, Mr. McMillian." Bailey pulled out files from her bag and handed one to Justin. "If you don't believe me, check these papers. They'll prove federal and state monies are attached to the Broughton Inn. Some are old, before Floyd's time as owner."

Justin noticed his crew creeping closer to the porch. The men had cut the distance in half twice, no doubt curious. He didn't blame them. This was their livelihood, too. He wouldn't let them down or allow Bailey Cole to screw up this project any more than she had.

He opened the folder, eager to prove her wrong. Except…

The first page listed the inn's grant awards. Not one, several. Federal and state funding had been provided to the inn.

His neck stiffened, the cords of muscles tightening and coiling like electrical wire. He turned the pages, one after another. Each was a death knell to his plans for the inn, smothering his hope for success, throwing the resort company's future ownership in doubt.

It now made sense why Floyd gave them only forty-eight hours to make a decision about purchasing the inn. The man had been trying to pull a fast one. Not trying, succeeding. Damn.

Talk about a crook. Paige, everyone at McMillian Resorts, had been duped. If Justin couldn't fix this, his parents would sell the company and ride off into retirement

without ⸺
spent their ⸺ thought to their three ⸺
Not about to ⸺ng and working at the ⸺
the papers. "We we⸺ and working at the ⸺
appreciate copies at y⸺ustin straightened, ⸺
"I'll get those to you a⸺ed this informatio⸺
Grady took the file out o⸺venience."
copies made. You need to get o⸺
"I will." She ground out the wor⸺Bailey said.
back teeth. "I have to return the artwor⸺"I'll have
"So, what's the approval process so we⸺
project?" Justin asked Grady.

The officer looked at his sister. "That's Bailey⸺
tise."

Great. She was the last person who would offer help⸺
but too much was at stake for Justin not to ask. "Care to
enlighten me on the steps?"

"Gladly." She leaned against the railing, but her casual
position didn't match the sharp, predatory gleam in her
eyes. "First the intended project plans must be presented
to the Advisory Council on Historic Preservation."

Not insurmountable. Justin released a quick breath.
"That doesn't sound so bad."

"No, but that's only the federal portion of the process."
Bailey flexed her knee with the injured foot, then straightened her leg. "After the feds check off on the plans, you
need input from the State Historic Preservation Office."

Each approval would take time. Not good. He scratched
his chin. Too bad he couldn't itch away the problems with
the inn. Or her. Bailey explaining the process without prod-
ding worried him. She might have a hidden agenda. Or
maybe she liked knowing more than he did. "Is that all?"

"After state approval, you'll need to present the plans to
the Haley's Bay Historical Committee in order to receive
your city permit."

...d im-

"Seems straightforward." Except the timin... ...pletely. ...busy sum-

pact the schedule, possibly change their pl... ...Paige ASAP

His parents wanted the inn to open b... But also a plan B.

mer season next year. He neede..." Grady added. That

and figure out not only dama...ficer's voice seemed to ...n pulled.

"My sister is head of th... ...ists. He wasn't into violence,

wasn't the cherry on...oyd Jeffries. The man had told

imply, but a gre... inn would be as easy as crushing

Justin's b...hrough three groups could take days,

but he...en months. Who knew if they'd allow ...e torn down so a new one could be built?

Jus...ing Miss Bailey Cole would be readying her ...a battle.

...ley's I-know-something-you-don't smile suggested she could read Justin's mind. "You realize if you do anything without getting approval—"

"I understand what's at stake, Ms. Cole." His words sounded harsh, but he'd lost patience. He couldn't keep his cool any longer. This so-called diamond in the rough, aka the Broughton Inn, was nothing more than a piece of fool's gold. He and his sisters looked like amateurs for not thinking the inn's fire-sale price came with strings of steel.

Ones that might handcuff them for months, maybe years, in a web of approval procedures. Ones that might destroy their lifelong dream of running McMillian Resorts.

He gave a nod to Wyatt and the crew. "Pack it up, boys."

For now.

Bailey Cole might be smiling, but he would show her who was in charge. His parents, too. This approval process delay wouldn't change the inevitable. The old inn was coming down. A luxury five-star boutique hotel would be built on this spot.

No one, including Bailey Cole, was going to stop him. McMillian Resorts would succeed. No matter what Justin had to do to make that happen, including charming the silly slippers off the mess of a woman standing in his way.

Chapter Two

An hour later, Bailey eyed the dark, ominous clouds gathering over Haley's Bay. The approaching clouds carried big fat raindrops, ones that could turn this already horrible morning into a complete catastrophe. But cracking jokes and drinking coffee seemed to be the construction crew's priorities this morning. Unloading the artwork from the semitruck parked on the street and carrying the pieces back into the inn, not so much.

She half hopped, half hobbled to the truck's ramp. Her left foot was swelling like the water at the mouth of the bay. But she had more things to worry about than her injury. "Hurry. We need to get the art inside before the storm hits."

"We're going as fast as we can, miss." The foreman, Wyatt, used only one hand to carry Faye Rivers's four-foot-tall sculpture composed of driftwood and colorful glass floats collected from the beach.

"Hey, that's glass." These bozos had no idea what they were doing. "Be careful."

"I've got it." Wyatt stepped off the ramp, snagged a cup of coffee from the hood of a pickup truck, then glanced her way. "Want some coffee?"

The scent of French roast teased. Her sapped energy level longed for a jolt of caffeine. But forget about asking for a cup. No fraternizing with the enemy.

"I'll get one later." After the artwork was safe.

Wyatt juggled Faye's sculpture with one hand and his coffee with his other.

"You guys are going to pay if anything gets damaged." Bailey sounded like a Harpy, but she would keep nagging until they finished the job. Too much was at stake to play nice.

"Nothing has been damaged, and nothing will be." Justin came around the end of the truck. His scruff of blond stubble could be called bad-boy sexy, except his shorter hair looked too corporate. It was messy at the moment, but a sweep of a comb would have him looking a little too neat, even with whiskers. "Relax."

"Wish I could." Bailey was rethinking turning down the cup of coffee and not bringing a chair to take weight off her throbbing toe. "I'll relax when the artwork is inside."

He hopped on the ramp with the ease of an athlete and walked into the trailer. His steel-toed boots would have come in handy when she woke up this morning. Brown pants hugged muscular thighs, and the tails from his light blue button-down peeked out from beneath his tan jacket.

He leaned his right shoulder against the truck's wall and stared down at her. The casual pose contradicted the hard look in his eyes. He definitely had that I'm-hot-and-know-it demeanor. Sexy, if you liked that type. She didn't, but he was easy on the eyes. A good thing she was immune to men like him.

"Patience." His tone wasn't condescending, but she

couldn't tell if he was teasing or not. "You wouldn't want us to drop anything."

"Of course not." Now he was being a jerk. This wasn't a gallery of painted rocks. "But there's no need to move in slow motion. Unless the crew is following orders."

"Be careful." His voice contained a hint of warning. "Or you might find the guys going in reverse."

Grrrr. "I bet you'd enjoy telling your crew to do that."

A grin exploded like a solar flare, making her forget to breathe.

"Just give me a reason, Ms. Cole. That would be the bright side to this dark day."

"This isn't my fault. Blame Floyd."

She wasn't about to let Justin McMillian's threats get to her. The rest of the crew was on its way to the inn or already inside the building. None of them wanted to be caught outside when the rain hit. She would have to take care of this herself.

"Unload the truck faster. There may not be damage yet, but the weather—"

"Don't lose your purple slippers over this."

Justin's you-know-you-want-me attitude annoyed her. Yes, the man was attractive. She appreciated the way the features of his face fit together. Rugged, yet handsome. Her fingers itched for a pencil to capture the high cheekbones, the crinkles around his eyes and his easy smile when he joked with the crew. But she wasn't here to admire the eye candy.

She pinned him with a direct stare. "The rain will be here in five minutes. That's my concern."

He raised an eyebrow. "You the local rainmaker?"

"Not maker. Predictor."

"Artist, history buff and the town's weather expert."

"I'm from a fishing family. We learned to read the clouds

MELISSA McCLONE 29

before we could count to ten. Predicting rain is a necessary skill when you're out on a boat trying to earn a living."

"But you're a…"

"Girl?" Bailey finished for him with a tone she would call "ardent feminist."

She knew his type. The last man she'd dated, a wealthy guy named Oliver Richardson from Seattle, hadn't been a chauvinist, but was just as arrogant. He'd thought his job, condo, city and artistic tastes were better than everyone else's, including hers. Turned out her greatest dating asset to him was her oldest brother, AJ, a billionaire computer programmer. Since then, she hadn't felt like dating any man—rich or otherwise. Who needed that crap?

"Haley's Bay might be small and full of old-timers with big fish tales, but working women thrive here, Mr. McMillian. One day, my younger sister Camden will be the captain of her own boat."

"You might be a rain predictor, but you're not a mind reader." Justin laughed.

The sound made Bailey think of smooth, satin enamel paint, the expensive kind, no primer required. She'd used a gallon on her kitchen walls. Worth every penny and the peanut butter sandwiches she'd eaten to stay in budget.

"I was going to say 'artist.' That has nothing to do with your gender. I'm not a chauvinist, as you quickly and wrongly assumed." Justin sounded more annoyed than upset. "I have two sisters. Smart, capable, hardworking women, but without the smarter-than-you attitude."

"You think I have an attitude?" Maybe she did, but so did he. The guy was full of himself.

"I don't think. You do."

Standing on the trailer bed, he towered over her, but she wasn't intimidated.

"Your attitude is entitled," he said. "You assume you're correct. You assume I'm an idiot. That I can't recognize rain clouds. Hell, I live on the Oregon coast. Let me do my job, and we'll get along fine."

Bailey's muscles tensed, bunching into tight spools that weren't going to unravel any time soon. He might have a point, but she didn't like Justin McMillian, and she wasn't good at faking her feelings. "How we get along isn't important."

"You're the head of the historical committee. We'll be working together."

"I sure hope not." The words flew out faster than a bird released from captivity. "I mean… Oh, who am I kidding? That's exactly what I meant."

His surprised gaze raked over her. "You're honest."

"Blunt. Like my dad."

"I'll go with honest. For now." Justin picked up a painting, one of hers.

Bailey reached up for her piece. She loved the seascape, sketched on the beach early one morning, a morning like this one with a sky full of reds, pinks and yellows bursting from the horizon and a sea of breathtaking blues. But turbulent and dark clouds were moving in, matching the mood at the inn. She longed for the return of the calm, beautiful dawn.

"I'll take that one." She trusted herself more with one leg than him with two.

He kept hold of the frame. "I've got it."

"Be careful."

"This one more special than the others?"

"They're all one-of-a-kind."

Bailey pressed her lips together to keep from saying more. She should stalk off into the inn and check on the artwork that had been unloaded, but something held her in place. Something—she hoped not vanity—made her want him to notice her painting, to like her painting, to compliment her painting.

His studied the work in his hands. "Not bad if you like landscapes."

She bit her tongue to keep from uttering a smart-aleck remark. No way would she piss him off with her painting in his hands.

He looked at her. "It's one of yours."

"Yes."

The colors in the painting intensified the brightness and hue of his eyes.

Bailey's breath caught. The man was arrogant and annoying, but his Santorini-blue eyes dazzled her. She thought about the tints she'd use to mix the exact shade. Not that she would ask him to model. His ego was big enough. But she would paint those eyes from memory.

He lifted her painting slightly to keep the frame out of her reach. "This is the last one."

"Good." The dark clouds came closer. The scent in the air changed. She knew what that meant. "Get inside now. The rain's going to hit."

"How can you tell?"

"The smell." She reached forward. "Give me the painting."

"I've got it. You can barely walk in those slippers." He carried her painting down the ramp.

"There isn't much time."

He walked past her. His long strides and her bum foot made keeping up with him impossible. He slanted the canvas so any falling rain would hit the back, not the painted side. Nice of him, but she wanted her piece indoors before drops fell.

Wyatt came out of the inn. "Any more?"

Justin handed over the artwork. "Last one."

The spool of yarn in her stomach unraveled. She exhaled. Her muscles relaxed. Bailey's painting and the oth-

ers were safe. If only saving the inn would be as easy...
"Thank you."

Justin stood near the porch. She was just reaching the walkway. "Told you I'd beat the rain."

Dumb luck, but she wasn't about to complain.

A step sent pain shooting up her foot. She squeezed her eyes shut to keep from crying out. Darn toe. She needed ice, ibuprofen and a barista-poured fancy cup of coffee with a pretty design made in the foam. Who was she kidding? She'd settle for black sludge at this point. She needed to get the artwork back to the rightful owners first.

"Hey there," he said. "You okay, Anubis?"

Her eyes popped open. "Anubis? The Egyptian god?"

"Protector of Egyptian tombs from raiders and destroyers. Fits, don't you think?"

The edges of her mouth twitched upward. She managed a nod, just barely. That Anubis was half jackal didn't seem to matter to him. A drop of water hit her cheek, followed by another.

Bailey took a step. Pain, jagged and raw, ripped up her left foot. She hopped toward the inn like a human pogo stick. Big, fat raindrops fell faster and faster.

She stumbled.

Strong arms swept her off the ground. "Hold on."

She stared into Justin's concerned eyes. Her heart thudded. He carried her to the inn and looked down at her as though he cared.

Maybe there was more to Justin McMillian than she realized.

She should tell him to put her down. But a part of her didn't want to say a word.

Rain pelted her face, but she wasn't cold. Not with his body heat warming her. The pain faded. Her insides buzzed. Something she hadn't felt in...forever. She closed her eyes, trying to remember the last time she'd been in a man's arms like this.

Too long ago.

"What did you do to your foot?" he asked.

Her eyes opened. This wasn't any man carrying her onto the porch and into the foyer, but the guy who wanted to destroy the inn. "I'm not sure if it's my foot or toe or a combo."

"Did you hurt yourself here?"

"At home." Water dripped from her hair. Two minutes ago, she didn't think she could have looked any worse, but now she was a wet Medusa. "Worried I might sue you if I'd injured myself here?"

"Nope. I was wondering if you normally strut around town in fuzzy slippers."

"They were the only shoes my foot would fit. And just so you know, I don't strut. Sauntering or sashaying is more my style."

"You seem like the strutting type."

"If anyone struts, you do."

"That's right." He carried her into the dining room, right off the entryway and lobby. "I wasn't dissing you. Can you stand?"

"I've been standing all morning."

"Which is why your foot is hurting. You should have stayed home and done first aid."

He sounded like one of her five overprotective brothers, telling her what to do and who not to date. Didn't matter that two were younger than her. "I jammed my toe. A sprain. That's all."

"Looks like you may have broken something." Justin placed her feet on the floor, causing her to suck in a breath. "Hold on to me until you're steady."

She dug her fingers into his jacket. The padding couldn't hide his muscular arms. His chest was solid, too. Fully dressed, he was hot. Naked, he would be a specimen worthy of a master sculptor, Michelangelo or da Vinci.

She imagined running her hands over the model to get the right curves and indentations in the clay. Her pulse skittered, and her temperature rose. His body shouldn't impress her, not after she'd sketched and painted male models who were as good-looking, if not more classically handsome.

Uh-oh. Time to go on a date if she was getting worked up over a guy like Justin. His company's name shared his last name. That meant he likely had money—Oliver Richardson all over again. Wealthy men wanted more money or connections, such as with her brother, and would use women to get them. No, thank you.

So what if he knew a little Egyptian mythology and carried her out of the rain without getting winded? She saved historic sites. He toppled beautiful old buildings. Someone like him would never be right for her.

She let go of his arm. Looked around. Fell over.

He grabbed her. "What?"

"Gone. Everything's gone."

A dozen dining tables gone. Over fifty chairs gone. Antique buffets, rugs, draperies gone.

"It's all in the truck," Justin said.

His words brought zero relief. Seeing the empty room hurt worse than her toe. Only the scent of lemon oil and memories remained.

Oh, Floyd. Why? Why would you sell the inn?

"For over a hundred and forty years, guests have eaten meals here." She stared at the empty room where she'd dreamed of having her wedding reception someday. "That will never happen again."

"Guests will be back when the new Broughton Inn opens. We'll have a café, a bar and a restaurant with a view of the bay."

Her lungs tightened. She took a breath, then another. "It won't be the same."

Bailey rubbed her tired eyes, trying to keep their stinging from turning into full-blown tears.

"Sit," Justin ordered.

Getting off her feet sounded wonderful, but she had a job to do. "I need to inventory the artwork."

"You look like you're about to pass out." He pointed to the floor. "Sit. Five minutes won't kill you."

She hesitated. A Cole never shirked responsibility. Even AJ, who had left town eleven years ago and moved to Seattle, had done what he could to help their family when the economy soured and they were on the verge of losing their boats.

But Justin was right. Five minutes wouldn't change anything. Bailey slid to the floor, careful of her foot, and stretched her leg out in front of her. She leaned back against the wall.

Oh, wow. This felt better. "A couple of minutes."

The construction crew seemed to have disappeared. Maybe they were off in another part of the inn. Maybe they'd left. She didn't care. Fewer people around meant fewer chances of bumping and damaging the art.

Justin sat next to her. He stretched out his long legs. She waited for his thigh or shoulder to touch hers, but that didn't happen. Thank goodness he understood the meaning of personal space. She was too tired to deal with anything more this morning.

"How long until the artists pick up their stuff?" he asked.

He was calling her life's work "stuff." How quickly her fantasies about an intelligent man who worked Anubis into a discussion were dashed. But then again, he wanted to tear down the inn.

"While you were taking your time unloading the truck,

I called and left messages. The artists have jobs and families. They'll be here as soon as they can."

He glanced at his cell phone, but she couldn't tell if he was checking the time or a text. "Can you be more specific as to when?"

"Got big plans, like working on the approval process?"

"Something along those lines."

"I'm here. You don't have to hang around."

"I do. I own the inn." Justin motioned to her foot. "Besides, you're hurt. You can't do this on your own. You need help."

"Resting is helping." Not really, but she wouldn't admit how much her foot ached. "I'll stay off my feet. There's no reason for you to stick around."

"I need to lock up when you're finished."

"I've got a key."

"Floyd gave you a key to the inn?"

Justin's incredulous tone matched the look in his eyes. He and Oliver could be twins separated at birth.

"No, his late father, Clyde, did." She shouldn't feel the need to explain, but she did. "I started working here when I was sixteen."

"Front desk?"

"Kitchen." She glanced to the doorway on the right where she'd spent so many years. The imagined smell of grease was as strong as if the fryers were going. "I was a cook until a few years ago. Then I partnered with Floyd to open the gallery. We hold art events here. Held them, I mean."

The gallery no longer existed. The inn, either.

The truth hit her like a sneaker wave, knocking her over on the beach and dragging her out to sea. The coast guard couldn't rush in and save the day. No one could. The inn as she knew it was gone.

The news devastated her. This was the place where

she'd figured out how to bring artist and art lovers together. Where she'd worked in the kitchen and grown up amid a staff that treated her as an equal, not a kid. Where she planned on getting married... She struggled to breathe.

Returning the art was only the first thing she had to do today. She needed to find another venue.

"What kind of events?" Justin asked.

She flexed her fingers. "Shows, exhibits, classes. I'm supposed to hold a Canvas and Chardonnay class here tomorrow."

"Canvas and Chardonnay?"

"That's what I call my paint night. The class appeals mostly to women, though a few men join in. People socialize, drink wine, eat appetizers, and I show them how to paint."

"In one night?"

"Everyone paints the same subject. We go step by step. It's fun and easy. And the inn was the perfect location for the gathering." She leaned her head against the wall. "The results are amazing. Each person leaves with a smile and takes home a finished canvas."

Bailey didn't know why she was going on about her painting classes. He didn't care what she did. She would sit for sixty more seconds, then get things done, not chitchat with her nemesis.

He glanced at his cell phone again.

"You need to go," she said. "Work. I'm fine here by myself."

"It's Wyatt, seeing where things stand." Justin typed on his phone. "I'm staying."

His words meant only one thing. She reached into her pocket and pulled out her key ring. The ache in her heavy heart hurt worse than her toe. "Then I don't need my key."

A part of her wanted to hear the words *keep it*. Wishful thinking. He said nothing.

Bailey's fingers fumbled. She worked to remove the key that she'd carried with her eleven, almost twelve, years. She managed to unhook the key. "Here you go."

Her fingers brushed the skin of his palm. An electric shock made her drop the key onto his hand. She pulled her arm away. Must be static electricity in the air.

"Thanks." He stuck the key in his pocket. "Thought you'd put up more of a fight."

"You own the inn."

"I do, but you act like I've done something wrong."

"Architectural and historical preservation is vital, but you've ignored basic—"

"This architecture isn't anything special." He made a sweeping gesture with his hand. "The renovations over the years have nothing to do with the original design. It's a hodgepodge of trends over the past century."

"Hodgepodge? Thought was put into every change." Red-hot heat flowed through her. She should have known he'd never understand. "Did you know the materials used in the renovations have been salvaged from all over the Northwest, the United States and Europe? Each piece has a history aside from the inn. Stained glass and lead glass windows from old churches. Beams and flooring from nineteenth-century buildings."

"Don't romanticize being cheap." His tone made tearing down a historic landmark sound like a public service. "The inn has lost its appeal over the years. What character remains isn't enough to make up for everything else that is lacking. Don't get me started on structural concerns or electrical issues. The wiring is a mess, as is the plumbing."

She scooted away from him to put distance between them. He might be a pro at justifying his plan, but that didn't make him right. "If you feel that way, why did you buy the inn?"

"To turn the place around. Make a profit."

"By flattening the building with a wrecking ball?"

A muscle twitched at his neck. "Given the low sale price, if we hadn't purchased the inn, someone else would have."

Maybe, but something felt off here. She didn't know if it was Floyd or Justin. "Someone else might not have torn down the inn."

"I'm not the bad guy here." His voice sounded sincere, but he would never convince her that he and his company had the inn's best interest at heart. "I'm just doing my job."

"That makes two of us." Or she wouldn't be sitting here hurting and looking so frightful. "As head of Haley's Bay Historical Committee, I'll do everything I can to make sure this inn remains in all its hodgepodge, character-lacking glory."

Three hours later, Justin walked another lap around the inn's dining room, ignoring the urge to check the time on his cell phone again.

Bailey leaned against the wall on the other side of the room, talking with a gray-haired artist who introduced herself as Faye. The two women had been chatting for over twenty minutes. Not that he had anything better to do than wait for them to finish.

The older woman had been the last to show up, and he was stuck until she left. He'd never spent this much time anywhere unless he was working or sleeping. Sure, he'd sent texts, made calls and done what research he could on his smartphone, but he needed Wi-Fi and his laptop. The two things Justin had achieved this morning were memorizing every inch of this room and every inch of Bailey Cole.

She laughed. The sound carried on the air and drew his gaze to her once again. Her coveralls were finally dry, no longer clinging to her body. Okay, her chest.

Yeah, he'd looked. What man wouldn't? More than once, her shift in position gave him a better view and rendered him mute. Not his fault. He was a guy, one who'd been too busy working to date regularly.

Her feminine curves sent his body into overdrive. Looking made him think of holding her. Carrying her the short distance through the rain had felt so right. Too bad he wouldn't be touching her again.

Bailey's sharp glances and pursed lips suggested she wouldn't mind punching him once or twice. The thought of her getting so worked up, the gold flecks in her eyes flashing like flames, amused him.

She was driven, cared about things other than herself. The opposite of his ex-wife, Taryn. Passionate beat dismissive any day. Not that he was interested in a relationship. Marriage wasn't for him. Too much work and compromising.

Plastic crinkled. The other woman covered her sculpture.

"Thanks for coming on such short notice." Bailey bent her knee so her foot didn't touch the floor. "I'll let you know about tomorrow night's painting class."

Faye picked up the sculpture. "You'll find a place."

"Would you like help carrying that to your car?" Justin asked.

"Heavens, no. But thank you." Faye smiled at him. "This is light compared to the driftwood I drag across the beach. Bye." She walked out of the dining room.

Bailey slumped against the wall, her eyelids half-closed. Slowly, as if exerting effort hurt, she pulled out her cell phone. Her shoulders sagged, the worry over the inn seeming too much for her now. "Darn. The battery died."

"You can use my phone."

"Thanks. I want to text my family. I'm going to need help getting out of here."

Justin nearly flinched. Why was she calling someone else when he was right here? He'd carried the painting. Hell, he'd carried her. He had this. "I'll help you."

"Thanks, but…" She rubbed the back of her neck.

"What?"

"It's not getting the paintings or me to the car." She looked down at the floor. Her energy had drained like her cell phone. "My foot. I don't think I can drive myself home."

He'd only spent the morning with her, but she had a backbone and strength. She had to be hurting badly to admit she couldn't drive.

Bailey sat without being told. That worried him. She leaned her head against the wall. That concerned him more.

He walked toward her. Her face looked pale compared to earlier, her eyes sunken. "This isn't only about your foot. You don't feel well."

"My fault."

Her reply surprised him as much as her admitting she couldn't drive herself.

"I haven't eaten," she added.

"Since breakfast?"

"Um…since lunch yesterday."

"You haven't eaten in over twenty-four hours. Why not?"

"When I get into a painting I lose track of time. That's what happened yesterday. I don't think I went to bed until two. And then my grandma called me early this morning."

"I've done that myself when I'm working on a new design. I'll drive you home in your car. One of the crew can pick me up."

"No, you don't have to."

Take the out. Walk away. That was the smart thing to do. Except she looked as if she might pass out. "I'm taking you home now. You need to eat. Sleep."

"And shower."

Justin imagined how she would look naked with water dripping from her hair and down her skin. He tugged at his collar. Getting a little warm in here. Time to turn off the video in his mind. A full view of her strange outfit would do the trick. His gaze ran the length of her. "So this isn't your normal style?"

Bailey framed her face with her hands. "What? You don't like the psychotic nutcase look?"

"I've never been a big fan of nutcases or clowns."

"Me, either. I'm glad there aren't any fun-house mirrors around. I'd scare myself."

"You don't scare me." He hadn't meant to flirt with her. Maybe she didn't notice. "I'll help you to your car, then come back for your artwork."

Her wary look changed to resignation. "I can carry a painting."

"It would be easier if I carry you."

Bailey might be on the fashion police's Most Wanted List, but if he got to carry her out of the inn, this day would rank up there with a Seattle Seahawks' Super Bowl win.

"What do you say?" he asked.

Chapter Three

*S*o much for carrying Bailey.

Outside the inn, Justin adjusted his grip on her framed painting. Plastic wrap crinkled beneath his fingertips. He could tell this piece meant more to her than the others, so he would be extra careful. But the woman herself…

He should have known better than to get worked up over *her*.

Passionate, yes, but stubborn to the nth degree.

He'd offered to carry Bailey to the car, then go back for the artwork. She hadn't wanted to do that. He'd then suggested getting her car and picking her up in front of the inn. She'd said no again. Mules had more sense than Bailey Cole.

She moved at a snail-pace wobble, her steps unsteady on the wet sidewalk. Any second, she might go down and hit the concrete. She would probably want him to let her fall than risk damaging her art.

She might be one of the most annoying women he'd ever met, but she worried him. "You okay?"

Bailey shot Justin a glare, one he'd become familiar over the past few hours. Her lips should thin in three... two...one...

And they disappeared. A line of chalk was thicker than her mouth. As easy to read as the Sunday comics. Too bad her lone-wolf act didn't make her curves less appealing.

"I told you." Her know-it-all voice grated on his back teeth. "I'm fine."

Sure she was. And he had complete control of the Broughton Inn project. What a pair they were. Well, a pair for however long this situation took to get resolved.

He supported the canvas between his far arm and body, in case she needed help. "You're back to looking like you're going to fall over."

"You have bigger things to worry about than me."

True, but he needed to get rid of her before he could deal with the rest of the mess. "Until I get you home, you're my biggest concern."

"It won't be for much longer. Five-minute drive, max. I'll be home long before I come close to losing it."

Whoa. His gaze ran the length of her. Maybe he hadn't figured her out. "Did you just admit you're on the verge of a meltdown?"

She didn't shrug or shake her head. "Maybe."

That was more than he thought she'd admit. Bailey Cole had ruined his day, but given her injury, she was a trooper—make that a general—who had defeated him. He couldn't wait for a rematch and to come out on top. Still Justin had a strange desire to comfort her, a feeling not only due to her killer curves.

She shortened her stride again. "If you don't mind adding a couple of minutes onto the drive to my house, I'd be grateful if you swung by the Burger Boat."

"They sell burgers on a boat?" he asked.

"Nope. Local fast food place. On land, not water. They have a drive-through, so we won't have to get out of the car. Not that I could." She glanced at her foot with a want-to-start-the-day-over look. "But it's past lunchtime. I'm starving and my cupboards are bare."

Her words reminded him of the "Old Mother Hubbard" nursery rhyme. Not that they had a dog to feed. Thank goodness the mutt was gone.

Thinking about a rhyme should seem odd, but wasn't given the way she was dressed and how strange today had been. "No eating. No food at home. You don't take very good care of yourself, Miss Cole."

"I take good care of myself." Her tone was an interesting mix—defensive and honest. She inched toward the curb. Exhaustion creased her face. "Except when I'm wrapped up in a project. Then my plans, like grocery shopping, get pushed aside. Most days bring a surprise or two."

Surprises, indeed. She'd surprised him.

"You might find a healthy meal and sleep a boon to your creativity."

"I'll remember that the next time."

"No, you won't," he said.

"I was trying to be polite."

"You sound annoyed."

"I'm that, too."

"Because you're hungry." He didn't wait for a reply. "A burger sounds good. I need to pick up lunch because Wyatt gave the dog my turkey sandwich."

Bailey stopped. "Where is the dog?"

"No idea. Dined and dashed. Probably headed home."

A look of concern returned to her face. "He could be a stray."

Nope. Justin wasn't going there. She might want to drive around and try to find the damn thing. Then they'd have to call Animal Control and wait. Again. He'd wasted his morning. He wasn't about to lose the entire day.

Time to change the subject. "Which car is yours?"

She pointed toward a four-door hatchback with a bright yellow exterior and black upholstered seats parked on the street.

"Looks like a bee." Tiny cars were annoying to drive, but this one was the color of a hot rod. He might not mind the leg cramps headed his way.

Bailey nodded, then stumbled.

He grabbed her with his free hand. "I've got you."

"Thanks."

He should be thanking her. Warmth and softness pressed against Justin, making him think of lazy autumn weekend mornings spent in bed, the brush of flannel sheets against skin, the feel of someone else's heartbeat and the sound of another breath.

Yes. He needed to get out more. Nothing serious, just for fun.

He helped her into the car, closed the door, then walked around to the hatchback and loaded the painting. "Tell me about this burger place. Good food?"

She turned and leaned between the front seats. "Best fries in town, thanks to a special seasoning mix. A little spicy, but not too much."

"I don't mind a little heat."

His words came out more suggestive then he'd intended. But what could he say? That image of a bed and tangled flannel sheets was burned on his mind.

She faced forward. "There are bungee cords, if you want to secure the painting."

Justin battened down the frame, then slid into the driver's seat. His right knee crashed into the steering wheel. "Knowing that was coming didn't help."

He expected her to laugh at him, tease him at the least, but no mocking laughter appeared in her eyes.

"That had to hurt." Her nose crinkled, her forehead, too. "You okay?"

"That's supposed to be my line." He didn't like being on the receiving end of her seeming to care. She was the enemy and would lose this fight to save the inn. "I'm fine."

"That's my line."

"Now we're even." He adjusted the seat so his legs half fit, then saw the stick shift. "You managed to drive a clutch with your injured foot."

"You're changing the subject."

"Damn straight I am." The woman was unbelievable. But he knew that. "Did you even consider staying home or at least off the roads?"

"I had no choice. If I hadn't come, there wouldn't be an inn."

So much for a truce. "If you'd been bleeding with your foot torn to shreds—"

"That's what rolls of gauze and bandages are for."

"You're either dedicated or insane."

"A little of both."

Her admission surprised him. "Seriously?"

"No one completely sane chooses to be a full-time artist. The market's as fickle as the economy, creativity comes and goes and making a living is hard. But I give lessons, put on events and sell an occasional piece. Somehow things work out."

Her car sat lower to the road than any car he remembered driving. Not a bumblebee. More like a battery-powered toy. He fastened his seat belt. "You must be doing okay, given this car."

"I'm not a starving artist, even if I look like one. I travel back and forth to a gallery in Seattle. I need a reliable vehicle. This one fits the bill."

From crazy to practical in less than thirty seconds. She must drive her boyfriend to the brink of insanity.

But what a way to go, a voice in his head whispered.

Justin ignored it. He drove up the block to the inn and parked at the curb. "I'm going to bring out the rest of your artwork. Won't take me long."

Five minutes later, he was back behind the wheel. "Which way?"

"Follow Bay Street until you reach Third Avenue. You can only turn right. You'll see the Burger Boat on the left."

He glanced at the digital clock on the dashboard. "Think you'll be able to hold yourself together that long?"

"Guess we'll find out."

He couldn't tell from her tone if she was joking or warning him.

Justin drove past the marina. Many of the slips were empty. The fishermen and charter-boat captains who made a living on the sea must be hard at work. People like Bailey's family.

Across the street sat stores and cafés, one after another. The buildings looked newer, not just with a new coat of paint, but updated facades to add to the quaint, coastal feel of the town. One restaurant had a crow's nest, but no drive-through window.

People, dressed in shorts or sundresses, filled the boardwalk running the length of the Bay Street shops. The little town of Haley's Bay was a big draw with Cape Disappointment and Long Beach nearby.

A boat-shaped building with a giant plastic hamburger for the ship's wheel caught his attention. Must be the Burger Boat. The blue-and-white paint job looked new, as did the windows. But the architecture screamed early 1970s tacky and retro-cool.

"Follow the anchors painted on the pavement to get to the drive-through window."

He did and stopped behind a silver minivan. There was no intercom system with a digital screen to display an order, only a window. "What do you recommend besides the fries?"

"The pirate booty burger is good if you have a big appetite. The hazelnut chocolate shakes are amazing."

"You know the menu well." He expected a shrug, but didn't get one.

"I eat here once a week. Have since I was a kid. They add seasonal shake flavors like pumpkin in the fall, and occasionally change up the Catch of the Day burger, but pretty much the menu has stayed the same for as long as I remember, a lot like Haley's Bay until they put in new shops on Bay Street."

"You don't like the changes."

This time she shrugged. "They are tourist spots, necessary for a service-oriented town, but not practical shops for those who call this place home. I miss the old places like the hardware store and pharmacy."

"The familiarity?"

"Consistency."

"To balance the not-always-stable life of an artist?"

"I guess. Maybe I'm just stuck in my ways."

The minivan pulled away from the window. Justin released the brake and drove forward.

"I'll have a dinghy burger, fries and root beer." She dug through her yellow shopping bag and pulled out a twenty-dollar bill. "Lunch is on me. I appreciate the ride home and not having to wait for my family."

Justin had two choices. Accept her offer or say no, thanks. He weighed both options. One would piss her off. Both might. But she was tired, and they were hungry. No sense aggravating the situation more. And she had ruined his day. A free lunch wouldn't make up for the mess she caused.

He took the money.

Loose strands of hair curled around her face and caught the light. The color looked coppery like a shiny new penny. His stomach tightened. That had nothing to do with being hungry.

She wasn't sweet or nice. She was a pain in the ass.

Still, he couldn't take his eyes off her.

The fast-food place's drive-through window slid open.

"Ahoy, matey. Welcome to the Burger Boat." A man in his early twenties with a chipped front tooth and a sailor cap grinned. "What can we reel in for you today?"

Justin gave their order and paid with Bailey's twenty.

A foghorn blared inside the restaurant, the nautical sound effects matching the place's boat theme.

"Here's your change. I'll bag up your catch." The window slid closed.

"Did you ever work here?" Justin asked her, trying to fill the silence in her car.

"No, I thought being under a chef would teach me more than how to grill burgers and blend milk shakes."

"Smart thinking for a teenager."

"I like learning as much as I can about what I do."

She had more going on in her head than what subject to paint next. She hadn't known what she'd faced this morning, but she'd arrived prepared with files and paperwork.

Unlike him.

The window opened again. The man passed over the drinks. "Here's your order."

Justin put the drinks in the cup holders between their seats, then handed her the bag of food. She gave him directions to her house. He pulled forward and turned out of the parking lot.

The scent of burger and fries made his stomach grumble. "Smells good."

"Tastes better." Bailey opened the bag, removed a couple of fries and lifted them to his mouth. "Here."

"Thanks—"

He hit the brake to let pedestrians cross the street.

Her fingers bumped into his chin, then slipped away, leaving a trail of heat.

A blush rose up her neck. Sexy.

Easy, guy. Justin needed to add "fingers" to the list of her lethal body parts, along with her breasts and her brain.

"Sorry," she said.

He reminded himself to swallow. The spice hit the back of his throat. "Eat. We're down to the final thirty seconds until you lose it."

Bailey ate French fries, then a bite of her burger. "I feel better already."

On her street, a man dressed in cargo shorts and a stained T-shirt stood next to Officer Grady Cole in front of a blue-painted cottage. Colorful flowers filled every space that wasn't covered by grass, including the basket of a rusted bicycle leaning against the outside of a white picket fence.

The house looked surprisingly normal, though Justin hadn't known what to expect. A run-down shack? A padded room? "That looks like your brother."

"Two brothers. Grady and Ellis." Bailey leaned forward. "Both should be at work."

What now? Justin gripped the steering wheel. "How many brothers do you have?"

"Five, and one sister."

"Where should I park?"

"The driveway is right past the police car." She dragged her upper teeth across her lower lip. "I hope nothing's wrong."

He reached out, touched her forearm. A gesture of comfort, except he wasn't 100 percent certain that was all. "Hey.

I'm sure everything's okay. Grady knew you injured your foot. They're probably checking up on you."

She nodded, but doubt remained in her gaze.

Justin switched on the blinker, turned into the driveway. Her brothers glared like wolves protecting their pack. His fight instinct kicked into high gear. He parked the car. Two against one. He'd faced worse odds and come out ahead.

"My brothers don't look happy," she said in an under-stated voice.

Justin recognized their don't-mess-with-my-sister expression. He pulled the key out of the ignition. "Let's find out why."

Seated in her car, Bailey sipped her root beer. She needed one more fortifying drink of sugar to face her brothers. Ellis and Grady's body language suggested they wanted to take someone out. They'd looked the same way when they found out she'd lied about going to a sleepover and snuck down to Seaside during spring break to hang out with college boys from the University of Washington.

No worries. She needed to stay calm and settle her brothers down. Fast. Or someone—namely, Justin—was going to get hurt.

Ellis, the second-oldest and married with kids, opened her car door. "Where have you been? We've been calling."

"The inn." She unbuckled her seat belt. "Grady knew where I was. Grandma, too."

"Grady told me you were at the inn, but you didn't answer my texts. When I called, all I got was your voice mail." Ellis sounded like their dad, only more caring.

"Long morning. My cell phone died." Bailey moved her legs out of the car. Her fingers dug into the seat fabric. She sucked in a breath. Oh, boy, that didn't feel good.

"You're hurt. And you look a mess." Ellis touched her shoulder. He turned to Grady. "You're right about her foot."

Grady nodded. "Told you."

"Excuse me." Justin pushed forward, moving her brothers out of the way, and picked her up. "Bailey's injured. Whatever you're here for can wait until I get her inside."

"Who are you?" Ellis asked.

"A Good Samaritan helping your sister," Justin said. "Out of my way."

Ellis grabbed the shopping bag from her hands. "Do you need anything out of the car?"

She nodded. "The artwork and our lunch."

"On it," Grady said.

Uh-oh. Her brothers were being too nice and not giving Justin a hard time. Something was up.

Justin carried her toward the front door. His strong arms cradled her. Her pulse quickened.

She didn't like what Justin McMillian intended to do to the inn, but her heart melted a little. No guy had ever stood up to her brothers. Not that Justin had caused a confrontation. But he'd shown concern for her without worrying about the repercussions. That was new. And seeing Ellis and Grady get out of the way was funny. They were as stubborn as she was.

What Justin did for a living stole a building's soul. But she was glad he was here. Pain and hunger must be softening her standards. "I appreciate the help."

"I figured you needed to get inside. Not answer a lot of questions."

Justin handed her the keys.

She pretended to unlock the door, not wanting another lecture from any man, brother or stranger, about forgetting to lock the front door, then opened it.

He carried her inside. "Is the couch okay?"

"Perfect."

He set her down. Being horizontal felt good. If only her foot would stop hurting.

"Put your leg up on the back of the couch." He eyed one of her paintings on the wall. "Nice artwork. You're talented."

Tingles filled her stomach like a flock of swallows. She wished his words didn't mean as much as they did. "I love what I do."

"You work here."

She glanced at the paint-covered drop cloth and easel with an unfinished painting. All she'd wanted to do today was complete the piece, wash clothes and grocery shop. So much for plans. "Yes."

Ellis set her yellow bag and lunch on the coffee table. He helped himself to some fries. "I'm Ellis Cole."

"Justin McMillian."

Ellis kneeled next to her. "How ya doing, sis?"

"My foot is killing me, but the inn is in one piece." She smiled, proud she'd saved the structure from demolition, then grabbed more fries. "A good day."

"Depends on your perspective," Justin said.

Grady set a painting against the wall. "I texted Mom. She's picking up Grandma. They'll be right over to take you to the hospital."

"Urgent Care will be fine." Bailey eyed her brothers. "Why aren't you guys at work?"

"Tyler called. He wanted me to find you," Grady said in his no-nonsense police voice. A world away from the wild kid he'd once been.

"Tyler is my cousin," she told Justin. "He's the only lawyer in Haley's Bay." She looked at her two brothers. "If this is about me introducing him to one of the girls in my painting class—"

"It's not." Grady's gaze ping-ponged from her to Justin. "I'm here on official business with news about the inn."

Justin rocked back on his heels. His face tightened. "What news?"

"I'm sorry, Mr. McMillian, but your company is the victim of a fraudulent real estate transaction," Grady said.

"Fraudulent?" Justin asked.

Ellis nodded. "You got conned."

Bailey sat up. "What are you talking about?"

"Floyd Jeffries sold the inn to two buyers on the same day," Grady said. "One buyer was McMillian Resorts. The other was represented by Tyler."

Justin swore. "You're joking, right?"

"I wish I was," Grady said.

Justin's face contorted, turned red. He started to speak, then stopped himself.

She didn't know what to say to him. But the news made her dizzy. She leaned back against the sofa pillow. "That's not the kind of person Floyd is. The man drives ten miles an hour below the speed limit. He's no criminal."

"Was," Ellis said. "He changed after he met that girl on the internet. I heard he canceled all the upcoming events at the inn."

Bailey's body stiffened. "He didn't cancel my paint night tomorrow."

"You ran the art events, not Floyd," Ellis said.

"I don't know him as well as your sister does, but there must be a mistake." Justin paced the length of the couch. The lines on his forehead deepened, more like canyons than wrinkles. "We have a top-notch team of lawyers. We might have misunderstood the permit process, but they're professionals. They'd never fall for a scam deal."

"Well, I heard Floyd gave the employees three days off with pay. Never told them the inn had been sold or they'd lost their jobs." Ellis sat on the sofa arm. "That's why no one was there last night or today."

Oh, no. The staff. Bailey had been so worried about the inn itself she hadn't thought about the employees. Floyd had worked with some of those people since he'd been a kid.

None of this made sense. "That doesn't sound like Floyd. He cares about those who work for him. He bought my senior prom dress when Dad wouldn't pay for one without sleeves."

"I know the guy was good to you." Ellis's voice softened, his tone compassionate. "Floyd bought fish from us for all these years, was often our biggest customer, but he's not the same person. He's changed."

Justin shook his head. "Floyd might not have disclosed everything about the inn, but my sister negotiated a legal deal. She would never have paid cash otherwise."

"Tyler's client was a cash buyer, too. Part of Floyd's requirements," Grady said.

Ellis whistled. "That's a lot of money."

"No." Bailey didn't care what Grady said happened. "Floyd wouldn't do that to me—to this town—and all the people who trusted him."

"You're right." Ellis rolled his eyes. "Floyd headed to Belize with his twenty-five-year-old internet girlfriend and a suitcase of cash because of the good weather down there."

"Floyd is fifty-five and he's never married. He's been lonely." Bailey knew him better than her brothers did. "He's been wanting to settle down for years."

"With a woman less than half his age? The man has more money than common sense," Ellis countered. "But now he's added another zero or two to his net worth and he's laughing all the way to some tropical island paradise with no extradition treaty."

"Innocent until proven guilty," Grady cautioned.

"Guilty, bro. You know it." Ellis sounded convinced. "Tyler will prove Floyd is nothing more than a two-bit criminal. His parents and grandparents must be rolling in their graves."

Justin stopped pacing, pulled out his cell phone and

looked at Grady. "I have to speak to our attorneys. Is there anything you need from me right now?"

"No," Grady said. "But don't dispose of anything you took from the inn. I'll need you to return everything."

Justin's face paled. "The truck's here in town. I'll have my crew unload the contents."

The on-edge tone tugged at Bailey's heart. The day had gone from bad to worse for him. Justin might want something completely different for the inn than her, but that didn't matter right now. The guy looked as if he'd been knocked over with his own wrecking ball. She wanted to reach out to him, but she didn't dare in front of her brothers.

"Thanks for driving me home," she said instead. "I'm sure Ellis or Grady can give you a ride back to the inn if you don't want to walk."

"I will," Grady offered.

"Thanks," Justin said, sounding anything but grateful.

Grady waved. "See you later."

"Wait." Bailey looked over the back of the sofa. "You never said who else bought the inn."

Ellis and Grady exchanged a knowing glance. Both shifted their weight.

Uh-oh. "What?"

"We were hoping you wouldn't ask," Ellis said. "But since you did, AJ said it was okay to tell you."

"What does AJ have to do with this?" she asked.

The lines on Justin's forehead deepened. "AJ?"

"He's our oldest brother," she said.

"AJ Cole?" His voice matched the dumbstruck look on his face. "Your brother is the internet guy?"

Ellis nodded. "He's the buyer Tyler represented in the second deal."

She straightened, ignoring her foot. "Why would AJ want to buy the Broughton Inn? He's never talked about owning a hotel."

"AJ didn't buy the inn for himself." Grady looked as if he was about to jump out of a cake and yell surprise. "He bought the inn for you. Happy early birthday, sis!"

Huh? She blinked, Grady's words echoing in her head as if she were standing on the edge of a canyon. *Bought. Inn. For. You.* She tried to make sense of the words, but failed as if this were a precalculus test and not a simple conversation she was trying to understand.

"Say what?" she asked.

Ellis beamed. She hadn't seen him smile so brightly since his son Maddox hit a home run at a T-ball game last week. "The inn is yours."

"Not so fast." Justin raised his hands. "McMillian Resorts purchased the inn."

"There are two owners for now," Grady said. "The lawyers and the court will have to decide the true owner."

Her gaze met Justin's and held it for a long moment.

He looked away.

Bailey rested her head back against the sofa. She wanted to be independent, make her own way, not rely on her billionaire brother, but he'd come through in a way she never could have expected. The last thing she wanted was anything to take her away from her art, but at least now she could save the inn and jobs of everyone who worked there. *Way to go, AJ.*

"What do you have to say?" Ellis asked.

Ideas swirled through her brain, but first things first. She looked at Justin. "I want my key back."

Chapter Four

Two days later, Justin stood outside Tyler Cole's law office on Bay Street. A breeze rustled the leaves in a nearby tree. The cool morning air made him want to walk back to the B and B where he was staying and crawl in bed. He yawned, stretching his arms overhead.

A horn honked. Kids in a passing car waved at him. He gave a mock salute. That was all he could manage at the moment.

Worry over gaining possession of the inn was messing with his sleep. Random thoughts about Bailey Cole in her rain-soaked coveralls weren't helping. This quaint little town and its residents could be his ruin.

Cell phone against his ear, he popped another breath mint into his mouth. Should have picked up antacid tablets instead. But he doubted anything in a bottle would lessen the unease in his gut.

The unanswered ringing plucked his patience. "Pick up, Paige."

The line clicked.

"About time," he said.

"Ready for the big meeting?" His sister sounded way too cheerful under the circumstances.

"I was about to ask you that question. You're supposed to be here." Justin had better lower his voice. Kent Warren, one of McMillian Resorts' buttoned-down, Brooks Brothers–wearing lawyers who worked with Paige, was nearby. If Kent went running to Justin's parents, this whole thing would turn into a bigger mess. "Where the hell are you?"

"The office."

He pictured Paige sitting behind the impressive mahogany desk, her brown hair pulled up in a French twist, manicured nails tapping impatiently and her face puckered with an annoyed look. A hundred bucks said his annoyance level was higher.

"The meeting starts in five minutes." He didn't hide his anger. "Unless you've discovered a way to magically transport yourself, you're going to be late."

"I'm too busy. Mom and Dad have no idea what's going on. I have to keep them in the dark. That means staying in Lincoln City."

Paige acted as if she ran the company already. Not far from the truth. He and Rainey—their twenty-five-year-old younger sister—worked off-site much of the time. That left the hamster wheel of meetings, negotiations and fires needing extinguishing to Paige, but she thrived on pressure. Looked forward to it.

"You should be here in Haley's Bay," he said.

She clicked her tongue. "You don't need me. Kent knows everything about the deal. All you need to do is represent the McMillian name and reputation while we try to fix this deal before Mom and Dad find out."

She might be twenty-nine and the opposite gender, but

her tone and word choice sounded exactly like their father. Too bad she hadn't developed the same sixth sense their dad had to know that Floyd had been scamming them.

"You tried to make me the fall guy with the Seaside remodeling fiasco. I'm not going to let you do that again." The misadventure with foundation issues had cost them big money and made their parents question their capabilities. If Justin and his sisters lost the company, he wasn't going to be the only one they blamed.

"No reason to bring up the past."

"It's the perfect reason. Both places were your deals." Justin wished he'd never supported buying the Broughton Inn, but the bay view from the inn had captured his imagination, and any issues they'd found in the inspection didn't matter in a teardown. "You should be here cleaning up the mess."

"One for all, bro. Suck it up and represent." Her attempt at joking fell flat. "Stay in Haley's Bay. Make sure we end up with the inn. Otherwise…"

"I know what's at stake." The big reason behind his sleepless nights. "If we lose the Broughton Inn, we lose McMillian Resorts. You, me and Rainey will be out."

Out of the company. Out of a job.

Out of the one thing that mattered most to him.

The business was as much a member of his family as his parents and sisters. Without the company, they would never see each other, let alone talk. Everything would be different. His family would be forever changed. And not for the better.

A lump the size of the ugly, outdated chandelier hanging in the inn's foyer formed in his throat. His entire life had revolved around McMillian Resorts. Working for their parents wasn't easy, but the siblings' dream had been to run the company themselves, to pass on their legacy to a future generation of McMillians. Not possible if their parents cashed out by selling the business and firing them.

"Don't fail," Paige said. "Rainey and I are counting on you."

"Doing my best. We're up against deep pockets."

"AJ Cole doesn't care about the inn. Focus on his sister. She's the one we need to make give in."

Bailey. He pictured her warm green eyes, the look of pure delight when she bit into a French fry.

"Use your infamous charm on her," Paige continued. "You have a way with the ladies."

Kent cleared his throat, flashed the time on his cell phone.

"Gotta go," Justin said. "The meeting's about to start."

He disconnected from the call and entered the law office, located in a small, converted house and decorated with quilted chairs and black square tables. A metal magazine rack hung on the wall. The smell of coffee filled the air.

A thirty-something brunette with an easy smile greeted them, motioning down a hallway. "They're in the conference room. First door on your left."

"Thank you." The carpet muted Justin's footsteps.

"Smile," Kent ordered in a courtroom defense attorney voice. "You look like your dog died."

"I was never allowed to have a pet because we lived in hotels."

Kent's gaze hardened, making the lawyer look like a beady-eyed shark about to bite off a limb. "Those hotels will belong to someone else unless you pull yourself together. This morning, you're the face of McMillian Resorts."

Justin stopped at the conference room doorway, glanced back at Kent. "Fine. Sucking up on demand."

Two people sat at an oval table—a man in his early thirties and a woman who looked as though she belonged in a Renaissance painting. Copper corkscrew curls. A close-mouthed smile. Gorgeous face. Striking green eyes.

Justin smiled at her. Being stuck in this meeting didn't seem like a chore now. Was she Tyler Cole's paralegal or personal assistant? Another lawyer?

Justin searched for something witty and charming to say. He took a closer look. Familiar-looking. The laughter in her eyes matched her grin and reminded him of…

"Looks like we're all here now." Her voice was instantly recognizable.

Bailey. His pulse accelerated like an electric drill switched to the fastest speed. Man, she cleaned up well.

"Hi." Eloquent, no. But the two-letter word was safer than the others coming to mind. Sweat dampened the back of his neck. His collar shrank an inch, maybe two.

The man seated next to Bailey stood, then shook Justin's hand. "I'm Tyler Cole. I represent Bailey and her brother AJ, who couldn't be here today."

"Justin McMillian." The firm grip suggested the opposing counsel worked out. "This is Kent Warren, one of our company's attorneys."

Kent shook Tyler's hand, then Bailey's. "Nice to meet you."

Justin tried to think of more than one or two words to say to Bailey. "How's your foot?"

"Not broken. I got lucky."

He wouldn't mind getting lucky with her. His gaze met Bailey's. Something churned, then settled, in the pit of his stomach. Too much breakfast or too little coffee? "Glad you didn't break any bones."

"Me, too."

Kent cleared his throat.

Damn. Justin was staring. An artist or a siren? Right now he'd go with the latter. Not good. He couldn't let himself be distracted. One of them would walk away from this situation empty-handed.

Not him.

He sat on the opposite side of the table.

She drummed her metallic-blue short fingernails on the table, drawing his attention once again. Cuts and scars marred her hands. Working hands, like his. But her life seemed to be a contradiction, given she'd received an inn for a birthday present.

"Let's get started." Tyler handed out half-inch-thick documents. "Police reports have been filed by both parties. According to an update this morning from Detective Hanson, Floyd left the United States on Tuesday evening, but he never entered Belize. His whereabouts are unknown. AJ Cole has hired a private investigator."

"So has McMillian Resorts." Kent scanned the documents.

Bailey leaned forward over the table. The gap in the neckline of her pink blouse provided a glimpse of lavender lace and creamy, soft skin.

Justin's mouth went dry. He forced himself not to leer, but took another look. Not a good, long look, more like a glimpse.

"Have you spoken to Floyd, Justin?" Concern tinged each of Bailey's words.

His gaze flew up to meet hers. He wasn't sure whether she'd busted him or not, but his cheeks warmed, something that hadn't happened in…years. "I spoke with Floyd on Tuesday afternoon. I haven't heard from him since. His phone goes straight to voice mail."

Tyler jotted a note. "Both properties closed on the same day. Different title companies were used. No financing was involved in the private contracts, Floyd waited three days, then took the money and ran."

Bailey's nose crinkled. "This is so out of character for Floyd. I don't know why he'd do this."

"We believe an individual who recently came into Mr.

Jeffries's life may provide his motivation." Kent removed a file from his briefcase. A photo of a beautiful young blonde was clipped to the front. "Our investigator turned up information on Mr. Jeffries' girlfriend, Sasha Perry. Not only does she date older, wealthier gentlemen, she has been investigated for fraud four times over the past three years. The various DAs lacked evidence for any indictments."

Tyler squinted, reached for the picture. His face paled. "That's the woman who handled AJ's closing."

"Ours, too," Kent admitted.

Tyler swore. "So we both have a title and what appear to be legal copies of the signed documents."

Kent shuffled his papers. "Yes."

Lines creased Bailey's forehead. "What does that mean?"

Justin wanted to reach across the table and squeeze her hand, an inappropriate response under the circumstances. *Focus, McMillian.*

"Good question," he said. "We both can't own the inn."

Kent removed another legal-size file full of paperwork. "You both hold titles and own the inn. For now."

"So, will the court decide ownership?" Bailey asked.

"Yes, but a ruling will take time," Tyler said. "That leaves the inn closed and staff unemployed."

Bailey's face pinched. "The employees and vendors rely on the inn."

"We have other options such as mediation, relinquishing rights or a buyout," Kent offered.

"Wouldn't a buyout mean one party ends up paying more money?" Bailey asked.

Kent shrugged, but that sharklike look returned. Justin didn't like that Bailey was the intended prey.

"Paying more isn't an issue if someone wants the inn badly enough," Kent said.

"Only forty-eight hours have passed since we discovered what Floyd did," Tyler said. "We need to understand the extent of the fraud and legal implications before any settlement options are decided upon."

Kent didn't flinch. Of course not. The guy dressed as if he stepped off the glossy pages of a magazine, with his hair supergelled into place. He was the one who'd taught Paige to be cool and calm before she went in for the kill during negotiations. Justin wondered how being scammed made Kent feel. The guy never showed weakness or emotion.

"Just putting one possibility out there," Kent said.

"I don't want to sell," Bailey said, to Justin's surprise. "I want the inn."

He leaned back in his chair. Bailey didn't need the inn. Not when space for her art events and classes could be found elsewhere. But the determined set of her jaw reminded him of when she told him she wouldn't move away from the wrecking ball. This could be a tough battle.

"So, what happens next?" Justin asked.

"You first, Kent," Tyler deferred. "You're more experienced in these matters."

Kent's expression didn't change, but he tapped the end of his pen against the table. The less their adversaries knew, the better. "We've filed a civil claim with the court, but getting restitution from Jeffries is unlikely with his whereabouts unknown. The police are investigating criminal charges. You and Miss Cole need to decide how you want to proceed."

Bailey dragged her upper teeth over her lower lip. "Can't we temporarily open the inn so people can have their jobs back?

Kent shook his head. "There would be liability issues to deal with and money needed to fund temporary operations."

"From a legal standpoint, it's not something I recommend," Tyler added.

"So we just wait? And the inn remains closed?" Bailey's

frown matched the frustration in her voice. "What about the employees?"

Kent smiled. "They are eligible for unemployment benefits."

Her lips thinned. "That's not the same as a job with pay."

Kent's smile vanished. "Miss Cole. If you are close to the inn's staff, I suggest you not raise their hopes of the inn reopening any time soon. Looking for new employment will be in their best interest."

She looked at Tyler. "Is that true?"

Her cousin gave a slight nod. "We need more information before we can proceed."

Her lips drew into a thin line. Anger flashed across her face as clear as the lights on a fire truck. The opposite of her poker face when she'd hid her pain at the inn the other day. Which was the real Bailey?

"How long are we talking?" she asked.

"It's hard to say," Tyler said.

She blew out a breath. "So this meeting was only a formality."

Another nod from Tyler.

"Is there anything I need to know or do right now?" she asked.

"No. Not today." Kent looked at Tyler. "But I'd like a few minutes of your time, counselor."

Tyler straightened his papers. "I'm free until ten."

Bailey rose. "I'll be going home, then."

All three men stood. Tyler pulled out her chair. "Do you need help out?"

She looked up at her cousin, adoration in her eyes. The Coles seemed to be a close family. "Thanks, but I'm good."

She walked out of the office with only a slight limp. A gray walking brace covered her left foot. She wore a flat sandal on her right. Her floral-print skirt flowed back and forth with the sway of her hips.

Let her go.

But Justin didn't want to. Not yet.

"I'll wait for you outside." Justin ignored the startled look on Kent's face and quickened his steps to catch Bailey. "Wait up."

She stopped in the hallway, glanced over her shoulder. "I didn't mean for everyone to leave."

"I got tired sitting at the grown-ups' table."

The concern in her eyes remained, but she smiled. Her curved lips looked soft and tasty. Yeah, he wouldn't mind a nibble. Anticipation thrummed to his core.

He motioned to her brace. "You're walking better."

"Staying off my feet. My family has been hovering, not letting me do anything."

"Annoying you?"

"You have no idea."

Being around Bailey made him want to forget everything but her. "I might. I have two sisters and we work for my parents."

"Then you do know." She blew out a puff of air. "I love my family, but I'm not used to being around people all the time. Talk about exhausting."

Justin bit back a smile.

"What?" she asked.

"You're different."

She struck a pose. "Crazy-clown-lady different."

"Not today." In the time he'd spent with Bailey Cole, two things were clear. Honesty and integrity defined the woman. He glanced around the parking lot. The sun was shining, but no sign of her yellow bumblebee car. "Did you drive?"

"My grandmother dropped me off. My family has taken to chauffeuring me around."

"You can't drive?"

"I can. They think I shouldn't."

He remembered when his younger sister, Rainey, needed surgery on her knee. Her parents had been busy with a resort's grand opening. He and Paige had rotated caring for their youngest sibling. Bailey was lucky to have a family who cared about her.

Bailey removed her cell phone from her purse, a colorful, summery bag with circular designs in pink, lime green and yellow. "Better text for a pickup."

"Have a cup of coffee with me first." The offer tumbled from his mouth, driven by intrigue and attraction. Fraternizing with an adversary was not on Paige's to-do list. Probably shouldn't be on his, but he'd asked. No reason to take back the invitation. "There's a place across the street. If you can't walk, I'll carry you."

She eyed him warily. "Thanks, but I can walk."

"Let's go, then."

She gave him a look. "I didn't say yes."

"You didn't say no."

"True, but…" She glanced back at the law office. "Given the circumstances, do you think us hanging out is a good idea?"

Her question surprised him. She didn't seem like the cautious type. "One coffee. No big deal."

She looked at the coffee shop across the street. "I guess."

"Don't worry, I'm not trying to woo the inn away from you," he teased, though the thought had crossed both his mind and Paige's.

"Good to know, but I'd never fall for that tactic."

Bailey sounded jaded. He didn't like the idea someone had hurt or taken advantage of her. Maybe he was reading too much into her tone.

"Come on," he said, wishing they could call a truce. "Let's get some coffee."

Bailey grabbed a table for two by the front window at the Java Cup while Justin waited for their drinks. The scent of roasting beans, brewing coffee and baking treats filled the air. Normally the small shop felt like an extension of home, thanks to the friendly greetings from familiar faces, but not today.

Justin leaned against the counter. His black shoes screamed *Italian leather*. He wore gray slacks and a blue button-down tucked in. His hair had been combed into place and the stubble shaved from his face. The result... dazzling—if she liked that kind of dressed-up guy, but she'd had enough of sharp-dressing men who flaunted their wealth and acted as if they knew everything.

She hadn't seen that side of Justin yet, but she preferred his work clothes to business attire. Not that what she liked mattered where he was concerned, except she seemed to be the only woman here who felt that way.

A twenty-something blonde barista batted her eyelashes as if she were a butterfly, trying to show off beautiful wings. She said something to Justin.

He laughed. The deep, rich sound filled the air and drew attention to him. More female gazes turned his way.

The barista's cheeks turned pink, but she kept looking at Justin.

Bailey didn't blame the woman for wanting his attention. Men like him didn't walk into the corner coffee shop every day. Especially in a town the size of Haley's Bay. Her type or not, she couldn't deny Justin was good-looking. Gorgeous, really.

She needed to be careful around him for the sake of the inn and its employees. They were in a fight for ownership of the Broughton Inn. One of them would win; the other would lose. He might not be trying to charm the inn away from her, or so he claimed, but she couldn't let him distract her.

Justin looked over at Bailey, smiled. "Be right there."

Her tummy did a double twist as if she were a high diver. Nerves knocked against her insides like trick-or-treaters at her door on Halloween. This morning's overcast, windy skies and sense of foreboding in the air were better suited to late October than early July.

She should have said no to coffee. *N-O.* How hard could saying two letters be? Not that she'd said *Y-E-S.* Yet here she was.

Stupid, stupid, stupid.

She massaged her temples, trying to quell the headache threatening to erupt.

Justin might not be planning to "woo" her out of the inn, but he must have an agenda. To mine her for information or plant doubts that she could run the inn. This wasn't a date, because Justin wouldn't be interested in Bailey if he lost his bid for the inn. Or if he won, for that matter. He was only interested while the inn was in limbo; she had to keep that in mind.

Well, two could play that game. Maybe she could plant some doubts of her own.

"Hey, Bailey." Mrs. Caldecott, the wife of the town's butcher, stopped at the table. A pink baseball cap covered her white hair. She carried two coffees in a drink holder and a small brown bag. "Sorry to hear about your foot, but good to know you're looking out for the inn. I know you'll make sure everything turns out right."

"Thanks." More than one person had called or texted yesterday to lend support. Added pressure, yes, but that only firmed Bailey's resolve. "I'll do my best."

Mrs. Caldecott smiled warmly, the wrinkles on her face deepening. "You've always been a good girl, Bailey Cole. Just a little…different."

With that, Mrs. Caldecott left the coffee shop.

Different, huh? Bailey supposed that was a step up from odd. She'd been called that, too.

"Here you go." Justin placed a large white mug in front of her. "One cappuccino with a pretty flower."

"Thanks." Bailey studied the rosebud in the foam, complete with a stem and a leaf. "The baristas personalize their drink creations here. Bart, who works weekends, makes animal faces. He's a volunteer at the local rescue shelter. Puts out a jar for donations."

Cup in hand, Justin pulled out his chair. "I'll stop by on Saturday."

Her spine went steel-beam rigid. "You're staying in town?"

"For now." He sat.

The small, round table made for close quarters. His scent, soap-fresh and enticing, tickled her nose. She raised her cup to smell her coffee so she wouldn't want to sniff him.

Bailey's foot ached. She stretched her left leg and brushed his. She stiffened. "Sorry."

"My fault." He scooted back in his chair. "You need more room."

No, she needed distance from him. "I'm fine. We won't be here long."

Bailey drank her coffee. The warm liquid did nothing to help her growing unease.

"I'm putting together an improvement plan for the first approval committee." Justin raised his mug in her direction. "I appreciate the handy list you put together on the city's website to help approach the groups. Very thorough. Thanks."

"You're welcome." She chewed the inside of her mouth. Great. Her work would lead to the inn being torn down.

Okay, not really, but she needed to drink her coffee and leave before she gave him more helpful hints. "That's a requirement of my position."

"You're not anti-remodel."

"Not at all, but improvements need to be carefully considered so the historical significance isn't remodeled out of the property. Integrity of the architecture and intent of the design must be protected. Floyd…"

Saying his name squeezed her heart. She stared at the pink lip gloss mark on the rim of her cup.

Justin reached across the table, covered her free hand with his. The touch filled the empty places inside her with surprising warmth.

"What about Floyd?" Justin asked.

She stared at their hands. A sketch formed in her mind with lines and shadowing falling into place. The rough and calloused skin on his hands contradicted his style of dress. Her late grandfather and father and brothers—AJ, Ellis, Flynn, Declan and Grady—had similar hands. Her sister, Camden, too. Bailey's weren't much better.

"Floyd created the historical committee." She set her mug on the table. "He put together the committee to oversee property improvements. Wrote most of the rules and regulations. I took over for him a year ago."

For such large, scarred hands, Justin's touch was solid, safe, comforting. So what if pulling her hand from beneath his was the smart thing to do? She liked the feel of his skin against hers to deal with the consequences and rumors.

"His choice to leave the position or someone else's?"

"His. He wanted me to take over."

"Doesn't sound like the same guy I talked to. He was all for tearing down the old and making way for the new."

"Floyd was raised at the hotel. Loved that old building. Cared about the employees. His girlfriend must have pressured him to do this."

"You keep surprising me, Bailey Cole."

She glanced up, meeting Justin's gaze. "Why?"

"Most people want Floyd to rot in jail."

"I've known him my entire life." Bailey expected Justin to lift his hand off hers. He didn't. That surprised her, but in a good way. "Floyd let me open a co-op gallery at the inn and use the bar for my classes. I'm not about to condemn him without a hearing. I just wish I knew why."

"You might not ever hear his side or get the answers you want, but his reason could be as simple as falling in love with the wrong person."

"Yeah, his girlfriend sounds like a loser. That relationship has been full of red flags from the beginning."

"Lust can be addicting and dangerous. Powerful enough to make people change, not always for the better."

Something about Justin's tone piqued her curiosity. She leaned forward. The table pressed against her rib cage. "Are you speaking from personal experience?"

Bailey waited for Justin to answer her question. His taken-aback expression told her she'd crossed the line. Wouldn't be the first time.

The bell on the coffee shop door jingled. A young couple—tourists, based on the camera bag one carried—walked in holding hands and gazing lovingly into each other's eyes. Sweet.

A part of Bailey longed for a partner, one in the truest sense of the word. She stared at Justin's hand still on top of hers. Oliver had never comforted her with a touch. He was too worried about the solvents on her hands ruining one of his expensive manicures.

Why had she gone out with him? Oh, yeah, her sister-in-law Risa had set her up. The guy had been wrong for Bailey from the start, but she had liked having someone to go out with when she was in Seattle—AJ was always too busy—but as soon as Oliver began spouting his opinion about what she should be doing with her money or talking about his newest client and wanting to be introduced to AJ, the fun ended. Being on her own was so much easier.

Still, she found herself drawn to Justin in a way she hadn't been before. The little things he did, like having a hand ready if she stumbled or a kind gesture when she needed one most, were thoughtful, and she liked hearing what he had to say, even when she disagreed. But nothing would change their situation with the inn. No reason to complicate matters. Or chase heartache.

She pulled her hand from beneath Justin's. "So..."

Justin did a double take at her hand at the edge of the table, as if he hadn't realized he was still touching her. Maybe he'd enjoyed the contact as much as her.

Best not to go there.

He put his hand under the table.

Then again, maybe not.

With his other hand, he ran his thumb along the cup's handle. "We're talking about Floyd, not me."

"Didn't mean to pry."

"Yes, you did."

"Okay, I did." Bailey nearly laughed. "Subtlety isn't my strong point. But I'm trying to understand."

"Floyd?"

"And you."

His thumb continued moving up and down, up and down. "I wouldn't waste any time trying to figure out Floyd's actions. Sometimes those we think we know turn out to be complete strangers."

"Sounds like some woman did a number on you."

He flinched. "Excuse me?"

His shocked expression made her want to giggle. She'd caught him off guard. Again. "From what you're saying, I'm guessing it's not all about Floyd."

"I'm...divorced."

Interesting. Most women wouldn't catch and release such an attractive guy with a stable job who seemed relatively charming. Though she hardly knew him. He could be a weirdo for all she knew. Or a cheater. "Should I say I'm sorry or something else?"

"Sorry works. My ex wanted the divorce."

His voice held zero emotion. Over the woman or in denial? Hard to tell. Not that his past was Bailey's business.

"And no, I didn't cheat." He stared into his coffee cup, then met her gaze. "That's what everyone assumes."

"The thought may have crossed my mind."

"Our expectations of married life were different. She wanted to live in Portland. My work was on the coast, and job sites weren't always close to home. We grew apart."

"That's happened to a few people I know." But not Bailey's parents. They had been married for thirty-five years, through good times and bad times, and some horrible, want-to-forget ones, but they'd stuck together. That was what commitment—and saying "I do"—was about. But she'd never dated anyone for more than a few months, so what did she know? "You don't have to tell me this."

"You wanted to know."

"Yes, but that's small-town life for you. Hard to break the butting-your-nose-in habit, even though I don't like when people do it to me."

"Any more questions?"

"Are you still in contact with your ex?"

"No, she remarried and had a baby. She's happy now." A mutual friend had told Justin the news. "No reason for us to be in touch."

"Would you get married again?" Bailey asked.

"Hard to say, but unless I found a woman who either liked being on her own or traveling to job sites with me, probably not. I thought marriage would be easier, but it's a helluva lot of work. I have enough of that with my job."

How sad. Having to work at a marriage might be hard, but she believed the rewards would be worth the effort. Maybe Justin would realize that someday.

The conversation around them rose as silence took over their table. A man typed on his laptop. A woman stared at her smartphone. An elderly couple sat on a love seat and read the paper together.

A longing to grow old with someone rose within Bailey. She tapped it down.

"So my turn to ask the questions," Justin said. "How does an artist living in a small town end up on the historical committee?"

"Painter, and I love old buildings."

"What do you love? The design, the materials?"

"Those things are interesting, but for me it's all about the history." She wrapped her hands around her mug. The heat from the coffee warmed her palms, but she preferred Justin's touch. "The buildings are living memorials to the people who have been there before."

"Some are."

"Every single one." She thought back. "When I spent a semester in Europe, I climbed so many bell towers. The stone steps were worn smooth. You could see the paths people took, and that made me think of everyone who had climbed before me. Were they local or from far away? Recent or from centuries ago? What had they wanted to see when they reached the top? Were they with someone special or getting over a lost love?"

Justin leaned back in his chair. "You don't hesitate getting in someone's face, but you're also a romantic."

"I don't know about that." Bailey ripped the edge of a napkin into a symmetrical fringe. She couldn't believe he'd figured out that side of her. "My family would disagree. They call me hard-nosed."

"You're that, too," he teased.

He studied her like a scientist looking to identify a new virus. She forced herself not to move. "I wouldn't disagree, but hard-nosed and romantic don't exactly go together."

Maybe her brothers weren't the only reason she was

still single. Maybe she was as much to blame for driving men away.

"The traits go together in their own way." Justin's flirty smile raised her temperature ten degrees. "You know the past and see a future. You won't be bullied, but value artistry."

She sat taller, buoyed by a sense of purpose and pride. "I take my position on the historical committee seriously. And the inn…" From the time she was a little girl, she'd imagined getting married there someday. "…means a lot to me personally."

"Your actions are proof of that. The self-declared Guardian of the Broughton Inn."

"Thanks." Satisfaction bubbled inside her.

"You would take that as a compliment."

"I do." Her gaze met his. "You realize no matter how much you and your family want the inn, I plan on living up to that title. And winning."

"I have no doubt we'll fight to the end." His respectful tone held a challenge. "I'm up for it."

She raised her chin. "So am I."

Chapter Five

Bailey had thrown down the gauntlet, and Justin had taken it up. He leaned back in his chair at the coffee shop. He didn't want to think about the damage that would be done by the time he won this battle. "Enough about the inn."

She eyed him warily. "That's the only reason we're here."

Not him.

He'd never met a woman like Bailey Cole and wouldn't mind getting to know her better. Smart, attractive, she would prove a worthy opponent, but no matter how determined she was, she would lose. At the end, she would hate him, if she didn't already. He couldn't tell. That bugged the hell out of him.

"Doesn't mean the inn's all we have to discuss." The coffee shop door jingled. From his peripheral vision, he saw people entering, but his attention remained on Bailey. Justin rested his elbows on the wooden table. "Tell me about—"

"I'm boring."

"Haley's Bay," he said a beat after she spoke.

She blushed.

Hmm. Maybe she liked him a little or maybe she was egocentric. Either way, she amused him, but he kept his smile neutral rather than a blatant I-see-you're-interested-in-me grin.

Justin raised his cup, only to realize no coffee remained. He took a pretend sip. Bailey would be none the wiser, and that would keep them from saying goodbye too soon.

"Didn't you do a market analysis of the town before you purchased the inn?" she asked.

"For an artist and former cook, you know how business works."

"Common sense. And art is a business if you want to make a living with your work."

He liked her answer. Brains had always been a turn-on to him. "A market analysis was performed, but you live here. I want to hear what you think."

Bailey gazed into her mug, then looked up at him. "Haley's Bay is a typical Pacific Northwest small town. The name comes from a trader who anchored his ship in the bay. Fishing used to drive the local economy, but now tourism brings in the money. Population nearly doubles in the summer, thanks to tourists wanting to hang out at the beach or sightsee. The Lewis and Clark Interpretive Center appeals to the history buffs. And who doesn't like lighthouses?"

"Sounds like you gave me the Chamber of Commerce robot spiel."

A smile lit up Bailey's face. "Guilty. I'm biased, so I gave you the vanilla, glossy trifold brochure version."

"I want to hear the Rocky Road version."

"With nuts?"

"Of course." Some whipped cream would be nice, too. And a cherry. He undid the top button on his collar.

"Well…Haley's Bay is a small town with lots of history.

A couple of families like mine have lived here forever. Gossip is rampant. The women at the Cut, Curl & Dye Salon are the worst. I drive to Astoria if I need a trim, or do it myself. The guys who hang out at the Crow's Nest aren't much better. Conformity is applauded here. Being different means no one will even try to understand you, except family. And that's not always a given. High school was brutal for kids like me. Most grew up dreaming about leaving for the big city, but many of us stayed or came back. "

"You came back?"

"I never left except for college. My family, except for two older brothers, lives here. For all the town's faults, there's a sense of paying it forward in Haley's Bay I haven't found elsewhere. This is the only place I want to live."

At least she was honest about that fact, unlike his ex, who swore she wouldn't miss living in Portland. But Taryn had gone into the marriage thinking she could change his mind about staying on the coast. "You mentioned driving to Seattle."

Bailey nodded. "I oversee AJ's gallery. I'm up there a few times each month."

"More opportunity for art sales in the big city?"

"In the off-season, most sales happen through the Seattle gallery. I'm grateful for the extra exposure. So, you live on the Oregon coast?" She downed what remained in her cup.

"Lincoln City. My sister Paige works with my parents at our headquarters there. She's an attorney. My younger sister, Rainey, is an interior designer and spends her time at whatever resorts we're renovating."

"You oversee construction."

"And design. That's my favorite part."

"You're an architect who wears different hats."

He nodded. "Keeping the work in the family. All we're missing is a chef."

"Your parents should have had four kids."

"We joke about that."

Bailey glanced out the window to her right. She leaned toward the glass. "The stray dog from the inn is out there. He's so skinny."

Justin followed the direction of her gaze.

The thin brown dog sat on the sidewalk staring into the coffee shop. Mud covered the animal, but Justin saw the outline of the dog's bones beneath the dirty fur.

Bailey stood, took a step toward the door. "That dog needs medical attention."

He rose. "Where are you going?"

"To get the dog."

"Stay off your feet. I'll get the dog."

Her gaze narrowed. "You sure?"

Helping the dog might put him on Bailey's good side. "Positive."

How much trouble could a dog be? Justin stepped out of the coffee shop. The sun was brighter, the temperature at least five degrees hotter since they'd entered the coffee shop.

"Hey, dog." He looked at the pathetic, filthy animal that hadn't moved. "Hungry?"

The dog panted.

"You must be thirsty, too." Justin knew nothing about animals and couldn't believe he was having a conversation with a dog. But anyone with half a heart could see this one needed help. "Come here so we can get you fixed up."

The dog scratched himself with a hind leg.

"You know you don't want to be on your own out there. Let's get you some food. A bath. Flea medicine."

The dog tilted his head. Two brown eyes watching Justin.

He took a step closer. "Make me look good for the pretty lady looking out the window, and I'll get you a bone."

The dog didn't move.

"And a ball." He came closer. At least the dog didn't

seem to be afraid of him. "That's fine. Just sit there. I'll come to you."

Justin wanted to show Bailey he had this, even if he'd never owned or even walked a dog. He stood less than an arm's distance away. "Let's get you fed and cleaned up, buddy."

He reached for the dog, felt fur under his palm, then air. The dog bolted.

Justin lost his balance and hit the sidewalk, flat on his ass. So much for impressing Bailey.

"Oh, no," Bailey's voice sounded from the door to the coffee shop. "Are you okay?"

He sat on his butt, brushed off his hands. "Ego's bruised, but that's about it."

She joined him on the sidewalk. Her lips curved upward. "Not very experienced with dogs, are you?"

"You could tell."

A smile graced her lips. "Just a little, but nice try."

If she was trying to make him feel better...

She extended her arm. "Let me help you up."

He took her hand and found himself standing so close to her he could feel her breath on his neck. Her eyes locked on his. Her pink, delicious-looking lips parted.

Oh, yeah. He wanted a taste. A nibble would do.

If he angled his head slightly, he could kiss—

A bark cut through the air.

Bailey took a step back. "The dog."

Justin glanced around to see a flash of brown trotting away from them along the sidewalk. Not too fast, but a catch-me-if-you-can pace.

Bailey's nose crinkled. Concern filled her gaze.

Justin had a feeling he would regret this, but what the hell. Anything he had to do could wait until later. "Want to go after the dog?"

* * *

Bailey waited outside the coffee shop for Justin to return in his truck. Her stomach twisted like a glass-blown piece gone wrong. A part of her wanted him to take his time, except she wanted to find the dog. But she needed to cool herself down. Heat continued to burn her cheeks. She must look like one of Titian's blushing virgins.

How embarrassing. She'd thought Justin was going to kiss her when he stood up. Worse, she'd wanted him to kiss her. This was becoming more complicated by the second, and she wasn't the type for complications. Life was hard enough. She should say goodbye and not see him until their next meeting about the inn.

And she would.

After they found the dog.

Bailey scanned the street for a glimpse of the stray. Tourists packed the sidewalk, but no sign of the pup who needed food, water, medical treatment and to know someone cared.

She did.

If only her foot wasn't hurt, she could have run after the dog instead of being forced to wait for a ride. But she'd been standing too long this morning, and her entire leg ached. She sat on a nearby bench.

Glong. Glong. D-ding-a-ting-glong.

The bells chimed on her cell phone. She glanced at the screen. "Hey, Grandma."

"Hello, dear." The sound of waves could be heard in the background. "I'm in Long Beach. Do you need a ride home from Tyler's office?"

"I'm good." Justin would probably offer to drive her home after they found the dog. "Don't rush back for me."

"Okay, I'll bring lunch by later. I baked brownies this morning."

"Yum. My favorite. Thanks." Her grandmother loved

cooking for her family, especially her grandkids. "But I'm
going to gain five pounds if you keep feeding me so much."

"Men like women with curves."

Did Justin? The thought flashed in Bailey's brain. She
shouldn't care, but the more time she spent with him, the
more she did.

A large black pickup stopped at the light caught her attention. Justin sat in the driver's seat, looking like a cross
between a CEO and a cowboy. Her pulse stuttered. A totally inappropriate response when *not* seeing him again
was her smartest move.

She rose, swung her purse onto her shoulder and walked
toward the curb. "I've got to go, Grandma. Justin is here."

"Who's Justin?"

No. No. No. Bailey cringed. Had she really mentioned a
man's name to her grandmother? She hadn't opened a can
of worms; she'd released a vat of them.

"Bailey? Are you there?"

She swallowed around the lump in her throat, wishing
she could have a do-over. "I'm here."

"Is Justin your new beau?"

The hope filling Grandma's voice sliced into Bailey's
heart with scalpel-like precision. Having her grandchildren marry had become Lilah Cole's driving goal since
AJ fell in love with nanny Emma Markwell last August.
A big, billionaire-worthy wedding was in the works and
that delighted Grandma. At least her matchmaking was
subtler than Risa's, but Bailey wouldn't be surprised if the
two were in cahoots, along with her great-aunt Ida Mae.

Bailey knew she had to say something, but as little as
possible. "I hardly know the guy. He's the one who wants
to tear down the Broughton Inn."

"Then why is he picking you up?"

At least she had a good reason. "We're looking for a
stray dog."

"Is that a sex term?"

Bailey stiffened. "Grandma."

"What?"

"We're looking for a brown dog, covered in dirt and malnourished. Most likely a stray."

"Oh." Grandma sounded disappointed. Hard to believe the woman would be eighty-one in August. She acted much younger. "I suppose it's easier to keep your enemies close if they're good-looking."

"Have you met him?"

"No, but he's staying at Ida Mae's B and B. She said he was handsome."

Bailey was not going to discuss Justin's looks with her grandmother. Bad enough her great-aunt Ida Mae had mentioned him.

"Don't keep your young man waiting," Grandma added.

"He's not…" Bailey blew out a puff of air. Best not to go there when the truck was pulling up to the curb. "I'll talk to you later."

Justin jumped out of his truck and held open the passenger door. "Need a hand?"

"Thanks, but I'm fine." She climbed up using her good leg, but sensed him right behind her in case she fell. "It's okay."

"I'll move once you're buckled in."

"You don't have to play big brother to me."

"Trust me, my feelings for you aren't brotherly."

Her heart stumbled. He might not be her Mr. Right, but she was still female. Of course he could mean the exact opposite of what she was hoping—no, thinking. "Does that mean you're taking the term 'enemy' to heart?"

"I didn't say that."

But she didn't want to think of the alternative—that he might find her attractive. Something, maybe even desire, flashed in his eyes, as if he was imagining her naked and liking what he saw, made her feel pretty and wanted, and totally not in control of the situation.

The man was not only trouble, but also dangerous. The hair on the back of her neck stiffened, each one screaming to get the hell away from him. And she would. Once they found the dog.

Justin couldn't believe they'd spent an hour and a half driving around town with no dog to show for it. Not even a glimpse of dirty fur. He pulled into Bailey's driveway behind her car, the bee with tires.

"I'll keep my eyes out for the dog," he said.

"Thanks. I really thought we'd be able to track him down. I'll let Grady know so he can contact Animal Control. They take the animals they find to the local shelter." She yawned.

"Tired?"

"A little."

More like a lot. He turned off the ignition. "You haven't said much."

"I'm worried about the dog. And this is my first time out of the house since I went to the doctor. I'm not used to being vertical this long."

"Then let's get you inside."

"I can take care of myself."

"I know that, but if you fall, guess who'll get the blame? Don't you think being known as the man who wants to destroy the inn and got put into his place by Bailey Cole is enough infamy for one week?"

Her smile brightened her face. So pretty, though her look that other morning at the inn was endearing in hindsight. "People are saying that?"

"I might be exaggerating, but I don't want your brothers blaming me if you fall."

She reached up and touched Justin's cheek, surprising

him, but in a good way. "Oh, that would be bad. They'd mess up your nice face."

His chest swelled. "You like my face?"

Bailey jerked her hand away. Her shock widened his smile.

"I'm speaking as an artist." She looked everywhere but at him. "Your features are aesthetically pleasing and fit well together."

"You must have a good memory since you're not looking at me."

Her Mona Lisa smile hit him hard in the gut. He wished he could taste those lips. He grinned at the thought of doing just that.

She opened the front door. "What's so funny?"

He didn't dare tell her about wanting to kiss her on the sidewalk earlier. Not unless he wanted her to slam the door in his face. "This is the last place I expected to be again. Not that I mind. Your company is better than Kent's. The guy reads judicial briefs for entertainment."

Bailey stepped inside. He followed, closing the door behind him. "Kent's going to think you've gone missing."

"I texted him."

"Does he know you're with me?"

"I left that part out. Self-preservation."

She raised an eyebrow. "Sounds like a line I'd use with my family."

"Don't forget I have sisters. Paige routinely goes ballistic over less, but in this case she'd be firing words faster than bullets fly at a SWAT team's target practice."

"We have something in common."

"You sound surprised."

"Maybe I am." Bailey plopped onto the couch, resting her foot on a coffee table with designs burned into the wood and painted bright colors. "We're...different."

"Not really. We just happen to be on different sides with

the inn." Justin hadn't noticed the decorative table when he was here the last time. He touched one of the etch marks. "I like this."

"Bought the table at a garage sale for five dollars. A few doodles, wood-burning and paint...good as new."

Her modesty was endearing, but misplaced. "I'd say better than new. You could make an entire line of refurbished tables like this one and sell them for a shabby chic fortune."

"Listen to you." She held a pillow on her lap. "Tough guy resort developer talking shabby chic."

"We furnish every place I build or renovate." He pulled an overstuffed patchwork ottoman over and sat. "My sister might be the interior designer, but I know a thing or two about style. I also know you're a painter, but you have talent for furniture, too."

"Thank you," she said. "We're even for compliments."

He tugged off the sandal from her good foot. She hadn't asked, but his helping her felt strangely natural. "But I can hear in your voice that you're not interested in starting a business."

"It's not that. I sell what I make all the time, but I like to choose what I work on unless someone commissions a piece. I'd rather not be locked into making tables or anything else."

"Free-spirited."

"Sometimes. Other times not. Truth is, I'd let orders wait if I was inspired to work on a painting. I'd let everything wait, actually, which makes me wonder—"

Justin's hands still held her good foot. His fingers longed to rub her skin, soothe any sore muscles. He let go of her foot. "If you want to run the inn?"

Bailey frowned. "The inn has a staff to run it. I'm talking about, well...life. I'm different from my sister-in-law, whose life is her family. She volunteers, works out, cleans, cooks and gets mani-pedis. She's very happy, but I'm..."

"You worry whether you want a husband and family."

"*No*. Not at all. I worry I won't be good at it. That I'll put my art before everyone else, and then need to stop working altogether because I can't figure out how to balance the two."

The emotion behind her words startled him. He didn't understand her trusting him with something so personal when he was supposed to be the enemy, the rival for the Broughton Inn, the guy she stopped by standing in front of his wrecking ball. Or why he had the urge to move to scoop her into his arms and tell her she could handle marriage and a family.

He needed to get a hold of himself. She was a stranger, not his friend. But he'd tried the marriage route and failed. Maybe he could help her.

"Trust me, Bailey. Being a good wife has nothing to do with whether you work or stay home. It's difficult, no matter who you are. So is being a good husband. But you care about people and that's what matters." Reassurance came naturally, because the words were based on his experience. "That's my ounce of wisdom for the day."

"More like sixteen ounces of good advice." Gratitude filled her voice and her eyes.

He wouldn't swear an oath, but he glimpsed what might have been a tear. For the first time in a long while, he felt like a hero. Which made no sense, because he'd done absolutely nothing to earn the title, and had no right to give advice, given his divorce. "Do you want a glass of water or something to drink?"

"I could use some ibuprofen and water." She looked relieved at the change of subject. Well, join the club. He wasn't sure why the topic had come up. "The pills are in a white bottle on the counter. The glasses are in the upper cabinet right off the sink."

"Be right back.

"I'm not going anywhere."

Bailey's kitchen was like her—unique and comfortable. The Dutch-blue walls complemented the white cabinets with fused glass handles. Colorful pottery sat on top of the kitchen cabinets. Small seascape canvas paintings hung on the walls. The area was neat and tidy, except for two coffee cups in the sink. She must have had company this morning. Who?

He took a closer look and noticed lipstick stains. Not a guy. Then he remembered she'd said family members had been taking care of her. Her sister? Bailey talked more about her brothers.

Justin filled a glass with water and grabbed the pills. He stepped into the living room. "I've got your…"

Bailey's eyes were closed, a soft smile on her slightly parted lips. He took a step back. Okay, three.

Beautiful, yes. He'd been surrounded by attractive women his entire life. Hell, Taryn was gorgeous. But something about seeing Bailey like this took her appeal to a new level.

Her expression wasn't vulnerable. Nothing about her was needy, but at that moment, all he wanted to do was take care of her. Not in a caveman type of way. She was the last woman who needed protecting, with such a strong independent personality and surrounded by family as she was. But he wanted to make sure she had everything she needed and was…happy.

Happy.

Crazy and illogical, given the inn. He'd better get out of here before Paige found out. But first he wanted to do something.

Justin placed pills on the table and set the glass on a coaster. He covered her with an afghan from the back of a rocking chair. She didn't stir.

Okay, now he could leave. But a part of him wanted to stay to make sure she didn't wake up and need something.

He glanced around the living room. Seascapes with lighthouses. Landscapes with mountains. Photographs in hand-painted frames hung on the walls and sat on shelves, a glass jar full of painted rocks on one corner of the mantel, a bowl with seashells on the other and a colorful flowerpot with colorful, swirly lollipops sticking out on the window-sill near the front door.

Easy access for visiting kids, old and young?

He took a closer look at the photographs. One with Bailey and another woman on the beach caught his eye. The two resembled each other—her sister, Camden?—but their looks were the only similarity. Bailey was the image of femininity in a blowing skirt, tank top and no shoes. The other woman wore rubber waders held up with suspenders and a cap worn backward on her head. Bailey was the image of Mother Earth, while the woman next to her defined *tomboy*. He recognized Ellis and Grady in several of the pictures. The other men must be her brothers. Not identical facial features, but you could tell they were related. The lengths and shades of brown hair varied, but their heights only slightly so. He moved onto the next photograph, then another and another, making his way around the living room.

A slight knock sounded; then the front doorknob turned.

He'd closed the door, but hadn't turned the lock.

A short, white-haired woman entered, then closed the door. He'd seen her picture on the wall. She wore a green tracksuit and carried two bags. Her eyes widened. "Well, hello." She didn't look worried or surprised.

"Hi."

A welcoming smile deepened the wrinkles on her face. "You must be Justin."

How did she know his name? "Yes, I'm Justin McMillian." He motioned to Bailey on the couch. "She fell asleep."

"Doing too much too soon. Did you find the dog?"

"No."

"She'll be worried about that."

"I plan to keep looking."

"That'll make Bailey happy. Place a report with Animal Control so they're on the lookout, too. That'll impress her." The elderly woman walked into the room, her excitement visibly bubbling over. "I brought lunch. There's plenty for you, too."

So, what if he was supposed to meet Kent for lunch? Justin would rather stay here with a sleeping Bailey and her surprise visitor.

"By the way, I'm Lilah Cole, Bailey's grandmother."

"Nice to meet you, Mrs. Cole."

She shuddered. "Lilah, please. Mrs. Cole makes me think of my mother-in-law. Those aren't fond memories." She handed him one of the bags. "Come in the kitchen. I need help with lunch and while we work, you can tell me about yourself."

He stared at the bag in his hand. He could guess where Bailey got her strong personality. He had no idea what she would say to his hanging out with her grandmother, but he had a feeling Lilah would be nothing but smiles. That was good enough for Justin. Maybe helping Lilah prepare lunch would earn him some points with Bailey. He could use them. "What do you want to know?"

Chapter Six

Bailey blinked, allowing her eyes to adjust to the light. She wasn't ready to wake from her nap, but she'd heard something. Voices? Laughter? Except the TV was off. The radio, too. Maybe she'd dreamed the sounds.

She sat on the couch with her leg propped on the table. Light streamed through the front windows. The clock on the DVD player showed she'd slept over an hour. Felt like longer. She stretched her arms over her head.

An afghan, crocheted by Grandma, fell to Bailey's lap. She didn't remember covering herself. Had Justin done that? No, he would have left by now. At least she hoped he hadn't stuck around while she slept.

Bailey cringed.

She couldn't believe she'd confessed her personal worry to him. Shame poured through her, like the water rushing from the Columbia River to the Pacific Ocean. Tiredness and worry about the dog had lowered her defenses, allowed her to open up. That rarely happened, even with her family.

Laughter sounded from the kitchen. Female. Familiar. Grandma. She must have brought over lunch.

Bailey heard another voice. Male. Not one of her brothers.

Oh, no. Justin was still here. Her back straightened like a piece of rebar, no longer against the sofa. Seeing him would be too embarrassing after blurting out her feared ineptitude about having a family. Even if she'd appreciated his advice.

She glanced around the room, looking for an escape. The bathroom? Her bedroom? A closet?

And then she realized Grandma and Justin had spent time alone. Flutters filled Bailey's stomach like a bevy of blindfolded butterflies.

Her grandmother finding Justin here while Bailey slept could be the start of a Lilah-induced apocalypse. Instead of four horsemen, her brothers would ride in and wreak havoc. This was bad, so bad Bailey debated pretending to be asleep so she wouldn't have to deal with...

"You're awake." Her grandmother stood in the doorway to the kitchen.

Too late to play possum. Bailey forced a smile.

Lilah Cole was a short, wiry woman with white curls, wrinkles from a lifetime of laughter and a bright-as-the-sun smile. She would turn eighty-one next month, but she acted like a spry sixty-year-old, doing Jazzercise classes at the rec center twice a week.

"I must have needed that nap." Bailey fingered the edge of the blanket. "I didn't hear you come in."

"You were out cold. Big Foot could have stomped around, and you wouldn't have stirred. Justin kept me company. Such a nice man. So polite. And handsome, too."

Uh-oh. Bailey recognized the twinkle in her grandmother's eyes. That was how she looked when she talked about Emma Markwell, AJ's fiancée. If Grandma decided Justin was the man for Bailey...

Time for damage control. "Not nice. He wants to tear down the inn."

"To build a better one."

"A glass box to take advantage of the views, but a building with zero personality. I did an internet search, saw pictures of the remodeling job he did in Seaside. No, thanks." Bailey couldn't believe she was having this discussion with her grandmother. "Where is he?"

"In the kitchen doing dishes," Grandma said in a low voice. "We ate while you napped."

"Great." Not really. Bailey had no idea why Justin had stuck around unless he wanted to pump Grandma for info. "You always bring too much food."

"That's what grandmothers do. Feed our grandbabies."

"I'm way past the baby stage."

"Not in my eyes." A faraway expression filled Grandma's gaze. "Seems like only yesterday you were running around in a diaper and nothing else. Your grandfather would chase you down the hallway. You'd giggle. Two pigtails sticking out on each side of your head like Pippi Longstocking. Crayons in each hand. A giant grin on your face as you looked for something, usually a wall, to color."

Justin entered the room carrying a tray. "Braids and a grin, I can imagine. The crayons, too. The diaper, not so much."

This was going to be a problem. Bailey blew out a breath.

Grandma laughed. "Bailey wanted to be naked, but I had my hardwood floors and rugs to protect."

Heat spread up Bailey's neck. She bit the inside of her cheek. In less than ten seconds, her face would clash with her hair. "Grandma. You're as bad as Mom."

"What?" Grandma feigned innocence. "You've always been a free spirit. Nothing wrong with that."

Bailey's insides twisted while she kept a straight face.

Justin was looking at her, and she felt unusually self-conscious. "I prefer wearing clothes these days."

"You look wonderful in whatever you wear," Grandma said.

"Except for those paint-splattered coveralls." Justin handed Bailey the tray containing a plate full of lunch, utensils, napkin and glasses of lemonade. "If the fashion police had been patrolling the streets the other day, we'd still be trying to raise bail."

Bailey grimaced. "They aren't that bad."

"Yes, they are." Grandma's scrunched face matched her disapproving tone. "Please tell me you're joking about wearing them."

"I've only worn them once in public," Bailey admitted. "Satisfied?"

"Yes, but that was one time too many." Grandma motioned to the lunch—meat loaf with mashed potatoes, green beans and homemade biscuits. "You need to start chowing down. There are brownies for dessert."

"You made my favorites."

"Anything for you, dear. And Justin." Grandma picked up her purse. "I have to go."

Bailey's muscles tightened into a tapestry of knots. Her grandmother leaving them alone was a bad sign—a matchmaking sign. "We haven't visited."

"You see me almost every day." Grandma waved her off. "Risa is busy, so I need to pick up the kids from school."

"Amelia and Maddox don't get out of school for at least two hours. And they take the bus home whenever I babysit them."

"I'm a busy woman. Places to go. People to see." Grandma headed toward the door, then glanced over her shoulder. "Delighted to meet you, Justin. See you soon."

He nodded. "Thanks for lunch."

"I'll pick up the containers later. Have fun, you two."

With that, Grandma strode out the door, a small hurricane about to be set loose on Haley's Bay.

"The woman is a spitfire." He sat on the far side of couch. "She asked so many questions."

"I'm sorry. Grandma wants to know everything about everybody. She uses her newfound knowledge to meddle. Managing others' lives—well, trying— keeps her young."

"No apology needed. I got a great lunch and made a new friend."

"You don't mind that your name will be bandied about town? Might already be happening."

He moved to the cushion next to her, cutting the distance between them in half. His smile hinted of mischief and something else Bailey didn't want to name. "Your grandmother is a sweetheart, but I caught on fast that she was trying to pry me open with her charm."

"You should have woken me up. I would have run interference."

"You were tired."

"You didn't have to stay."

Justin shrugged. "Lilah asked for my help with lunch. I couldn't say no."

Bailey shook her head. "My grandma can whip up a meal for forty without blinking an eye."

"Yeah, she seemed to have everything under control."

"But you went along?"

"She's your grandmother. There's no other place I'd rather be right now."

The sincerity in his voice tugged at Bailey's heart. The last thing she needed from Justin. "What about Kent?"

"I texted him. He's at the courthouse." Justin pointed to her lunch. "Eat. The meat loaf won't taste as good cold."

She stabbed her fork into her lunch. Food would distract her from the man. She took a bite. Spices and flavors exploded in her mouth. "Mmm."

"Your grandmother's a good cook."

"The best." Bailey scooped up another forkful. "My mom conceded defeat in the kitchen, but one-upped Grandma by having seven children to her three. My mom, however, would never admit that was her reason for having a big family. She adores Grandma."

"Cole family gatherings must be interesting."

Bailey wiped her mouth with the napkin. "They are. Crowded and loud, but no fighting unless we're talking sports."

"Seahawks fans?"

"My brothers and sister are. Sundays at my grandma's house during football season are mandatory. Doesn't matter if you like sports or not, so I watch the commercials."

"Your way of fitting in."

Once again he'd said something that made Bailey think he could see right through her. Not about to admit anything, she focused on her lunch. Bailey ate. Maybe silence would convince him to leave. The seconds turned into a minute, then two.

"I reported the stray dog to Animal Control," he said.

She choked, coughed, grabbed her lemonade to wash down whatever had gone down the wrong way. She cleared her throat. "Did my grandmother tell you to do that?"

A beat passed. A sheepish grin appeared. "She didn't want you to worry."

Bailey's fork slipped from her fingers, clattered against the tray. "Crap. This is worse than I thought."

"Excuse me."

She took a breath. "My grandmother's picked you. For me."

Justin's eyebrows drew together. Lines crinkled his forehead. "She said that a minute or so after meeting me."

"Timing doesn't matter to Grandma. She's a romantic at heart. Love at first sight. Cupid's arrow." Bailey rubbed her aching temples. "My grandmother married my grandpa after knowing him three days. They eloped and were married for over half a century before he died. I bet she's over at the B and B where you're staying, telling my aunt Ida Mae that we're making out on the couch right now."

"We'd better get started, then."

Bailey ignored his joke. "Grandma's been wrong about her picks in the past, so I'll remind her about that when she brings you up."

He scooted closer, until his thigh pressed against hers. "Is that going to be before or after we make out?"

Bailey's pulse sprinted as if she were running a hundred-yard dash. "Very funny."

"You're smiling."

Was she?

He slid his arm around Bailey's shoulders.

His breath tickled her neck like a cat's whisker against her skin. *Speak up. Say something. Stand.*

But she couldn't. Because a part of her wanted to see what happened next.

Justin leaned forward.

She met him halfway, driven by a mix of curiosity and desire.

His lips touched hers. A spark flared, made her stiffen, but then the feel of his lips relaxed her, turning her into a mass of goo.

Heat, salt, wow. Justin's kiss tasted better than any she'd experienced or imagined. She arched against him.

His lips moved over hers.

Time stopped. Her brain short-circuited, not wanting to think but feel and enjoy. Her heart wanted more…wanted him.

He drew back. His gaze met hers. "Time for dessert."

Bailey's mind went straight to her bedroom. So. Not. Good. She looked away from him, touched her lips. The kiss was short, but hinted at...possibilities. "Why did you kiss me?"

"Because I wanted to. I've thought about kissing you since the first day we met."

"Even though I looked like a crazy clown?"

"You had your moments of normalcy. Though the clown look was a little endearing."

Her heart sighed. She needed to make it stop doing that.

"I'm glad I did." He smiled. "No regrets."

Her lips tingled from his kiss. She kept thinking how easy kissing him again would be. But she...couldn't.

The inn. The staff. Her family.

If she wasn't careful, this was going to erupt into a huge, tsunami-type mess. Cleanup could take years.

Bailey took a breath, then another. "Kiss me again and you'll have regrets. A lot of them."

He flinched, a surprised look on his face. "You didn't seem to mind when we were kissing. You seemed into it."

"Maybe I was. Now I'm not." Bailey swallowed around the lump in her throat. She had to get away from him. "Thanks for your help. But you need to leave. Now."

Before she changed her mind and kissed him and showed him what kind of dessert she'd prefer instead of brownies.

Seven days passed. Seven days Justin spent thinking about Bailey and her amazing kiss that made him want more. Seven days he looked for the stray mutt after finding out Animal Control had yet to catch the dog, so he'd have a reason to contact her. The damn dog must have worn an invisibility cloak because he hadn't seen a glimpse of dirty brown fur. Maybe Bailey had one, too. He hadn't seen or heard from her.

No texts, no calls, no meetings about the ownership of the inn or the dog.

His fault for kissing her, but he still had no regrets. Her

kiss had been both a surprise and electric. She'd met him halfway and her kissing him back had been a turn-on. Was that why she'd gotten so upset? Because she'd wanted the kiss as much as he had? Women had gotten mad over less. He guessed he would find out in a few minutes.

He parked his truck on the street in front of Lilah's stately, three-story Victorian that overlooked Haley's Bay. He glanced at the horizon to see the sun setting. The rhyme he'd learned from a fisherman in Depot Bay, Oregon about a red sky at night being a sailor's delight played through his mind. Tonight's red sky would please fishermen and boaters wanting to head out in the morning.

The invitation from Ida Mae to attend Bailey's Chardonnay and Canvas event at Lilah's house had come at the perfect time. Saying no had never crossed Justin's mind. He wanted a chance to see Bailey, to figure out why she'd gotten under his skin.

Colorful painted pots with blossoming flowers sat on the front steps. The bright color combination looked like Bailey's work.

This evening would be interesting. An artist, he wasn't. The only painting he'd done involved drywall. But to see Bailey, he'd happily pick up a brush and pretend to be Picasso for the next three hours.

A white swing hung on the left side of the porch, inviting visitors to sit and enjoy the view. He imagined Bailey out here, the breeze toying with the ends of her hair, her bare feet pushing the swing back and forth. He could almost smell her floral perfume.

A woman had never been on his mind the way Bailey was, not even his ex-wife. He and Taryn had met in college and become good friends. A romantic relationship had been the next step. After they married, they'd bought a bungalow in Lincoln City, but she soon tired of life in the small town on the Oregon coast with him away so much on job sites.

She wanted to move to Portland, where she'd grown up. He wanted to live near their company headquarters. Taryn decided to move without him. She hadn't cared about his job or anything except what she'd wanted. She'd filed for divorce shortly after that. Better off without her.

Justin stood on the welcome mat, stared at the word written in black script. Lilah and Ida Mae might want him here, but what about Bailey? A weird feeling settled in the pit of his stomach.

Sure, he was attracted to her, but he couldn't be distracted. He wanted life to return to normal, where his every thought didn't revolve around a pretty, copper-haired woman. He didn't want to be kept on his toes or have his emotions go from one extreme to another or be tempted to kiss her again. He liked being single and not having to explain himself to a woman.

He knocked.

The door opened. Lilah's white curls bounced. Her smile reached her twinkling blue eyes.

"You're here. Wonderful." She pulled him into the house. "I'm so happy Ida Mae invited you. We had a last-minute cancellation and she thought you'd be the perfect substitute. I hope you don't mind hanging with our garden club tonight painting flowers."

"Thanks for including me. I've been curious about Bailey's classes."

Lilah patted his arm. "You'll enjoy yourself."

Justin didn't need a PhD in human behavior to know grandmother-style matchmaking was afoot. Bailey had made him uncomfortable when she asked him to leave her home. His turn to do the same to her, but in a more fun way. "I'm ready to paint, though a mechanical pencil is more my tool of choice than a brush."

"You'll do fine. Bailey is an excellent teacher. She's

also a fantastic cook. Did you know she used to work in the kitchen at the inn?"

He thought Lilah might pull out Bailey's scrapbook next to show her winsome, braided, diaper-clad babyhood. He wouldn't mind. She was probably a cute, hard-nosed, in-your-face kid. "She told me, but mentioned something about being a better artist."

"Bailey's too modest. Have her cook you dinner. I promise you won't be disappointed with the meal she'll serve."

Subtlety wasn't the woman's strong point, just like her granddaughter. "I'm sure I would love it, but she shouldn't be standing in the kitchen while she heals."

"That's true. Tonight will be hard enough. But her brother Declan, one of the twins, dropped off a stool earlier for her to use."

Twins? Bailey had never mentioned she had twin siblings. But then again, he hadn't known her long. "She's lucky to have her family take such good care of her."

Lilah tsked. "Bailey is too independent to allow anyone to take care of her. Been that way since she was three and the twins, Camden and Declan, were born. But we help where Bailey allows. She's let us do a little more with her injury, which tells me how much her toe must hurt."

Justin wasn't surprised. Bailey's middle name could be self-reliance. He followed Lilah into a large room filled with long, rectangular tables holding easels, white plastic paint trays and brushes. A black apron hung over the back of each chair.

"A couple of my grandsons moved the furniture out earlier," Lilah said. "Good boys, though a tad on the wild side. They need to find good women to straighten them out."

Over toward the side of the room stood a group of white-haired women chatting, laughing and sipping wine. The average age appeared to be seventy-five, maybe eighty.

"Your garden club?" he asked.

Lilah beamed. "Friends since before you were born."

He didn't have many long-term friends. He'd grown up moving from town to town, as resorts were opened, never staying longer than two years in one place except when he went to college and then got married. Until he came to Haley's Bay and met the Cole family, his transient life these past few years hadn't seemed bad. After the divorce, he'd sold their house and rented a condo because he spent more of his time at job sites than at home. But now he wished he'd had…more.

"Chardonnay for the gentleman." Ida Mae handed him a wineglass. "So glad you could join us. Linda Ross had to cancel, and we didn't want her spot to go empty."

"Thanks for the invitation and the wine." Justin took a sip. He was a beer drinker—craft beer was his favorite— but this was tasty with a hint of oak and touch of vanilla. "I'm looking forward to tonight's class."

Especially seeing Bailey. He searched the crowd of women, but didn't see any copper ringlets. Maybe she was sitting…

"Justin?"

He turned toward the sound of Bailey's voice. His breath caught. She stood, as if a vision, in a maroon, ankle-length skirt, a slightly oversize T-shirt with colorful swirls and her hair pulled back in a loose braid. He hadn't conjured her in his imagination. She was real, standing in front of him within arm's reach.

"Hi." He forced a greeting from his dry throat.

Her gaze narrowed. "What are you doing here?"

Ida Mae raised her wineglass. "When I heard we had an open spot, I invited Justin. Much better than having him spend another night hunched over blueprints in his room. I want my guests to have fun while they stay at the B and B, not work all the time."

Justin fought a grimace. She made him sound like a

workaholic. "I'm new in town. Don't know a lot of people yet. And I have a lot of projects to finish."

Well, *start,* once they gained possession of the inn.

"Working is important, but you need to have fun, too. A good thing you have us to keep you company tonight." Lilah patted his arm. "Won't having Justin here be fun, Bailey?"

"Letting Linda's spot go empty would be a waste." Bailey sounded on edge. She dragged her teeth over her lower lip.

He remembered kissing those lips. "I've only painted on construction sites. I'll try not to be too much trouble."

"A man who looks like you has trouble written all over him," Ida Mae teased.

Lilah shooed her away, then looked at Bailey. "I'm going to check the appetizers and wine. Why don't you give Justin a quick intro about how tonight will work?"

Bailey watched her grandmother head to the food table. "I can't believe my great-aunt dragged you into my grandmother's scheme."

"Matchmaking?"

"Aunt Ida Mae is Grandma's partner-in-crime. Be glad my sister-in-law Risa isn't here or we'd be dealing with a trio instead of a duo."

He wanted to wipe the embarrassment from Bailey's eyes. Though he liked the cute blush on her cheeks. "Hey, no one dragged me. I'm curious about the painting class. Might be something to add to our guest offerings. And I'm honored your grandmother approves of me. Even if we both know nothing will happen between us with the inn's ownership at stake."

Relief filled Bailey's gaze. "You're really being nice about this."

Crap. Justin rocked back on his heels. Inn or not, he didn't want her to think of him as nice. Sexy, handsome, not nice. "How else would I be? I get a night where I'm the only man in a roomful of women."

"Into cougars?"

"These ladies might be considered lionesses."

"Word of warning." Bailey leaned toward him. Her warm breath against his neck made his pulse hiccup. "Don't let any of them hear you or they might attack."

He laughed, trying not to think about her lips so close to his ear. "I'll be careful. So, what's going to be happening during the class?"

She stepped back. "You want to do this?"

"I so want to do this, even if my painting will look like something a preschooler made. No laughing, okay?"

"Promise. Though am I allowed a giggle or two?"

The light in her eyes brightened her face. He wanted to snap a picture of her to capture the moment. She looked so happy.

"Three giggles," he said. "That's all."

"I can live with three."

He'd never understood people who danced without music, but he wanted to take her in his arms and swing her into a dip. He shook the crazy thought from his head, then noticed she wore an oversize sandal on her left foot. "You're wearing a shoe."

"Sort of. This one belongs to Grady. Never thought his big feet would come in handy, but they have this time. I can't wait to wear my own."

"You look great. Better than the last time."

"Thanks. My foot's healing." She glanced around the room, not meeting his gaze.

He wanted her to look at him. "Animal Control hasn't found that dog. They've had reports for a few weeks now."

Bailey's gaze met his. "Poor dog. I thought for sure he'd be in the shelter, maybe adopted by now."

"I've looked, but not seen him again." He took a quick

sip of his wine. "If I find him, I'll let you know. So tonight…"

"We socialize at the beginning. After that, everyone takes a seat. Each person has a canvas on an easel and supplies at a spot. Just follow the directions and at the end, you'll have a completed painting. We have dessert before heading home."

"Sounds easy."

"Painting is easy and fun." She glanced at the clock on the mantel. Her lips parted, making a perfect O. "I need to get the class started or we'll be here all night."

Spending all night with Bailey sounded good to Justin. He watched her cross the room, a sexy sway to her hips. If she was still limping, he didn't notice.

"Take your seats, everyone," she said. "Put on your aprons. It's time to begin."

Maybe after the class finished he could convince Bailey he needed private instruction. Not here, but back at her place, the two of them and a leftover bottle of Chardonnay and a few of the chocolate-dipped strawberries. Playful images filled his mind. He sipped the cool wine to keep his temperature from rising.

Would Bailey say yes? Or turn him down cold?

Wait a minute. He wasn't looking for romance. A relationship was the last thing he wanted.

Stop with all the r*-words.*

He downed the wine in his glass.

Focus.

He'd allowed himself to get worked up over Bailey because of not seeing her for a week. Now that he'd seen her…

No big deal, he told himself. All he had to do was concentrate on painting. Chat with the nice old ladies. Then he could return to his room at the B and B.

Alone.

Chapter Seven

"**R**eady to have fun tonight?" Bailey loved sharing her love of painting with people. These social art-and-wine events were a fun way to do that. She smiled at the eleven Garden Club members, women she'd known her entire life, sitting at the four rectangular tables her brothers had set up this afternoon.

Her gaze met Justin's. Held. His blue shirt brought out his eyes, deepened the color. Not quite cobalt…

Aunt Ida Mae coughed.

Oops. Bailey looked away. She hadn't expected to see him here. She'd been trying to forget about him, but the memory of his kiss lingered on her lips. She needed to focus.

"I've picked out a fun floral project." She lifted her sample from behind one of her supply bins and kept the painted side away from the guests. "I'll give you a clue what type of flower you'll be painting. Holland."

"Tulips," a woman named Sharon shouted.

"That's right." Bailey turned the canvas to show them her rendition of a Dutch-inspired landscape of a tulip field and optional wooden clogs in the front with a windmill. People would use her design to make their own. "This is what you'll be painting."

The Garden Club members oohed and aahed.

Justin peered around the canvas on his easel. "Wow. You did an amazing job."

Bailey ignored the urge to stand taller. His opinion didn't matter. But she wanted everyone, including him, to enjoy the project.

Mabel snickered. "Maybe you should think about becoming a painter instead of using your wrecking ball to destroy lives. My son worked the inn's front desk for thirty-three years. My granddaughter was a server there for five. Now they're on unemployment and trying to find new jobs."

Other women nodded or mumbled their agreement. Justin's smile no longer looked natural. Bailey wanted to say something, but she was supposed to be looking out for the inn, not comforting the man who wanted to destroy it. She clutched her canvas.

Aunt Ida Mae touched his shoulder. Her reassuring smile seemed to help Justin. The lines around his mouth relaxed.

Bailey needed to get these women painting ASAP. "Let's get started."

She instructed the class on sketching the design, then adding the first layer of paint. She discussed mixing colors, as well as techniques for loading brushes. She made her way to each table, watching first splashes of color appear on blank canvases. This was not a paint-by-numbers course. Here, creativity reigned.

"That's lovely, Faye." Bailey loved seeing how her friend, a sculptor, added texture with the paint. She moved on to the next person. "Great use of color, Mabel."

Getting around to each person wasn't easy with Bailey's injured foot, but she moved better today than this past weekend. Progress. She explained the next steps.

"Any questions on painting flower stems?" she asked.

Brushes in hand, the class set to work on their canvases, ignoring the full wineglasses sitting next to them. Plenty of time to socialize later.

Bailey returned to the three seated at the first table. She glimpsed the back of Justin's head, two rows in front of her.

Why was he here? Boredom? Maybe. Curiosity? She could see that. To annoy her? Most definitely. But a part of her—make that a small part—was happy to see him.

Bailey pointed to a flower on Darla Watson's canvas. "I like the shading you've done. If you use an even darker color along this edge, the flower will have more of a 3-D effect."

She continued on to the second table, then the third. Aunt Ida Mae sat next to Justin, no doubt trying to be her grandmother's ears and eyes during the painting class.

"Love the golden flowers, Aunt Ida Mae. Not maize, more like saffron. I also like the ochre shading with the pale yellow. The colors will match the breakfast room at your B and B."

"That's exactly where this one will go, dear." She worked on one of the stems. "Though I can't decide between a black and a white frame."

"I have some you can try and see which you like best." Bailey glanced at Justin's canvas, did a double take, gasped. She'd expected straight lines and a symmetrical design, given his architectural background. But this work of art brought a sense of wonder and awe. How could he have done this? Made her feel this way?

Her gaze traveled from the painting to Justin. "I thought you only painted walls."

He lowered his brush, stared up at her. The dazed look in his eyes spoke of being totally lost in his little world.

That was what she called being so into her work she forgot about everything else.

"Huh?" The surprise in his voice matched the confusion on his face. "I'm sorry. What did you say?"

Bailey recognized his clouded gaze and disorientation. She moved closer and gave him another minute. "You said you didn't paint."

"I don't. Unless you're talking construction." He used his brush to paint a pink tulip. "But I must admit, this is almost meditative. Stress-relieving."

"You know what you're doing," she said, trying to keep the emotion out of her voice. His painting affected her not only as a teacher, but an art lover. She didn't want to be impressed, but she couldn't help herself. Unlike other students, he'd used different colors for the flowers. No monochrome fields and rows. He painted the flowers with no pattern whatsoever.

He looked over his shoulder at her. "Thanks, but I'm using the trial-and-error method, one step above paint by numbers."

"Could have fooled me." She pointed to the top of his canvas. "I love how you used smoother strokes for the sky, then short, choppier ones that added texture to the tulip field. Your windmill is elaborate and realistic. Especially the perspective with the lattice-framework sails. They look like they'd spin off the canvas if I blew hard enough. You're a natural. I knew an architect could draw, but this..."

Okay, he'd talked about shabby chic that first day at her cottage. Justin knew who Anubis was, but he seemed more left-brain, a straight-lines-and-angles kind of guy.

"That's because I have a good teacher," he said.

"You have talent." Raw, sure, but that was part of the charm. His eye for color was first-rate. "The way you shadowed the flower stems is perfect. They look like they're blowing in the wind."

"Your directions were clear. I just added paint."

"There's nothing about art that involves just adding paint." Bailey peered over his shoulder, wanting a closer look. She touched his back, then realized what she was doing and stepped back. "I'd better see how everyone else is doing."

Walking away, she pretended not to notice Aunt Ida Mae staring at her with a can't-wait-to-see-what-happens smile. Grandma, too.

Bailey's stomach did a cartwheel. She'd given Justin attention for his painting, but the gray-haired matchmaking Mafia would exaggerate. Embellish. Embarrass.

This was part of being a Cole and living in Haley's Bay. For better or worse, her family cared. But how was she ever going to meet a guy, let alone date, with so many busybodies around? Not that she was interested in dating Justin. But if she were…

Grandma carried a bottle of Chardonnay and topped off people's glasses. "Want a refill on your wine, Bailey?"

She'd had a couple of sips to check the bottles when she'd opened them, but didn't drink while teaching. A good thing. She needed to be fully cognizant around Justin with her grandmother watching. Now that she saw his hidden talent, she was amazed and more attracted to him. "No, thanks. I'll stick to the sparkling cider."

"Sweet and bubbly." Aunt Ida Mae's lips spread into a curious smile. "You don't want to act silly or make googly eyes."

Her aunt spoke to Bailey as if she were fifteen and knew nothing about boys. Get a little wine in Aunt Ida Mae, and she was the one who got goofy. Bailey hoped Justin wasn't watching and couldn't hear.

She didn't dare glance his way. That would only play in to their shenanigans. She had never wanted a class to be finished early until tonight. "No worries about me doing either of those things."

"Too bad." Justin studied her as if she were a painting and he was analyzing the artist's usage of design and color. People looked at her all the time, and she'd been staring at him moments ago, but his appraisal bothered her. She shifted on the couch. Not wanting to care what he thought, but wishing she knew at the same time. "I was hoping to see some goofiness tonight."

Darn the man. He was playing along. She stuck her tongue out at him. "There you go."

Instead of waiting for a response, she headed toward the food table.

His laugh echoed behind her.

A ball of heat settled at the center of her chest and spread outward.

Don't say a word. Don't cause a scene.

She checked the desserts, plates and napkins. Sliced brownies, chocolate-covered strawberries and Snicker-doodle cookies filled a three-tiered serving dish. Leave it to Grandma to go overboard.

Bailey sensed Justin's presence behind her. Her nerve endings tingled with anticipation. Crazy, since the two were in a room with eleven other women.

She straightened the stack of napkins. No turning around or she might end up making googly eyes.

"I finished the painting." His voice rumbled over her, low and rich, delicious like the sweets on the table. "Earned my dessert."

"You did." She stepped to get out of his way, but he went in the same direction. She brushed against his chest. Fireworks exploded, surprising her with their intensity. She stumbled.

He placed his hands on her waist. "Be careful. Don't reinjure yourself."

Bailey nodded, not trusting her voice.

"I may have to try another," he said.

"Cookie?" she squeaked, aware of his hands touching her, even though she was standing fine now. Problem was, she didn't mind all that much. Everything she thought she knew about Justin McMillian was proving her wrong each time she saw him. His possessive touch ignited a flame deep in her belly. Her lips ached for another kiss. *Stop thinking about his kisses.* "There are plenty of cookies."

"I'm talking about another painting class."

"Oh." Being so close to him unsettled Bailey. At any moment, she might win the klutz-of-the-year award. Walking seemed hard around him. Sure, her foot made her clumsy, but her awareness of him made a simple task ten times harder. She didn't like that. "You should."

He let go of her waist, reached around her and snagged a Snickerdoodle. "Though I'm not going to turn down one of these."

His lips closed over the cookie. She watched him take a bite, wishing he was nibbling her.

What was wrong with her? Only a week had passed since he'd been at her cottage. Seeing him tonight was nothing, and no more kisses were on the horizon.

Talk to him about...his painting. Yeah, that would take her mind off his lips.

"Do you know where you're going to display your painting?" she asked.

"Probably my office. I'm there more than I'm home, unless I'm out in the field."

She took a cookie. Maybe the sugar would quench her craving for, well, him. "Must be hard being away from home so much."

"Part of the job."

"Your family..."

"We don't see much of each other because of work. Right

now Rainey is in Gold Beach on the southern Oregon coast redoing the interiors of a resort. My parents are at a property in Cannon Beach. Paige is holding down the fort in Lincoln City."

"Do you ever get together?"

"Not often. Everything in my family has always revolved around the business. Even when we were kids."

How sad. She couldn't imagine. "What about holidays and birthdays?"

"Sometimes, but holidays are big business when you're in the resort industry. Birthdays can be celebrated anytime."

She remembered having to work holidays at the inn, but she'd gotten off in time to attend her family's gathering here at Grandma's. "I forgot about that part."

"You'll remember quickly if you own an inn."

"I do own one. Well, half of one, for now."

"Funny, so do I. For now." His smoldering look sent her pulse into the stratosphere. "We have two choices. Remain serious or try silly."

Stay in control. "Silly is always more fun than serious. But the last time I made a fool of myself in front of a man, I was mistaken for a psychotic clown. That left horrible scars."

He brushed strands of hair from her face, and she almost swooned. "I don't see any."

"Internal scars, not external ones." She noticed women standing up. Her grandma said something to Aunt Ida Mae, pointed and smiled. That satisfied expression on her grandmother's face meant one thing—more matchmaking. "Dessert time."

"I'd better grab a brownie and get out of the ladies' way."

He did, then moved toward the tables with the easels. A part of Bailey wished he'd stayed, but then again, after Mabel's outburst, she didn't blame him for retreating.

Grandma came closer, leaned her head toward Bailey's and whispered, "Go talk to him."

"I just was talking to him."

"Not enough." Grandma placed a brownie in a napkin, then handed it to Bailey. "Give this to Justin. The way to a man's heart is through his stomach. Is he a good kisser?"

Bailey stared at her grandmother in disbelief. "That's not something I want to discuss."

"The night's still young, dear," Aunt Ida Maid said. "The two of you could have a lot of fun before the sun rises."

"Go for it," Faye encouraged. "If you can forget about the inn. If I were twenty years younger…make that forty."

The women laughed.

"Well, if you don't go over to him," Sharon said, "some of us will. He might like mature women."

"I'm game."

"Me, too."

Bailey wasn't going to say a word. She couldn't. Gossip would be raging in the morning, possibly by bedtime.

Brownie in hand, Bailey made a beeline for the other side of the room, wanting distance from everyone. She didn't need the Garden Club's advice about Justin. She didn't need to be pushed into talking to him. What she needed was chocolate.

She bit into the brownie.

This would have to do. For now.

Three hours later, Justin folded the legs of the last table. He and Bailey were the only ones still at Lilah's. No one had asked him to stay, but Bailey's pale face and the circles under her eyes bothered him. He wanted to make sure she didn't do any heavy lifting.

"Where do the tables go?" he asked.

"In the storage room, but Declan will be here in a few

minutes to help and then drive Bailey home." Lilah swept the hardwood floor. "It'll go faster with the two of you."

Declan, one of the brothers who would mess up Justin's face if he got too close to their sister.

"Should I be worried about meeting another one of your brothers?" he asked Bailey in a lighthearted tone, hoping he could squeeze a smile from her tired face.

She sat on the floor and packed away her supplies in two large plastic containers. She didn't look up at him. "Not if you behave yourself."

He had touched her at the dessert table. Having his hand around her waist felt natural. She hadn't seemed to mind. At least he hadn't kissed her, though he'd been tempted once. Maybe twice. Okay, a lot of times. But he knew better without an invitation.

"I always behave myself. But you might not agree with the behavior."

Bailey tilted her head toward Lilah, who seemed to be working extra hard sweeping imaginary crumbs. A not-now look followed.

The door opened, then closed. A twenty-something man wearing shorts, a ripped T-shirt and flip-flops entered the room. He looked like a modern-day pirate with a scruff of whiskers, shoulder-length dark hair and tattoos on his arms. He had green eyes like the other Cole siblings.

The guy gave Justin the once-over, didn't look impressed by what he saw. "You the resort guy who wants to tear down my sister's inn?"

That summed up the situation succinctly if you happened to be a Cole.

Bailey hung her head. "Declan…"

"I'm Justin McMillian, resort guy."

"Declan Cole, fishing guy and boxer." He didn't extend his arm. Must not be a shaking-hands type. "You an artist or do you just like hanging with older ladies…and my sister?"

"I'm not an artist. Architect." Justin kept his tone light. This guy didn't just talk tough. He was rough 'n' tumble and ready to fight, the kind of man you didn't mess with in a bar or anywhere. "Your aunt invited me. I'm staying at her B and B. But I must admit the Garden Club ladies are a fun bunch."

Declan cracked his knuckles. "And my sister?"

"An excellent artist and instructor."

Lilah stepped forward. "Justin's quite a painter, isn't he, Bailey?"

She looked up. "Yes, very talented. Surprised the hell out of me."

Lilah gasped.

Declan laughed.

Justin smiled. He could always count on Bailey being honest.

The front door opened. Grady or Ellis must be making an appearance. Justin looked at the doorway to see which brother had arrived. Tyler Cole entered. He wore dress slacks and a button-down shirt. No tie or jacket, but he looked as though he might have come straight from work in those clothes.

"Tyler." Lilah sounded surprised to see him. "What are you doing here?"

The lawyer rolled up his sleeves. "Thought I'd help move the furniture back in."

"Wonderful, wonderful." Lilah rubbed her hands together. She looked at her two grandsons. "Have you boys eaten?"

"No," Declan and Tyler said at the same time.

"I'll heat up dinner." With that, Lilah scurried from the room as if she were about to feed royalty.

Justin assumed that was how the woman saw her grandchildren. He loved seeing the family dynamic between the Coles. Ever since arriving in Haley's Bay, he hadn't felt like hired help, which was how his parents treated him and his sisters. Not only now, but when they'd been younger, too. What Justin wouldn't give for a family like Bailey's...

Tyler's gaze narrowed. He looked at Justin. "You decide to help out, too?"

The lawyer's less-than-curious tone suggested he knew Justin was going to be here. Those old ladies spread gossip faster than bees scattered pollen in the springtime. No wonder Bailey was so worried.

He wouldn't be deterred. "I attended the paint night, figured Lilah might need an extra hand moving tables. Didn't realize the Cole cavalry was riding in."

Bailey looked up from her storage. "The cavalry better be polite to the guests."

Her words didn't contain a warning, but a threat.

Hard-nosed and in your face, yes. But he liked that about Bailey.

Declan and Tyler exchanged a glance. Something was going on, but Justin didn't know what.

"Want to help me carry the tables to the storage room?" Declan asked him.

Justin picked up the one closest to him. "Lead the way."

Bailey stood. "I'll help."

"No," he and Declan said at the same time.

Justin motioned to Bailey. "Sit on the bar stool and relax. You've been on your feet too long."

Declan's chin jutted forward. He pointed to Justin. "Do what he says. Or you won't like the consequences."

Bailey's lips curved downward. She looked not only tired, but also fed up.

At least Justin might get out of here with his face intact. Spending an evening with Bailey and learning to paint was worth whatever happened to him. And his face.

He raised a table. "So, where do these go?"

* * *

Bailey put her paint tubes in the plastic supply box. Her foot hurt, so sitting on the floor was the best position for now. She'd caught a glimpse of Justin leaving the room from her peripheral vision. She hadn't wanted to look at him. Not when Declan seemed ready to pounce if Justin said the wrong word. And Tyler…

She glanced at him. "Why are you really here?"

Her cousin stood over her, casting a large shadow. "Mabel Sawyer called me. Told me McMillian was getting chummy with the other co-owner of the Broughton Inn. Thought I'd want to know."

"Did you?"

"Yes."

The one word spoke volumes. The kissing, the low-key flirting and her attraction to the man suddenly felt naughty and wrong.

"Why?" she asked.

"The inn."

"Tonight had nothing to do with the inn. Mabel is the one who mentioned it. And rather rudely, if you ask me."

"You shouldn't be around Justin without legal counsel present. That's me, in case you forgot."

"I know that."

Tyler kneeled. "You're an attractive woman, Bay. A guy like McMillian might try to take advantage of you. Put undue influence on you to gain possession of the inn."

Her cousin made her sound like an idiot. "I'm not some naive person, ready to be taken in by a scam artist from a developing country."

"I know that, but the last thing you want is an impropriety. You've got people counting on you. Any kind of conflict of interest is going to look bad."

"I didn't invite him tonight. That was Aunt Ida Mae and Grandma's doing."

"Matchmaking?"

Bailey nodded. "Single men between the ages of twenty-five and forty seem to be her target. Justin falls squarely in that range."

"I'll talk to Grandma, but you can't see Justin outside of any meetings I set up."

She rearranged the paint tubes in the box. "We haven't discussed the inn."

"Doesn't matter." Tyler's voice sharpened. "Got it?"

She nodded, even if her cousin's—make that her *lawyer*'s request—seemed harsh. She'd wanted distance from Justin. Looked as though she got her wish. So, why did she want another wish to come true instead?

Glong. Glong. D-ding-a-ting-glong.

The sound woke Bailey. She rubbed her eyes. The bells continued to chime. She needed to change her ring tone to something else.

Light filtered in around the window blinds. Bailey glanced at the clock—7:23 a.m. She yawned, stretching her arms over her head.

Better not be Tyler again telling her to stay away from Justin McMillian as if she were sixteen. Her cousin had loaded her art supplies and driven her home before anyone returned. She hadn't even said good-night to Grandma or to Justin.

Bailey's family needed to get out of her personal life, the conflict of interest about the inn aside.

She glanced at her cell phone on the nightstand. No name and an unfamiliar number. The 541 area code belonged to Oregon. "Hello."

"It's Justin."

Hearing his voice brought a smile to her face. Not a bad way to start her day. Except she shouldn't care if he called or be smiling when he did, at least according to Tyler. "How did you get my number?"

"An internet search on your Chardonnay and Canvas events. Sorry to call so early, but I might know where the stray dog has been hiding."

She sat. "Where?"

"The yard of an old deserted house on Bay Street."

"Mr. Potter's place. It's been deserted since he passed fifteen years ago. His son in Boise owns the house, but he hasn't been back to Haley's Bay since the funeral. The overgrowth could hide a family of five."

"Or a stray?" Justin asked.

"Definitely."

"When I was driving home from your grandmother's last night, I saw something—looked like the stray—dart into the yard. I stopped, but it was too dark to see anything."

"Last night is a long time from today when you're talking about a stray dog."

"I know." He hesitated. "I drove by this morning. I didn't see him, but it's worth taking a look."

She glanced at the clock again. "Have you called Animal Control?"

"They haven't had much luck, given all the sightings."

"So, are you going to give Animal Rescue a try?"

"Thinking about it."

She had to give him kudos, given his lack of dog experience. But she'd seen last night how much more there was to Justin McMillian. Still, she didn't want him to fail. For the dog's sake. "Need help?"

"That's why I'm calling. I've never had a pet. I know dogs bark and wag their tails and shouldn't be fed chocolate. I could use someone with dog knowledge."

Tyler's words about staying away from Justin echoed through Bailey's head. But an image of the dirty, skinny dog was there, too. Right next to one of Justin.

Focus on the dog. Who had probably taken off for somewhere else by now. She bit her lip. "When?"

"Ten minutes."

Not the answer she expected. She glanced down at her nightshirt, touched her tangled hair. But if there was any chance they could help the dog… "Sure. I'll be ready."

Bailey disconnected from the call. She thought about texting Tyler, but he would tell her not to go. Better to keep quiet and apologize later if someone happened to see her. She hoped no one did.

Crawling out of bed, she remembered her plan for today—painting. Oh, well…how long could catching a dog and going to the shelter take?

Chapter Eight

Eleven minutes later, Justin pulled into Bailey's driveway. He hadn't expected her to be ready, given that she sounded as though he'd woken her up, let alone waiting for him on her front step. Yet there she was. The woman continued to surprise him.

Bailey wore a pair of faded jeans that hugged her hips. The bottom of a blue shirt hung out of her green fleece jacket. Cute. Typical Northwest attire and perfect for being outside this morning. There was no heavy coastal fog, but the temperature was cooler than yesterday when he'd gone for a run in shorts and tennis shoes.

He jumped out to open the passenger door for her. "Good morning. I swung by the Java Cup. There's a coffee in the cab for you."

"Thanks."

Her lopsided ponytail bounced. She climbed into the truck. "I hope the dog didn't wander off again."

Her voice held a note of worry, but something else...anxiety. She sounded…impatient. He wanted to make her feel better, but a hug or another kiss seemed wrong right now.

He'd asked for her help. He didn't want to take advantage of her.

"Me, too." He climbed into the cab, backed the truck out of the driveway, caught a glimpse of Bailey biting her lip.

The gesture gave her up. He'd learned to read tells and Bailey was an open book. "Your foot okay?"

"Almost good as new." No relief over her recovery showed on her face. Only worry.

He drove toward the bay. "You look…stressed."

"I'll feel better once we get the dog."

The dog was a means to an end for Justin, a way of spending time with Bailey. Seeing her this morning was a great way to start his day. Maybe they could grab breakfast after they took care of the dog.

"There is something you should know." She picked up her coffee from the truck's drink holder. "Tyler told me not to see you without legal counsel present. That means him."

Justin tightened his fingers around the steering wheel.

"He's concerned about a conflict of interest and jeopardizing the inn," she added.

"Seems strange he didn't say this before."

"Mabel contacted him after the paint night."

"I remember Mabel."

Bailey flicked her fingernail against the cup's sleeve. "I'm sure you do."

"Mabel has a reason to be upset. I get that."

She looked at him. "You do?"

"Yeah. Usually by the time I start working on a place, time has passed. Employees are long gone. But jobs are difficult to find these days. No one wants to see loved ones out of work."

He sure didn't. But the longer the question of the inn's ownership dragged on, being fired by his parents seemed more likely. His mom and dad were the dream destroyers. Or would be when the pink slips got handed out.

Once the company was sold, Justin had no doubt his sisters would move to bigger cities with more job opportunities. Portland, Seattle, maybe San Francisco. He'd never see them or his parents, who wanted to spend their retirement traveling the globe. All would leave Lincoln City without a glance back, the way Taryn had left.

Not Justin. He might not have a hometown where he grew up, but he considered the entire coast home. He wasn't leaving. He'd find a way to keep his family together and show them work wasn't everything. Maybe they could be more like the Coles, watching Sunday football games and eating dinner.

If only they could locate Floyd Jeffries... But the man seemed to have disappeared. No sign of him, his shady girlfriend or the money. Private investigators were searching, and half-jokingly said the pair was probably on some tropical island sipping cocktails.

"Mabel shouldn't have run to Tyler like a tattletale."

"So I shouldn't call Tyler and tell him you're with me?"

Bailey tightened her ponytail. "This is about the stray dog, not the inn."

Yes, but her hunched shoulders weren't normal. Everything from her facial expression to her posture looked off. "I know your family means a lot to you. I don't want to make this harder on you. Let's agree not to mention the *I-N-N*, okay?"

"Sounds good." She took a sip of the coffee. "This hits the spot."

"I'm on my second cup." He'd needed more caffeine. He hadn't slept well. Too much thinking about Bailey and painting.

He parked his truck in front of 717 Bay Street. Weeds

and twenty-five-foot-tall overgrowth hid whatever house might be on the property. "Ready to go dog-hunting?"

Bailey placed her coffee back in the cup holder. She pulled two plastic baggies from her jacket pocket and handed one to Justin. "I watch Declan's dog, Chinook, when he goes out of town. I brought some of her treats for the stray."

Justin tucked the bag into his pocket. "I knew I called the right person."

"I'm guessing I was your only choice."

"There was Animal Control, but you're cuter."

She smiled, unbuckled her seat belt. "Cuter or not, don't know that we'll have better luck than them."

"They look for lots of animals. We only need to find one."

A twisted gate hung on one hinge barely attached to a dilapidated, fence post with its paint peeling. Two-thirds of the fence was cracked or missing. What once was lawn gave way to a jungle of huge shrubbery, a mix of green and brown, up to his neck.

"Can't imagine anyone wanting to live here," he said.

"Some animals don't have a choice. They have nowhere to go. Every day is a fight to find food to eat and survive. Chinook was a rescue dog living in a hoarder situation, but you'd never know it looking at her now."

By the time Justin rounded the truck to help Bailey from the cab, she was already at the gate. She gave a push.

The hinge creaked.

She jerked her hand away, looked at him. "I can't believe the gate didn't fall off."

"Failure looks imminent."

"The gate, yes. Too soon to know about the dog." Bailey stepped through, her feet tromping on weeds providing a strange backdrop, but she looked beautiful in the morning light. "Here we are. Two enemies blazing a trail like Lewis and Clark."

"I'd say we're more like frenemies."

"I can go with that."

She tripped on a root but caught herself before he could act. His smile faded at the missed chance to touch her.

"Be careful," he warned.

"I'm trying, but this place is a jungle." She headed toward the left. "If I remember correctly, the backyard is this way."

He eyed the two-foot-wide passage through the plants. If Bailey was game, so was he.

Halfway in, a wayward branch scratched his jacket. No rip, but a mark remained. Walking through the tall walls of weeds reminded him of the corn mazes at pumpkin patches, only this wasn't planned. "I hope the dog is here. Somewhere."

The gap narrowed ahead. Bailey walked sideways. "I remember a staircase that leads to the back deck. We can stand up there and look for him."

Justin followed her up the steps, enjoying the view from behind. This was his first time seeing her in jeans. He wouldn't mind trading places with the denim cupping her butt. Sexy and a turn-on.

She stood at a wooden rail. "The backyard is worse than the front, but maybe we can see the dog walking around."

He stopped next to her. A view of the bay greeted him.

"Wow." If the Broughton Inn had a million-dollar view, this one was worth double. Given the waterfront location, this property was a find. "I wonder why Mr. Potter's son hasn't sold his dad's old house."

"Wanting to buy up the entire town now?" Her voice sounded stiff, almost suspicious.

"Curious, that's all."

Justin's father had taught him to keep his hand hidden

from both friend and foe. The distance to the water and elevation of the bluff where the house sat was far enough to stave off high tide or storm surges. He estimated the lot size to be a quarter of the Broughton Inn, but the bay frontage more than compensated and a smaller rolling lawn could be added.

"Any sign of the dog?" she asked.

He'd forgotten their reason for coming. He scanned the yard. "No, but I'll take a closer look."

That would give him a chance to get a better feel of the slope to the shoreline. He wondered if he could find the exact dimensions of the lot on one of the town websites.

"I don't see the dog." Bailey sounded disappointed. "Here, puppy."

No dog appeared.

The breeze tossed the ends of her ponytail about. She shook her bag of dog treats. Nothing. She gave the bag another shake. No movement below. She whistled.

Bailey's gaze met his. "I don't think he's here."

"Look at the brush down there. If he's skittish…"

"I just wish we could find him." Her lips parted slightly, pink and soft and smooth.

He needed another taste of her, a longer one. "I wish…"

"What do you wish?" she asked.

He lowered his mouth to hers. Slowly. To give her time to decide if she wanted a kiss or not.

She didn't say no or back away. Justin took that as a yes.

He covered her mouth with his, the urge to kiss her stronger than common sense.

Her kiss was as sweet and as warm as he remembered, a tasty confection he wanted to devour. His lips moved over hers, but he kept his hands at his side. He'd made the first move. Twice now. He was leaving the next one up to Bailey.

This time she didn't stiffen, but leaned into him. Her muscles remained loose. She pressed against his lips, kissing him back. Her eagerness surprised. Now, this was a real turn-on.

Heat roared through his veins.

Her hands didn't touch him. Lips locked together, but nothing else.

He wasn't complaining. Her kiss was as spectacular as she was. Unique. Perfect.

She wrapped her arms around him finally. Her breasts pressed against his chest.

He circled his arms around her, pulling her closer. This was what he wanted. All he needed.

A moan escaped her lips. She backed away from him, her eyes clouded, her lips swollen.

"Kissing isn't going to help us find the dog." Her tone was stunned, amused.

He'd take it. "No, but consider the kiss a warm-up for our search."

"You think we needed one?"

He shrugged. "When it comes to you, I have no idea what we need."

She'd crashed into his life like a runaway train. Okay, she'd been standing there, unmovable, but he hadn't been the same since that morning at the inn.

Justin knew one thing…he was happy he'd kissed her again. "I do know this kiss was better than the first one. I can't wait to see how the next one turns out."

Bailey's mouth gaped. She was speechless, a memorable occurrence.

He bit back a smile. "I'm going to check down below. Care to join me?"

Join him? The man had some nerve. That was the last thing Bailey wanted to do. Her ragged breathing matched her rapid pulse. Cheeks burning, she didn't want to acknowledge how much she'd wanted to keep kissing Justin.

Her lips didn't tingle. They throbbed. Her body ached for more.

She clutched the deck railing, thankful the weathered wood was smooth beneath her palms, not full of splinters. Her skin felt hypersensitive as it was.

What had she done? And what was she going to do now?

Justin McMillian had kissed her again, unexpectedly and thoroughly, as if she were his to command with a touch of his lips. Worse, she had been willing, eager, hungry. Responding to him like a woman starved for kisses. She'd wanted to gobble him up. A part of her still did.

Stupid. Stupid. Stupid.

For all she knew, her reaction was exactly the response he wanted. Tyler's warning seemed more ominous post-kiss. Nothing good would come from spending time with Justin. Conflict of interest. Uh, yeah. Kissing was not exactly professional behavior. The inn's staff and their families were counting on her to win.

She needed to keep her distance from him and keep her guard up. He could be playing her. Why wouldn't he? A charming hotelier and construction hottie who oozed sex appeal must be good at that kind of game.

Thank goodness she'd remembered the dog or she might still be kissing him. And happily enjoying the kisses.

She tightened her grip on the railing. Her gaze narrowed on Justin heading down the stairs. He looked like a fashion model, handsome in his worn jeans, Henley shirt and flannel jacket. His boots were durable enough to withstand the weeds and rocks below. Handsome, check. Capable, check. Under control, check.

The opposite of her.

The urge to bolt was strong. So what if doing so would be rude? But she doubted she could walk home without doing some serious damage to her foot, and she had the dog to consider.

Justin waved from the bottom of the staircase. "I want to see if the dog is by the shoreline. Come on down if your foot's up to it."

Her foot was fine. Her heart, she wasn't sure.

Bailey gave him a half wave but didn't answer. Her nerve endings jangled as if they were dancing and wanted a new song.

He disappeared into the weeds.

She breathed a sigh of relief. A second kiss changed nothing. This was a spur-of-the-moment action brought on by worry over the dog. Once they found the stray or confirmed he wasn't here, she wouldn't see Justin until another meeting at Tyler's office or in a courtroom. That made the most logical—

"Bailey," Justin shouted. The way he said her name made her stomach drop. "I need your help."

His words rushed out.

Concern shot through her. She hurried down the staircase and followed his path, mindful of her foot. The mix of weeds and rocks and uneven ground made walking difficult, but she didn't slow down. "Justin?"

"Over here."

A moan.

The deep guttural noise prickled the hair on the back of her neck. "Are you okay?"

"I found the dog. He's stuck in some rocks. Hurt."

Oh, no. Picking up her pace, she followed the sound of Justin's voice talking to the dog until she found him, one knee on the ground. He steadied the dog's head with his hands. The scruffy dog lay next to him, barely moving, covered in mud and dirt and burrs. So thin. Her heart broke.

"I freed a leg that was caught between two rocks, but there's a bad gash on his back leg. He doesn't have much strength."

She kneeled and let the dog sniff her hand. "Hey, pup."

A lick was her reward.

"What a sweetie." She removed her jacket and covered the animal, careful to avoid the injured leg. "You're a nice doggy."

The dog's tail wagged.

"That's a good sign," she said. "How did you end up here?"

"No collar."

"A vet can check for a microchip. That's the easiest way to see if he has, or had, an owner."

Justin scratched behind the dog's ear. "You're going to be fine, buddy."

Bailey hoped so. She rubbed the dog's dirty face. "Some doggies don't like to go to the vet, but you look brave."

Justin looked over at her, an odd expression on his face. "You're good at this."

"I watch Chinook and babysit my niece and nephew." Bailey eyed the wound on the dog's injured leg. "We need to get to the vet now. You carry the dog. I'll call to let them know we're coming."

"Come here, buddy." He picked up the dog.

The stray yelped, a pathetic sound that physically hurt Bailey to hear; then a soft whine emerged, constant, but fading.

Justin cradled the dog as if he were a fragile, premature baby, only bigger and covered with fur.

His tenderness and concern melted her heart. Nothing solid remained, only a warm puddle. He might not have had a pet before, but he was kind and gentle and caring with the dog. She had a feeling he would be the same way with children.

With their children. Her pulse quickened. Everything she'd dreamed of having suddenly felt in reach. All because of this poor stray dog.

He continued to talk to the dog.

Cell phone in hand, she followed Justin to the stairs. "I'm calling Declan's vet. It's nearby."

The dog rested its head on Justin's arm. The whining had become quieter, not more than a whimper.

"Let's hurry." He speeded up. "The pup's not looking so good."

Bailey opened the door to the animal clinic. Justin carried in the dog. A gurney was waiting.

"What happened?" a scrub-clad vet tech asked.

"He's a stray. His paw was caught between rocks. There's a bad gash."

"We'll take a look." She pushed the gurney through a door that closed automatically behind her.

"I need some information about the dog," the receptionist behind the window said. "Name."

"Buddy," Justin said without any hesitation.

"You said the dog's a stray."

He whipped out his wallet and handed the woman a credit card. "As far as we know. Do what needs to be done with him. I'll cover all expenses."

Bailey whispered, "Vet bills can be expensive."

He smiled at her. "I can afford it."

Not only kind and nice, but also generous. Justin's actions warmed her heart. "That's very thoughtful of you."

The receptionist nodded. "Would you mind filling out this treatment authorization form?"

Justin did. Bailey went to sit. The smell of freshly brewed coffee filled the air in the waiting room, slightly masking a lemony-bleach scent. A television hung on the wall, a home-and-garden channel playing with the sound muted. Phones rang and doors opened and closed in the distance.

Bailey sat on an upholstered chair. The thin layer of

padding didn't offer much comfort, but she was in a better place than the dog.

And Justin.

For the next hour and a half, he paced the length of the waiting room, staring at the screen of his smartphone. He'd been checking missing pet websites trying to find info about "Buddy," the name he'd given the dog when they checked in. He'd also contacted Animal Control again, too, who had little information on the dog other than multiple sightings since spring.

The bell on the door sounded. A man entered the clinic with a black Lab on a leash.

Too bad Tyler wasn't here. If her cousin saw Justin in action today, he might change his mind about the guy trying to take advantage of her or exert "undue influence" to get the inn. Okay, she still had concerns. His being worried about a dog wasn't enough to make her dismiss all misgivings, but she liked this side of Justin. Liked it a lot.

He sat next to her. "No one has reported a lost or missing dog that looks like him."

"The vet should know soon if he's got a microchip."

An elderly couple with a meowing cat in a pink carrier checked out at the receptionist counter.

"They're taking a long time. I hope he's okay." Justin stared at the door to the exam area. Lines on his forehead deepened. "I thought we'd hear something by now."

The worry in his voice tugged on Bailey's heart. She reached toward him, then pulled her arm back, resting her hand on her lap.

Yes, she wanted to comfort him, but she was unsure if that was okay or crossing a line or giving him the wrong idea. Boy, that second kiss was messing up her thought process. "We should hear something soon."

Justin rubbed his lips together. "I've never been to a vet office before."

"Tests and X-rays take time. Just like with people," she said. "I'm sure they want to be thorough with the exam and not jump to any conclusions. He looks like he's been on his own for a while."

"Makes sense." He stared at the closed door leading to the exam rooms. "But I wish I could do more."

"You found him. You're paying for his medical treatment. You're doing plenty." Her words didn't change the serious expression on Justin's face. Bailey wished she could bring back his smile. "And this is an excellent vet clinic."

"I knew you'd pick the right place."

She straightened. His words meant more than they should. "Want another cup of coffee?"

"No, thanks."

"The Burger Boat is across the street. I can get sodas or milk shakes."

"Appreciate the offer, but I'm not thirsty." His gaze returned to the closed door. "Buddy's paw didn't look that bad. All he needs is a bath and a few good meals to put some meat on his bones. He'll be fine."

She recognized something in Justin's tone. Years ago, she'd sounded the same way after finding a baby bunny in the field by their house. She'd waited for hours for the mother rabbit to return, but that never happened. She'd begged her parents to let her bring the young bunny home. Instead her father took the bunny to a nearby farm, saying their house was already too much of a zoo. He'd never told her where. She'd cried for days. "You seemed to hit it off with Buddy."

"Yeah, it's weird." The edges of his mouth curved slightly. "I hadn't considered getting a dog. But Buddy's all I can think about. Crazy?"

"Yes, but I'm all for crazy."

His mouth swooped down for a quick kiss. "Figured you would understand."

She was the one smiling now. "I do, but if you're serious, you need to take some time and think about it. Adopting a dog isn't something you do lightly or temporarily. Dogs get attached. They can be expensive and need attention. You'll need to figure out what to do with him when you're at a job site. Or here in Haley's Bay. My aunt doesn't allow pets at her B and B. So there are logistics you'll need to work out. If you're not committed—"

"I am." A surprised expression flashed across his face. "I can't believe I said that."

"Why not?"

"I haven't committed to anything in a long time. But that mangy mutt…"

"Stole your heart."

His gaze met hers. "Yes."

Her heart melted. "Everything happens for a reason. That's what my grandma always says."

Bailey expected him to look away. He didn't.

"This feels…right," Justin continued.

Being with him felt that way. She kissed him. He tasted the same as he had before—delicious, one minute some fresh-from-the-oven baked goods, then a gourmet entrée the next. His warmth seeped into her as if she was home, comfortable and warm, wrapped in a bed of handmade quilts.

His lips took hers, awakening something deep within, a longing for…more. He brought his arm around her back. A fire ignited low in her belly. A wanting heat. She leaned into him to get closer.

A ding sounded. The clinic's door.

Bailey jerked away, nearly falling off her chair, but Justin caught her. A blue carrier was being brought inside. A cat meowed. Next came…

Risa. Her sister-in-law.

No. No. No. Bailey slid down in her chair, wishing the

door to the restroom wasn't next to the receptionist's desk where Risa stood.

"What's wrong?" Justin asked.

Bailey placed her finger at her mouth. "Shh."

By dinnertime, every single Cole, including Tyler and AJ, would know…whatever Risa had seen when she entered the clinic. Bailey didn't want to make this worse.

Risa turned. Her gaze met Bailey's. "What are you doing here?"

"Found an injured dog over on Bay Street." She didn't like the way Risa studied Justin, as if he were on display in a department-store window. "How about you?"

"Annual exam for Skippy." Risa gave Justin another once-over. "Who's your friend?"

He stood and approached her. "I'm Justin McMillian."

Risa looked impressed. "McMillian Resorts?"

Justin nodded, shook her hand.

"I'm Risa Cole. Bailey's sister-in-law."

"She's married to Ellis," Bailey said in case he didn't remember.

"I met your husband last week," Justin said. "He's a lucky guy."

Risa grinned as if she'd won a year's worth of mani-pedis at the nail salon. "Why, thank you. Grandmother Cole was right when she said you were sweet as her graham-cracker pie."

Great. Bailey leaned back. Her head hit the wall. The result—a dull ache.

He was at her side in an instant and touched her shoulder. "You okay?"

"That's Bailey for you. Always acting without thinking." Risa's attention hadn't left Justin, nor had she missed him touching Bailey. "So you're here for the Broughton Inn?"

"I am." He tilted his head toward Bailey. "Except your sister-in-law is trying to get in the way."

Bailey raised her chin. "And I have succeeded."

"For now." His wink caught her off guard.

"Bailey, like all of the Coles, tends to see things from only one side. They'll fight you to the end whether they're right or wrong."

"When have I been wrong?" Bailey asked.

Risa and Justin shared a glance and a smile.

A vet tech called Skippy's name. Risa headed toward the door. She glanced back. "I'll be wanting to talk to you later. Don't do anything I wouldn't do."

The door shut. A call from her mom should be coming in, oh, five or six minutes, followed by one from Grandma.

Laughter gleamed in Justin's eyes. "So that's your grandmother's matchmaking apprentice? Guess I should expect a call for dinner soon?"

His words brought a much-needed smile to Bailey's face.

"Risa is as subtle as your grandmother and great-aunt," he continued. "I was waiting for her to ask my height, weight, IQ and yearly income."

Bailey grimaced. "My family is insane. The women set me up, and the men scare the guys away."

"Does your sister fix people up?"

"No way. Camden's not interested in having a relationship at all. All she cares about is fishing."

"So then it's not the Coles who like setting people up, but the ones who marry into the family."

"I hope that means I'll never become one of them. But related by blood or not, they are family, and I'm stuck with them."

"They care about you."

"In a nosy-I-know-what's-best-for-you way." She thought about kissing him. A flush of heat went up her neck. "Do you think Risa saw us...?"

"No. Only the cat. So unless Skippy can talk or was wearing a GoPro camera to film a cat's view of a vet visit and be the next YouTube sensation, we're safe. Unless you want to kiss me again."

"No way. Not with Risa here. I already know she's going to tell my family I was here with you."

"Could be some major fallout."

"Grandma and Aunt Ida Mae will be happy."

"Don't forget Tyler."

Bailey had. "Oh, no. He's going to flip."

This was not going to be good. For her. She looked at Justin. Or for him.

Chapter Nine

Justin had paced the animal clinic's waiting room so many times he knew the length and width and had a pretty good guestimate of the height. Bailey sat on one of the uncomfortable chairs, a worried expression on her face.

Buddy? Her family? A combination?

All Justin knew was his relief at having Bailey here with him to wait, to hold his hand, to kiss him. If not for Bailey and her family, he doubted he would want to adopt a dog.

Hell, he wasn't even sure what he was going to do with Buddy. But if no owner claimed him and he recovered from whatever they'd spent hours working on him in the back, Justin wanted him.

A forever home. That was what Bailey had called it.

He could do that.

Maybe Buddy would give new meaning to the word "home," too.

A blonde who looked to be in her early thirties and wore

green surgical scrubs entered the waiting room through one of the doors. She carried a clipboard.

"I'm Dr. Nora Hayworth." She had bright green eyes. "You brought in Buddy?"

"Yes." Justin stood and helped Bailey up, not that she needed his assistance, then introduced them. "How is he doing?"

"For what he's likely gone through, he's holding his own. We didn't find a microchip, and Buddy's unaltered."

"Unaltered?" Justin asked.

"Buddy hasn't been neutered. Most owners spay or neuter their animals, which means he's likely abandoned or always been a stray." The vet ran down her notes. "We've cleaned him, run blood tests and taken X-rays. His leg isn't broken, but his wound is infected. He's also underweight and dehydrated. We've given him subcutaneous fluids. Once he's more stable and closer to a proper weight, we can discuss vaccines, heartworm medicine and flea treatment, since we don't have any medical history on him."

Justin's tension lessened. "Whatever he needs."

"So Buddy needs to stay overnight?" Bailey asked.

"Yes, he's been on his own for a long time. Possibly since birth. We can make sure he's hydrated and eating. Small meals are best for now. He's also going to need to wear a cone so his wound can heal properly."

All in all, that didn't sound too bad to Justin. "So, what do I need to do?"

The vet looked at her paperwork. "We can call Animal Control—"

"No," he said quickly. "If the dog doesn't have an owner, I want him."

"Justin's interested in adopting Buddy," Bailey said. "Is there anything about Buddy's personality that he should be aware of?"

"Not that I've seen so far," Dr. Hayworth said. "Buddy's

quite friendly and wants to play. He isn't that old. Based on his teeth, approximately nine months old. Still a puppy. Likes other dogs and cats and gets along well with the vet techs. His behavior indicates a good disposition."

Justin felt as if Buddy had brought home a report card full of A's. "That's what I wanted to hear, Doc."

Bailey nodded. "I wish we knew how he ended up alone and injured."

"Sometimes people don't understand the responsibilities that go with pet ownership. Puppies are cute, but more work than some realize. Or a person picks the wrong breed for their lifestyle. That leads to dogs being given away, dumped or surrendered at shelters. Other times a dog will escape or get lost. Often a stray will have a litter of puppies." Dr. Hayworth looked at her notes again. "Any other questions?"

"None from me." Justin looked at Bailey. "Do you have any?"

"Nope."

He laced his fingers with Bailey's and squeezed. "We're good for now. Thank you."

"Always a pleasure to see a happy ending. You're more than welcome to visit him each day he's here. If there's a change in his condition, we'll contact you. Make sure reception has your number." Dr. Hayworth left the waiting room.

Justin released a loud breath and Bailey's hand. "Sounds like Buddy's going to be okay."

"Great news." Her grin made him feel warm, as if he were still touching her. "Looks like you're a doggy daddy. Congrats."

"I'm going to have to go shopping."

"You have a couple of days."

"Right, but I need to find a place to stay that allows dogs."

"Buddy can stay at my place while you're in town."

Justin straightened. "What about Tyler?"

"This isn't about the inn. Though I'm sure he won't be happy." She tilted his head. "I'll go out when you visit him. That should solve any conflict-of-interest problems."

"I'll want to spend a lot of time with him." Justin would like to spend more time with her, too. "I don't want Tyler to be upset at you."

"I love dog-sitting. This will be fun for me. And that's what I'll tell my cousin."

"Thanks so much." Justin's smile spread across his face. "That'll be better for Buddy than boarding him until I go back to Lincoln City. Especially given his condition. You're the best."

"You are, for giving Buddy a home."

"I need a book on being a dog owner."

"Lots are out there."

He put his arm around her. "Plus, I have you."

Each day, Buddy got stronger, put on weight, healed. Thanks to help from Bonnie, the clinic's receptionist, Bailey timed her visits to avoid Justin. That was the only way to keep Tyler's wrath, Grandma's innuendos and her family's curiosity at bay. Even her mother was asking questions.

After Risa told the entire family at Sunday dinner about seeing Bailey with Justin at the animal clinic, Tyler had given her two more lectures. Not nice ones.

But Bailey had no regrets.

Buddy would be coming to her house soon. No one in her family would know that, a secret she wanted to keep. She crossed her fingers.

Bailey entered the waiting room from the back of the clinic and waved goodbye to Bonnie. "Thanks for the text about when to come in."

"I'll do the same tomorrow." The woman smiled warmly. "Though I don't know how much longer he'll be here."

"I'm getting my house ready." That meant dog-proofing

her cottage and trying to get all paintings done ASAP. She needed to put away her art supplies with a dog—make that a puppy—running around the house. No way would she chance Buddy getting into something toxic. "I can't wait."

"Or maybe you can't wait for Buddy's owner to pay a visit to your house."

Her cheeks felt warm. She recognized the flush of heat and hoped her face wasn't too red. "I'm sure Justin will want to see his boy."

"No doubt. He's here three times a day."

"I had no idea." But Bailey wasn't surprised. Even though she hadn't seen him in a couple of days, she'd picked up bits and pieces of what he'd been doing from people around town. Though she wondered why they thought she cared.

Okay, she did. A little.

The clinic door jingled. "Bailey."

A chill ran through her. Justin had arrived.

She faced him. "Hey. I was just visiting Buddy."

Justin's brow furrowed. "How is he today?"

"His leg is healing." She jiggled the zipper on her purse. "He's putting on weight, too. Handsome guy."

"Takes after his dad."

"Yes, he does." The words popped from her mouth like a champagne cork. *Oh, no.* Had she said that aloud?

His smug smile was proof she had. Great.

He moved toward Bailey, causing her to take two steps back until she bumped into a counter.

He placed a hand on either side of her. "You're…interesting."

She leaned back, afraid if she moved forward, he would kiss her. Or maybe she would kiss him. Not good with Bonnie watching them. "That's like saying I have a good personality."

"You do."

"Funny."

"Come on, I'm kidding." He leaned close enough that she could feel his warmth and smell the scent of his after-shave. "What I mean is you're passionate about what you do, yet have a practical streak at the same time."

She raised her chin, a satisfied feeling settling in the center of her chest. "Not many folks around here call me practical."

"It's true." He lowered his voice. "Got plans tonight?"

"What do you have in mind?" Oops. Her answer should have been yes, she had plans. She wasn't looking for a date.

"Takeout, then head over to the south point to eat."

"Hiding from the crowds."

"I'm not suggesting that for me."

Okay, more proof he was a good guy. He was aware of her family and others who might see them together. She should still say no. That was what Tyler would want her to do. Except she wanted to say yes. "Sure. Sounds good."

An act of rebellion or one of attraction? She had no idea, but Bailey wanted to spend more time with Justin.

"Burger Boat or Ying's Chinese?" he asked.

Dinner sounded like a real date, and that appealed to her. "Ying's. I feel like some orange chicken."

And she was curious to see what her fortune cookie said. Her life sure hadn't been the same since Justin came to town.

The sun dipped toward the horizon, and an evening breeze traveled over the water. Justin sat on the south end of Haley's Bay. Summer meant extended daylight. He wanted to make the most of this time with Bailey.

She sat on a rock, finishing up her dinner. "Did you get enough to eat?"

"Plenty. Egg rolls are one of my favorites. Good choice."

"I like Chinese food."

Another thing they had in common. "Me, too."

He only wished the Broughton Inn wasn't the biggest thing they shared. He stared at the buildings along the waterfront.

The quaint town of Haley's Bay was growing on him. He glimpsed the facade of the Candy Cove, lit up with white bulb lights. He couldn't decide if the peanut-butter fudge or the saltwater taffy was his favorite.

"You're quiet," she said.

"Long day. One full of surprises."

"That seems to be most of my days." Her gaze focused on the marina, making him wonder what artistic image her creative brain was conjuring.

"Come here often?" he asked.

She nodded. "Can't beat the views. It's a fun place to hike, too."

The wind teased her hair, but she didn't try to smooth or fix the blowing strands. Her casual, careless beauty appealed to him, but he also appreciated her sharp mind and caring heart. Three things that made him want more kisses. "You're a hiker?"

She wiped her mouth with a napkin. "Hiking is the closest thing I do to a sport, much to the chagrin of my athletic family. Though I enjoy watching the Olympics."

He laughed. "That'll keep you in shape."

"I stand for the National Anthem and jog to the kitchen for snacks during commercials," she joked. "Seriously if I don't keep myself busy, I morph into a couch potato. I'm trying to cut back on sugar, eat healthier. If not for good genes and a fast metabolism, I'd be in trouble. Unlike you. Let me guess. Runner?"

He nodded. "Triathlons."

"My brother Flynn does those."

"He's the one in the navy."

She nodded. "Swimming, biking and running on the

same day seems like torture to me, but he enjoys the challenge. You must, too."

"Nothing like it. Challenging and rewarding."

"I'll take your word on that." One corner of her mouth rose in a sideward smile. "My idea of a triathlon is parking my car in a compact spot, walking into the ice cream parlor and eating a Scoop-a-licious Super Sundae with two cherries on top. Of course, I'd need to be rolled back to my car afterward, so maybe I should call that a quadrathlon."

She really was something. He took a step toward her. "I've done those, too, with an added kayak, but I like your kind better. More fun and tastier. You're a unique woman, Bailey Cole. You start artist co-op galleries. Save old buildings. Babysit your niece and nephew. Take in other people's animals. What else do you do for yourself besides hiking and quadrathlons?"

"I paint," she said without any hesitation.

"That's your job."

"It's what I love to do." She glowed with an enviable look of contentment. "I'm fortunate to earn my living doing what I enjoy. Or will again, once my foot isn't holding me back."

"Wouldn't a couch potato sit when she paints?"

"You'd think so, right?" Bailey joked. "I sit when I'm working on smaller projects, but my current piece is too large, so I was standing before I got hurt. Declan brought over a stool. I tried sitting, but that affected my process. I need to keep moving and circling to bring the piece alive and see the various angles and lighting." Her cheek turned pink. "Sorry, I get talking about painting…"

"Don't apologize. I like hearing about your work."

The creative process—especially hearing about hers—fascinated Justin, reminding him of the times he'd designed outside-the-box prototypes. Those were his favorite projects, but they were rare. Some of his best work had never been approved by his parents or built.

Maybe he could do something on his own. It seemed a waste to not do anything with those designs.

Her smile spread to her eyes. "That's because you're thinking about your own process."

"Didn't know I had one."

"Maybe not consciously, but the interest has been sparked."

"Maybe."

"Definitely," she countered. "How does your painting look in your room at the B and B?"

"Very nice. Still can't believe I painted it."

"That's what's so fun about the Canvas and Chardonnay classes. People discover a hidden talent once a paintbrush is in their hand." She stared across the water. "The sun's starting to set. This was a good idea. No one around to bother us."

He'd also gotten a good view of the backside of the Potter property. But Justin didn't want to tell Bailey that. He didn't want business to be part of their…whatever this was. He might have considered trying to charm her out of the inn, but that was before. Before getting to know her better. Before kissing her. Before having her offer to take in his dog. Now he wanted only to spend time with her.

"We needed to celebrate," he said.

"What are we celebrating?"

"Buddy put on more weight. He should be released in a day or two."

"That's awesome."

"You sound happy."

"I am." Her grin lit up her face. "I can't wait for my surrogate doggy to come home."

"Won't be long until he's there. Though you'll have to put up with my visits."

She met his gaze, then looked down at the rock. Her face flushed.

Adorable.

"So, what do you think of this view?" she asked, changing the subject. He'd let her. It was either that or kissing her. On second thought...

He focused on the overgrowth and junkyard disorder of the Potter property.

"I—" Ideas exploded in his head. The structure, the landscape, a dock, everything. His fingers itched for a pencil and paper so he could sketch the designs running through his mind like a slide show. A smaller inn or B and B. Not one to match the Broughton Inn, but to stand alone and complement those plans.

Oh, hell. He looked from the lot to Bailey.

"What?" she asked.

Guilt coated Justin's mouth, the taste bitter compared to Bailey's sweet kisses. His design for the new Broughton Inn was one of his favorites, and if he added the Potter place to the mix, he had both a first and a second place for his best designs.

Forget kissing her again. That wouldn't be a good idea if he wanted to go after both properties.

She smiled at him. "You had an idea. For a painting?"

The hope in her voice stabbed Justin like a dagger.

Damn. She had no clue what he was thinking about doing. He didn't dare tell her. She might not understand. For all he knew, Potter's son would say no to him. "I was thinking about the inn."

She pursed her lips. "It's never far from my mind. The people who count on the inn for their livelihoods need jobs."

Justin picked up a stone and tossed it into the Columbia River. "You think about everyone but yourself."

"That's not true. I want the Broughton Inn for a consignment gallery. There's also the historical piece, the preservation and the beauty aspects."

He didn't agree with using the word *beauty* to describe

the inn, but he knew she didn't see the place as he did. "You've mentioned that, but those things can be preserved with pictures, special displays and placards."

Her nose scrunched. "You mean like a museum?"

"The Hotel del Coronado near San Diego, California, has a section that documents its history."

She thought for a moment. A wistful expression formed. "The inn has meaning beyond history books and architectural value for my family. My grandparents were married at the Broughton Inn. My parents went to their senior prom together there."

"Those memories will always remain."

Bailey started to say something, then stopped herself. "What about making new memories? Ones to add to the old?"

"Does the actual building matter? If not, people can still remember their experiences there and enjoy a new inn."

He waited for her to respond.

Finally she shrugged.

"It's clear the inn has special meaning for you and your family, but let me ask you this," he said. "Will owning the inn hold the same kind of passion you have for painting, or will it turn into an obligation you must uphold?"

Justin knew the question might not be easy to answer. He'd felt that way himself on occasion, wondering if there was more to life than building resorts and hotels so other people could relax. He didn't want Bailey to experience the same frustration when creating works of art made her happy.

"I don't know, but I'm willing to try." A faraway look filled her eyes. "Owning the inn is good for those around me."

"That's noble. I mean that in the most sincere way, but consider what you're taking on."

She raised her chin, giving him that stubborn look he'd

grown to know and not mind so much now. "I worked there for years. I know what's involved."

"As an employee, yes, but not as the boss signing paychecks. Details like payroll, insurance, benefits, profits and losses weigh on you, become a burden," he explained. "You care about people. Leaving their problems when you walk out the door will be difficult. If you can leave them at all. There's not much time to take a day off or go on vacation. Family gatherings and celebrations might have to wait."

"That does sound boring."

Taryn had said the same thing over and over again, but he thought she'd grow to understand what his job entailed and how the resorts were part of his family. But she could never understand why he needed to work so many hours and be away so much. She got angry when he brought work home. Would Bailey be the same?

Stop. He was getting off track. What Bailey thought about his company's business wasn't relevant to the discussion.

But an idea popped into his head, one that might solve both their problems. "What if McMillian Resorts offered to hire back the laid-off employees and maintain contracts with vendors?"

She pressed her lips together. "I didn't think we were going to discuss the inn after what Tyler said."

They shouldn't. Justin understood what the lawyers meant about conflict of interest. "Hypothetically."

"Hypothetically, I might be open to that if you preserved the original building. I've had time to think about the various additions. Much of those are dated and uninspiring, lacking historical significance or architectural detail. But the original portion is worth saving. You were wrong to include that in your teardown."

Another surprise. Maybe she wasn't as stubborn as everyone thought, if she could admit he was right about something and compromise. That kind of renovation didn't fit McMillian's business model. But he hadn't planned on adopting a dog or kissing Bailey, either. "Anything is possible. Hypothetically."

His thoughts flip-flopped between Bailey and the Potter place. She was a jewel with faceted edges and a brilliance that drew his eye time and time again. The lot across the bay was a rough stone with potential. He imagined everything—weeds, plants, house—bulldozed from the lot, leaving a clean slate, a blank canvas, to create something stunning that would take advantage of the location and views.

Would she object to that teardown, as well? The place was old and in disarray. Would she see reason? Would she ever see that new was not only easier and more comfortable, but *more* beautiful? Or would she be disappointed in his lack of vision and slam the door on them being friends or something more?

Justin wasn't ready to find out the answer.

He needed to get her home and stop talking about the inn before he did or said something he would regret.

Chapter Ten

The next morning, a knock sounded at Bailey's front door. She glanced at the clock on the microwave—nine o'clock—and wiped her wet hands with a dish towel. She wasn't expecting visitors, but that never stopped her family from dropping by. Calling wasn't in the Cole DNA. At least she'd changed out of her pajamas. Not that her ratty green sweatpants and ripped gray hoodie were much of an improvement.

She trudged from the kitchen. The traction on the bottom of her fuzzy socks kept her from slipping. She yawned, tired from dog-proofing the house and a sleepless night thinking about Justin. He hadn't kissed her when he dropped her off after dinner. He'd simply walked her to the door and said he'd see her tomorrow.

No biggie, she'd told herself. Just like the kisses. The only things she and Justin would have to discuss in the future would be Buddy and the inn. But she couldn't help from feeling a tad…disappointed.

Another knock.

"I'm on my way." She opened the door.

Justin greeted her with a smile. "You should keep your door locked."

"I, um…" Seeing him left her tongue-tied. She hadn't expected him to stop by this early. "What's the word on Buddy?"

"I might be able to pick him up tomorrow. Want to go dog supply shopping? I'm not sure what he needs."

The request was what a friend would ask, except they weren't friends. She wasn't sure what they were. Part of her wanted to spend more time with Justin. The other part kept thinking about what Tyler had said. She could write him a list of supplies, but that didn't feel right, either.

Bailey touched her hair, realizing she'd twisted the strands into a messy bun held in place by a paintbrush. She remembered what she was wearing. "I'm not dressed to go out."

"You look fine."

So said the man in the khaki pants and cornflower-blue polo shirt that did amazing things to his eyes and funny things to her insides. The guy looked good no matter what he wore. Unlike her.

But she supposed clean sweats were a step up from smelly, dirty coveralls. This was how she dressed when cleaning or doing yard work, and that was what she planned to do today, so why was she worrying about her clothes? Shopping at a pet store wasn't a date. "Okay. Let me grab my purse and a pair of shoes."

"Fuzzy ones?"

"Excuse me?"

"You like to wear fuzzy things on your feet. Socks, slippers, shoes."

"I hadn't noticed." Bailey was surprised he had. She thought about her choice of footwear. Interesting. He was correct. "But why wear boring socks and shoes when you can wear fun on your feet?"

His grin gave her chills, the good kind. "Until coming to Haley's Bay I've had a fun deficit. I've been sketching some landscapes. Being here is good for me."

"Buddy will give you the perfect reason to have more fun." She opened the door wider. "Come in. I won't be long."

She retreated to her bedroom, rubbing her hands over her arms. Chills were not a good response to having fun with Justin. Maybe she should start a list for herself—no throbbing lips, no chills, no kisses.

Even though kisses weren't on the agenda, she brushed her teeth—for general hygiene's sake—put on shoes, the nonfuzzy kind, and grabbed her purse. "I'm ready."

He stood in the empty dining room. "What happened to the drop cloths and your painting?"

The guy was more observant than she realized. "I put them away."

"Your foot is healing. You'll be able to stand and paint in no time."

"True, but I didn't want to take any chances with Buddy here."

Brow furrowed, he studied the empty dining room. His lips parted. "You put away the painting and supplies because of my dog."

She nodded, noticing a cloudy area that had been covered by the tarp. Something must have soaked through to the floor. She would have to see if denatured alcohol would repair the damage.

After Buddy left with Justin. Whenever that might be.

"Why?" he asked.

"Paints and brush cleaners are toxic. Didn't want to take a chance of Buddy getting into something he shouldn't," she explained. "I have so many other projects I can do while he's here, things that won't hurt him if he's the curious type."

"Thank you."

The sincerity in the two words made breathing difficult. The connection she'd felt when he held her hand at the vet clinic returned. Her every nerve ending went on high alert. Her lips tingled in anticipation. She forced the words "you're welcome" from her tight throat.

He reached for her.

Bailey wanted him to touch her, to kiss her, more than anything, but she knew that wasn't smart. She backed away, adjusted the strap on her purse. "There are two pet stores in the area. One in Astoria, the other in Long Beach."

"No rush." He held up his hand. "We have time."

"I know, but remember what Tyler said."

A sheepish expression flashed across Justin's face. "We're seeing each other because of Buddy."

"That doesn't mean we have to…"

He gave her a look.

Was he going to make her say the word? She waited. He kept staring at her. Fine. She would say it if he wouldn't. "Kiss."

Justin grinned. "I like kissing you."

At least she wasn't the only one, but she didn't feel better. "I like kissing you, but more kisses might complicate us resolving the ownership of the Broughton Inn."

Justin raised an eyebrow and grinned wryly. "So I'm a complication, huh?"

Yes, and a big distraction. But there was no need to answer. He knew that.

"Probably a good idea, then. No kissing," he added.

"Thank you." Except Bailey wished he hadn't agreed with her so easily. Wait. She should be relieved he had. When Justin McMillian was involved, she had no idea what was going on inside her head. "Astoria is the safest choice for dog shopping. Less chance of being seen."

"All set, but don't get your heart set on doggy designer wear. I will not be dressing Buddy in clothing."

"Come on," she teased. "No rain slicker for those wet days?"

"I'm a true Oregonian. I don't carry an umbrella. Buddy and I will both get wet."

She opened the door. "What about bunny ears come Easter time, or reindeer antlers for Christmas?"

"No way." Justin stepped outside. "A bandanna might be okay. Depends on the pattern."

"Picky."

"I must protect Buddy's dignity."

"At least until you decide to use a picture of him for your Christmas card and wrap him in garlands with a Santa hat on his head."

"Never."

"It's only July. Time will tell." But she would never know. Her heart panged with regret. She shook off the feeling, stepped out of the house and locked the door. "So, how do you feel about doggy booties?"

After having fun shopping with Bailey and spending more money then he'd ever imagined spending on a dog, Justin climbed the steps of the Astoria Column, a 125-foot-tall tower built in the 1920s and one of the most popular tourist attractions in the area. Of the 164 steps, they were about halfway to the top.

He glanced back at Bailey. "How's your foot holding up?"

"I'll let you know if it hurts."

She continued upward, a smile on her face and her breasts jiggling with each step. Too bad he couldn't walk backward.

"The view is worth the climb," she added.

The stop at the tower had been her idea when she found out he'd never seen the view from the top.

"I can't believe I'm the Oregonian, but someone from Washington brought me here."

"Then we're even because I've never been to the top of the Space Needle in Seattle."

"Spend time on the Oregon coast?"

"Some. Mainly Cannon Beach. It has such a strong artistic community, more so than on my side of the Columbia, which has been underserved by coastal galleries."

"Until you."

"That's right." Pride filled her voice. "The co-op gallery will be back one of these days."

"Do some tourists enjoy local art?"

"More than some," she said. "From my experience with the inn's gallery, people want to take home more than a souvenir magnet to stick on their fridge. A piece of art that captures their vacation destination is a memento to treasure."

"You're not like other artists I've met," he said.

"Should I take that as a compliment?"

"Yes, you should. You've done your research."

"Art is as much a business as a passion. After the Broughton Inn co-op gallery opened, art sales tripled. There's also been an increased interest in classes and art-centered events from both tourists and locals. That's huge, given the current economy."

He moved to the side to let a couple pass by on their way down.

"You're almost there," the man in a Mariners cap said.

"Hear that, Bailey? We're almost at the top." Two minutes later, Justin reached the final step and walked out onto the viewing platform. He looked past rooftops toward the bridge that connected Oregon to Washington. The water of the Columbia River shimmered, a contrast to the green shrubs and trees both nearby and in the distance. He saw the coastal ranch. "Incredible view."

"See Young's Bay?" She wore her sunglasses on her head. "Then there's the Pacific Ocean. It's quite a sight to see all the boats and ships sailing under the bridge."

He could imagine. The part of the bridge closest to Oregon was elevated. The Washington side seemed to float on the water.

"Breathtaking." Like the view of Bailey, her eyes bright and her smile wide. Beautiful. He couldn't stop staring at her. "Do you ever come up here to work?"

"Not enough room." She closed her eyes and tilted her face upward. The sun kissed her cheeks, making him wish he could have a turn. "Too many tourists, too."

"That's what we are today." Though she didn't look touristy at all. Someone looking at her would guess she was an artist or a cook, or maybe a writer.

She opened her eyes, then gave him a look. "You know what I mean."

Did he? Justin liked how she treated him like an artist, assuming he understood, when all he'd done was complete one painting. Still, he appreciated the way she included him. "I'm figuring it out."

"Have you done any more painting?"

"I knew you would ask that."

"So, what's your answer?" The dog-won't-let-go-of-the-bone tone had returned.

The wind blew off the water, stronger up there than on the ground. A large ship sailed under the bridge.

"I've sketched a few things," he said finally. She didn't need to know that he loved every minute, lost himself in the work and found himself refreshed when he returned to working on blueprints and resort designs. "I don't have the supplies to paint."

"Borrow some of mine. I'm not using any right now."

"Because of my dog."

"I want to see more of what you can do."

"That sounds like a challenge."

"Maybe." The wind tousled the ends of her hair. She moved out of the way so a young family could pass. "I'm excited whenever I find someone with natural talent."

He raised an eyebrow. "So you're only interested in my painting ability?"

She grinned wryly. "Your kisses aren't too bad."

Justin thought that might be an invitation, but she moved to the other side of the viewing plaza. He followed her. "You can't leave me hanging."

"Was just making a comment about your talents. Remember what we said."

"No kisses."

"How about a peck?" he asked.

She shook her head. "Semantics."

He wrapped an arm around her back. "So you'll let this amazing view go to waste."

"If we're kissing, we can't see the view." She scooted away. "You don't give up."

"Neither do you."

A thoughtful expression formed on her face. She stared at the horizon with a faraway look in her eyes. "Guess we have more in common than I realized."

"We'll have even more after Buddy gets released."

She half laughed. "Better enjoy your final day of freedom, Dad."

"You, too, surrogate Mom."

"We're almost a family." Her eyes widened, as if she hadn't meant to say the words aloud. "Well, a little like one."

"Yes. We will be." For as long as he was here. The idea appealed to him on a gut level. "Until I came to Haley's

Bay and met you, I had no idea what family was all about. I'm glad I met you, Bailey, and a few of the other Coles."

"Let's hope you feel the same way when you leave town."

He rubbed his face. "Still worried your brothers might mess up my face?"

"No." A wicked gleam lit her eyes. "That I will."

"Guess I'll take a rain check on those kisses."

"Smart thinking."

"I try." But he had to try harder when he was around her.

Buddy, Bailey and him. A family. Justin had to admit, the idea appealed to him. Too bad the Broughton Inn had to get in the way. And her family.

Two days later, Justin sat on Bailey's couch with Buddy at his feet. They'd come straight from the vet clinic that morning.

Best. Dog. Ever.

All dog owners probably thought that about their pet, but in Justin's case the words were true. Buddy was amazing. Still recovering, but now clean and fresh-smelling, as well as flea-free.

And most important, happy.

Buddy seemed thrilled to be inside, have toys to play with, his own doggy bed, food and a kick-ass colorful collar that Bailey had picked out at the pet store in Astoria. A part of Justin wished he were staying here instead of the B and B. But that had as much to do with Bailey as Buddy.

"You are such a good dog," Justin said. "A lucky one, too."

Buddy stared at Justin with big brown eyes and a look of total adoration. The dog panted, wagged his tail. Not even the cone bothered him.

"Sorry, boy. No more treats." Justin had learned within five minutes of arriving at Bailey's that Buddy could sit and lie down and shake. Food was the best motivator for the tricks, but the dog didn't seem to have an off switch when it came to eating. "You'll get a tummy ache."

The dog made a noise that resembled a whine.

Smart dog, but spoiled already. "Cry all you want. I'm not changing my mind."

Buddy looked at him, then lay down on the throw rug, not quite defeated. It was more like that he wanted to rest up for his next round of treats and rubs.

Yeah, one smart dog.

Bailey stepped through the kitchen doorway, a cup of strawberry lemonade in her hand. "Thought you might be thirsty.

She knew him well. Justin smiled. "I am."

"How's Buddy doing?"

"Great. Explored the living and dining room. Did a few tricks. Ate too many treats."

Bailey shot an accusing glance Justin's way. "Whose fault is that?"

He took the glass from her. "Just making sure he's comfortable."

"Looks right at home."

"Yeah, he does." Justin wanted to spend lots of time with Buddy so the dog was used to him before they went to Lincoln City. "Figured out in the first two minutes that he's addicted to petting. Thought I should warn you, one or two rubs aren't enough for my pup."

"If Buddy didn't know that before, he knows it now."

Justin sipped the lemonade. Tasty. Was there anything Bailey couldn't do well?

Buddy's ears perked up. He sat, looked at the front door, barked once.

"What is it?" Justin asked the dog.

The doorbell rang.

Bailey gave him a pat, then walked toward the door. "Good, Buddy."

"Knew he was a great dog." Justin was finding something new to love about Buddy every five minutes. "Expecting company?"

"No, but that doesn't mean someone won't drop by." She opened the door.

"Surprise," a group of people shouted.

Buddy barked.

Justin looked over his shoulder. A crowed gathered on the front porch. He recognized a few—Grady, Ellis, Risa, Lilah and Ida Mae. The others, including a couple of cute kids, resembled the people he knew. It looked as though the Cole family had come calling. They'd brought food and gifts.

"What's going on?" Bailey asked.

Risa beamed. "When I had to take Skippy back to the vet the other day, one of the techs mentioned Justin was adopting the dog you'd found and the receptionist said the dog would be staying with you so I thought a doggy shower was in order. So here we are with gifts and food."

Bailey's face paled. She clutched the doorknob. None of her family seemed to pay attention to her as they walked in, making themselves right at home.

As usual.

Justin held on to Buddy's collar. The dog sniffed the air but seemed content to stay near him. No growling or barks, just watchful eyes.

Two children, a boy and a girl, ran up. "Can we pet your dog?"

He remembered what Bailey had done yesterday when they found Buddy. "Put your hand out and let him sniff you."

They did.

Buddy licked each of their hands.

The girl giggled.

The boy pulled his hand back. "That tickles."

Buddy raised his paw so the little boy would shake.

"Wow." The boy's eyes widened to the size of silver dollars. "That's one smart dog."

"Can we play with him?" the little girl asked.

Even Buddy seemed to be waiting for an answer.

"Sure," Justin said. "But no running. He's got an injured paw."

The kids scrambled toward the kitchen with Buddy at their heels.

Justin joined Bailey as her family continued to stream in with food and presents and beverages. Even cousins, including identical twins, a frowning Tyler and his smiling brother, J.T., a firefighter, were there.

"I'm sorry," Bailey mouthed to Justin.

He helped her carry the presents to the fireplace hearth. "Wow. It's like Christmas."

She nodded. "You're going to have more dog supplies than you could ever imagine."

A tall, tanned fifty-something-year-old man entered the house. One look at Bailey in her yoga pants, old T-shirt and bare feet, and he grimaced. "Holy crap, Bailey. You've already got the whole artsy-fartsy thing against you. Please tell me you didn't go out in public looking dressed like a hobo. Do you know what people are going to say?"

She took a deep breath and another. "Love you, too, Dad."

So this was the patriarch of the Cole family. He looked like a fisherman, and someone you wouldn't want to upset or bump into in a dark alley. Not that Haley's Bay had any.

Justin extended his arm. "I'm Justin McMillian. Nice to meet you, Mr. Cole."

"Jack Cole." He shook Justin's hand. "Word of warning. That dog of yours better be the only thing sniffing around here."

"Understood. Feel the same way about my two sisters."

Justin wouldn't be surprised if the fisherman father had driven away more than one potential boyfriend.

Bailey sighed with twenty-seven years' worth of exasperation. "On that note, I'm going to crawl into a hole and die."

"Don't be overdramatic," her father said.

She winked at Justin, as if she weren't too upset, but playing along. "Fine. I'll go change into something too artsy-fartsy so you'll have at least one more thing to complain about, Dad." She kissed his cheek. "Remember the number one rule in my house…no fighting."

She walked to her bedroom.

Her father's frown deepened. Her brother Declan looked disappointed. Apparently battles were part of the family fun.

Justin bit back a smile. He'd wanted to know what a Cole family gathering would be like. Looked as though he was getting his chance. For better or worse.

Though this wasn't what he expected.

Tyler looked unhappy, and Declan looked ready to punch a wall. Justin hoped the Cole males remembered the no-fighting rule. For Bailey's sake. And his.

Bailey stood at the back door, staring out at her yard. Food covered the picnic table. Her family members and Justin occupied folding chairs setup on the lawn. They ate, drank and laughed. Buddy, the guest of honor, went from person to person getting pets.

Warmth balled in the center of her chest. She had to give her family credit. When the Coles threw a party, including an impromptu dog shower, aka an excuse to check out Justin, they went all out. Buddy had enough toys, supplies, treats and clothing to make him the most stylish pup on the West Coast.

She carried another pitcher of strawberry lemonade to

the drinks table, a folding card table with various sizes of plastic cups and a permanent marker to write someone's name on their drink. Three ice chests full of soda, juice boxes and beer were underneath.

Tyler grabbed a bottle of amber ale from one of the coolers. The serious expression he wore when he'd walked into her house remained. He was dressed like a surfer, but he still looked like a lawyer. "Buddy's staying here. Is McMillian?"

"No." She lowered her voice. "He's over at Aunt Ida Mae's."

"I texted AJ."

"About?"

"Justin trying to charm the inn away from you."

"He's not."

Tyler sipped his beer. "Looks that way to me. Ask anyone else here, and they'll agree."

Her cousin's words hurt. "You're wrong, and so are they. I'm not stupid or naive, Ty. I've been around the block a couple of times. I'm not going to give away the inn to some handsome sweet talker."

"It's been a while since you've dated."

"Not that long. Remember Oliver." Just saying his name left a bad taste in Bailey's mouth. "And just so you know, I'm not dating Justin."

Kissing and dating were two entirely different things. She looked over to see him surrounded by the Cole women—her grandmother, great aunt, mother, sister, sister-in-law and niece. They'd have a précis on him within the hour.

"We found Buddy at the Potter place," Bailey said. "Keeping Justin's dog has nothing to do with the inn. You know I like animals. I'm just trying to help."

"Knowing the McMillian reputation, chances are he'll want to buy the Potter property, too."

"What reputation?"

"The company is cutthroat when buying real estate."

"Justin isn't like that."

Tyler raised a brow. "You know him that well?"

"No." Nothing she'd seen so far gave her such an impression, though what she'd heard about his sister Paige made her wonder if she was the source of rumors.

"It's a moot point anyway." Tyler wiped off the condensation dripping from his beer. "Phil Potter has shown no interest in selling in the past. He won't now."

"Maybe they'll make Phil an offer he can't refuse," she countered. "He hasn't been back to Haley's Bay in forever. The place is a hazard. There's no reason for him to hold on to the property."

"What about sentimental reasons?" Ty's gaze narrowed. "That was something you understood before spending time with Justin McMillian."

"I still understand that. Why do you think I want the inn? But if McMillian Resorts buys another property, they might not want the inn. Then it's mine."

He lifted his bottle. "Still dreaming of saying 'I do' there, cuz?"

Justin joined them. He refilled his cup with strawberry lemonade. "What's this about 'I do'?"

Oh, no. Please no. Her gaze implored Tyler not to say anything, but the devilish smile on her cousin's face made one thing clear—he was going to spill.

Her stomach churned with a potent mixture of dread and embarrassment. "Ty—"

"For as long as I can remember, Bailey has wanted to get married at the Broughton Inn," Ty said.

"Like your grandmother?" Justin asked.

Bailey nodded, heat rushing up her neck. Declan approached, eating a brownie. Oh, no, she didn't want him to get in on this conversation, too.

If a big earthquake were going to strike the Pacific Northwest, this would be the perfect time for the fault lines to shift. Everyone was outside. Nothing to fall on them. No one would remember the topic of discussion.

Except Justin was waiting for an answer.

She took a breath. "Most girls dream about weddings."

Declan grabbed a beer from a red ice chest. "Not all eight-year-olds put on a wedding and make their brothers and cousins attend."

"That was a dress rehearsal, not a wedding," she clarified, praying the ground would start rocking and rolling any second now.

"She made us wear paper bow ties," Tyler said.

Declan laughed. "And black hats. I'd forgotten about those."

Ty grinned. "We must have looked like idiots standing on the gazebo in funny hats with a boom box playing the 'Wedding March.'"

So much for an earthquake. Might as well go all in. She squared her shoulders. "You were wearing top hats. And the music was Bach's 'Jesu, Joy of Man's Desiring' and Pachelbel's 'Canon' in D."

Justin's eyes twinkled. "A formal affair."

"Oh, yeah," Tyler said, seeming to enjoy her discomfort. He and J.T. had no other siblings, but both treated her and Camden like sisters. "Bailey wore a white nightgown and borrowed a friend's First Communion veil."

"She had on white gloves and shoes, too," Declan added. "Mom was so pissed she scuffed up those shoes before Camden could grow into them."

Bailey remembered that. "I was grounded for a week and was assigned extra chores when they found out I cut Aunt Ida Mae's white roses for my bouquet."

"I thought Camden did that."

"She did, but she was my maid of honor and younger. I

couldn't let her be punished when this was my idea." Bailey smiled at the memories, both good and bad. "I don't think I wore white shoes for the longest time after that. But I got to play bride, so the punishment was worth the crime."

"Sounds like an elaborate rehearsal," Justin said.

She nodded. "Important stuff when you're little."

Declan looked from Justin to her, an odd expression in her brother's green eyes. "All Bailey needed was a groom to make the wedding complete."

That hadn't changed. There was still no groom.

She forced herself not to glance Justin's way. "I asked one of you to stand in, but had zero takers."

"I was too short," Declan said.

"You were lucky we showed up at all." Tyler walked away. Declan followed him.

Justin stared over the lip of his cup. "Do you still want to get married at the Broughton Inn?"

Buddy nudged her leg. She bent over and rubbed his back, trying to avoid the cone secured around his neck as well as Justin's questioning gaze. "He's doing great with all these people around. Did you see him playing with the kids?"

"Answer the question."

The firmness in his voice made her look up. He stared intently at her. She swallowed around the lump in her throat. "Yes. That's what I meant about making new memories."

"I see."

He did? Maybe he would consider sharing what he saw. "Any other questions?"

"No, but the gazebo could stay."

"Huh?"

"The gazebo wouldn't have to be torn down. The structure could be repaired and strengthened. Painted, too."

Bailey thought about what Tyler had said about the inn being charmed out from under her. "Hypothetically?"

"I'm trying to make sure you get what you want."

Her pulse skittered, matching her erratic heartbeat. No one had ever done that for her. Oh, AJ tried. His way to make up for staying away for ten years, perhaps? She'd been the middle child with three older brothers and three younger siblings. The forgotten one. Her older brothers were always giving her—not to mention their parents—a hard time. The twins and Grady had needed constant supervision. No one had time to think about Bailey's desires, just her basic needs.

She struggled to find the right words. "Thanks, but I can take care of that myself."

He glanced around the backyard at her family until his gaze reached hers. That connection she'd felt was stronger now.

"I know you can," he said. "But you shouldn't have to. Not all the time."

Tingles poured down her spine and she knew then what she'd been denying all along. Justin McMillian might be the wrong man, but she was falling for him anyway. Falling hard.

And if the Broughton Inn was coming between them, she might have to choose. The question was…which one would she pick?

The first answer that came to mind surprised her. Justin couldn't be the right one…or could he?

Chapter Eleven

For the first two days after Buddy arrived, Bailey left her house when Justin visited. She knew that was what Tyler, her family and everyone else in town wanted. Saying hello followed by goodbye a minute later got old fast, but she was trying to do the right thing.

Except leaving home each time wasn't the right thing for her.

Or Justin, who wanted her to stay.

Or Buddy, who tried to block the door when she was leaving.

On day three, when Justin came over, she gave in and stayed home. Tyler didn't call. None of her family showed up. No one seemed to notice, let alone care. So she did the same thing the next time. And the time after that.

One week passed, then another, each day sweeter than the last. Bailey was getting attached to Buddy. She looked forward to Justin's visits. Their no-kissing mandate fell by the wayside.

When he was at her house, she could almost believe the three of them were a family. A part of her—a big part—longed for this arrangement to become permanent.

Crazy? Yes, but she didn't care.

Bailey was happy in a way she hadn't been before. Not with any former boyfriend or date. Nothing came close to this. She didn't want the feeling to end. If only she didn't have to worry about the inn...

But she wouldn't think about that now. She had chocolate chip cookies to make. By the time Justin finished playing with Buddy in the backyard, she would be finished baking and they could spend time together.

The ingredients sat on the counter. Parchment paper lined the cookie sheets. The oven was preheating. She reached into her kitchen cupboard and pulled out a large mixing bowl.

"Whoa. That's commercial-size."

She glanced over her shoulder toward the sound of Justin's voice. He stood in the doorway and looked way too good in his khaki shorts and green polo. A good thing she'd decided to wear a skirt and a tank top, rather than her work-around-the-house clothes. She knew he didn't care, but she did.

Buddy peered around Justin's legs. The pup sniffed the air.

"I haven't started yet," she said to the dog.

"How many cookies do we need to make?" Justin asked.

We. The word made Bailey's heart sigh. She hadn't asked him to help. She'd assumed he wouldn't want to bake when he could be playing with Buddy. "Ten dozen."

"I had no idea the Coles were related to Cookie Monster."

Grinning, she stuck out her tongue. He made a silly face in return.

She placed the bowl on the counter. "Sorry to disappoint you, but there are no fuzzy blue relatives in the Cole family tree."

"Only fuzzy blue shoes."

"Purple fuzzy slippers."

He exhaled, louder than a sigh, as if he were exaggerating the sound on purpose. "I have fond memories of seeing those slippers for the first time."

"Revising history?"

"Embracing it."

Bailey wished he'd embrace her. She felt as if she'd known Justin longer than a few weeks. He fit so perfectly into her world. Or would, once the problem with the inn's ownership was resolved.

She pulled out her measuring cups and spoons.

"So why ten dozen?" he asked.

"That's how many Grady asked me to make for his department's barbecue tomorrow night."

Justin shook his head. "I can just imagine what Paige would say if I asked her to bake cookies for me."

"What about Rainey?"

"She would go to the nearest bakery and buy them. None of us learned to cook growing up. It wasn't something my mom had time to teach us." Justin put on the apron hanging from a hook. "What do you need me to do?"

He really was a good guy. Too bad Tyler couldn't see this side of Justin. "Thanks, but you don't have to help. Go play with Buddy."

"I want to help. Buddy, too. He'll be happy to clean up anything that drops to the floor." Justin walked toward her. "You're going to need help making twelve dozen cookies."

"Ten."

"Twelve." He rubbed his stomach. "The other two dozen are for us. Well, me."

Smiling, Bailey faced the counter and scooped flour

into a measuring cup. "I might be able to stretch the dough into more cookies."

"Might?" Justin stood behind her, his chest pressed against her back. "What's it going to take to get you to say you will?"

A thrill ran through her. She was ready to bake twenty dozen cookies, if that was what he wanted. She'd do anything to make him as happy as she felt. "I…"

"Need more convincing?" He showered kisses along her neck. "How's this?"

A moan escaped her mouth. Talk about talented lips. She leaned back against him to give him better access. "I could make an extra half dozen."

"Only six more?" Justin nibbled on her ears. Sensation shot from her earlobe down to her toes. "That won't do."

"No?" Her voice sounded husky.

"Nope." He turned her so she faced him. "Two dozen."

She held the measuring cup full of flour between them. "How about a dozen? I can't stretch the recipe any more without having to pull out a calculator and refigure the ingredients. Math was never my best subject."

"A good thing it was mine." He ran his fingertip along the side of her face. "I'll help you calculate measurements. And whatever else you need."

He brushed his lips across hers, the kiss feather soft.

A list with several more kisses on it formed in her mind. "I might need a lot."

"That's okay." The desire in his eyes matched the way Bailey felt. She arched toward him.

Justin pulled her closer.

Something pressed against her stomach. Huh? The measuring cup slipped from her hand and crashed to the floor. The sound echoed in the small kitchen. Flour flew up, a cloud of white dust.

Justin jumped back.

Bailey reached for a dish towel. "Sorry. I forgot I was holding the cup."

"If our kissing made you forget, then it's worth the cleanup."

"Good point." She stared at his legs. His feet were completely covered in white. "You've got flour on you."

"So do you. All over."

Bailey glanced down. She was covered in white from her waist down. She laughed. "At least it can't get any worse."

Buddy bounded in between them. Flour went flying again, all over them and the dog.

Justin laughed. "It's worse."

The dog ran in circles, spreading more flour around the kitchen and on them.

"He thinks this is a game," Justin said.

"Well, he won, if that's the case." She laughed. "So much for wowing you with my cookie-making skills."

"You've wowed me with all your other skills. And you've cooked for me already. I know your cookies will be killer."

His words sounded genuine. Her cheeks warmed, a regular occurrence around Justin. "Thanks."

"Thank you." He gave her another kiss. "You taste like flour."

"I must have touched my face."

He grabbed a roll of paper towels. "I'm going to put Buddy in the backyard so we can get this mess cleaned up. He'll need a bath, but we have cookies to make."

"Yes, twelve dozen is a lot." She grabbed a dish towel. "If you're good, I'll let you taste the dough."

"Oh, I'm always good."

Smiling was so easy to do around Justin. "I had a feeling you'd say that."

"Cookie dough is one of my favorites." His grin spread. "What's yours?"

She liked the cookie dough, but she liked tasting something better. "You."

On a Saturday morning under an overcast sky, Justin sat at the picnic table in Bailey's backyard. He tossed a neon-green ball toward the fence. Buddy ran after it.

She was inside on a phone call to one of her brothers. Justin had no idea which one. Keeping track of all the Coles in Haley's Bay could be a full-time job.

Buddy barked. Now that the uncomfortable cone was off and his leg healed, running and chasing had become his favorite playtime activities.

"Bring the ball here."

The dog picked it up in his mouth, but decided to take a roundabout way back.

Justin preferred going the direct route, point-to-point. He didn't make a habit of sniffing every blade of grass like Buddy. But his dog seemed to be having fun and enjoying the journey, not speeding by to arrive at the destination. Maybe the dog could teach him some new tricks. Bailey, too. "Come on, boy."

Buddy ran and dropped the ball.

Justin threw the drool-covered ball once more. He'd yet to reach the point where the dog gave up first. Maybe that wasn't in Buddy's nature. "Wait until you see your new house. It's on the beach. You can chase balls into the water."

The dog was more interested in running after the ball than listening to him. Justin didn't blame Buddy. Playing was more fun.

Staying in Haley's Bay had been fun. The quaint coastal village had a different vibe than his hometown, Lincoln City. He wouldn't miss the everybody-knows-your-business factor here, but he would miss the everybody-knows-your name part. And Bailey.

He might be ready to go home, sleep in his own bed and introduce Buddy to his new home, but he would miss the pretty, kind artist who'd opened her home to his dog and, by default, him.

Buddy ran toward him with the ball once more.

Justin's growing attraction and affection were too deep to think of Bailey as only a friend. Romantic was the only way to describe his feelings.

But they were stuck in some kind of limbo, which he hated. Buddy drew them together. The Broughton Inn kept them from becoming closer. The thought of leaving Bailey and going back to Lincoln City depressed him. She'd mentioned visiting, but that didn't make him feel any better.

The dog dropped the ball. Justin threw it again, this time aiming for the opposite side of the yard.

He tried to think of reasons he needed to stay in Haley's Bay longer, but things were winding down.

The property inspections, done by two different inspectors, each hired by one of the "owners," showed typical problems with a building that age, but nothing on the reports required demolition.

Of course not. A teardown recommendation would have made this too easy. But now that he knew what the inn meant to Bailey, a part of him was glad her dreams for the place hadn't died. And maybe there could be a solution where they both got what they wanted.

While Justin fine-tuned the renovation applications for the various historical committees, he'd tasked Paige with finding Mr. Potter's son in Boise, Idaho, and buying his land. So far, the man had turned down two offers, but Paige had gone back with a third. The guy would be a fool if he said no.

Justin had blueprints he'd drafted in his free time, but

he'd wait to show them off until the deal closed. No reason to jinx the project to stroke his ego. Or, if he was being honest, open himself up to criticism.

Bailey's opinion of his plans meant more than he understood. Sure, she had a style he admired, but the need for her to appreciate his work borderlined on pathetic. Yet he kept the stupid tube in his truck, in case she asked what he'd been up to in the time they were apart.

She hadn't asked.

He hadn't told her about trying to purchase the Potter lot or the blueprints.

A bird swooped down over the grass. Buddy dropped the ball and went for the bird that wisely flew into the neighbor's yard.

Justin shook his head. "You'll have better luck with the ball."

His cell phone beeped, signaling a text message.

He glanced at the message from Paige displayed on the screen: Phil Potter said no to third offer. Told me not to call again. It's dead. Get the Bro. Inn deal closed. NOW!

Not the news Justin wanted to hear.

He and Bailey had avoided any discussion of the inn since the dog shower. But the sooner this was resolved, the sooner he could figure out where he and Bailey stood, now and in the future.

"Hey." Bailey sat next to him. "That was AJ. His private investigator might have a lead on Floyd in South America. Someone matching his description was in Cartagena."

"Let's hope they find him."

She stared at the dog. "Buddy looks like he's having fun."

"That makes one of us."

"You bought the bag of balls."

"Who knew a triathlete's arm could tire from fetch?"

She wasn't smiling. "Something wrong?"

"Not wrong." She moistened her lips. "It's just… I've been thinking. That's why I wanted to talk to AJ today. He told me to go through Tyler and formally present my offer, but it's Sunday and you're here, so I'll just tell you what I told my brother. If McMillian Resorts agrees to put in an art gallery that I could lease, hire the former employees, maintain vendor contracts and keep at least a portion of the main building in the new remodeled design, I'll give up my ownership claim."

Wow. And like that, it was done.

Still, her words shocked Justin. He searched her face to see if she was uncertain about her decision, but she looked almost serene. "You're positive?"

"Yes." She didn't hesitate. "I've been thinking about a compromise for a couple of weeks now. I think this would work."

"You're full of surprises. I never would have guessed."

"I do my best pondering when I'm alone. Or with Buddy." She rubbed the dog's head and he gave her an I'm-in-love pant and lick combo. Buddy being able to touch her made Justin almost jealous.

Definitely jealous.

"I'm an artist. I've never wanted to be an employer or manage people." A gleam entered her green eyes. "And I want to do this without feeling like I'm doing something wrong and letting people down."

She leaned toward him and kissed him on the mouth. Hard.

Oh, man. Him, too. Her warmth, her sweet taste. He wrapped his arms around her, pulling her close. Her hands splayed across his back. She kissed him with a hunger that matched his own. He wove his fingers through her hair, relishing the feel of her mouth.

Buddy barked, jumped on top of Justin so he fell back away from Bailey.

She laughed. "Someone is jealous."

Better you than me. Buddy panted. He looked happy, not upset, and gave each of them a lick.

"Guess he wants kisses, too." Justin petted the dog's head. "We'll have to do some training."

"He's too cute."

The dog wasn't the only one. Justin's gaze locked on Bailey's. Funny, but a shared glance was as much of a turn-on as one of her kisses.

"About the inn…"

"I'll have Paige draw up a contract."

"Sounds good." Bailey gave Buddy another rub. "AJ's hoping they can track down Floyd and get some restitution. But I can't let this drag on any longer. The employees need to know what's happening, and so do the artists. The inn is the best place for the co-op gallery. And the truth is, I'm ready to move on."

So was Justin. But he wasn't sure what he wanted to move on toward. Renovating the inn wouldn't take as long as new construction, but he would have to draw up new plans. His part wouldn't last as long. After that…

No complaints. He had the Broughton Inn and Bailey. What more could a guy want?

Three days later, Justin sat in the company's conference room in Lincoln City. He skimmed through the contract Paige, Kent and the two other attorneys had drafted for Bailey—an inch-thick worth of mumbo jumbo legalese.

The growing tension behind Justin's eyes spread down his neck. He dropped the contract onto the mahogany table. The papers hit with a thud. "I'm not giving this contract to Bailey. This piece of crap has enough loopholes to confuse the Supreme Court. She made us an offer with conditions, but those are nebulous at best with the contract wording you used."

"You received a verbal offer." Paige lifted her chin. "This contract ensures that the Broughton Inn will be ours. You can't expect us to hire just anyone without knowing whether they meet the McMillian Resorts standard of customer service or locking ourselves in to unknown vendors who could cut into our profit margin by raising prices. We also both know a gallery is not what the inn needs."

"I'll concede the first two points, but you're wrong about the third." He rolled his shoulders, but the movement bunched his muscles more. "A gallery would give the inn a local look, invest in the community and lead to more event business."

"Don't let an infatuation cloud your judgment," Paige said. "Bailey Cole is an artist. She's too flaky to run a gallery."

"She did a great job running the gallery until we purchased the inn."

"There's no business plan. She brings nothing to the table except her limited experience with Floyd Jeffries. Look how well that turned out."

He leveled his gaze at Paige. "The same could be said about your experience with Floyd."

"What's going on?" Her eyes narrowed. "All you used to care about was getting a project completed on time and under budget. Not even Taryn got in the way of that. Now your priority is some artist and a gallery. You need to keep our business interests the priority. Not hers."

Until today, Justin had never paid attention to what his sister and the other lawyers did to close a deal. He took over once they'd obtained the property. Negotiating wasn't his area of responsibility. This wasn't his concern. But Bailey's warm, enthusiastic smile appeared in his mind. He couldn't let this go. For her sake and his.

His gaze traveled from Paige to the two attorneys. "There has to be a way to make this deal fairer."

"The contract was written for McMillian Resorts' benefit." Kent leaned forward over the edge of the table. "The company has the sole option of deciding if any of Miss Cole's conditions will be met, and if opening a gallery is in the best interest of the inn or not."

"Not," said one of the newer attorneys, a man Justin had only met once and whose name he couldn't remember.

His sister and the rest of the attorneys laughed.

The hard knot in Justin's stomach grew into a large rock capable of damaging a keel and causing a boat to capsize. He felt unbalanced, uptight, out of place. All he could see was a beautiful woman with copper ringlets, expressive green eyes and a go-to-hell attitude. "These terms aren't what Bailey had in mind when she made her offer."

"So?" Paige gave him a look, the kind she hadn't given him since they were teenagers and he was about to get caught by his parents for sneaking out of the house past curfew. "This is the contract we're offering. The 'we' includes you."

That was the problem. Justin eyed the contract. He was a part of this because he'd brought Bailey's offer to Paige, and each page was an affront, a selfish grab on the part of his company—really, his family. He'd wanted Bailey's appreciation and gratitude over the formation of a partnership with the art gallery, one that could exist beyond business. But the terms would only make her see McMillian Resorts as an adversary. Not only the company, but him, too. "That still doesn't make the terms right."

Kent twirled a pen between his fingers. "Bailey will have Tyler look over the deal. He can counsel her on whether to sign or make a counteroffer. Negotiations rarely are settled the first go-round."

"That wastes time and money," Justin said.

The pen froze on Kent's fingertips. "Her brother's

money. AJ Cole could use hundred-dollar bills for kindling and not miss them."

"That's beside the point." Justin didn't like any of this.

Paige rolled her eyes. "Don't let a pretty woman mess with your head. This is what we've always done in the past and what we'll continue to do to make McMillian Resorts successful."

Maybe he hadn't cared how deals were carried out or turned a blind eye in the past. But the underhanded tactics now made him sick to his stomach. How many other people had been confused or even…swindled? He wasn't sure he wanted to know the answer. "Success at what price?"

"Any price." Her voice hardened. So like their father. "That's how it's been. And will be. You should know that."

"I do now." The words tasted like sand.

Relief filled Paige's eyes. "The only person standing in our way right now is Bailey Cole. Once she signs this contract, the inn is ours. Thanks to you."

Victory. That was what he wanted, what he'd been working toward these past weeks, so why did winning feel hollow? He felt off his game, as if he'd been playing by different rules. But Paige was correct about one thing. McMillian Resorts needed to salvage and close this deal. Should he change how he normally operated because he'd fallen for a passionate artist, one he'd only known a few weeks? If a gallery at the Broughton Inn didn't work out, couldn't AJ help Bailey out? She would understand, right?

"Do you want to take the contract to Bailey or do you want us to courier it to her?" an attorney asked.

Logically Justin knew the contract was necessary to ensure the inn's success and protect McMillian Resorts. This was business, nothing personal, but he wanted to make sure Bailey knew that. "I'll deliver the contract."

He could explain what was going on, make her see… What? That McMillian Resorts cared only about the inn?

No, that might be the truth, but he wanted Bailey to know that he cared about the art gallery and her.

Especially her.

The next day, Bailey sat on her living room couch with Justin and a sleeping Buddy. The ride up the coast to Haley's Bay, followed by chasing birds in her backyard, had worn out the dog.

She flipped through the thick contract, scanning the pages. "Seems a bit much for a few conditions."

Justin dragged his hand through his hair. His heavy eyelids matched his tired eyes.

His quick trip home to Lincoln City hadn't seemed to agree with him. He was more relaxed when he was here with her in Haley's Bay.

"You know lawyers. They are the definition of anal." He leaned back against the sofa. "Have Tyler review the contract so you understand what you're signing."

"Trying to pull a fast one to get the inn," she joked.

"Not me, Bailey. I—" He covered her hand with his. "I want this to work out."

"Me, too." She glanced from the contract to him, a weird feeling in her stomach. "So, why do I feel there's a 'but' coming?"

"There isn't, but promise me you'll review the contract with Tyler before putting pen to paper. Understand what you're signing. I can't stay much longer. I need to drive back to Lincoln City today."

She stiffened. "You drove all the way up here to deliver the contract?"

"I wanted to see you, too."

But an hour wasn't a long enough visit. She'd hoped they'd have the whole day together. Should she tell him that?

"Hey," he said. "Don't be sad."

"Okay. I know something that will make me feel better."

She brushed her lips over his. Forget chocolate. He was her favorite flavor. One she could easily become addicted to if she wasn't already. "I wish you could stay."

"I'll be back in two days. We'll go out."

She waved the contract. "And celebrate."

He held her hand. "I'm going to miss you until then."

"Same here."

"I want you to know that when I'm with you, I can't imagine being anywhere else. When I'm not with you, I can't wait until we're together again."

Tingles shot through her. *So sweet.* "I can't wait, either, but sounds like you have it bad."

He nodded slowly.

"Good," she said.

Justin drew back. "Good?"

"I feel the same way."

"What are we going to do about this?"

"No time to do anything today, though you could kiss me."

"Happy to oblige."

He pulled her into his arms and lowered his mouth toward hers. His kiss was gentle, not as raw and on-edge as before. She recognized the familiar urgency and desire, but this time a new tenderness to his kiss made her think of picket fences and forever, not sweaty sheets and one night.

This kiss. This man. This feeling of completeness was what she'd been waiting for. Oh, she had a good life, a career, a home and a family who loved her. But Justin brought something different, something new, something totally unexpected and welcome. Buddy, too.

Justin pulled her closer. She went willingly, wrapping her arms around him.

His kiss made her feel as if she could conquer the world, whether creating a new work or taking on a project for the historical committee. Sure, she'd felt that way before, but this was better. She wasn't alone. Oh, she had her family, but she'd wanted someone not related to her to care. Not just humor her. She had never known the boost this kind of unconditional support could give her.

She gave into the sensations pulsing through her, ran her fingertips through his clipped hair. He wasn't the kind of man she thought she would end up with, but he was exactly the kind of man she wanted, needed, loved.

Love.

She loved him.

Bailey had known she was falling for him, but somehow in this mess Floyd had made for them, she'd completely fallen in love with Justin McMillian. Only time would tell what would happen, but so far so good.

Especially if he kept kissing her this way.

Slowly he dragged his lips from hers. "I wish I could stay, but I need to head back to Lincoln City for another meeting."

"Business or family?"

"One and the same when you're a McMillian."

"Your family is so different from mine. My mom gets upset if we talk too much business."

"Your mother is a smart woman. I see where you get your beauty and brains from." He brushed his lips across Bailey's hair, then woke Buddy. "Be back soon."

Everything was coming together. Finally. Bailey never thought she'd want to thank Floyd Jeffries for his criminal behavior, but if not for his breaking the law by selling the inn to both AJ and McMillian Resorts, she would never have met Justin.

She wiggled her toes, her excitement growing. Instead of the Broughton Inn pushing her and Justin apart, the old hotel was bringing them together. This was the start of something new, something big.

Her, Justin and Buddy.

Cole and McMillian.

A family.

The next day, Bailey sat on the opposite side of Tyler's desk. Tapping her toes, she opened her mouth, then pressed her lips together. She'd arrived at her cousin's office confused. After listening to him, her understanding hadn't increased.

"I must be missing something. The contract reads like there's no guarantee of anything I asked for, including an art gallery."

"That's correct." Tyler rested his elbows on the desk. His serious eyes and expression made him look every bit a lawyer and not the cousin who used to have who-can-burp-the-loudest competitions with her older brothers. "The contract is written strictly for the benefit of McMillian Resorts with more escape routes than the latest tsunami evacuation plan. Based on the convoluted verbiage, I'd say the inn will not hire past employees, honor current vendor contracts or have an art gallery when it reopens."

Bailey's heart cracked wide open, the newly found love she felt for Justin bleeding out. Her world tilted. She gripped the sides of her chair to make sure she didn't fall off.

She hadn't wanted her first impression of him to be right. She wanted to be wrong. Dead wrong.

"I don't understand." Her voice shook. "Those were my conditions if I gave up my ownership claim."

Each breath hurt. She blinked to keep the tears at bay. No way was she going to cry over Justin McMillian. Not in front of Tyler.

"I'm sorry, Bay."

She nodded, not trusting her voice when her insides felt as if they'd been mixed up in a food processor. Her fingers dug into the chair. It was a good thing she wore her nails short or she'd cut through the leather upholstery.

"What were your exact words to Justin?" Tyler asked.

His harsh tone startled her. She leaned back. "I... I don't remember."

"You should have come to me. We could have officially presented an offer with your conditions."

"That's what AJ said to do, but I didn't want to bother you over the weekend."

"Doing legal stuff like this is my job, Bailey. And given their contract, the offer you made to Justin may have put your claim on the inn at risk, whether you agree to their terms or not."

Her muscles seized. "What?"

"No one with half a brain would sign this contract. They know that. So that means they expect us to make a counteroffer or..."

She slumped in her chair. "Why do I have a feeling I don't want to hear the *or* part?"

"Or," Tyler said, "depending on how you worded your offer to Justin, the McMillian legal team may claim you've verbally forfeited your claim on the inn."

She jumped out of the chair. "What?"

"No worries yet." Tyler motioned for her to sit, but she didn't...couldn't. "That's only one possibility, given the scenario."

"Let's hope it's not the one they go with."

"You care about Justin."

"I don't believe he planned to screw me over. I really don't. He'd been too shocked and happy about my offer. But his family..."

"He's part of that family."

"I know." Justin had chosen not to fight his family over her and what she wanted, even though he had seemed to say he would. But family came first, a lesson she'd known but pushed aside because of her feelings for him.

"I'm sorry." She tried to control her breathing. "I should have listened to you and AJ. I did so many things wrong."

She might love Justin, but he wasn't her Mr. Right. As long as he retreated into what was safe for him, work and the family business, he was Mr. Wrong. Words about needing her were easy to hear, but his actions told the truth. He didn't care as much for her as she did for him.

"All we can do is start over. I can't promise anything, but I'll do my best," Tyler said. "This contract tells me McMillian Resorts plans on playing hardball. You should resign yourself to a protracted legal battle. Likely a messy one. Your relationship with Justin McMillian may come up."

"My fault. I'll deal with it."

The contract changed nothing with the inn. Not yet anyway. But something had changed with Justin. She couldn't keep seeing him. Not knowing what she knew now. He wasn't the man she thought he was. Her heart panged at the loss.

Bailey should have known better than to put her heart and the inn on the line. "I accept full responsibility. The complete blame."

She felt like an idiot for stupidly risking the inn for a man. She blinked away the tears. Crying was not going to happen. "Let them know I'm not interested in their contract."

"Do you want to make a counteroffer?"

Bailey raised her chin. "No. I'm all in. I'll fight until the end."

Tyler looked proud of her. That had to count for something, right?

"Go buy yourself a cup of coffee and a donut while I make the call," he said. "Bring me back a maple bar."

"Yes, counselor." She tried to joke, but her voice sounded flat. That was the same way she felt inside, pummeled by a semitruck. "One maple donut coming up."

She forced her feet to move, to keep a smile plastered on her face, to pretend that her world hadn't spun off its axis and rolled into a different dimension. She went to the donut shop first, then headed to the coffee shop. She wasn't ready to face Tyler yet.

Fifteen minutes later, she still wasn't ready, but slowly made her way back to the office. Somehow she managed to carry her coffee without spilling—okay, the cup had a lid—and the bag of donuts without sneaking a bite. Not that she had an appetite.

The emptiness inside threatened to swallow her whole. Bailey's splintered heart cut like shards of glass. But she wasn't giving up hope. She couldn't. Perhaps this was a mistake. Tyler would have good news, and she could laugh off the way she'd believed Justin would betray her.

She entered the law office. Tyler sat on one of the upholstered chairs in the waiting room. He stood when she entered.

Bailey raised the bag. "That hungry for a donut?"

Her cousin took the food and drinks from her hand.

She didn't need a PhD in rocket science to decipher the look on Tyler's face. "It's bad."

"As soon as I told them you weren't signing, Paige McMillian said they were petitioning the court that the verbal agreement between you and Justin nullified your ownership rights to the inn."

Bailey's stomach roiled. She staggered back until she fell into a chair. "That's… I didn't. There were conditions."

"We'll fight them."

She trembled. "Is this Paige's doing? Or Justin's?"

"I don't know," Tyler said. "But this is only the beginning."

The fight over the inn might be in the early stages, but things between her and Justin were over. "I—I should have—"

"Don't think about what you should have done. You can't change the past."

No, the past was set, but she could change. A part of her had been trying to change by making that compromise to Justin, but her stubbornness and drive to be independent put the inn at risk.

"Hang in there." Tyler touched her shoulder. "The Mc-Millians don't know what they've taken on. We Coles are fighters."

She nodded. "I'm not giving up without a fight."

The inn was one thing, but Justin…

Her dreams about the two of them and Buddy went *poof*, disappearing like a child's bubble blown into the air. Her eyes had been opened to the man she'd fallen in love with. He wasn't who she'd believed him to be. She forced herself to breathe.

Her heart felt trampled upon, battered and bruised, but only time would let her know the full effect. The inn, however, would be lost forever. Replaced by a modern monstrosity and a staff not from here, and that was her fault. All the employees and Haley's Bay residents had been counting on her. She'd let them down. She was the one responsible for following her heart and not her head. For thinking she knew better when she didn't. She'd been warned. And now she felt like a complete fool. She had only one person to blame—herself. But she never wanted to see Justin McMillian again.

Chapter Twelve

"Hey, it's Justin." He left a voice message on Bailey's cell phone. "Wanted to confirm dinner plans for tomorrow. Call me back."

He disconnected from the call, then checked his text messages. No reply from Bailey. Where was she? His calls today had gone straight to her voice mail. Weird. She usually called right back. Maybe she was teaching a class he'd forgotten about, but he missed hearing her voice.

Paige bounced into his office, reminding him of when she was eight and had pulled out a tooth. "We won!"

"Won?"

"The inn."

His pulse accelerated. He stood. "Bailey didn't tell me she signed the contract."

"She didn't."

"Then how…?"

Paige shook her head. "Tyler Cole called. The guy acted

so put out. Turned down the contract we offered. Said no counteroffer would be made."

"Wait a minute." Justin rubbed his chin. "Without the contract, how do we win?"

She didn't say a word, but her I've-got-a-secret-gleam gave him a funny feeling in his stomach.

"Tell me what's going on," he said.

"This morning we filed a claim for sole ownership."

"On what basis?"

"The verbal agreement made between you and Bailey where she relinquished her claim to the inn."

"There wasn't a verbal agreement. She made us an offer, one that came with conditions that you and your legal crew ignored."

"Not true. We took her words very seriously. Giving her that contract gave us time to get everything finished on our end."

"What you're doing isn't ethical. It's wrong."

Paige shrugged. "We'll let the court decide. Bailey may decide to give up her fight."

"Give up?" Frustration threatened to overwhelm Justin. "The Coles of Haley's Bay do not give up. Tyler will go after you like this is a personal attack, which it is, since you're twisting Bailey's offer. AJ has enough money to fund a war. They aren't going to let this drop. Why did you do this?"

Paige looked perplexed. "Why wouldn't I? Our dream, our jobs are at stake. Whatever it takes."

"Not like this."

"This is what I always do. What Dad taught me to do. I get whatever property you want. Just because you don't see the fallout or backroom dealings doesn't mean there aren't any."

He stood speechless.

"The Broughton Inn is going to be ours, so you'd better get busy with the approval process," she said. "A complete teardown is what we're after, but if not, do your best to make the old look brand-new."

He couldn't shake Paige's words about how his family did business or stop wondering if Bailey knew what had happened, and that was why she hadn't called or texted. She must know if Tyler knew.

Paige touched his shoulder. "Hey. What's wrong? I thought you'd be excited. You look like you've lost your best friend."

Justin hoped he hadn't. "I'm wondering how Bailey's going to feel about this."

"Come on," Paige said. "Did you not learn your lesson with your divorce about dating women who are the opposite from you?"

"Bailey's not opposite. We're quite similar."

"You're kidding yourself. Can you imagine what Mom and Dad would think of her?"

"I hope they'd like her because I do." But if that was the case, why hadn't he driven down with Bailey and introduced them? Because of the inn? Or was there more? "I'm heading up to Haley's Bay with Buddy."

"Better bring a hazardous waste suit. There may be fallout."

That was what Justin was afraid of. He only hoped the inn wouldn't be what kept he and Bailey apart, because he wanted them both in his life. He didn't want to have to settle for only one. And wouldn't if he had the choice.

The knock at Bailey's front door made every muscle tighten, including ones she hadn't known existed. She rolled her neck, but the action did nothing to relax the tension gripping her like a straitjacket.

She didn't have to peek out the window to know Justin was standing on her welcome mat and rapping his knuckles against her door. Buddy had barked, and four people had texted they saw Justin driving on Bay Street. That was life in a small town, where everyone knew not only her business, but also her secrets and, in this case, her pain, broken heart and shame.

She walked to the door, keeping her head high, each step moving her closer to a confrontation that wouldn't be pleasant but must be done. She wasn't prepared.

How did a person prepare herself for saying goodbye to someone she'd come to care about...come to love? And Buddy. She didn't want to say goodbye to the sweet dog.

Focus. She'd been played for a fool. Forget about the good times and magical kisses they'd shared.

Not magical. Stupid. They no longer mattered.

She squared her shoulders. His excuses would not sway her. If he even made any. Time to get this over with.

With her hand on the doorknob, Bailey took a deep breath. She opened the door. Buddy ran inside.

"Hey." Justin's smiled loosened the lines around his mouth. "I wasn't sure you'd be here."

The relief in his voice poked at her heart. She tightened her grip on the doorknob. "I'm here."

He stepped inside. "You never called back or replied to my texts."

She closed the door. Better to do this in private than in front of the watchful eyes of her neighbors, who were likely timing the length of the visit so they could report in to her grandmother and Tyler.

"I thought you lost your phone," Justin continued. "Or might not want to talk to me."

"I..."

Bailey knew what she wanted to say, but words failed her. All her practice had been for naught with him standing so close to her and looking far too handsome for her own good. The urge to fling herself into Justin's arms and forget the mess she'd made was strong. She had to be stronger.

Bailey swallowed. Twice. "I didn't want to talk to you."

He flinched. "The inn."

She nodded once.

"You spoke to Tyler."

"At length." She moved into the living room, wanting to put distance between them. "How could you lie about my offer to you?"

"I didn't lie. Paige and the legal team decided to do this on their own. I had no input."

"So you're not guilty, just complacent."

"You don't understand." He brushed his hand through his hair. "You're a free-spirited artist who doesn't care what anyone thinks of you. My parents expect me to live up to certain expectations."

Bailey wasn't buying his words. "You still could've stopped them."

"No, I couldn't. My family is at stake here."

She struggled to remain in control and not lose it. "Your company. Not family."

"It's the same thing when you're a McMillian. Paige didn't tell me about filing until after the fact. You have every right to be upset, but it's just business."

Baily's mouth gaped. She couldn't believe him. "If this goes to court, you'll be forced to testify under oath."

"We'll settle before this ends up in court. That's what we always do."

She wasn't sure if he sounded confident or cocky, but she didn't like his tone. Or any of this. She stared down her nose at him. "That doesn't make your tactics right. And I'm not settling."

He didn't flinch. His facial expression didn't change. "I told Paige you would fight."

That surprised Bailey. "Not just fight. I'm going to win,

so you'd better start practicing for your deposition, since it'll be your word against mine. And I'm not the one who'll be lying on the witness stand."

He reached for her. "Bailey."

She leaned away so his hand only found air. This...*he* wasn't what she wanted. Not any longer. "Don't touch me. I don't want you to touch me again. Or contact me."

"Is that what Tyler said to say?"

"Oh, he told me that weeks ago. I foolishly didn't listen. But I won't make that mistake again."

Justin's forehead creased. "You're willing to let the inn come between us?"

"Us?" She half laughed. That was better than crying. "There's never been an *us*. You've wanted the inn from the beginning for your family. I happened to be the way for you to get what you wanted."

"That's not what—"

"Nothing you say or do will convince me otherwise."

"These past weeks, we've shared something special."

Her eyes stung. She blinked. "Special? Not from my perspective. I understand you putting your family first. I should have listened to mine, but you're no better than Floyd. And like him, you have no idea what you're losing by doing this. I deserve so much better. So does the inn."

"That's not how this is."

"It is. I trusted you. That's why I made the offer." Her voice cracked. Darn, she needed to stay in control. "I thought..."

"What?"

That they had a future together. But she'd die before she admitted those words to him. She raised her chin. "It's too late, but I wish I'd never gotten involved with you."

He flinched.

Good. Except it wasn't. Not really.

He straightened. "Let's talk about this over dinner."

"Your family is trying to steal the inn using lies about my offer. I have nothing left to say to you." She motioned to the door, hoping her fingers wouldn't tremble the way her insides were. "Please go, and don't come back."

His eyes darkened. "So that's how you want things to be."

She hesitated, crossed her arms over her chest. "Yes."

Justin called for Buddy. She hugged the dog and kissed his head. Oh, how she would miss this adorable furball.

Without a word, Justin grabbed Buddy and walked out of the cottage. Out of her life.

An engine started. She waited until she couldn't hear the car's sound anymore. She slid to the floor, buried her head in her hands and let the tears fall.

The sun rose each morning, but Justin found getting out of bed and heading to the office harder and harder to do. Nothing satisfied him. Today had been the most difficult. All he could think about was Bailey. Her pretty, warm smile and gorgeous, caring eyes were imprinted on his brain. Whether his eyes were open or closed didn't make a difference. He still saw her.

Wyatt—Justin's foreman and closest friend—spit out a sunflower seed shell. "That artist girl got under your skin."

Justin nodded, but Bailey had done more than that, She'd found her way into his heart, too. He'd kept telling himself he liked her when the truth was, he'd fallen in love. Fallen headfirst. Fallen hard. Every cliché rang true where she was concerned.

Damn. He hadn't been this messed up by his divorce. He hadn't felt this emptiness inside, as if someone had ripped out his heart and not put anything back in its place. "I don't know what to do about it."

"You got over Taryn. You'll get over this one."

"Her name is Bailey." Justin didn't like the way the people closest to him ignored her existence. She was more than an artist or the obstacle standing between McMillian Resorts and the Broughton Inn. She was a daughter, sister, aunt, friend. A kind, beautiful, intelligent woman. Damn, she was right. He had it bad. "And I'm not sure I will."

Wyatt eyed him warily. "Never seen you like this."

"Never been like this. Not even with Taryn. I—" Justin shook his head, trying to dislodge Bailey from his brain. "The only place I want to be is Haley's Bay."

"Not at the inn."

"I wish I'd never heard of the Broughton Inn. No, that's not true. I wouldn't have met Bailey. Too bad my family is hell-bent on seeing this project through to the end."

"You were spearheading that mentality."

"At the beginning, but now…"

"Because of her."

He started to say yes, then stopped himself, because she wasn't the only reason. "Bailey is the biggest reason, but my family's tactics to close this deal…"

"Dude, that's how it's always been. You never cared. Or maybe you didn't pay attention."

Justin hadn't. He'd focused on the result. The means hadn't mattered. A part of him had known or guessed how the legal team operated, but he hadn't let that stop him. Not until he'd seen the repercussions. Years of not paying attention, of focusing on his role and no one else's, had caught up to him. Their method of business and the resulting damage was too much. "I don't like it."

"So tell them."

He should, except…nothing would change. No matter what he said, the course was set. He knew that in his heart.

Because he'd been the same way with Taryn.

She'd wanted him to work less and spend more time with her. Move to Portland, away from his family and their company. He'd said no. That they could figure out another way.

But what he'd offered to save their marriage hadn't been enough. No wonder Taryn had left. He'd wanted his wife to do all the work and make all the compromises. Exactly what his family was asking of him now.

Taryn hadn't been the one to blame for their divorcing. He was responsible, but he hadn't realized it until now. Crap.

Justin didn't want to make the same mistake this time. The way he'd felt about his ex didn't come close to his feelings for Bailey.

He didn't want the inn. He wanted her. "I screwed up."

"What's new?" Wyatt joked.

"Nothing. That's the problem. I'm finished." Justin rose from behind his desk. "I can't keep doing this."

Wyatt's brow furrowed. "Do what?"

"Let McMillian Resorts ruin my chance at love and happiness again. I didn't see it the first time with Taryn. I do now. Time to make a change." He walked out of his office toward the conference room where he knew his family would be assembled. His heart pounded with purpose; every fiber in his being agreed.

"Took you long enough," his dad grumbled as he entered.

"Now, now." His mother patted his father's hand. "Justin's here. We can get started."

Rainey, his younger sister, the baby of the family, fingered the pendant on the chain around her neck. Dark circles under her eyes and her pale complexion made him wonder when she'd last had a full night's sleep. She needed a vacation.

Paige tapped her fingers against the table as if she'd rather be somewhere else. He knew how she felt. He was impatient, too. He wanted this over with now.

His father motioned to an empty leather chair. "Sit. Now that the three of you have shown us what you're capable of doing, we're ready to sign over ownership of the company to you and retire."

Justin stood in the doorway. His and his sisters' dream handed to them on a platter of lies. Unbelievable.

The only thing he knew was this company. He'd never worked anywhere else. This was his family, but until going to Haley's Bay he hadn't realized how much business defined them, as individuals and a collective group. Living like this was no longer enough. Family should mean more. And being without Bailey was not an option.

He sucked in a breath. Exhaled. "I quit."

His father laughed. The gut-busting sound echoed through the conference room. "Stop being an idiot and wasting our time. Take a seat."

"I have at least two months' vacation and personal time off. Wyatt knows where all the projects stand. He's overqualified but can step into my position without any problems."

His family stared at him, mouths gaping.

His mother pursed her lips. "You can't be serious. We're giving you the company."

"I am serious. I don't want a company that's run this way. I'm in love with a woman named Bailey. She's the other owner of the Broughton Inn."

His father's nostrils flared. "If this woman's got half a brain, she won't want an unemployed bum for a boyfriend."

"She's very smart, and I won't be unemployed for long once I tell my side of Bailey's so-called verbal offer to the judge."

Paige's face dropped. "You wouldn't."

"Don't be so sure about that."

A weight lifted off Justin's shoulders. He had no doubt he was doing the right thing.

He tossed his office keys onto the table. They clattered against the wood. "I'm sure this will take time getting used to, but I hope we'll be over this by the time the holidays roll around."

His mother stood. "Justin—"

"I've got to go."

"Where?" Rainey asked.

"Haley's Bay."

His father frowned. "This artist is more important than your own family."

"You're important, too," Justin admitted. "But I've lost one woman to McMillian Resorts. I won't lose another, especially one who means as much as Bailey does to me. I need more in my life than work. I need her."

The words *I'm sorry* were on the tip of his tongue, but he wasn't going to apologize for wanting more, wanting to be loved, wanting more from a family than sharing a common work interest.

"I love all of you, but I love Bailey, too. I need to tell her and hope that's enough for her to give me a second chance."

"And if it's not?" Paige asked.

Justin hadn't thought that far out. He shrugged. "I'll keep trying until I convince her or she has me arrested."

Rainey beamed. "A good thing we have an attorney in the family. Though sounds like a bail bondsman might come in handy."

"Likely. Bailey's youngest brother is a police officer."

Paige shook her head. "This isn't going to end well."

"I've gotta try." And Justin would. Because he didn't want to live with the *what-if.*

The phone vibrated against the living room end table. Bailey rolled her eyes. What part of "no" didn't Justin McMillian understand? He'd been texting and calling all morning. She should have turned off her phone instead of only muting the sound.

A stupid mistake. One she would remember not to make again.

As she stood on a plastic tarp in her dining room, her vision blurred, the colors on the canvas blending together in an odd-shaped rainbow. Distractions always made her lose sight of a project. One reason she liked being alone.

She just needed to keep reminding herself that.

And forget about how much she missed having Buddy around, and…

She blinked until the canvas came into focus, the landscape of her grandmother's house as clear as the robin sitting on the bird feeder outside the window.

More vibrating. That one sounded like a text.

A week ago Bailey might have been flattered. Okay, she would have been. But now Justin's attempts at contacting her left her aching heart hurting more.

She hated that, hated…

No, she didn't hate Justin.

But she was angry with him. A part of her felt sorry for him. But she didn't hate him. She kept trying for indifference, but so far that hadn't happened.

Stop thinking about him.

She needed to finish this commissioned piece if she wanted to pay her mortgage without having to dip into her savings.

Bailey used her forearm to push stray hairs off her face with her forearm. Paint splatters covered her hands. She didn't need paint on her face.

Another text from Justin arrived. She would turn off her phone once she washed her hands.

She wasn't interested in anything he had to say. She didn't need him. Or anyone.

Bailey had what she needed to be happy—a loving family, her own home, a career that might not make her rich, but one she loved. So why did she feel so miserable?

She knew the answer, a six-letter word that started with a capital *J* and ended with a small *n*.

Not fair.

But her brothers, all five of them, would tell her life wasn't fair. As they'd always done.

She got back to work. If she concentrated on finishing the painting, then she wouldn't have to think about anything else. She could put everything into her work, including her heart.

Time seemed to stop. Minutes…hours…she had no idea how long she'd been working.

The front door opened. Three of her brothers—Ellis, Declan and Grady—walked in.

"See?" Grady said. "I told you she would be working and her door wouldn't be locked."

Declan double-checked the lock. "Not broken, which means you didn't lock the door again."

A headache threatened to erupt. "I'm working. Go away."

Ellis looked at her painting. "Pretty good, but you haven't answered your phone for two days."

Declan picked up the cell. "Sounds off. Battery's almost dead."

"Go away." She focused on her painting. "I need to finish this."

"Mom sent us over," Grady said. "Worried you were upset over breaking up with Justin. She wanted to make sure you were eating."

"Sleeping," Ellis added.

"Not crying nonstop." Declan studied her. "Your eyes look a little red, but I thought they'd be swollen."

"Oh, man," Ellis said. "Remember the time Bobby Steele dumped you for that hot blonde?"

"Cecilia Remming." Declan whistled. "As much as I love you, sis, can't say I blame the guy."

Bailey sighed. "Just because a girl has a D-cup in high school doesn't make her the be-all, end-all. You do realize Cecilia ended up having breast reduction surgery last year because of back trouble."

Declan checked her empty water bottle, then tossed it to Grady. "Don't ruin the fantasies."

"Fine. I take it back." Bailey wasn't a dream crusher. That title belonged to Justin. She waved her paintbrush, sending splatters of coral pink onto the tarp beneath their feet and causing her brothers to step back. "As you can see, I'm fine."

"You don't look so good." Grady raised the water bottle. "I'm going to refill this."

Ellis dug through the candy wrappers on the floor. "When did you eat last something that wasn't all sugar?"

"Showered?" Declan sniffed. "I'd say at least two, maybe three days, based on the smell."

Her shoulders sagged. Bailey straightened. She wasn't about to answer them. If she did, they would know that she wasn't exactly fine, but she was doing okay. Surviving. Hoping the emptiness inside would go away sooner rather than later.

"I'm working." She motioned to the almost finished canvas. "I'll do those things as soon as I complete my painting."

Ellis studied her. "So the way you look, how messy your place is, has nothing to do with Justin?"

Bailey fought the urge to say something sarcastic or biting. No fighting with them, either. She counted backward from five. "This is how I work."

And it was, except work usually left her feeling refreshed, able to stay up late and wake early. This painting hadn't done that. If anything, work was draining what energy she had left.

"It's okay if you're upset." Declan stacked empty cups lying on the floor. "We know you liked Justin."

Ellis nodded. "You were different with him."

"Yeah, not such a hardnose all the time," Grady teased.

Declan glared at their youngest brother. "Shut up, Grady."

"We're not trying to butt in." Ellis folded the throw she'd used for a nap. "We're your brothers. It's our job to take care of you."

"No, that's my job." Bailey placed her brush on the easel. "I appreciate the concern, but I'm not a kid anymore. My heart's been battered, but this isn't the first time I've lost in love. This won't be the last."

At least she hoped not.

"You've been hiding out," Ellis said.

Her shoulders sagged. "What part of working don't you understand? I'm not doing a spin-art project. Creating a painting takes time. I lose track of things, including staying in contact and time. Go tell Mom all is well and as soon as this painting is finished, I'll be over there."

Her brothers exchanged glances.

"Really," Bailey added for emphasis, then motioned them to the front door. "Go. Risa is expecting you home, Ellis. I'm sure you two single guys have hot dates tonight."

Declan winked. "A lukewarm date, but no complaints if the night ends the way I expect."

"I'm giving a talk at a Boy Scout meeting, then calling it an early night," Grady said. "I'm on duty in the morning."

Their little brother sure had grown up. All of them had. Bailey gave each one a hug. "I'll charge my cell phone. But I'm not answering until the work is finished."

"Fair enough," Ellis said.

"And, sis—" Declan reached out to her "—we give you a hard time, and you can be a pain in the ass sometimes, but McMillian's an idiot for letting you get away."

The tension wrapped around her chest loosened. "Thanks. I appreciate that."

Her brothers filed out of the house, one by one. She closed the door.

"Lock it," the three said in unison.

Bailey bolted the lock, then leaned against the door. She loved her family, and how her brothers wanted to take care of her was sweet. But she wished someone other than her siblings wanted to watch out for her. She wished she had someone to kiss good-night and wake up to each morning. She wished she had finally found her Mr. Right.

Being disappointed by Mr. Wrong, time and time again, was getting old.

Chapter Thirteen

"I don't know what I should do next." Justin sat in his parked truck with the windows rolled down. The temperature in Haley's Bay had cooled to the sixties as soon as the sun had set. "Probably shouldn't go back to Bailey's house again."

He'd been twice. No answer when he called her. No replies to his text.

"She's shut me out of her life completely. I miss her."

He stared at his cell phone charging. Not many options remained except giving up. He wasn't ready to admit defeat. Not yet.

Buddy sat in the passenger seat. The dog had been the definition of loyal.

Justin rubbed his dog. "So glad I've got you."

Buddy placed his head on Justin's leg.

He rubbed the dog. "I screwed up. Took me too long to stand up to my family. But I'm the reason I lost her. Can't blame anyone else."

His throat was dry. He'd finished his last bottle of water an hour ago. No wonder he was thirsty. He checked Buddy's portable water bowl—full. "I'm going to grab a drink. I'll be right back. Stay."

Buddy sat for a moment, then lay down.

The side and back windows were open. Buddy would be cool enough.

Justin saw the sign for a place called the Crow's Nest, what looked to be a dive bar, halfway down the block. One beer; then he'd find a place to stay for the night that allowed dogs. Or he and Buddy could sleep in the back of the truck.

A night's sleep would help him regroup. He'd try something else in the morning.

Inside the place, the smell of beer and grease filled the air. The place was crowded, but a few open spots at the bar remained. The jukebox's sad country-western song about lost love matched his mood and situation.

He took a seat at the bar and ordered a beer on tap from a local microbrewery. The bartender set the pint in front of him. "Here you go. Compliments of Declan Cole."

Justin looked over his shoulder. Declan sat at a table for two, but only one glass was at the table. Justin picked up his beer and walked over. "Mind if I join you?"

"Seat's empty."

"No date tonight?" Justin asked.

"She canceled."

"There's always tomorrow night."

"Gonna cut this one loose. She's got commitment on the brain. All I want to do is have fun."

Justin took a sip. The beer felt cool going down his throat. Might as well get the one question he had off his mind. "How's Bailey?"

"Working hard on her newest painting and trying to convince everyone she's fine."

"Is she okay?"

Declan's jaw tensed. He raised his glass. "Do you care?"

"More than you know." Justin stared into his beer. "I want her back."

"Tell her."

"I've tried. She won't answer my texts or calls. She wouldn't answer the door tonight. I tried the knob. Locked."

Declan laughed.

Justin took a long drink. He might need two beers. "Go ahead and laugh at some other guy's pain."

"No, it's Bailey. She finally listened to us about locking her door."

"Wish she would listen to me."

Declan raised his pint. "What would you say to her?"

"I messed up. I was wrong to let my family try to take advantage of her offer. That I quit."

Declan pinned him with his gaze. "You quit your job?"

"I don't approve of the way my family does business."

"How'd they take your resignation?"

"No idea. I didn't stick around. I drove up here. No one's called or texted, so I'm guessing they're still getting used to the idea."

Declan stared at two women who'd entered the bar, then looked at Justin. "What are you going to do now?"

"Figure out how to get Bailey to talk to me. She won today, but I'll go back for more rejection tomorrow. Maybe try a new tactic."

A blonde waved at Declan. He shook his head. "Like what?"

"No idea. I'm hoping inspiration strikes tonight." He stared at the white foam in his beer. No answers there. "Got any ideas?"

"You think I'm going to help you get my sister back after you broke her heart?" Declan sounded incredulous.

"I didn't ask for your help, only ideas."

"She would never admit it, but she likes fairy tales. And

romance. Big into that. But if you say that I told you, I'll deny it, then beat you up."

"Fair enough." Justin took another sip. "I'm sure Bailey would see past any suit of armor or white horse. She prefers wildflowers to cut ones. And she's been trying to cut back on eating sugar."

Declan stared over his beer. "Bailey doesn't diet."

"No, but giving her chocolates would tell her I wasn't listening. I've got enough cons against me. Not going to add any more."

Declan studied him.

"What?" Justin asked.

"You like my sister."

"Yeah, I like her." Justin downed the rest of his beer. "I'm pretty sure I'm in love with her. Not that I can tell her."

"Want another?"

"Nope. One's enough. I need to find a motel, then put together my plan for tomorrow."

"Your plan?"

"To get Bailey to listen to me for five minutes so I can tell her how much I love her. I'm assuming that's as long as she'll give me. So I need to be prepared." He removed a diamond engagement ring from his pocket. "I hope this will be enough. Thanks for the beer."

"Hey. Skip the motel. I have a spare bedroom."

"I've got Buddy with me."

"He can play with Chinook," Declan said. "I'll call my brothers and cousins. Maybe we can give you some ideas."

Justin's heart pounded. "You'd do that?"

"Hell, yeah. Any guy stupid enough to spend money on a ring for my sister when she won't text him gets bonus points in my book. But I swear if you hurt her, you'll—"

Justin raised his hands. "If I hurt her, you're free to do whatever you want to me."

Declan pulled out his cell phone. "I'll text the boys to meet at my place. Camden, too."

Amazing. Justin had Bailey's family on his side. Well, at least one of them. All he had to do was get her on his side, too. He wasn't superstitious, but he crossed his fingers. He was going to need not only help from the Coles, but lots of luck, too.

This had better be good.

6:00 a.m. was too early to be up on a Saturday. The rising sun provided enough light for Bailey to see the paved walkway at the Broughton Inn. She'd much rather be in bed after another restless night. She doubted she'd slept more than two hours each night this week. But Grady had said meeting him this morning was vital to the future of the inn, so here she was.

Her steps barely sounded against the stones. Dew clung to the grass and dripped from the lights that normally lit the way. They were off today. Electricity must have been turned off until ownership of the inn and someone's name went on the account.

The past few days had crystalized her thoughts about her future. Yes, she wanted to find love, but she also wanted to do something more to help artists in Haley's Bay. She wanted to open an art center, one that housed a gallery, classrooms, even a retreat. Ideas had been exploding in her mind like fireworks. She would figure out a plan once she knew if this was all a pipe dream. But thinking of something other than Justin helped her broken heart.

Better not think about him or she might cry. She'd wasted too many tears already.

Bailey headed toward the gazebo. She loved this place, even if the structure needed repairs and a new coat of...

She looked up. Froze.

The gazebo had been painted white and the flower boxes

hanging off the sides filled with colorful blossoms. Tule and miniature white lights had been draped around the top and along the rails. Her heart beat in triple time. Exactly the way she imagined her wedding day.

She blinked. Closed her eyes. Opened them.

Nothing had changed. The gazebo still looked like a dream come true. "Grady?"

Justin stepped from behind the gazebo. He wore a tuxedo. Buddy, wearing a black bow tie, was at his side.

Her heart slammed against her rib cage. She opened her mouth to speak, but words wouldn't come.

He looked handsome, mouthwateringly good, even though she shouldn't care what he wore or looked like. But she did, and didn't like that.

A million questions ran through her head. She went with the most obvious one. "Where's my brother?"

"Grady, along with Declan, Ellis, J.T. and Tyler, is standing watch. I don't want to get arrested for trespassing on private property, even though we both own this place. For now, at least."

She glanced around at the decorations gracing the gazebo. "Did you boys decide to play decorator?"

"Risa was happy to help. She had the supplies in her craft room, and tying bows is beyond these hands of mine. Camden joined in, too. Your sister is amazing with a paint sprayer in the dark."

Bailey wanted to believe she was dreaming. That she wasn't standing in a place set for a wedding with the man she'd dreamed of marrying. This was too…much.

Tears stung her eyes. She turned away. "I have to go."

He touched her shoulder. "Five minutes. That's all I need."

She didn't have five minutes. Five seconds were going to be difficult enough. She rubbed her eyes, trying not to lose it completely.

Justin lowered his hand. "Please."

She nodded, not trusting her voice. Breathing was automatic, but right now she felt as if she had to remind herself not only to breathe, but to also think and stand. Nothing seemed to be functioning except her tear ducts.

"I'm sorry." His voice cracked. "The more times I go over what's happened, the sorrier I am."

The regret in his eyes pushed her back a step until she bumped into the gazebo's railing.

"I've been focused on work for so long, I couldn't see what was in front of me." His gaze met hers. "You."

Her breath caught in her throat. "Justin—"

"Until I met you, I put McMillian Resorts first. That was a mistake. I couldn't let my family and the inn come between us. I quit."

Bailey gasped. "You quit your family's company?"

"I couldn't continue to work there, knowing what they'd done to you. You're not the first. I turned a blind eye, but not any longer. I'm not going to lose you."

"What about the inn?"

"They won't ask me to testify for them now. That means they have no case. If you still want the inn, I'll do everything in my power to make sure it's yours. I'd suggest you have Tyler call Paige ASAP. My family members are most likely ready to make a deal themselves."

Bailey was having trouble thinking straight. "What will you do now?"

"Find a new job. Start my own business. I haven't thought that far ahead. All I've been thinking about is you. We have something special. I'd like another chance."

"That's what this is all about? Trying to charm your way into my heart?"

"I was hoping I was already there, but I figured this couldn't hurt."

She wanted to scream yes, jump into his arms and kiss

him hard on the lips. Fear held her back. Justin had messed up her nice, not-so-neat world. She didn't want him to do that again with even worse results. Together, they were good, but he also pushed her buttons, made her want things, want him. "I…"

The twinkling lights covered by the white tulle caught her attention. Common sense told her to say no. No good would come of trying again. She'd followed her heart once and ended up possibly losing the inn. What would she risk this time?

But, her heart countered, what could she gain? Was she willing to walk away from the possibility of something wonderful and awe-inspiring? She had done so in the past, but now she wasn't sure she wanted to do that again.

"I'm scared," she admitted.

He held her hand. "I am, too. But life is scary. It'll be less scary with the two of us together."

"You sound confident."

"I am." He squeezed her hand. "I love you, Bailey."

Heat pulsed through her, and joy overflowed. Had he really said that he loved her? She wanted to hear the words again. To be sure. "What did you say?"

"Your expression tells me you heard me the first time, but I'll say the words again. I love you. I love your passion and your creativity. The way you care so deeply about the people, animals and the things in your life, including your family. You're unique, and I can't imagine being without you."

She'd longed to hear those words. She just hadn't thought they'd come from him. But let this man go? No way.

"I love you, too. Even when we disagree. I love how you gave Buddy a forever home. I appreciate how you hear my side, and don't try to change who I am."

"I would never want to change you."

"Just every building you see."

"Not every single one. I have a feeling you're going to like some of my new ideas."

"For the inn?"

"For the Potter place," he said to her surprise. "Phil Potter turned down three of Paige's offers, but I'm not going to give up. The spot is perfect for a gallery and small inn."

"An artist retreat center."

"That works."

Of course it would. Because she and Justin were meant to be. Grandma had always said everything happens for a reason. She was right once again.

He held out his arms. "Come here."

Bailey did with Buddy at her heels. She kissed Justin hard until she couldn't think straight and clung to his shoulders to keep her knees from giving out.

He drew back. "I've missed everything about you, especially holding you in my arms and kissing you. We'll have to do more of that."

"Most definitely." But something kept her from being totally ecstatic over reconciling. "What about your family? Aren't you sad?"

"This is the right decision for me. They'll see that, too. I doubt my leaving will make them change the way they've done business, but maybe they'll rethink how they close deals in the future. Everything in our family life has always revolved around the business. Whether I'm involved or not, won't matter."

"I love you."

"You don't know how long I've waited to hear those words."

"As long as I was waiting."

He laughed. "I have one more thing to ask you."

"About the inn?"

"This has to do with you and me. I want you to know I'm serious and want to make a commitment." He kneeled and showed her a black velvet ring box. "Will you marry me, Bailey Cole?"

Her heart skipped four beats. She covered her mouth with her hands. "I… I…"

He opened the box to show a gorgeous diamond engagement ring; its setting was not traditional, but an asymmetrical, artistic one. So…her.

"I love it."

"Is that a yes?"

"Yes." She extended her hand. He slid the ring on her finger. Satisfaction pooled in her chest. "I know we'll create a wonderful life together here in Haley's Bay."

Buddy barked.

She gave the dog a rub. "All three of us will."

* * * * *

Don't miss Sarah Morgan's
next Puffin Island story

Some Kind of Wonderful

Brittany Forrest has stayed away from Puffin Island
since her relationship with Zach Flynn went bad.
They were married for ten days and only just
managed not to kill each other by the
end of the honeymoon.

But, when a broken arm means she must return,
Brittany moves back to her Puffin Island home.
Only to discover that Zac is there as well.

Will a summer together help two lovers reunite or
will their stormy relationship crash on to the
rocks of Puffin Island?

Some Kind of Wonderful
COMING JULY 2015
Pre-order your copy today

Join our *EXCLUSIVE* eBook club

FROM JUST £1.99 A MONTH!

Never miss a book again with our hassle-free eBook subscription.

★ Pick how many titles you want from each series with our flexible subscription

★ Your titles are delivered to your device on the first of every month

★ Zero risk, zero obligation!

There really is nothing standing in the way of you and your favourite books!

Start your eBook subscription today at www.millsandboon.co.uk/subscribe

β